PRAISE FOR *MURDER LEADS TO MARRIAGE*

"*Murder Leads To Marriage* by Shannon Peeples was compelling and exciting. The events were descriptive and easy to visualize. It was fast-paced, and the chapters flowed into each other. The story was so well-written that I immersed myself in the tale and couldn't believe it when it was over. It was much more than I expected."

—Readers' Favorite (starred review)

"I have nothing but admiration for *Murder Leads To Marriage* by Shannon Peeples. I was struck by how engrossing the plot was. Once I started reading the book, I found it impossible to put down for various reasons. The outstanding character development was another feature that had me smitten. The book was a delightful read with a perfect rating of 5 out of 5 stars."

—OnlineBookClub.org review (starred review)

SHANNON PEEPLES

MURDER
LEADS TO
MARRIAGE

ISBN: 979-8-9883712-0-5
LCCN: 2024900851

Printed in the United States of America

Mom, I can still see you sitting in your favorite
chair, surrounded by library books, magazines,
and the daily newspaper. You used to say,
"As long as you have something to read, then life is good!"

My brother **Tommy** started his reading career
with comic books, and oh how I loved to sneak into
his room and read them when he was away.

What they both taught me was there are very few
things in life more enjoyable than a good book.

I only hope they have e-books in heaven.

Skylar Smith *hung up the phone slowly and gave a deep sigh. "Is that what you wanted me to say? That poor woman. I can't believe you made me say those things to her." She turned and looked at the person sitting on her couch. "I've paid you back and then some. You need to get out of here. Now. And don't ever again say anything to me about Melissa. You were just as much at fault as I was."*

"Are you sure you don't want to have one last fuck? You know, for old times' sake?"

"You. Disgust. Me. I wouldn't fuck you if you were the last person on Earth."

She'd forgotten how quickly he could move. He grabbed her chin with just enough pressure that she knew she would bruise.

"Don't piss me off. You really don't want to do that. And you were a horrible lay anyway. I get more satisfaction using my hand. At least it moves."

"Get out. Now."

Skylar stared at him, silently willing him to leave her apartment.

At last, he went to the door. He turned to Skylar and said in a menacing tone, "You do not want to tell anyone about this. Bad things happen to little girls who squeal."

Only after her apartment door was shut and locked did Skylar begin to relax. She sank down to the floor and put her head in her hands. "Oh my God, what have I done?"

For the next three weeks, Skylar tried to go about her normal routine, but it felt impossible. She was a nervous wreck; positive she was being followed everywhere she went. She thought constantly about the phone call she'd been forced to make, and deep down she knew she was going to have to tell someone about it. She just wasn't sure who. She didn't want to bring her family into this mess—she was afraid of them getting hurt—but she was also too afraid to go to the authorities. While she was pretty sure she hadn't committed a crime, she was afraid the police would uncover the real reason she'd agreed to make the call . . . and that had been a crime.

On the last night of her life, Skylar decided she had finally had enough. She was exhausted, frightened, sick to her stomach, and truly at her wits' end. She made up her mind; she was going to go talk to her oldest sister, who was an attorney at one of the larger law firms in the city. Since it was Friday, Skylar figured if she got to her sister's house around 7:00 p.m., there would be a good chance her sister would just be getting home from work. Skylar knew she was being paranoid, but she didn't want to call her sister first to tell her she was coming over. She was too afraid her phone had been bugged, and even though her rational mind tried telling her that was impossible, her scared mind was taking no chances. Skylar knew first-hand how dangerous he could be.

"After all," she thought, "look what happened to Melissa."

Skylar took a shower, dressed in her typical black jeans and black T-shirt, and as she was combing out her hair, she thought she heard a noise in the living room.

"He's here," she thought. *"I need something to defend myself with."*

She saw her phone on the counter behind the sink, and with trembling hands, she picked it up and put it in her back pocket. She held her breath and looked desperately around the bathroom for a weapon, anything she could use to protect herself. She grabbed a pair of scissors from the drawer and crept to the door. She was so scared that she could hardly move, but she had to see if anyone was in her apartment.

She slowly opened the bathroom door and looked down the hall to the living room and kitchenette. There was no sign of him. Skylar let herself exhale. She started to go out into the hall when she heard a noise from the bedroom. Before she could turn, a familiar rough hand grabbed her around her mouth so she couldn't scream and pulled her back against him.

"You bitch," he growled. "I knew I couldn't trust you. Who were you going to go talk to? The cops?"

Skylar frantically shook her head back and forth, trying to bring the scissors up to stab at the hand covering the lower half of her face. His other hand grabbed her wrist and viciously twisted so she had no choice but to drop the scissors. The hand over her mouth shifted to also cover her nose so she couldn't breathe.

She began bucking and throwing herself back against him, grabbing and pulling on his hand, anything so she could breathe again. She felt his other arm encircle her throat, and her last thoughts before everything went black were, "I am so scared," "I am so sorry," and, "I want my mom."

CHAPTER ONE

DAISY KNEW IT WAS GOING TO BE A BAD DAY before she even opened her eyes. She recognized the heavy feeling in her chest and limbs, a feeling she had become all too familiar with in the last two years.

Jesus. Two years. She still couldn't believe such a terrible thing had happened to her. She'd woken up one day as a happily married woman, and by nightfall, she'd been a widow. All because of a stupid, tragic, bad-luck accident. She knew it had been an accident. Enough people had told her that. She told herself that. And most days, she could believe it. But she couldn't get past wondering if there was something *she* could have done to prevent it. If maybe she had ordered a cup of coffee before they'd started home that night, then she might not have been dozing in the passenger seat. Or if she had taken the car in to be checked, and they had found the flaw in the airbag . . . though who would have even suspected that the airbag was defective? That was something you didn't find out until it was too late, as Daisy was now well aware. And all the wondering, all the replaying that night in her head was eating her up inside. Especially now, after that phone call. She still got physically sick to her stomach every time she thought of it. What did that girl mean?

With a sigh, Daisy rolled over and got out of bed. She pulled on her robe that had been thrown over the foot of the bed and went into the kitchen to make coffee. Making coffee in the morning was only one of the small things that had changed so much in her life. Tommy had always made the coffee, mainly because he was always up before her. If that man spent more than five hours in bed, he felt like he was wasting the day, or "burning daylight," as he liked to say. She used to love walking out into the kitchen to the smell of freshly brewed coffee. Now she walked into a dark, not-smelling-like-coffee kitchen, and the grief hit her anew every fucking morning.

She sighed again and made herself begin her daily mantra. "I *will not* sigh. I *will not* cry. I *will not* go around with a frowny face scaring small children. I *will* smile. I *will* be open to any new opportunities that come my way. I *will* try to be happy." And then the tears came, just like they always did.

Usually, Daisy would indulge herself with a good five-minute cry, but on this day, Daisy angrily wiped the tears away and actually yelled in her not-smelling-like-coffee-kitchen, "ENOUGH! Jesus, ENOUGH, Daisy! Tommy would kick your ass if he knew you were going around acting like this every day," she told herself. "He's dead, yes. And I'll miss him every day, but I have to get my life back. Or I might as well get it over with and join him in the ground. So maybe I'll start drinking tea. That would solve at least one of my problems!"

Of course, she had given herself these little inspirational pep talks before, and they never really worked. But today seemed different somehow. Maybe it was because her sister, Lilly, had told her about an opening for a unit clerk at the hospital where Lilly worked. When Daisy had asked what the qualifications were, Lilly had said, "I think you just need to be able to work a computer and have some common sense. Heck, some of the people who have been there forever have neither of those qualities and they still manage to keep their job. Why don't I send you the notice and you can follow up on it if you want?"

For the first time in what seemed like forever, the thought of that unit clerk job sparked a tiny flame of interest—though despite what Lilly had said, Daisy wasn't sure she was qualified for the position. She had worked as a preschool teacher until Tommy was killed. Since that night, she had just *floated*. That was how she thought of it. *Floating.* She floated through life, bouncing off her family and friends, never really allowing herself to feel anything or think about anything too deeply. It was just easier that way.

But if she was honest with herself, she was tired of floating. She was turning into someone she never would have liked or tolerated when Tommy was alive— drab, uninteresting, and not at all fun to be around. Tommy and she had used to make fun of people who just phoned it in, people that weren't engaged with life. *God, we were smug,* Daisy thought. *But we had reason to be smug. We did have a great life.*

CHAPTER TWO

A WEEK LATER, after a lot of mental scolding, Daisy finally contacted the point person at the hospital to inquire about the unit clerk position. To her amazement, after two interviews, she got the job. She'd almost backed out, but Lilly had told her, firmly, that it was finally time for her to re-enter the world.

When Daisy got ready for bed the night before she was to report for her new job training, she set her alarm for six so she would have plenty of time to be at the hospital by eight. And it was a good thing she had. After waking up at 1:10 a.m., then 2:15, then 4:40, she'd finally fallen into one of those dark rabbit hole dreams where bizarre things happen. She'd dreamt about people she had gone to high school with, a childhood friend from the neighborhood where she had grown up, even the librarian at her old library.

When her alarm went off at six a.m., it took her about five minutes to get reoriented and out of bed. *Wow, what was my subconscious trying to tell me with that dream?* she thought as she shampooed her hair. *Maybe all those people from my past were trying to tell me I am making a HUGE MISTAKE!*

When Daisy got to the hospital at 7:45 a.m., she was very glad Lilly had told her exactly where to go on the third floor. Otherwise, Daisy would have wandered around like an idiot and probably would have been late for her very first day of unit clerk job training. And she was nervous enough without having to ask numerous people where the training room was.

Daisy looked into training room 312 and saw an older lady who was self-consciously looking down at her notepad and two younger women who were, of course, looking at their phones. When Daisy entered the room, all three of them looked up expectantly at her. Daisy laughed as she closed the door behind her and said, "Don't look at me. I'm here for training, just like you guys! My name is Daisy, and I do not have a clue what's going to happen today."

The older woman said, "Oh my gosh, I am so glad to hear that! I've been out of the workplace for so many years, it's ridiculous. I finally sent my last grandchild off to kindergarten, and I needed something to do with my time. My name is Miranda. I used to work in a hospital years ago. I ran the gift shop, you see, so I thought I would maybe do the same thing in this place. But I think they're just going to have me volunteer. I've been here for about thirty minutes because I was so afraid of being late!"

Just when Daisy thought Miranda was going to start pulling out pictures of her grandkids, the door opened, and a tall woman walked in. She introduced herself as Laura Kennedy and said she was the head of human resources. And with that, the training began.

———

A month later, Daisy walked through the front door of the Methodist Hospital, took a right that led her to the elevators, got in, and pushed the button for the third floor. Daisy stored her purse in the employee locker room and got a cup of coffee from the Keurig. Daisy had never seen a Keurig before working there, but after using it once, she was hooked. *I've got to buy one,* she thought. *That'll solve the problem of standing in my kitchen, waiting for the coffee to brew, and crying about Tommy.*

Daisy went out to the floor and sat down at her desk. There had been a couple of admissions during the night, and the orders were stacked neatly next to her computer. After spending two weeks shadowing an experienced unit clerk, today was Daisy's first day by herself on the job, and she was pretty nervous. She really wanted to make a good impression and not seem like a total ass who hadn't been in the workforce for a couple of years—even though that was exactly what she was. *PMA, Daisy. PMA.* Daisy could hear her father saying those letters in her ear, since that was what he'd said whenever one of the girls would get into a negative mood. "PMA. You can handle just about anything with a positive mental attitude."

So she would fucking PMA herself silly today. With that thought, she straightened her shoulders and began entering the routine orders into her computer.

CHAPTER THREE

ROSIE THREW UP HER HANDS in frustration, sighed, and pushed away from the computer. "Why is this so hard? Why can't I get this to come out right? How do Stephen King, Liane Moriarty, Curtis Sittenfeld, Donna Tartt, Elizabeth Gilbert—I could go on and on—all manage to write such wonderful books year after year?"

She turned to Big Shirley, who was trying to squeeze her entire body into the space under Rosie's desk. It would never happen, but the 130-pound Newfoundland was eternally hopeful. Whenever Rosie sat at her desk in the guest bedroom, Shirley would spend the entire time trying to maneuver into the space.

"You will never admit defeat, will you?" Rosie asked.

Shirley's tail beat a rhythm on the floor as she looked at Rosie with devotion.

"That's because you are as stubborn as I am. Although I don't think your motivating stubbornness factor is to become famous. You just want to get under the desk, whereas I . . ."

Rosie sighed. If she were honest with herself, she did not want worldwide fame. Mainly, she just wanted to prove to herself that she could write a book. Rosie couldn't remember a time when she hadn't wanted to write a novel. It had always been in the very back of her mind, and now that she had the time to do it, she was dismayed at how hard it was to put pen to paper—or fingers to keyboard, as it were. "Shit," she said out loud. "Maybe if I get some pens and legal pads, I might actually accomplish something."

"Did you say something?" Rosie's sister asked from the other room, having just come in through the unlocked front door. "Or are you talking to Ms. Shirley again?"

At the sound of her name, the Newfie got to her feet and ambled out the door to greet Lilly, Rosie's older sister. Next to Rosie, Lilly was Shirley's favorite person. Probably because Lilly was one of the few people who didn't mind the thick strings of drool occasionally hanging from Shirley's mouth. Lilly had learned to always keep a towel handy to wipe them away.

Rosie had adopted Big Shirley a year ago from a farm in South Carolina. The Newfoundland Rescue Society had contacted Rosie about Big Shirley because they knew Rosie had put down her ten-year-old Newfie, Lucy, the summer before. Lucy had been her first experience with Newfoundlands, and Rosie had fallen in love with the gentle, laid-back, life-is-good breed. She mourned Lucy, but she always felt better when she remembered all their happy times. When the Rescue Society called, Rosie was going to refuse to consider three-year-old Big Shirley, but when she opened the picture they'd emailed of the black Newfie with the soulful eyes, Rosie felt her heart lurch and an involuntary smile spread across her face. She looked so much like Lucy!

"Of course she looks like Lucy," Rosie's younger sister, Amy, had said. "All Newfies look alike! Black, hairy, and drooly, with a penchant for being a couch potato—have I missed anything?"

Amy had a point. With their domed heads and deep-set black eyes, along with the pink tongues that were always poking out, it was sometimes difficult to tell one Newfie from another. Not only was Amy the only sister out of the four of them who didn't have a flower name, but she was also the only one pragmatic about dogs. She did love them, but she certainly didn't tolerate the hair and drool that accompanied dogs, especially Newfoundlands, the way Daisy, Lilly, and Rosie did.

Rosie still grinned whenever she thought back to the day Shirley arrived. The dog service had agreed to bring Big Shirley to Texas from South Carolina, and when she'd arrived, all Shirley had with her was a towel. No toys, no dog bowl, no leash—just a towel. And the first time Shirley shook her head back and forth and the drool went flying, Rosie understood the importance of that small towel.

"Yes, I'm talking to the dog. At least she understands me." Rosie got up and walked out to the kitchen, where her sister was pouring herself a cup of coffee. Lilly was two years older than Rosie and happily married to Keith O'Rourke, a lawyer in town specializing in estate planning and bankruptcy. Keith always joked that what he really wanted to do was specialize in medical malpractice, but he wanted to marry Lilly, who was a nurse, even more, so boring bankruptcy became his job. Lilly and Keith had been married for eight years and had two children, three-year-old Luke and eighteen-month-old Lacey.

"What's going on today? How did you escape the looney bin, the place that used to be such a haven of peace and quiet until you and Keith decided to repopulate the world?"

Lilly smiled, put her hands over her head, and stretched. "Keith's mom offered to watch the kids, and I'm no fool. I took her up on the offer and skedaddled out of there. Do you want to go on a run?"

"God, I want to, but I really shouldn't. I told myself I was going to plant my ass in my office for the entire day and work on my book, which lately, I'm thinking should just be a short story. How can you have writer's block when you don't even have the first chapter finished?" Rosie asked.

"Come on, you need to get out of the house, if just for thirty minutes. We'll do a quick run over to the woods, and you'll come back with a whole new attitude. And besides, it's one of the first gorgeous April days we've had."

"All right, whatever. It's not like I'm accomplishing anything sitting here staring at the computer. Let me go change." Rosie headed down the hall to her bedroom, and Big Shirley began to follow her but thought better of it. Why go to all that trouble when pets from Lilly were only a few steps away?

CHAPTER FOUR

HER FINGERNAILS were the first things he'd noticed. They were cut short and slightly rounded. There was a clear coat of polish on them, but that was it. No flowers, no two-toned polish, no stars and stripes, no tiny jewels, no letters that were supposed to spell out some esoteric message. In short, they looked like what fingernails were supposed to look like.

Actually, the fingernails were the second thing Ren had noticed, but he was having so much trouble processing what he was seeing that he focused on the nails. His brain could not make sense of the scene before him. A woman was lying on her back, about two feet off the path. Her hands were folded neatly on her chest, and if it weren't for the way her head was tilted grotesquely to one side, he would have thought she was taking a nap.

There was no blood Ren could see, no disorder to the area around her. She was dressed in black jeans, sandals, and a generic black T-shirt. Ren estimated that she was around twenty-five years old, and he was certain he had never seen her before in his life. So, what was she doing in the woods behind his house and office? Ren leaned forward and felt for a pulse on her neck. Her skin was cold and felt stiff.

Rigor mortis? Ren thought. *Like I know what the fuck rigor mortis feels like in a person. Probably the same as an animal. What am I doing standing here? I need to go call someone.*

As he was thinking this, Ren noticed something coming at him out of the corner of his eye and jumped back, away from the body. One hundred and eighty pounds of Great Dane skidded to a stop next to him and bent down to sniff at the body. "Shit," Ren yelled. "Walter, get back. SIT."

Walter immediately dropped to his haunches and looked at Ren with something like reproach in his eyes. Ren never yelled at Walter, and besides, Walter was only going to sniff at the object laying on the ground. It smelled funny.

Ren was just grateful it was Walter that had come down the path and not Walter's sister, Marilyn. Marilyn would have totally ignored him. Ren often thought Marilyn was born with the balls in the family, not Walter.

Ren stood up, and, with one hand on Walter's collar, he fruitlessly patted his pockets, hoping in vain he had brought his cell phone with him. Ren knew he'd left his phone in his office because he was just taking a brief stroll in the woods before his afternoon appointments, but he had to try anyway. Ren was a veterinarian, and he had taken over the practice from a very popular vet who had retired the year before, so he was usually very busy.

The morning had been crazy, with a couple of emergencies making a mockery of his schedule. A small stray dog had been hit by a car and found on the side of the road by Claire Graham, the teenager who helped in his office. Claire said she'd seen the car hit the dog, and it hadn't even slowed down. She'd told Ren it had been a black car, and that she'd even memorized the license plate, sheepishly adding that memorizing license plates was just a weird thing she always did. She'd been able to get the dog out of the street and into her car, but by the time she'd brought the dog in, and Ren had gotten the dog on the table in one of the exam rooms, the dog had died.

Then Mrs. Cramer had brought in her cat, Tom—*such an original name*, Ren thought—who had to be at least twenty years old and was surviving on a wing and a prayer. Ren had brought that cat back from the brink of death so many times in the last year, he had lost count, but he knew the cat was the only thing Mrs. Cramer still cared about, so he kept treating Tom and kept his mouth shut about the possibility of euthanasia.

At the sound of voices, Ren tightened his hold on Walter and turned to face whoever was coming up the path. It sounded like two women, each slightly out of breath but still talking a mile a minute. When Lilly and Rosie came around the corner, they saw Ren standing there, a gigantic Great Dane by his side. Walter let out a loud HARUMP, and Lilly and Rosie both stumbled to a stop.

"He won't hurt you," was the first thing Ren said. A dog the size of Walter usually inspired both fear and awe, and Ren had learned early on to put people at ease. "Do either one of you have a cell phone? I don't have my phone and, well, there's a problem." Ren moved sideways off the path, and Rosie and Lilly saw the young woman for the first time.

"Oh my God, what happened?" Rosie asked. "What's wrong with her head? Is she dead?" Lilly started toward the woman, but Rosie grabbed her arm. "What are you doing?" she asked.

"I need to see if I can help her."

"I'm pretty sure she's dead. I don't think we should screw up the crime scene," Ren added.

"How in the hell do you know she's dead? Did you feel for

a pulse?" Lilly's voice was rising. "And who the hell are you? Just what the fuck is going on? Did you hurt her? Kill her?"

"Christ, no, I didn't kill her. What a stupid question. Do I look like a murderer? I've never seen her before in my life! I just came from my office and found her about two seconds ago." Ren didn't blame the women. The scene before them was something out of a nightmare and totally beyond comprehension.

Rosie knew if Lilly was saying "fuck," then she was seriously upset, and she could hardly blame her. The whole situation was bizarre, and Rosie was beginning to feel the first frisson of fear.

"Neither of us has a cell phone," Rosie said.

"My office is just up the hill. Do you guys feel okay staying here while I go call the police? Walter will stay here with you if I tell him to. I will feel better if he stays, just in case."

"Just in case the murderer comes back? Is that what you're thinking? Just in case the nutcase in the hockey mask comes around the corner, looking for more victims?" Rosie's voice was also rising. She always talked too much when she was stressed, and she was very stressed at this point.

"We all need to calm down and think this through," said Lilly. "Yes, whoever you are, please go and call the police. We will stay here, and I think Walter should stay with us. Please hurry!"

Ren ordered Walter to sit and stay, then took off up the hill without another word.

Lilly and Rosie looked at each other in shock and then both looked at Walter, as if he could fill them in on what had happened in the last couple of minutes. Walter just looked back at them and snorted as if to say, "Get with the program. Do something constructive!"

"Good thing we're not afraid of dogs, although I would say this one qualifies as more of a horse than a dog."

Lilly didn't reply. She started over to where the young woman's body was laid out.

"What are you doing? I think what's-his-name is right. We don't want to mess up any clues."

"What, do you think the CSI people are going to pick up the one leaf I step on, and when they analyze it at the lab, discover I screwed up the only clue needed to find the killer? Although they do manage to solve murders from just a tiny piece of cloth on TV, and we all know everything we see on TV is true." Lilly was basically just talking to herself while she took in the dead woman.

"What is the matter with us?" Rosie asked. "Why aren't we in hysterics? There's a dead girl not more than five feet from us. Her neck and head are twisted. Oh, that must have hurt! Do you recognize her at all?"

"I think we're having a hard time digesting this because it's so surreal. And the fact there's no blood or gross stuff coming out of her is making this seem totally unreal. Like we stumbled onto a movie set or something. And she does kind of look familiar to me, but I can't really place her." Lilly stopped about a foot away from the girl and squatted down on her haunches, being careful not to touch anything.

"Lil, I know you're a nurse, but aren't you freaked out?"

"You know, it's weird. Why isn't this whole area totally messed up? If someone did this to her here, you would think it'd look like a tornado hit or something. She must have been killed someplace else and moved here. I wonder why?"

"Truly, who the hell cares? I just want to get out of here! Do you think we should have let that guy leave? Maybe he's the killer?"

"For some reason, leaving Walter here to protect us doesn't seem like something a killer would do. He could have made his dog attack us or something."

"I don't think that would happen," said Rosie. "He's too gentle." Rosie had gone over to Walter and was scratching him behind his ears, and Walter, doing what all Great Danes liked to do, was leaning his entire body against her with his eyes closed. "He would have to take a nap before he could take us down."

Walter's ears pricked up, and he turned his head in the direction Ren had gone. Lilly and Rosie then heard Ren running back down to them. He came around the corner, cell phone in one hand and a pistol in the other.

Lilly rose from her crouch. Rosie turned and said, "Uh, what in the hell are you doing with that?"

"The cops are on their way, and I grabbed this out of my office just in case we need it. I don't have a clue where the person is who did this, but I don't want to take any chances." He lowered his voice and went on, "But I gotta be honest with you, I don't even know if it's loaded."

"Give it to me," Rosie ordered. "Let me see it."

"You know about guns?"

"Yeah, I've been around guns all my life."

Ren at least knew enough to give the gun to Rosie butt first. It was a standard Smith & Wesson revolver with all six rounds. Rosie brought it down by her side and admitted to herself she felt better with it in her hand.

They could hear the faint sound of an approaching siren, and they all stood awkwardly on the path, not really wanting to look at the body but helpless to stop their eyes from drifting back to her.

"I wonder who she is and how she got here," Ren said. "I mean, it's obvious she wasn't killed here. Everything is so neat around her. It looks like she just laid down to take a nap. I mean, if only her head wasn't twisted like that."

"We noticed," said Rosie. "That's probably what stopped us from karate chopping you and everything. That's what we would have done if we thought you had killed her. We're a lethal team, you know."

Ren looked at Rosie and opened his mouth to respond but then closed it. His look said it all. *You are a nutcase.*

"Don't mind her. Her mouth starts spouting random stuff when she's weirded out," Lilly said. "Way too much imagination for her own good."

Just then, three uniformed police officers came down the path, and Ren, Rosie, Lilly, and Walter turned toward them and gladly let them take charge of the scene.

CHAPTER FIVE

REN FINALLY GOT BACK TO THE OFFICE around four p.m. He had called the office and told them about the murder, and his office manager had rescheduled most of his patients. There were a few she'd been unable to get a hold of, and they were waiting in the exam rooms.

"Do they know who she is?" asked Claire. "I wish you would have let me go down there."

"The cops said they didn't want a crowd, and you probably wouldn't have been able to see anything anyway. By the time the coroner got there with his crew, it was too crowded to see anything."

"Still, how cool. A murder. I don't think we've ever had one in this town."

"Good," said Julie Jones, Ren's office manager and secretary, who had just come into the back office with charts. "I'm glad I live in a place where you can say that. I just feel sorry for her and any family she has. What a terrible thing to have happened! And now I hate to say it, but there are patients waiting." Julie ran a tight ship, and Ren would never admit it, but she kind of intimidated him. She had an answer for everything, and nothing seemed to faze her.

"Bring 'em on back," Ren said as he went around the corner to wash his hands.

Dwayne Cooper was sitting in the examination room with Leonard, his English bulldog, at his feet when Ren walked into the exam room. Ren was always puzzled when he saw the pair. For one thing, Leonard was a girl dog, and Dwayne Cooper didn't look like a person who would think it was funny to give a girl dog a boy's name, but he obviously had. For another, the two were just an odd couple. Leonard had the typical bulldog face, like it was left in the oven too long and melted. Her underbite jutted out with a somewhat sideways turn, and truthfully, she didn't look too bright. But she was a lovable dog, and Ren really got a kick out of her.

She marched across the room with the pugnacious walk all bulldogs have and plopped down at Ren's feet with an audible grunt. Her corkscrew tail was wagging, and she looked at Ren as if to say, "Please pet me and tell me I'm cute. My owner never does that and it's bugging the shit out of me."

Truth be told, Ren did not care for Dwayne. He was prissy in nature and always had something negative to say. He never really acted like he *liked* his dog, which was not a typical dog owner in Ren's opinion.

"What can I do for you today?" he asked Dwayne.

"Well, I knew when I was in last week your girl didn't give me the right ointment for her rash, so here I am again. I certainly hope you won't charge me an additional office visit, when if you had got it right the first time, I wouldn't have had to come back in."

Ren thought of many things to say to Dwayne but held his tongue and bent down to look at Leonard. She tried to lick his face, radiating happiness that someone was talking to her. "Okay, we'll get her fixed up. And, of course, there will be no charge."

After Dwayne and Leonard left with samples of the same medicine with a different label glued on free of charge, Ren went into the second examination room. There he found a dog owner that was the exact opposite of Dwayne. Maggie Redcamp and her constant companion, Lois, were sitting patiently on the seat in the exam room.

Lois was a rescue dog, and the three-legged Scottish Terrier had the most winsome face Ren had ever seen. No one knew why Lois's back leg had been amputated. She was about six years old when she had been found on the side of the road by an elderly couple driving to the store. They had taken her to the local animal shelter, and the shelter had contacted Maggie, who sometimes fostered animals. In this case, Maggie decided to adopt Lois after fostering her for only a month. Maggie always said, "Lois has only three legs and I have only one arm. Together, we make a whole person!"

Maggie's right arm had been amputated above the elbow after a farming accident when she was five, but once you got to know Maggie, you realized it didn't make any difference to her. She just did the same thing with one and a half arms that everyone else did with two.

"What's going on with the Scottish lass today?" Ren asked, trying to use a Scottish accent but failing miserably.

Maggie just smiled at him. Lois reacted to Ren's voice by wagging her tail so furiously she was in danger of falling over.

"Hey there, girl," Ren said, squatting down to pet Lois. "You need to slow that back end down!"

"I'm probably being too overcautious, but she's been off her feed the last couple of days, and I just want to make sure she's not coming down with something."

"Well, let me take a look at her. She certainly looks like she feels okay. I might run some bloodwork, just to cover all bases."

"I don't want to be a ghoul, but did you really find a dead girl in the woods today?" Maggie asked. "How terrible for you, and for the girl!"

Ren knew the town gossip machine had been working overtime since the murdered girl had been found, but he was still surprised Maggie had heard about it already. She lived on a rather deserted country road a couple of miles out of town and, as far as Ren knew, really didn't socialize with too many people.

"I stopped in at the grocery store before coming here and that was all anyone was talking about," Maggie explained. "Did you recognize her?"

"No, I swear I've never seen her before. Then again, I've only been here for about a year, so I don't know everyone in town. I got the impression the cops didn't recognize her either, although maybe they were just being cops and didn't want to give out any information. The whole thing was so strange. When I first saw her, it took me a minute to really realize what I was looking at. And when my brain finally made the connection there was a dead girl in front of me, all I could think was that it sure wasn't like what you see on TV. It actually looked . . . peaceful, as strange as that sounds." Ren shook himself out of his thoughts and picked up Lois. "Let's get this girl taken care of."

CHAPTER SIX

THE NEXT MORNING, Rosie was back at her computer with Big Shirley once more trying to squeeze under the desk. "Is this going to be how the rest of my life goes?" Rosie asked Shirley. "Staring at my computer, trying to force words out of my brain and onto the paper, slowly going crazy because it isn't working? Am I trying too hard? Is my motivation for trying to write a book too self-serving, so the word gods are denying me? God, just shut up and write!" But instead, Rosie leaned back in her chair and turned her thoughts back to the bizarre events of the previous afternoon.

Rosie knew one of the policemen who had made their way down the path. She had gone to school with Danny Wright and briefly dated him before she left for New York three years ago. When Danny and two other officers had come around the corner, they'd stopped and assessed the situation. Ren and Walter had been standing to the right of the girl, with Rosie and Lilly slightly behind them. The older officer had knelt next to the girl, felt for a pulse, then began speaking quietly into the radio on his shoulder. Danny had turned and spotted Rosie.

"Hey, Rosie. What in the heck are you doing in town?" Danny had asked, looking at her with a puzzled expression. "And Lilly. How are you? What are you guys doing here?"

"Hi, Danny. Um, I moved back about six months ago, and

Lilly and I were out for a run. We came around the corner and saw him." She'd gestured to Ren by looking in his direction. "And, well, here we are. Oh, and Danny, I have a gun." She'd brought the revolver up and handed it to him. "It's his."

Danny moved his gaze to Ren. "Sir, is this your gun?"

Ren nodded and told him he'd just brought it down for protection. Danny's look told Ren what he thought of that idea, but he said he would return it to Ren after they made sure it had not been fired recently.

"Did you touch the victim?"

"I just felt her neck to see if there was a pulse, but other than that, I didn't touch a thing."

"Sir, if you would just step over here, I would appreciate it. I am going to need to ask you a few questions. And sir, I need you to make sure you keep a strong hold on your dog. Lilly and Rosie, please walk over to Officer Clifford." Danny had indicated to the third officer. "And tell him what you all know about this situation."

Walter had just been standing there, looking back and forth between Danny and Ren, as if he was listening to both of them. But Rosie could tell Walter was making Danny nervous. She had forgotten until now that Danny was not a big dog lover. That probably explained why they had only dated a short time.

Ren had shot Rosie a "thanks a lot" look. "Certainly, officer. My dog won't hurt you." *Unless I tell him to*, he'd wanted to add, but decided to keep his mouth shut.

They'd moved slightly up the path, and Danny had taken out a notebook and begun questioning Ren. Rosie couldn't hear what he was saying, but although Ren had looked a little worried, he'd been answering the questions without any hesitation.

The next couple of hours were spent giving their statements and watching the coroner give a cursory exam to the body and direct the evidence collection. They'd been told they could go home, but to probably expect another call from the police to tell them when and where they would need to go to formalize their statements. When Danny said this, he'd looked at Rosie. She could tell he'd wanted to say more to her but had thought better of it. "I'll talk to you all later," was all he'd said, and then turned back to the crime scene.

"I always wondered what happened between you and Danny," Lilly had said as they'd made their way back down the hill. "You guys have a lot in common, so I really thought it would work out."

Rosie had sighed. "Yeah, it was maybe too comfortable with him. I mean, I have known him since grade school. It's hard to get excited about someone when you know they saw you wet your pants in first grade because the stupid teacher wouldn't let you go to the bathroom."

Lilly had laughed. "Oh, that. God, I totally forgot about your urinary dysfunctions when you were a kid! You did have a couple of mishaps, if I remember right!"

"Gee, thanks for reminding me. No wonder I can't go anywhere without scoping out where the bathrooms are first. I'm scarred."

"More like you're scarred because every time we would go somewhere new, Dad would tell you there was just one thing they forgot when they were building the place and that was a bathroom. And you believed him!"

"I was kind of a goober, wasn't I?"

Rosie grinned to herself when she thought back to that conversation. She knew she was blessed to be such good friends with all her sisters. She was perhaps the closest to Lilly, mainly because Lilly was just two years older, and they'd shared a room growing up. That's not to say they didn't fight like cats and dogs most of the time during their teen years, but Rosie always knew she could turn to Lilly for just about anything. Who else would have taken her to the bathroom in the middle of the night because Rosie had just known that the boogey man would come down the hall at the exact moment she sat down to pee?

Wow, come to think of it, I was obsessed with my bladder, Rosie thought.

Daisy was six years older than Rosie, and their relationship was more of the big sister/little sister type, although now that Rosie had moved back to town, she found herself becoming closer to her eldest sister. Amy was the youngest of the four girls, and she was three years younger than Rosie. To this day, the girls never could figure out why their mother had decided to forego the flower names and name her Amy. They were never able to ask their mother because she died after giving birth to Amy. According to their father, she'd begun bleeding heavily a few hours after the delivery and sustained a heart attack due to the blood loss. Their dad had always said even though the nurses and doctors were right there and did everything they could, it must have been her time because they were unable to save her.

The Hurley sisters had grown up in Brunswick, Texas, which was about fifty miles east of Dallas. They'd had somewhat of an idyllic childhood. Their father, Jack, was the editor of the *Brunswick Chronicle,* one of the newspapers in town, and the girls had been exposed to all sorts of interesting and intellectual happenings on a daily basis. Even when the girls were young, their father would talk to them at the dinner table about current worldly events.

Rosie had always known she wanted to follow in her father's footsteps into some kind of profession that dealt with words, and so she'd been ecstatic when she'd received an internship at a fledgling newspaper in New York after she'd graduated from college. Little had she known at the time, the three years she would spend in New York at the *Times Express News* would be some of the best years of her life—and also some of the worst.

CHAPTER SEVEN

LILLY HAD BEEN A REGISTERED NURSE for the last ten years, and normally she enjoyed her job. But today, she was tired. Tired of the unrelenting stress of taking care of patients and their families, who expected one-on-one care and didn't understand Lilly had four other patients to deal with. Tired because she hadn't slept well the night before. She'd kept seeing the murder scene in her dreams and would jerk awake with a gasp every time she tried to focus on the girl's face.

In her dreams, the girl had a covering over her face. Lilly practiced amateur psychology on herself and decided her subconscious was trying to tell her she knew the girl. She had this underlying feeling that maybe she did know her, but just couldn't come up with a name or even where she would have seen her. Lilly worked in the Coronary Care Unit at the Methodist Hospital, and her patients were usually older people with heart problems. Possibly a family member? Maybe a nurse from another floor?

Her musings were cut short when the unit secretary called her phone and told her Mr. Thompson in room 112 had a complaint about his IV. *What else is new?* Lilly thought. Mr. Thompson complained about everything. And if it wasn't him doing the complaining, it was his wife. Unfortunately, Mr. Thompson was a fairly prominent businessman in the city and had donated a substantial amount of money to the hospital. Not that Lilly would treat any of her patients differently just because they were rich, but when even the doctors kowtowed to him, she knew she had to tread lightly.

Although come to think of it, not all the doctors bow down to Mr. Thompson. Dr. Jonathan "Dickhead" Booker (that was what Lilly had always secretly called him. She just hoped she didn't blurt it out one day when she wasn't paying attention) *doesn't care who anyone was. He's such an asshole himself that any clues regarding social niceties are lost on him.* Lilly smiled to herself at the thought of her frequent daydream where she told Dr. Booker exactly what she thought of him. Though her smile always faded when she thought about how she would have to tell Keith she just got fired from her job. Why did reality always have to stick its nose into her happy thoughts?

"Tell Mr. Thompson I'm on my way," Lilly said to the unit secretary as she rounded the corner to go to his room. "And please let it be just a simple empty IV bottle," she prayed under her breath. "I really don't have time today to restart his IV."

Of course, his IV had clotted off, and forty-five minutes later, after she'd had to listen to Mr. Thompson and his wife make some snide comments about why it took her a total of three times to restart his IV, she was heading into the medication room to catch up on her morning meds when she ran into Janet Franklin, one of her best friends in the unit. "Hey, Lil. Do you have a minute to help me with Mrs. Smith?"

"Let me get some of these meds passed, and I'll meet you in there. Give me ten minutes."

"Okay, hurry up though. I want to hear all about it!"

Lilly figured she was talking about the murder. She was surprised it had taken this long for someone to mention it.

Fifteen minutes later, Lilly met up with Janet at the bedside of Mrs. Smith, a seventy-six-year-old who had suffered a massive stroke about a week ago. She was in a vegetative state but was still being treated aggressively. Lilly and Janet both knew it was just a matter of time before only palliative measures were going to be ordered. Lilly had taken care of Mrs. Smith when she was first admitted and had grown fond of her three daughters who were constantly at her bedside. Lilly could tell the daughters were just beginning to realize their mother was not going to make it. It was a cold hard fact many people never were able to comprehend.

"Oh my God, so did you really find that dead girl?" Janet asked. "Tell me everything! Do you have any idea who it is?"

"You know, that's what's been bugging me since yesterday. I feel like, not that I knew who she was, but maybe I had seen her somewhere at some time. I've been racking my brain trying to re-member, but it's, you know, right on the tip of my tongue. It's driving me crazy!"

"Don't even think about it, and then it will come to you. If you do think about it, don't concentrate on trying to remember her name." Janet had graduated with a psychology degree before going to nursing school, and Lilly sometimes thought she felt she was qualified enough to hang out a shingle.

"Well, I'll keep you posted if anything pops into my head. But right now, I have to run. I'm so far behind, I'm never going to get out of here on time."

Lilly was almost at the end of her shift, and she was congratu-lating herself for making it through the day without pissing some-one off or doing something totally stupid when she rounded the corner and ran right into Dr. Dickhead. He dropped the chart he was carrying, and the pages went all over the floor. Lilly did a juggling act with the apple she was carrying and managed to grab it before it hit the floor.

"Oh my gosh, are you all right?" Lilly asked Dr. Booker.

"Of course I am. Are you okay? Is there a fire somewhere you're running to? Or away from?"

"Uh, well, no fire. And I wasn't really running . . ." She was trying to convey without words that she thought he was being an asshole, but she could tell it wasn't working.

Dr. Booker just bent over and started picking up the scattered pages. "Well, if there's no fire, maybe you could fill me in on something. Were you really involved in finding the murdered girl yesterday in the woods? That must have been very frightening for you."

Lilly was so astounded; she could only gape at him. Their conversations had always stayed strictly in the back and forth regarding the medical information for the patient. Lilly sometimes thought he was a robot, or better yet, some creature from outer space. She could never figure out why some space creature would want to work at a hospital, but it didn't stop her from thinking it. He came onto the hospital floor, discussed his patients, and left. No chitchat like some of the other doctors. Which Lilly preferred, if she was being honest with herself.

"Well, um, yes, in fact, my sister and I did stumble onto the dead girl. And it really wasn't scary, which is so strange. The whole scene was peaceful, which is even stranger."

"Well, I'm glad you're okay. Now, I trust you will slow down the next time you're running around like a chicken with its head cut off." He started down the hall, and even though Lilly could not see him, he gave a small chuckle to himself.

Lilly just stood there and stared at his retreating back. God, what world was he from? Running around like a chicken without a head? He sounded like he was ninety years old, but Lilly knew he was just a few years older than herself. Lilly often wondered if he did these things deliberately because he thought it was a hoot how mad she got. Perhaps he had a mental bet with himself that one day she was just going to explode around him. *Yep, I couldn't have run into anyone else. It had to be the dickhead!* she thought. *Let's just finish the day and get out of here before you get yourself fired.*

Because Lilly worked a twelve-hour shift, she didn't get home until around eight that evening. Keith, God bless him, had already fed and bathed the kids. She went upstairs and found Lacey asleep in her crib and Keith rocking a very sleepy Luke. She bent down and kissed Luke on his forehead, then gave Keith the same chaste kiss.

"That's all I get?" Keith whispered.

"You're lucky you even got that. I am so tired; I can barely keep my eyes open. I'm going to shower and go to bed. Is that okay? I promise I'll do diaper and bath duty tomorrow night."

"Lightweight." Keith smiled at her. "Go to bed. You look like crap."

As Lilly went into the bathroom to take her shower, she admitted to herself she was one lucky gal. Keith was probably the most even-keeled man on the planet and didn't seem to have a problem with taking over so many of the chores other men might deem "for the wife to do." She had heard enough from some of the nurses she worked with to know Keith was probably one of a kind. *How did I get so fortunate?* she asked herself.

She was still thinking how happy she was with Keith when he pulled open the shower curtain and said, "Do I get a thank-you fuck for taking care of our kids?"

She just smiled and held open her arms.

CHAPTER EIGHT

AMY WAS STANDING IN HER CLOSET trying to decide what to wear. Her small closet wasn't exactly the neatest place in her house. For one thing, Amy liked to try things on but absolutely did not like hanging them back up, so the clothes gravitated to a couple of piles on the floor. One pile was shirts, the other pile was skirts—or maybe it was skirts and jeans together? It was kind of hard to tell. She couldn't even fool herself that there was a method to the mess. It was just a mess.

Amy wanted to wear something that looked pulled together but not something that looked like she had spent a lot of time thinking about it. Today was such an important day, and she really didn't want to start off on the wrong foot. Although she seriously doubted anyone was going to care what the heck she had on. *Today is the first day of my own personal hell. Why, oh why, oh why, did I do this to myself?* she thought.

Today was her first day of law school, and Amy was both excited and scared out of her mind. She figured everyone would be too petrified of saying the wrong thing in class or not having prepared enough to even notice her. She had read *One L*, for God's sake— the book by Scott Turow, detailing his first year at Harvard Law. So, she knew all about the Socratic method, and how everyone was only out for themselves, and how the pressure to get the best grades was so intense it made people do horrible things like hide cases that were needed for class, and truthfully, it was making her stomach hurt.

Amy had taken two years off after high school to earn money for college and worked every entry level job possible. She worked at McDonald's, at Macy's, at the various food court restaurants at the mall, as a lifeguard during the summer at the local YMCA— and she had even worked for two memorable weeks on a construction crew, holding the stop and go signs out on Highway 24. It had been hot, it had been smelly (mainly it was her that was smelly because she stood in the burning sun and sweated like a pig), and to top it off, she almost was hit a couple of times because, of course, no one wants to put down their phone, not even for a second. Regardless of the fact they were driving a car. Amy always told her sisters those two weeks "on the chain gang" were what had convinced her to go to college.

Amy had gone to a small liberal arts college in the Northeast and loved every minute of her college experience. She'd joined the Phi Pi sorority and made a ton of friends, both boys and girls. To her surprise, she found she enjoyed studying, and especially making good grades. She had done okay in high school but certainly nothing to write home about. College had seemed to bring out the competitive side of her nature, and kicking butt in the classroom had really appealed to her.

"Get a move on," she muttered to herself. She pulled on a clean pair of jeans, tucked in her shirt, and stuck her feet in her favorite cowboy boots. "Now they'll know they're dealing with a cowgirl. Don't mess with Texas, as they say!"

Amy pulled into the parking lot of the law school and took a deep breath. She had called Rosie on her drive to school, knowing her older sister would cheer her up and put this day into perspective.

"You're smart, you aced the LSATs, you're pretty darn cute—and I can say that because you look like me—and, if I know you, you have on your lucky cowboy boots! You have all the bases covered! Besides, I sincerely doubt they're going to haul you up in front of the class on the very first day and interrogate you," Rosie said.

"I know. *I know.* And I really don't think they'll start right in on us, at least I hope not. It was just crazy the amount of stuff they expected us to read before classes even started. And you hear all sorts of stupid crap from people, you know? Like, 'Well, my boyfriend's sister's best friend went to law school and didn't even make it the first week.' Why do people say shit like that? It's like Lilly always saying how people will try to one-up you in medicine. If you're diagnosed with an ulcer, then there's someone who will say their uncle had three ulcers and it killed him. Shit, I'm rambling."

"Yeah, you are. But that's okay. Get all the bad karma out of your system before you go into class!" Rosie laughed. "Gotta run. I'm meeting with Danny to talk some more about the dead girl we found. See, there are worse things than going to your first day of law school. You could be that dead girl!"

Amy was right. Rosie *always* found a way to put things in perspective.

CHAPTER NINE

THAT EVENING THEY ALL MET over at Daisy's to have some drinks and dinner. About once a month the sisters liked to get together and catch up on each other's lives. Everyone was so busy, they'd found that if they didn't make a concerted effort to get together, then months would go by without all of them seeing each other.

"You will absolutely NOT believe what I found out today," said Amy.

Daisy, Lilly, and Amy were seated around Daisy's round wrought iron table on the patio. Amy was drinking a beer, and Daisy and Lilly were having glasses of red wine.

"I can't wait for Rosie to get here to tell you," Amy went on. "Besides, she's always late. Okay, how weird is this? The dead girl you guys found about a month ago?" She looked at Lilly. "Her sister is going to be in school with me. I heard some people talking about it. Her name is—er—was Skylar Smith. Isn't that weird?"

"Skylar Smith? Skylar Smith. Why does that sound so familiar?" Lilly asked herself. Suddenly, her eyes widened, and her eyebrows practically went up to her hairline. "Oh my gosh! Are you sure?"

Amy nodded.

"I knew I had seen her before! I'm taking care of her grandmother at the hospital. Her daughters and grandkids have been in and out the last couple of weeks, that's where I saw her. I think she's a granddaughter. Or a great-granddaughter. I have been racking my brain trying to remember where I knew her from. Wow, that poor family."

"Hellooo," Rosie yelled from the kitchen.

"We're out here," Lilly called. "Grab yourself a drink and sit down."

Rosie appeared a moment later at the back door carrying her favorite drink, Hendrick's gin over ice. No vermouth, no yucky olive juice, no tonic. Just Hendrick's and a slice of cucumber if she wanted to take the time. Tonight, she didn't.

"Hey, I met with Danny Wright today about that dead girl we found, and I know her name."

"We know it too! Her name is Skylar Smith. Her sister is going to be in class with me. Lilly knows her too."

"What are you talking about?" Rosie looked at Lilly. "You said you didn't know her."

"Well, I kept thinking I had seen her somewhere before, and then when Amy said her name, I remembered her from the hospital. I'm taking care of her grandmother. Or great-grandmother, I don't know which. And it doesn't really matter! What did Danny say about her? Did they find out who killed her?"

Rosie snorted. "Well, if he knows who killed her, he's certainly not sharing it with me. I had to practically drag her name out of him. He is not being very forthcoming with information."

"He's not going to tell you anything but the basic facts," said Amy. "You had to practically browbeat him into meeting with you. Although I'm not so sure you had to twist his arm too hard. He did just break up with his girlfriend, and he has always had a thing for you."

"Oh, get out. We went out eons ago, and he wasn't too broken up when I ended it with him. I think he wanted to say it was my loss, but he knew I would kick the shit out of him if he did."

"Hey, Daisy. Daisy. Are you okay?" Lilly was looking at Daisy, and the other two sisters both turned to her. "What's wrong? You look like you're going to faint or puke."

Daisy was about the color of congealed oatmeal, and she had her hand on her chest. Lilly squatted beside her. She took her wrist and felt for her pulse, then asked her if she was having chest pain. Daisy shook her head no and opened her mouth like she wanted to say something, but then just sat there, shaking her head. Tears were starting to form in her eyes.

"Your pulse is a little fast but not bad. Honey, what's wrong?"

Daisy looked at her three sisters, who were all crowded around her with the same expression of concern on their faces. "I . . . um . . . I don't know what to do." She took a very shaky breath and then burst into tears. "I just . . . if only Tommy was here. I really didn't know what she meant. I didn't know what to do, and so I didn't go, and now that girl is dead." She gulped some air, then put her head down in her arms and sobbed.

"What the fuck?" Amy said, and the three sisters all looked at each other.

"Okay. Rosie, go get her some water and a washcloth for her face. Amy, bring me my drink. Daisy, we're here to help you, but you have to let us know what's going on. You need to stop crying and tell us what's the matter." Lilly had her best "nurse in charge" voice going, and everyone did what she asked.

After Rosie gave Daisy some water, Daisy wiped her face with the washcloth and took a big drink of her wine. She looked at each sister in turn and sighed. "I really don't know where to start. I—well, okay, here it is. I got a phone call from that Skylar Smith about eight weeks ago."

"What?"

"What did she say?"

"How does she know you?"

All the sisters were talking at once.

Daisy held up her hand. "Just let me tell you what I know, which isn't much."

"Okay. We will try to keep our mouths shut, but this is so bizarre!" said Lilly.

"Yeah, tell me about it." Daisy sighed again and looked down into her wine. "Do you remember the night Tommy died?" she asked slowly.

The sisters looked at each other with puzzled expressions.

"Yes, of course we remember," Rosie said gently. "But what does Tommy have to do with this girl? Did he know her?"

"I don't think so, but I don't really know. She didn't say that. She—" Daisy paused. "She called on a Tuesday night, I remember that. I made some notes after I hung up. Let me go get them. Maybe you all can make some sense out of it." Daisy hurriedly pushed her chair back and went into the house.

The three girls looked at each other in stunned silence.

"I don't know about you guys, but I'm having a hard time taking this all in," said Amy. "How did this girl even know Daisy? And Tommy's been dead for two years. Why now?"

"Maybe this will explain some of what has been bothering

Daisy. I mean, I know the accident and Tommy dying was terrible, but I thought lately there was something else bothering her. Like she was keeping a secret from us, and it was tearing her apart."

"Damn it, Rosie, you always look for the mystery in everything. I think she's been coping pretty well, all things considered."

"She's been doing great, but I don't know, it's like she hasn't been able to put the whole thing with Tommy behind her, and now this." The girls were whispering to each other and looking at the door so Daisy wouldn't be able to hear what they were saying.

"Put it behind her? How in the hell is she supposed to do that?" Lilly hissed at Rosie. "Tommy was the love of her life, and, well, with no kids . . . I think she has been doing remarkably well."

"Stop it, both of you," Amy said. "Let's wait and see what her note says."

Daisy came out onto the porch holding a sheet of plain white paper folded into an envelope. "Here it is." She put the paper in the middle of the table, grabbed her wine glass, and went out into her backyard, one arm folded around her waist, like she was hugging herself.

The other three girls bent over the lined sheet of paper, and Lilly read out loud:

Called me Daisy.
Said she knew what I did that night.
Said I caused Tommy's death, and she's going to go to the police with her information.
Said Tommy's death was all my fault.
Said Tommy was tired of me and in love with her. Said Tommy wanted a divorce.

At this, the girls gasped in unison.

"What was this bitch talking about?" Amy asked.

Meet me Sunday afternoon.
West end of Glenndale Park.
3:00 p.m.
Said her name is Skylar Smith, but I don't know her.

Daisy still had her back turned to the girls. A blue jay landed in the tree above her, going on and on in bird talk about some wrong that had been done to her. The day was still hot, and the cicadas were starting to sing their evening song. None of the girls knew what to say; it was all so inconceivable. Daisy? Their Daisy? Daisy and Tommy, who had such a wonderful marriage? Daisy, who was the gentlest of all the girls and who had taken over their mother's role after she died?

The girls moved as one and went over to Daisy. Lilly put her arm around her shoulder, and Rosie and Amy moved to the other side of her, as if to surround her for protection.

"Was this some kind of sick joke?" Amy asked. "I can't even imagine what the hell this girl was talking about. So you didn't go meet her? That would have been about eight weeks ago, right? Why didn't you let us know she called you and wanted to meet with you? One of us could have gone in your place."

They all looked at Daisy, who continued to stare out into the yard. Her body was rigid, and the girls could tell she was trying to hold back tears. "You know I loved him more than anything else, don't you? I know he's gone, but I still expect him to walk through the door every night, and when he doesn't show up, my heart breaks all over again. I hear his voice; I smell his aftershave;

I feel his leg next to mine in bed. I would never have intentionally done anything to hurt him." She was openly sobbing now and looking at each of her sisters, as if begging them to agree with her.

"Daisy, of course we know how much you loved him and how much he loved you back." Rosie smiled gently at her oldest sister. "Truth be told, we were all a little jealous of what you two had with each other. We know you would never have hurt him."

"Come on, let's go sit down and see if we can make some sense of this," said Lily.

They led Daisy back to the table and they all took their former seats.

Daisy looked at her sisters for a long moment, then let out a long, shaky sigh. "I never told you all exactly what happened the night Tommy died. I—well." She paused with a faraway look in her eyes. "It's so hard for me to go back to that time. I just try to block it out. And I hit my head when the car hit the tree, and, well, I sometimes think I stayed unconscious on purpose, so . . ."

Her voice caught then, and she continued so very softly, "So I wouldn't have to see him like that. It's hard enough to see him in my dreams, where he's alive and he's holding me, and I can forget, for just a minute, that my life has turned into this hell." All the girls were crying now. "If I had to see him how he was at the end of that night . . ."

"Hush, hush now, hush. It's all right. We'll fix this. It's okay," said Lilly. She was holding Daisy in her arms and slowly rocking her from side to side, murmuring soft sounds of comforting words. Rosie and Amy were rubbing Daisy's shoulders and swaying along with Lilly.

After a few minutes, Daisy lifted her head and smiled sadly

at her sisters. "I don't know what I would do without you all. You have kept me sane; you know that, right?" She settled back into her chair and closed her eyes for a moment. "So, does anyone have any brilliant ideas as to why this girl would have called me, and who killed her, and do you think I'm in any trouble? God, why didn't I go meet her? At least I would know what she was talking about."

"I don't blame you for not going to see her. Such a traumatic event like that. No one would want to relive it," said Lilly.

"But do you know what this girl was talking about? This Skylar person?" asked Rosie.

Daisy sighed again. "I really don't know. That whole night is just a blur now. I mean, maybe I did do something. Maybe I did cause Tommy's death." She looked so stricken at the thought and kept opening and closing her mouth, like she couldn't even begin to formulate words.

"Why are you saying that? It was an accident." Lilly took Daisy's hand and said very gently, "The car went off the side of the road and hit a tree. Your airbag went off, and Tommy's did too. Although the police did think there was something wrong with his airbag . . . that maybe it didn't go off as quickly as it should, or it didn't expand as much as it should have. But remember? We talked about looking into it, but you didn't want to. You said it wouldn't bring him back, so why bother? Do you think this letter has anything to do with that?"

"God, I don't know. Do you think we will ever know?"

CHAPTER TEN

AMY SPENT THE THIRTY-MINUTE DRIVE HOME from Daisy's lost in thought. The whole evening had been surreal, to say the least. To think *anyone* could believe Daisy had anything nefarious to do with Tommy's death was ludicrous. Preposterous! Asinine! Absurd! Bizarre! Stupid! *Fucking stupid*, Amy amended. She had run out of synonyms, and she was just left shaking her head in disbelief.

She needed to think of something, anything, they could do next to get some answers. She supposed Rosie could try and pry some answers out of Danny to see if any information had come up about this Skylar Smith. And certainly Dad could look up any old records at the newspaper to see if she popped up anywhere, although Amy thought she should check with the sisters first before getting Dad involved. *He'll hit the roof when he finds out,* she thought. He had always been so protective of the girls, but especially with Daisy.

And maybe Lilly could check with the coroner at the hospital who'd done the autopsy on Tommy, just to make sure nothing was out of the ordinary with Tommy's death. *But,* Amy thought to herself, *wouldn't the coroner report anything unusual?* She assumed Daisy must have received a copy of the autopsy, but undoubtedly, she hadn't read it and just stuffed it in a drawer somewhere. Not that Amy could blame her. Who would want to read that about your husband?

And what could Amy do? The fact that she was in law school—well, the *first week* of law school—certainly didn't give her any insights into the legal field. Just reading a case in her criminal law book took forever because she had to keep going to her law dictionary and looking up words. *It's going to be a very long three years,* she thought with a grimace.

Amy pulled into her one-car garage and doused the lights. She put her head back against the head cushion and breathed a sigh of relief. Amy truly loved her little house and always felt so safe and secure when she was in it. It was in a cul-de-sac in a very family-oriented neighborhood, and she knew she was lucky to have found it. She had not been looking to buy a house, but she would frequently drive through the neighborhood on her way to her favorite Starbucks, and she always admired the well-established trees shading the homes and the well-kept yards.

One day last year, she'd been driving down the street and realized she had forgotten her phone in her apartment. She turned around in the cul-de-sac and there was this little house, smaller than most of the houses in the neighborhood, with a "for sale" sign in the front yard. It was painted a dark moss green color with cream shutters. There was just something about it that had made her slow down and then stop altogether. She'd written down the name and number of the realtor, and within three months, she'd been the proud owner of the small green house.

Even now, it still shocked her that she was a homeowner. She always thought she was too cool to live in the suburbs—though she would never tell anyone that because, truth be told, she was not cool. She still told anyone who asked the only reason she'd bought the house was because it was a good investment, but she knew it was because she felt a sense of rightness and completeness whenever she came home. *Sue me,* she thought. *I am a nerd and proud of it.* With that thought, she got out of the car and went into bed.

CHAPTER ELEVEN

JACK PUSHED AWAY from his computer. He stood up and stretched. At six foot three and with his still-full head of silver hair, people sometimes commented he looked just like that older actor—you know, the one who has the deep, scratchy voice. No one could ever think of his name, but everyone thought he looked just like him. Jack was just glad people compared him to an actor instead of to their grandfather or elderly uncle. Of course, they always did say "that older guy," but Jack figured it came with the territory. He was sixty-five, after all, even if there were times when that number totally took him by surprise. It sounded so *old!* His brain certainly thought it was still young, even if his body knew the truth.

Jack walked out of his office and looked around the newsroom with satisfaction. There were three reporters' desks along the far wall and an editing room opposite. Although the editing room was typically where a sub-editor, the person who would do all the fact-checking to make sure everything was legal and correct, would sit, because this was a small newsroom, everyone pitched in to help and wore many hats. Jack, being the owner and ostensibly the boss, did a little bit of everything. He didn't go out in the field as much anymore, but he was known to grab a camera and head out if need be. Although truth be told, he was just as happy staying in the office and doing all the millions of things that needed to be done before a story could go out. He had always been a details man.

"Hey, Andrew. What do you have on the murdered girl who was found about a month ago?" Jack asked Andrew Foley.

Andrew was the newest reporter on the team. Andrew was twenty-seven and pretty green. He had graduated from the University of Missouri's journalism program in the spring and made his way down to Brunswick a couple of weeks ago. When Andrew had shown up looking for work, Jack hadn't had the heart to tell him no. Jack knew it was difficult to get work as a reporter these days, mainly because there were very few reporter jobs to be had. Jack's first boss had hired him when Jack was new and naïve, and Jack never forgot that kindness, so he tried to help out when he could.

Andrew turned to his computer and pulled up his notes. "Well, her name was Skylar Smith, according to Officer Wright. They're trying to get some background information on her."

"Did you ask about the time of death and the cause? What about any suspects or motives? Any idea if she was killed there or if the killer moved her body?"

Andrew shook his head and continued looking at his notes as if he could find an answer in them. He repeated what Officer Wright told him. This told Jack that Andrew hadn't thought to ask any follow-up questions, and he had to tamp down his irritation. The kid was new to reporting, after all.

"Okay, grab your stuff and come with me. Let's go talk to Officer Wright together and see if we can squeeze any more details out of him. Remember, kid, cops will not give you any unsolicited information. You gotta dig for it. You gotta push them into a corner. Ask those questions that will make them reveal more than what they want to." Jack knew he sounded like a caricature of an old-time newspaper reporter. He felt like he should have one cigarette smoldering at his desk and another one dangling from his lips to go with a stained and rumbled shirt and loosened tie, as if he had been sleeping at his desk. *The good ole days,* thought Jack with a smile.

"Let's go."

CHAPTER TWELVE

IT HAD BEEN ABOUT TWO MONTHS since Skylar's body was discovered, and Rosie was no further along in writing her book than she had been on the day they went out for a run and found the body. Rosie loved books and reading, even as a child. The day her dad took her to the public library and she got her first library card, Rosie knew she wanted to have a job that had something to do with words. For the longest time, her dream job was to be a librarian, probably because Miss North was the first librarian she knew. She'd actually just wanted to *be* Miss North, who was tall and beautiful and smelled like lilacs.

As she'd grown older, her dream job changed frequently, but it had always involved words of some sort. She'd wanted to be Nancy Drew at some point, as long as Nancy could write about her mysteries as well as solve them. Wanting to be an editor of *Seventeen* had factored into the mix for a couple of years, until she'd seen Erin Andrews and decided she wanted to be a TV news reporter. That job was still actually floating around in the back of her head, but again, it had more to do with wanting to *look* like Erin Andrews than anything else—shades of Miss North all over again.

Rosie looked at her watch and shut down her computer, telling Big Shirley, "If I am not going to be productive with my book, then I will be productive with my body."

She changed into her yoga clothes and stopped in front of the mirror on the way out. At five foot nine, Rosie was the tallest of the sisters. Her hair was a light brown, with streaks of blonde, some natural, some not (thank you, Tamara at the Slim Lines Salon). All the sisters had inherited green eyes from their mother, and they were blessed with long and lush eyelashes. Well, except Amy. She always complained she got screwed not only by not having a flower name but by also having stubby eyelashes. She'd become *very* adept at applying false lashes at an early age.

Rosie drove to the gym a couple of miles from her home. It was a small neighborhood gym with limited classes, but Rosie discovered she liked that about the place. When Rosie first got back in town, she'd signed up to go to one of the huge mega-gyms popping up around town, figuring she would be able to do a variety of classes. She tried a few body pump classes, and they were okay, even if the music was a bit too loud. She then went to a hot yoga class and boy, was she ever surprised. She had taken yoga classes before, but she discovered hot yoga was a world unto itself. And not one she wanted to join.

First of all, the people taking the class were a *lot* more serious than normal yoga people. And the room was very hot, which was why it was called hot yoga. Duh. But Rosie felt like you were trying to earn some weird badge of honor by being able to stay in a room where the sweat started dripping from your face before you even got your mat situated properly.

And the people who were seriously into hot yoga? Especially the men who were seriously into hot yoga? Rosie could barely focus on what she was doing due to the two men in front of her who were wearing skimpy speedo-like bottoms and nothing else. When they did a downward dog, all Rosie could think about was what heat does to certain body parts. It made certain body parts droopy and hangy, if there was such a word. And when they threw their arms wide and the sweat droplets landed on her mat and her arm, she knew this was not a place for her. So back to the neighborhood gym she went.

Rosie especially liked the eight a.m. yoga class held on Mondays, Wednesdays, and Fridays. The instructor, Audrey, made the class a pretty good workout, and she loved having the class hold poses for a long time. She'd said she liked seeing everyone's arms shaking.

Rosie walked into the class about ten minutes early and was glad to see her favorite place still open. She liked to be in the back row, right in the middle. She had texted her yoga buddy, Rachel, before she'd left her house to see if she was coming to class. Rachel was going to be there but would be a bit late and had asked Rosie to save her a spot. Rosie put a block down next to her for Rachel, then laid down and closed her eyes. She tried to empty her mind, but all she could think about was the conversation she'd had with Rachel last week. She'd told Rachel that while researching for her book, she'd come across some yoga terms, and the one that stood out was "Ashwini Mudra," which was the practice of contracting the anal sphincter. When she whispered this to Rachel, they had started giggling and snorting. Audrey had thrown them a look that said, "I like you guys, but you are distracting everyone around you!"

Rosie felt Rachel lie down in the spot next to her, and Rosie said in a low voice, "I have conquered the practice of sphincter contracting."

A male voice said, "Wow, you can do that and fire a gun! You're a multi-talented girl!"

Rosie's eyes flew open and there was Ren, sitting on a yoga mat in Rachel's spot, grinning at her. "They sure know how to raise you Texas girls right!"

"What the hell are you doing here? And why are you sitting in Rachel's spot?"

Ren looked around and said innocently, "I didn't realize you had assigned seating. Besides, you were lying there grinning to yourself, so I thought I would try to get in on the joke. I was not aware it had to do with private body parts."

"Oh my God, can you go someplace else? Rachel always sits there. And besides, do they even allow guys in here?"

"Hmm, I guess you should ask the other three guys in this class." Ren lay back on his yoga mat and closed his eyes, saying with a smile, "Don't bother me now. I am going to concentrate on that area that could always use a good contraction or two." He slanted his eyes over to her to see if she thought he was funny and he could tell she was fighting a smile. "How did that topic even come up in normal conversation?"

"I was just doing some research on it the other day. For my book," she added.

"Wouldn't think there would be much of a market for a book about that topic, truth be told."

Rosie was going to tell him her book was *not* about that, but just then, Audrey came in and the class started. Rachel finally came into class and set up her mat across the room from Rosie, giving her a look that said, "Okay, who in the hell is in my spot? He is cute!"

Rosie eye-messaged her back, saying, "I'll tell you all about him after class."

Rosie was aware of Ren all through the hour-long class and was impressed with how flexible he was. He didn't have that look on his face most guys had when taking a yoga or Pilates class—the look that said, "I'd normally be in the weight room benching 350 pounds; I'm only doing this because I have a stiff back." When he quietly got up during savasana and left the room, she had to admit she was a little disappointed. If only because she wanted to clear up the topic of the ass puckering.

Rachel waited for her by the door, and as they walked to their cars, she asked, "Who the heck was that?"

"I told you about him. The vet with the Great Dane? When we found the dead girl?"

"You told me more about his dog than him. And you didn't tell me how cute he is. Are you going to ask him out?"

"Rachel, I know nothing about him. He could be married for all I know. And besides, I am not interested in love at this point in my life."

"Yeah, right. Who wouldn't want to have a steamy love affair with the local vet? Oh, that's right. I forgot. You swore off guys because you had one bad—and I assume it was really bad—relationship with some asshole, and now you think all males are jerks. You know, there are some good ones out there."

"I know." Rosie sighed. "I just don't know if I'm ready to start it all back up again."

"Rosie, it has been almost a year since . . . since everything that happened in New York. Maybe it's time?" When Rosie just looked at her, Rachel said, "I'm just saying. He is a vet, so maybe he has the proverbial horse you need to get back up on."

"I know. It might be time. But even if I did ask him out, he'd probably run the other way." Rosie told Rachel about the inadvertent "sphincter contraction" comment, and after she stopped laughing, Rachel said that guys liked girls who were "one" with their bodies. And told her to call him!

CHAPTER THIRTEEN

THAT NIGHT, all the sisters were again gathered at Daisy's house, brainstorming what more they could do about Skylar. Rosie told them she'd shared Daisy's and Skylar's phone conversation with Danny Wright, and he said he was going to investigate the matter. So far, he had not contacted Daisy, so Rosie said she would call him the next day to check up on any progress.

Daisy had given Lilly the autopsy report, and according to Lilly, nothing unusual stood out.

Amy thought they should bring their dad in on the mystery. If nothing else, Amy argued, since he was the chief editor of the *Brunswick Chronicle*, he would be the best person to research Skylar's background. Maybe he could find out something about her that might shed some light on the totally bizarre turn of events.

Daisy seemed to be calmer and more at peace than she had been the other night, as if sharing her worries with her sisters had lifted a load off her shoulders. That, plus the fact that she was really enjoying her work at the hospital. She said everyone had been very nice and supportive so far. Lilly snorted and told her to just wait until she met Dr. Dickhead.

Amy looked at her watch and let out a groan. "Okay, I got to go. I have a hot date with a Supreme Court judge. Of course, he's been dead for a couple hundred years, but hey, a girl can't be too choosy! Let me know what you guys decide to do. I can talk to Dad if you want."

After Amy left, Daisy agreed that they probably should let their dad in on what had been going on. They made plans to meet for dinner next week, and Rosie said she would text Jack and tell him to join them.

The next Tuesday found all the sisters together again at Daisy's house, and this time, their father, Jack, was there. They had a quick dinner, and afterward, Lilly took the bull by the horns and told Jack everything that had been going on with Daisy and the decidedly weird phone call from Skylar.

The first thing Jack did after hearing the story was cross the room to Daisy and pull her into his arms.

"I am so sorry you are having to go through all this. I know this is just bringing up all those painful memories. I promise you we will get to the bottom of this."

Daisy nodded and gave her dad a squeeze. "I'm just glad we all know about it now. And you know what? I feel like I can handle just about anything lately, especially with my main man and my sister squad behind me!"

They decided Jack would do some research on Skylar and comb through any news items around the time of Tommy's accident to see if there was something, anything, that stood out. The Hurley family was prominent in Brunswick, so the newspaper covered the tragedy thoroughly. But everyone was so grief-stricken at the time, none of them really paid much attention to the media. There could be a clue that was missed the first time around.

After Jack left, the girls had one more drink and talked about their dad. They frequently discussed trying to get him to start dating again, but Jack never acted like dating was a big issue for him. He'd told Daisy once their mom was the only woman for him, and besides, what would he want another woman for? He had four of the best girls around to take care of him, so he was happy! He also joked if he started dating again, his "boyfriends" would be upset because it would interfere with their weekly Saturday and Sunday golf game. Jack played golf every weekend with Matt, Perry, and Kevin, and woe to any woman who tried to disrupt that tradition!

CHAPTER FOURTEEN

UNLIKE MANY DOGS, Big Shirley loved going to the vet. Rosie thought it was because everyone made such a fuss about her. And she certainly was fussible! She ambled into the waiting room, looking both ways as if to say, "Yes, I am bigger than anyone else in this room, and a lot cooler too."

Unfortunately, instead of a whole crowd Shirley could entertain, there was just one other family in the waiting room. There was a mother and father with a young boy and what looked like a rat. Of course Rosie knew it was not a rat, but that was how she tended to think about those small, yappy dogs. As far as she was concerned, if a dog didn't weigh over one hundred pounds, they weren't a real dog. There was also a parrot striding back and forth on the counter, looking for all intents and purposes like he was patrolling the waiting room.

True to form, the yappy rat dog barked ferociously at Big Shirley, but the Shirls kept her dignity and looked at Rosie with an "Are you kidding me?" expression.

The young boy ran over to Big Shirley and stopped just in front of her, looking at her with big eyes.

The mother hurriedly got up and came over, putting a hand on the boy's shoulder before saying, "Tyler, remember, we always ask before we pet someone else's dog."

"Can I touch him?" Tyler asked.

Rosie told him it was okay to pet Shirley, and Tyler tentatively reached out a hand and lightly patted Big Shirley on her side.

"What kind of dog is this?" the mother asked.

"She's a Newfoundland," Rosie answered. "They're the most laid-back dogs in the world."

Tyler piped up and said, "He looks like a great big bear. And he has a lot of hair! Look, Mom. He has a slobbery mouth!"

Rosie wanted to tell the little boy the very small amount of drool hanging from Shirley's mouth was a mere drop in the bucket, but Tyler had already jumped up and ran across the room to the whistling and talking parrot.

"Beautiful dog," the mom said over her shoulder as she walked over to stand by Tyler.

"Of course, she is," Rosie mouthed to herself and turned her head just in time to see Ren grinning at her from the door to the exam room.

"Rosie, why don't you bring your Newfie in here." He turned and went into the exam room, holding the door open for Big Shirley and Rosie. Ren closed the door behind him and said with a smile, "You know, she is a beautiful dog!"

Rosie opened her mouth to respond, trying to think of something to say that wouldn't make her look even more foolish than she'd looked in yoga class, but then shut it when Ren continued.

"Seriously, she is a showstopper!"

And with those words, Rosie decided he was an okay guy after all.

"So how have you been?" He really wanted to make some funny comment about the body part they had discussed in yoga, but he also did not want to get off on the wrong foot with her. Because Ren was internally thanking whatever entity it was that brought her to his office. He had been trying to think of a way to talk to her again. He had even been to a couple more yoga classes, but Rosie hadn't been there. Needless to say, he'd been very happy when he'd seen her name on the roster.

"You haven't been to yoga," Ren said, and then thought to himself, *Way to just jump in there, big guy.*

"I've actually been extraordinarily busy." Rosie then thought to herself, *Since when did I become British?*

Then they both began talking at once.

Ren laughed and held up his hand. "Okay, you first. What brings you here today? Is something wrong with your dog?"

"No, there's nothing wrong with her. But we moved back to town a while ago, and I've been needing to get her established with a vet."

By this time, Ren was sitting on the floor with Shirley, running his hands over her legs and stomach. He chuckled. "I don't think you could have picked a better name. Big Shirley. It just works for her!"

"My sister is the one who named her—or renamed her, I guess. I adopted her from the Newfoundland Rescue Foundation, and her name was originally Midnight, which I mean, really? What a dumb name for her, or any dog, for that matter. We tried out a couple of different names, but none of them seemed to fit her. So then my sister remembered a comic strip that had a huge dog in it, but you never really saw the whole dog. Just a nose here, or a leg there. But you knew it was a really big dog and it was named Big Shirley. The rest is history."

"Well, your sister certainly hit the nail on the head with that name," he said, smiling at Shirley. "Okay, the first thing I think we need to do is get a baseline established with her. I'll send the tech in to draw some blood, get her weighed, maybe trim her toenails. Does that sound like a plan?"

"Works for me."

After Ren walked out of the exam room, Rosie sat down next to Shirley. *Well. So much for him falling all over himself for me,* she thought. *Maybe I scared him off with my split personality. One minute, I'm the pretty, funny yoga girl with a thing for unmentionable body parts, and the next time he sees me, I'm over-sharing about a stupid comic strip.*

Thirty minutes later, Rosie was paying at the front desk. She had the heartworm pills, along with the flea and tick preventives, and she was talking to Julie Jones about how glad she was to be back in Texas.

Just when she thought she was going to have to make up another reason for Shirley to see Ren, he came around the corner leading Marilyn, Walter's sister. "Hey, I'm glad you haven't left yet. I know you met Walter a couple of weeks ago, so I wanted to introduce you to his sister."

"Oh gosh, she's beautiful! What's her name?"

"Midnight."

CHAPTER FIFTEEN

ROSIE WAS STILL SMILING to herself later that afternoon about Ren's "Midnight" comment. She had certainly walked right into it, but she didn't mind. She liked guys who could joke around. *Unlike Steve*, she thought. He had been great at dealing out the jokes but certainly hadn't liked it when it was the other way around.

"Nope. Stop it. No Steve thoughts now." She didn't want anything to spoil her mood. She was meeting Ren for happy hour at a local bar in an hour. He had said it was time they put their heads together to try and make some sense out of what they had found a couple of months ago.

She'd called Rachel on her cell after Big Shirley's appointment to tell her she was going out with Ren.

"Well, it's about time," Rachel had said. "I was going to have to take pity on the poor guy and give him your number. It was obvious he was looking for you when he came to yoga. Of all times for you to decide you had to concentrate on your writing!"

Rosie had laughed. "For all the good it did me. I think I advanced my book by approximately one hundred words. Big deal."

Rosie was surprised to find herself looking forward to seeing Ren at the Brooksider for happy hour. It was true what she'd told Rachel about not being interested in a relationship at the present time, but what she hadn't told Rachel was how deep her hurt went. Steve had really done a number on her self-esteem, and even though she told herself *repeatedly* he was an asshole and what he had said and done to her did not matter, she knew deep down it did. To protect herself, she had built a shell around her heart and told herself she could lead a very productive and enjoyable life without a man. And sometimes she even believed it.

Ren was sitting in one of the back booths nursing a beer when Rosie arrived at the bar. It was still early, so the bar was quiet. Ren looked up from his phone when she walked in, and his eyes met hers as she walked across the room.

What she saw in his eyes (or at least what she hoped she saw in his eyes) was a look saying, "I think you are very attractive, and I hope we can get to know each other better." Of course, the look could have also said, "I think you are hot, and I want to jump your bones tonight," but she decided to take the high road and hope for the best.

She was smiling at her thoughts when she slid into the booth across from Ren.

"I can't decide if your enigmatic smile is telling me you're glad to see me or that you're already formulating an excuse to leave in ten minutes."

"Well, I do feel a migraine coming on." Rosie laughed at his startled expression. "I'm kidding! Hmm, I think I like being a mysterious person. Much better than telling you all about how a certain unmentionable body part works!"

Ren laughed. "That yoga technique does cross my mind at the oddest times, I must admit. Usually, it is when I am doing an exam on an animal and have to take its temperature. I'm sure no one can figure out why I smile when I'm back there!"

They both were laughing when their waitress, Katie, came up to take her order. Katie had been a friend of Amy's during high school, so they spent the next couple of minutes catching up. Katie didn't know Amy had started law school, and she told Rosie to tell Amy to come in for a free drink whenever Amy felt like she needed some down time. She left with Rosie's order for the house merlot.

"I know we need to talk about our mystery," Ren started. "But I really want to know why you came back to town. Weren't you in New York?"

So much to Rosie's surprise, she spent the next thirty minutes talking about herself, which was something she usually tried to avoid. She told him about growing up in Texas and how Brunswick used to be so much smaller than it is today. She told him about her three sisters, about her dad and how he still loved being the editor of the newspaper, and how being around the newspaper business all her life had led her to be a writer.

When he asked her about her time in New York, she just laughed. "My gosh! I am totally going against the rules of every how-to-get-a-guy magazine article by being the conversation hog and not asking *you* about yourself! So how did you end up here?"

"It's a boring story, but in a nutshell, I grew up in Kansas City, Missouri, with my two sisters and my mom and dad. My dad is a pilot for Southwest Airlines, and my mom is the CEO of a small orthopedic company. My one sister is a year older than me. She's married and still lives in KC. My younger sister is a buyer for Ralph Lauren, and they just moved her and her husband to Houston, so it'll be nice to be able to visit her on the weekends."

"When did you decide to become a vet?"

"We always had animals in our house growing up. Usually,

at least two dogs, a couple of cats, rabbits, turtles, goldfish—you name it, we had it. After I graduated from KU with a degree in biology, I accepted a job selling cardiac monitoring equipment to operating rooms, ERs, and some doctors' offices. And I found out very quickly that while my mom might be this great salesperson, I *definitely* did not inherit her selling genes. I hated it!" He laughed. "My mom would always tell me I had to work on 'closing the deal', but as soon as the buyer would tell me they were not in the market for my product, I was out the door. I just never knew what to say to make them change their mind. Used to drive my mother *crazy!* So, I had a long talk with myself about what I'd like to do with the rest of my life, and being a vet was pretty much the number-one idea that came to mind. I was accepted at Kansas State and spent the next four years loving vet school. When I graduated, I was lucky to get hired at the same veterinary practice we used to take our dogs to. I stayed there for a year, and when I heard about this practice down here being for sale, I decided to give it a go. And the rest, as they say, is history. Now we need to refill our glasses and decide if we are going to be the Baby-Sitters Club or the Hardy Boys. And don't say you want to be Nancy Drew because Ned was a big nerd!"

CHAPTER SIXTEEN

DAISY WAS IN THE BREAK ROOM getting coffee when she heard someone enter. She turned around and saw a man in a white coat getting something out of the small refrigerator in the corner of the room. Daisy mentally kicked herself when she automatically assumed he was a doctor. She had been training herself not to jump to conclusions every time she saw a man in a white coat. He could be a lab technician, or food service, or housekeeping, or maybe just someone who had horrible fashion sense and thought a white coat was cool.

The man turned to Daisy and held up an apple. "Just getting my breakfast I left here a week ago, although this apple is looking awfully sick. Are you new here? I don't believe I've seen you before. I'm Jonathan Booker, by the way." And he held out his hand. If Daisy ever wished she had a poker face, now would be the time. It was Dr. Dickhead!! The one who was so mean to Lilly! She was sure her face was revealing every thought in her head, but Dr. Dickhead didn't seem to notice anything out of the ordinary.

"Uh, yes, I am here new. I mean, uh, I mean, I am new here." Daisy took a breath. "My name is Daisy Wolf, and you're right. I just started here a couple of months ago." Daisy gave him what she was sure was a pretty weak-ass smile and thought to herself, *Just please do not blurt out "dickhead," please do not blurt out "dickhead," please do not blurt out "dickhead."*

As it turned out, she didn't have to worry about getting into an involved discussion with him because he just saluted her with his apple, smiled, and said, "Glad you're on board. Nice to meet you." Then he walked out of the break room.

Daisy lowered herself into the chair and let out a sigh. *Just wait until I tell Lilly!* she thought. Although she had to admit to herself that she had been expecting Dr. Dickhead to look totally different. For one thing, he was probably her age, maybe a year or two older. And for some reason, she'd been expecting him to be some old, crotchety man with thinning white hair sticking out everywhere, pants pulled up to underneath his armpits, and old man shoes. Instead, he had, well, nice hair that wasn't thinning at all. If anything, it was a nice dark brown color, maybe a bit too long on the sides, but it gave him something of a rebellious look and contrasted nicely with his blue eyes.

Okay, wait a minute. Am I really sitting here thinking about his hair and blue eyes? Am I so desperate to get back into the normal world that the first time—in a long time, I must admit—an attractive man says hello to me, I start in on his hair and eyes? I'm going to have to chalk it up to being so surprised he wasn't the fire-breathing ogre Lilly made him out to be.

She was deep in thought, so when she heard, "Hey, Daisy!" she practically jumped out of her chair. She turned and saw Miranda standing in the doorway.

"My God, you scared the crap out of me, Miranda! I was a million miles away!"

"You sure were! Do you have a minute to help me? I'm pushing the library book cart around, but there's something wrong with the wheel."

"Let me help you with that." Daisy got up, gave herself a mental headshake, and went to help Miranda.

CHAPTER SEVENTEEN

AMY WAS IN THE LAW LIBRARY studying when she looked at her watch and was astonished to see it was 11:05 at night. For one thing, she was surprised time had gotten away from her because she was studying criminal law and she *hated* criminal law. Well, she didn't hate it; she just could not stand the professor. He took the Socratic method just a tad bit too far. It seemed his main goal in life was not to instruct the students but to humiliate them as much as possible. And lately, she didn't like going out to the parking lot at night by herself.

For the last couple of weeks, she had been getting this creepy feeling, like someone was watching her. Amy usually was very aware of her surroundings, because if there was one thing her dad stressed to Amy and her sisters, it was to not put yourself into a situation that could get ugly. She could hear him saying:

Listen to your gut and use common sense.

Don't wait to pull your keys out of your purse—do it BEFORE you get to your car and use them as a weapon.

Don't be materialistic—throw your purse at them and RUN!

If all else fails, pull the 357 Magnum out of your purse and blow the fucker away! (Of course, Amy never could figure out how she was going to get the gun out of her purse if she threw it, but she didn't want to get too hung up on details.)

Now she was listening to her gut and trying to use common sense, but that didn't get her any closer to getting into her car and home to her bed. And she didn't have her gun with her, though she did have a concealed carry permit. So she did the next best thing. She put her keys between her fingers and started walking to her car.

The lot was basically empty except for a dark red truck parked about twenty spaces from Amy's car. *That's weird,* Amy thought. The truck didn't have its headlights or interior lights on, but Amy could hear the low rumbling of the motor. And she could just make out an outline of someone sitting in the front seat. *Shit. That truck has been here for the last week, parked in the same spot. Screw it. I'm running!* She took off, and when she got to her car, she pressed the unlock button, jumped in, and locked the doors after her.

She was panting like she had run a mile at full speed. She put her head down onto the steering wheel and tried to catch her breath. *What the heck is the matter with me? I typically don't get so weirded out about—*

Just then there was a loud *KNOCK* on the passenger door window. Amy looked over, and all she saw was the outline of a person bending over trying to look into her car. Amy let out a scream and instinctively laid on the horn. She was fumbling with trying to get her foot on the gas pedal when she heard someone yelling her name over the blare of the horn.

"AMY! AMY! It's me. It's Joe! It's okay. Lay off the horn!"

Amy turned and saw Joe Westgate, one of her law school buddies, bending down looking into the passenger side window. "Hey, open up. What the heck's going on? Are you okay?"

Amy put her hand to her head and let out a very shaky sigh. "Jesus, Joe. You scared the shit out of me!" Amy unlocked the passenger door.

Joe opened the door, threw his backpack into the rear, and folded his six-foot-four frame into the passenger seat. "Can you give me a ride home? And why don't you get a bigger car?"

"Where the hell is your car? And beggars can't be choosy. I should knock the shit out of you! You scared me to death, knocking on my window like that!"

"I tried to get to you before you left the library. When I got to the door, all I saw was you flying down to your car. I didn't think you could run that fast! Did you sprout wings? Who were you running from?"

"I don't know. I've just been making myself crazy the last couple of weeks. It's just . . . I don't know . . . hard to explain. Do you ever feel like someone is watching you?"

"Miss Amy, girls are *always* watching me. You just get used to it."

Amy rolled her eyes and told him he was an idiot. But he did have a point. He was tall, with a full head of dark hair and a great build. He'd played lacrosse in undergrad, and he still worked out a couple of times a week. He was also extremely smart and very nice, and he happened to have a steady girlfriend who, incidentally, was a very good friend of Amy's. They were all in the same section in school and had formed a very close study group.

"Where's Brooke tonight?" she asked. "I looked for you guys when I got to the library. Although it was probably just as well I was by myself. I really needed to go over that damn model penal code and all the various distinctions. It's driving me crazy!"

"I know what you mean. We can hit it tomorrow in the study group. Brooke and I are both having a hard time with it. Hey, what did you mean when you said someone's watching you? Is someone giving you a hard time? Is it that creepy guy in section A? What's his name? Donald? Brooke thinks he's weird too."

"No, it's not him, but Brooke's right about him being a weirdo. I'm glad we're not in his section. No, it's probably just my imagination. There's nothing concrete, and nothing has happened. I don't know. I'm just losing my mind, that's all."

Joe looked at her. "I don't see you giving yourself the heebie-jeebies unless there's a reason. Just be careful, okay? Like maybe don't stay at the library until midnight by yourself. I'm just saying! I know you're a tough little Texan girl, but listen to your gut and use common sense."

"Have you been talking to my dad?"

CHAPTER EIGHTEEN

AFTER HER FIRST "DATE" with Ren during happy hour at the Brooksider, Rosie went home and called Lilly. When Lilly answered, Rosie started to talk to her then promptly burst into tears.

"Rosie, what's the matter? Are you okay? Are you hurt?"

"No, Lilly, I'm fine." Rosie took a deep breath and let it out. "I really don't know what in the heck is wrong with me. I'm actually . . ." Rosie let out another shaky breath. "I'm, well, happy, I guess."

"Wow. Don't call me if you're sad then. Does this have anything to do with drinking with the handsome vet at the corner pub?"

"Holy shit! How did you find out about that? I just got home from there."

"I have my sources," said Lilly, sounding very smug. "Nothing escapes my attention! Okay, Keith's mom was in the back of the bar with some of her bridge buddies. They had just finished a hot game and decided they needed refreshments after all that card counting. She saw you and texted Keith. Do you want to know what her text said?"

"I know you'll tell me anyway, so lay it on me."

"Her exact words were, 'Rosie is here in the Brooksider, and she is with a very handsome man. Tell her she looks fabulous!'"

"I always knew there was a reason I liked her. And yes, I do look fabulous!" Rosie had laughed. "Oh, Lilly, I had so much fun. Maybe fun isn't the right word. It was like we just clicked or something. He is so easy to talk to." Rosie hesitated. "Of course, Steve was easy to talk to at first."

"Rosie, do *NOT* go there. I mean it. I don't know how this thing with Ren will play out and neither do you. You may go on another date with him and decide he's a douchebag. Or decide he's the love of your life. Whatever. But what I don't want you to do is let Steve get in your head and destroy any chance you might have with this man. Steve was a very bad guy. He did a number on you, and I hope you'll tell me about it when you're ready. I know you've been wary of getting close to any guy since you got home from New York. And I blame him for it. But I also know that you are one of the smartest girls I know, and you deserve to be happy. Either with this guy or with someone else or just by yourself. It's time to exorcise the ghost of Steve from your head and your heart!"

There was silence on the other line. Lilly was afraid she had said too much, but she was so tired of watching Rosie beat herself up about the failed relationship. Rosie had blamed herself for whatever had gone wrong in their relationship instead of laying the fault on Steve, where it belonged. It was really making Lilly angry. Of course, since he was dead, it was easy to make the memories tell a different story. If he was still alive, his true asshole colors would have inevitably shown themselves to Rosie, and she would have kicked his sorry ass to the curb.

"You're right! Of course, you're right! And trust me, you are not saying anything to me I haven't said to myself a million times over. Maybe this time it will work, huh? And maybe I should take a page out of Daisy's book. Have you noticed anything different about *her* lately? All of a sudden, she seems to be walking around a whole lot more chipper than she has in, like, two years?"

"Don't think I don't know you're trying to change the subject. I'll give you a pass this time, but I'm reserving the right to come back to this subject. And yes, Daisy seems happy, or if not happy, then certainly content with life. I really think she's having a lot of fun at work. I see her talking and laughing with all the nurses on the floor, and she has gotten to be pretty good friends with Miranda. I can tell they all really like her. I think she just needed to get back into the world. Doesn't that sound like some great advice? Sometimes those gentle nudges do work wonders, right?"

"I hear you loud and clear, Captain! I love you!"

CHAPTER NINETEEN

THREE MONTHS LATER, there was, well, absolutely nothing going on. At least, nothing regarding the death of Skylar or the girls' fervent desire to break the case wide open. They still hadn't solved the puzzle of how Skylar had known Tommy and how she knew he'd died in a car accident. Jack had gone over all the newspaper coverage of the accident and found nothing out of the ordinary. Lilly even gave the autopsy report to one of her coworkers to see if she could find anything amiss, but there was nothing.

Meanwhile, Daisy was happy. She realized this one morning while she was getting ready to go to work. She had slept great the night before, gotten up, taken a shower, and while she was drinking her coffee from her brand-new Keurig machine, she admitted to herself that while she was not quite ready to do a happy dance in the middle of the hospital lobby, she was satisfied with her life at the moment. Getting back into the workplace was something she should have done a long time ago.

The sisters were lucky in the sense that none of them really needed to work. Their grandfather on their mother's side had made his money in oil, and he had left all his assets to her. After their mother died, Jack took over managing the portfolio and made some astute investments. He also set up structured settlements for the girls. That was how Amy was able to buy a house and how Daisy could live without working for a couple of years after Tommy died. Jack had always been open with the girls about their wealth but instilled in them the desire to be self-sufficient and make their way in the working world.

Daisy also had some new friends at the hospital, which was doing her a world of good. Daisy had never realized until recently how most of the friends she and Tommy had known together had quietly slipped away. Daisy was honest with herself and knew she was to blame. After Tommy died, Daisy had just been numb. Even thinking about calling one of her old friends and making the effort to go out had seemed insurmountable in those first couple of months. After the first-year anniversary of Tommy's death, during a rare time when she'd thought she might want to reconnect with her old friends, she'd convinced herself no one really wanted to go out on the town with the poor sad widow. And besides, she had her sisters and her dad, so it wasn't like she was alone in the world. *Well, those lonely days are gone for good. This is the new Daisy, so look out world!*

That afternoon, while Daisy was finishing the last set of orders on the five new patients admitted to the floor, Dr. Dickhead came around the corner. Daisy hadn't spoken to him since that time in the break room, but she watched him closely whenever he came onto the floor. Daisy kept trying to see the bad guy Lilly insisted he was, but she was pretty sure Lilly had pegged this guy all wrong. He treated everyone the same, from food service to the head of the department. The nurses on the floor all liked him, even though they admitted he was very quiet and kept mostly to himself. Daisy had been around the nurses enough to know if they didn't like a person, you'd know about it.

Daisy was surprised when Dr. Booker came over to her. "Daisy? I don't know if you remember me, but I'm Jonathan Booker. We met in the break room a while back?"

"Sure. I remember you. Uh, is there anything I can help you with? Is there something you need ordered?"

He stared at her with a bemused look on his face. Finally he said, "I can't believe I didn't see it before. You have got to be Lilly O'Rourke's sister. I thought I heard her sister was working here in the hospital. You look a lot like her."

"We get that comment quite a bit, although I think she looks more like my younger sister than me."

He started to laugh. "Has she told you what a terrible person I am?"

"What? Of course not! Why would she do that?"

"Because I seem to get under her skin whenever we're in the same vicinity. And it cracks me up that she gets so angry."

"Well, I really don't think she's angry. I think you must, I don't know, do things that upset her. I know my sister, and she does not arbitrarily decide to be angry at someone. She is very level-headed!"

"She is a great nurse; I will give you that. But I always think she's holding back what she really wants to say to me. It's like I can see the wheels turning in her head. I think one of these days she'll finally let me have it."

Daisy could feel herself blushing, and at that moment, even when her brain was saying, *Do not say anything. Do. Not. Say. Anything. It could get Lilly in all sorts of trouble!* she knew what she was going to say even before she opened her mouth. "Well, there has to be a reason she has nicknamed you Dr. Dickhead."

Daisy could not believe she'd said that. All she could do was stare up at Dr. Booker with what she knew was a horrified look on her face. "I'm so sorry . . ." But before she could finish the apology, Dr. Booker threw back his head and let out deep belly laugh.

"That is absolutely great! I knew she wanted to call me names, but that one is great. Dr. Dickhead? Perfect!"

"You're not mad? Is she going to get in trouble? She would *kill* me if she knew I said that. And I apologize. It was completely unprofessional and uncalled for."

"No, truth be told, I probably deserve it. For some reason I get a kick out of pulling her chain, mainly because you can tell exactly what she's thinking. Give your sister some advice. Tell her to never play poker for money!"

"Oh my God. I still cannot believe I said anything. Seriously, I do not go around telling people I don't even know things like that! I don't know why I said it! I don't even tell people I *do know* stuff like that!"

"Don't worry about it. I am being completely honest with you when I say I probably deserve it." He stopped for a moment and gave her a look Daisy couldn't read.

"What? Did you change your mind and now you're thinking of turning me into the unit secretary police force, if there is even such a thing?"

"Nooo," he said slowly. "You said you don't tell people things like that when you don't even know them. I think we should go out for a drink, then you'll get to know me, and then you can tell me all the other stuff your sister's said about me. What do you say?"

Daisy was so astonished by this she just blurted out, "Are you asking me out for a drink? Me? I mean, wow, okay, um, I am really sounding like a total idiot here. You just are surprising the heck out of me."

Jon smiled. "Yes, I'm asking you out for a drink. And I think we need to get to the bottom of your irrational fear of the unit secretary police."

Daisy looked at Jon for a moment, as if considering his offer. "Okay. Let's start over. Yes, Lilly is my sister. She thinks you are the best doctor in this hospital and would never, ever think about calling you any names. She actually calls you 'sir' when she mentions you. Seriously." Daisy then said something that surprised her. "And yes, I think I would like to go get a drink with you."

"You know, you're funny. I like that. What time do you get off?"

Daisy contemplated calling Lilly when she got home that night but decided against it. For one thing, she wanted to savor the evening and go over in her mind everything they had talked about. Jon (Daisy would never think of him as Dr. Dickhead again) was a great person to talk to. There had been none of the initial awkwardness that usually accompanied a conversation where two people don't know each other. He had a terrific sense of humor, and Daisy spent a lot of the night laughing. Some of his funniest stories had to do with his patients, but he was never mean or belittling. He'd asked a lot of questions about her and her sisters. He had even persuaded Daisy to tell him some of the stories Lilly had told her about him, but Daisy could never finish because she would start laughing at all the stuff he added to the story, making it even more humorous.

When Daisy had finally looked at her watch, she couldn't believe it was nine p.m. already. "Holy crap! I've got to get going."

"Why, are you going to turn into a pumpkin? Is this past your curfew?"

"Ha, aren't you funny. It just so happens that I have another date."

"Oh, you do, huh? Tell me, does he make you laugh like I do? Can he make you do that little snorting thing you do when you are really giggling?"

"I don't snort! Are you on drugs? Any snorting going on was coming from your side of the table, not mine. And yes, Leo makes me laugh all the time!"

"Leo, huh? Is he my competition?"

"Well, I hate to burst your bubble, but there's no competition. Leo wins hands down."

"Hmm. You are really breaking my heart here. What does he look like, so I know what I am up against?"

"Let's see. He has the most gorgeous blond hair ever, he's muscular and strong, he can run very fast, he's loyal and loves me more than anyone else . . . um . . . oh yeah, and he drinks from the toilet and loves to chase squirrels. Can you do all that?"

Jon laughed. "I can never catch those damn squirrels, and to be honest, the whole toilet water thing was giving me terrible heartburn, so my doctor advised me to quit that habit!"

Daisy was still smiling to herself the next morning when she woke up and looked over at her *date* from last night. Leo had somehow managed to wiggle all the way up to the pillow on her right side, and he was still sound asleep. His entire eighty-five-pound body was sprawled on the bed. He was snoring softly, and every now and then, his paws would twitch like he was running.

"Chasing those squirrels again, huh?"

CHAPTER TWENTY

IT WAS A GORGEOUS DAY, about three weeks before Christmas. Amy knew she should be studying for finals, but she just could not make herself sit down with her law books. She had been hitting the books and meeting with her study group almost every night, and she thought she deserved one day away from the stress.

Heck, they all needed a break. Brooke had started crying last night while they were going over property problems, saying if she had to think about the rule against perpetuities one more time, she would lose her mind. She'd said she did not understand it, could not understand it, did not want to understand it, no matter how many times they went over it! And Amy had to agree with her. It was maddening.

Amy decided to take a mental health day. She called her dad and told him she was going to take him to lunch, and then she was going to get a manicure and pedicure. God knew her nails needed it. She was going to sit in the chair and read a magazine and not think about anything more stressful than whether Kim Kardashian was going to have another baby or not.

Jack was sitting in his office and talking on the phone when Amy came in. He saw her and held up his finger to let her know he had to finish the call. Amy nodded and sat in one of the chairs by the door.

She closed her eyes and inhaled the scent of the newsroom. It brought back so many memories of her childhood. She remembered all the Saturday afternoons when Jack would bring them down to the office and give them chores to do. Daisy would sweep the floor, Lilly would straighten the reference books that covered one whole wall, Rosie would somehow get out of doing any actual work because she said she was going to be a writer so she had to practice on the typewriters (yes, that was before the days of the PC), and Amy would just go from sister to sister, and they would let her do whatever she wanted.

Amy smiled to herself, thinking about those days. Jack would finish up whatever project he had going on and take the girls to the local pizza parlor for dinner. Amy was thinking about what a fun time that used to be (not like now, when every waking thought was spent worrying about flunking out of law school) when someone said, "Excuse me, do you need some help?"

Amy opened her eyes to see a young man standing before her. He was of average build, with curly brown hair and some very cute green eyes looking at her from behind a pair of wire-framed glasses. "Can I help you with anything?" he asked again.

"No, I'm just waiting for my dad to get off the phone."

"Oh. Well, since Jack is the only other person in here besides me, I take it he's your father?"

"Yes, he is." Amy stood up and held out her hand to shake. "My name is Amy Hurley."

He shook her hand. "I'm Andrew Foley. It's nice to meet you. Jack talks about his daughters all the time. I'm assuming you're the law student?"

"Oh God, don't remind me. I'm trying to forget all of that for just one day! I don't think I'm asking too much, do you? Just one day? Do I have to feel guilty about it because I'm taking my dad out to lunch? Well, do I?"

"Uh . . . I guess not. If you don't think so . . ."

"Don't try to reason with her, Andrew," Jack said as he came up beside Amy. "She's in the midst of her first year of finals, and I think, quite truthfully, she's losing her mind. What do you think?" Jack put his arm around Amy and grinned down at her.

"I think you hit the nail on the head. I am losing my mind." She looked at Andrew. "I usually am very calm and rational sounding, but wow, today I just sound crazy! Come on, Dad, you need to feed me!"

Jack told Andrew he would probably be back within the hour and to call him if anything came up needing his attention. They left the building, and Amy told Jack she had been reminiscing about their Saturdays in the office. Jack laughed and said he assumed then she wanted to eat at the pizza parlor, since she was walking down memory lane. "You read my mind! Pepperoni pizza, here we come!"

Once they were settled into their favorite booth, and after Jack had let Amy vent about upcoming finals and Amy let Jack talk about the article he was struggling to write regarding the local zoning commission, Amy said, "So, Dad. About this Andrew guy?"

"Andrew? What Andrew? Oh, you mean *that* Andrew. What about him?"

"Come on, Dad. How long has he been working for you? I thought you weren't going to hire any new reporters this year."

"Well, I wasn't. But he sent me a resume and letter requesting a meeting and there was just something about it. He kind of reminded me of me, you know? And Bill is going to retire at the end of the year, so I figured, what the heck. Give the kid a chance. And since when do you keep track of who the reporters are in the office?"

"I was just saying. You can hire who you want. He's just not the run-of-the-mill reporter, in my opinion. I am just looking out for you," she said primly, folding her napkin into a tiny square.

"And would you be looking out for me if Andrew was a bald, paunchy, fifty-year-old? Hmm?"

"Yes, I would!" Amy laughed. "Okay, maybe not. And maybe my brain is just fried from all the studying I've been doing. It's not like I need or even want the distraction of a boyfriend right now. If I'm not studying by myself or with my study group, then I'm sleeping. I am not exactly a barrel of fun here."

They came to the compromise that once Amy had finished her finals and *if* Andrew was still around (Jack thought he might move on due to the lack of any ground-breaking news in Brunswick), then maybe Amy would come to the newsroom and talk some more to Andrew. Of course, she made Jack swear not to try and do any matchmaking in the meantime. Amy said if Jack tried to set her up with Andrew, then she would give her Torts professor Jack's phone number. Amy thought her professor was neat and would be a good fit for her dad, but she knew Jack was very much against being set up with anyone, so she figured it was a good threat to make him be quiet.

CHAPTER TWENTY-ONE

CHRISTMAS TIME IN THE HURLEY FAMILY had always been special. Claudia, the girls' mother, had loved decorating for the holidays. She'd usually been the first one on the block to get the decorations going for Halloween. Jack had always said that if she could have strung up the ghosts and witches from the trees right after Labor Day, she would have. And while she had loved Halloween and Thanksgiving, Christmas was her favorite.

For Jack though, Christmas was bittersweet. Claudia had been eight months pregnant with Amy on their last Christmas together, and Jack remembered how Claudia had struggled with the whole decorating madness that year. Having three small children, plus being massively pregnant, had slowed her down. And she'd been so pissed about it, Jack remembered with a smile. He'd kept telling her she would have many other Christmases to put up decorations, and oh, he would give anything in the world if only that had been true.

He hated thinking about the night they had an argument over the Christmas decorations. He'd promised Claudia he would come home early to help her, but there had been a major fire in the stockyards on the south side of town and a couple of the reporters had already left the office, so Jack had covered the story himself.

He'd called Claudia and told her he would not be home until

later that evening and that they could do the decorations the next day. When he got home, Claudia was asleep on the couch with the boxes of decorations scattered around the floor. Jack could remember the irritation he'd felt when he saw the boxes. He couldn't figure out why she'd been so hell-bent on putting up the tree and the ornaments by herself. After she died, he always worried she'd had some premonition and wanted their last Christmas together to be special. He knew thinking along those lines was a sure way to lead to some of the blackest thoughts he ever had, but some days, he just couldn't help himself.

That was why Jack made sure to treat every holiday as something very precious. He involved the girls in all the planning, decorating, caroling, cooking—you name it, the Hurley girls did it for Christmas. Even now that they were older and each girl was so busy with their own lives, the Christmas traditions that had started when they were young were still the law of the land come December.

Jack thought this year could be a special year. The last two Christmases had been overshadowed by Tommy's death. Daisy had been so heartbroken, she couldn't even pretend to enjoy the holidays, especially that first year. But Daisy seemed to have turned the corner on her grief and appeared to be truly enjoying the holidays this year. Jack wasn't quite sure what the reason was, but he was grateful for it. Rosie also seemed to be in a much better place emotionally. Jack knew something bad had happened to her in New York, but he was willing to give her space and let her process it at her own speed.

He knew Rosie was spending time with her vet, and while Jack had only met him once, he certainly approved of him. Rosie was going to bring him over to the house for Christmas Eve, and Jack was excited to get to know him better. Amy had finished her finals and was just loving spending the holidays doing absolutely nothing. And the best news of all was that Lilly was pregnant again! She had only told Jack, swearing him to secrecy because she wanted to surprise Keith on Christmas Eve night with the news. Jack, who kept a running conversation with Claudia in his head, looked forward to telling her this would be a hell of a Christmas!

As per custom, everyone met at Jack's house on Christmas Eve. Jack never did move out of the big house the girls had grown up in. He would talk about it from time to time, but the sisters always suspected he was holding onto it because he hoped it would eventually be filled with lots of grandchildren. Everyone always congregated in the dining room. The table seated twelve, with extra chairs squeezed in if needed. It was situated in front of a huge picture window that looked out onto the front yard. With the Christmas decorations in full swing, all the trees in front of the house were covered with twinkling-colored lights. The lights made such a beautiful pattern on the lawn.

Amy got there first, and while she was a little annoyed to find her dad had invited Andrew without asking her, she really wasn't surprised. Their Christmas Eves had evolved from family-only to inviting anyone and everyone who had no other place to go. Jack frequently shared with his daughters how fortunate he was to have them in his life, and he wanted to share some of the love and happiness of the season with people less fortunate than him.

Jack also liked to play matchmaker (Amy knew her father, and she suspected this was his ulterior motive in inviting Andrew), not only in the affairs of the heart but also in trying to pair people up.

One year, an entire family—father, mother, two daughters, and three boys—who were struggling to pay the bills after the father had been laid off from his work had been invited to Christmas dinner—along with a farmer who'd been falling behind in his work because he hadn't found reliable help. Jack knew both of the parties, and he'd been sure they would be able to help each other out. Sure enough, it'd been a win-win for everyone. Nothing made Jack happier than solving problems of the heart and the pocketbook.

Amy noticed Andrew standing by himself in front of the tree, so she took pity on him and brought him a glass of wine.

"What do you think?"

"About the tree? It's gorgeous. Although I'm not sure how you guys got all the ornaments to fit. The tree's only about twelve feet tall!"

"I know. My dad just can't help himself. And he can't throw anything away either, so some of those ornaments go back years! Truth be told, neither can I nor my sisters. Decorating the tree is one of our traditions I doubt we'll ever break. Supposedly, my mom was the world's best holiday decorator, so we just carry on and try to do it justice in her memory."

"Well, the tree is fantastic, so you guys must be doing a good job following in her footsteps. So not sure I should bring this up, but how did the finals come out? Or is it too early to talk about it?"

Amy laughed. "Don't worry, I'm not going to go ballistic on you again. Finals were terrible, no good, awful, horrible, and I'm just glad I got through them with my brain intact. And my hands! Typing an essay for over four hours tends to make your hands cramp! I felt like an old witch with claws for hands by the time it was all over!"

Lilly came into the room and announced it was time for dinner. The dining room table had been extended to its maximum length and still the chairs were crowded together. Ren and Andrew, along with Perry and Matt, two of Jack's golfing buddies who were both divorced, were the non-family members this year.

Jack experienced a deep sense of satisfaction while looking around the table. Rosie and Ren were trying to be subtle about the way they felt about each other, but it was obvious to Jack something serious was happening with those two, and he couldn't be happier about it. While Jack didn't know the entire story of what had happened to Rosie in New York, he knew enough to know Rosie had been deeply hurt by some asshole guy named Steve. Rosie had promised Jack that one day she would tell him the whole story, so Jack had to be content with that.

Daisy, his sweet Daisy, was looking about as happy as he had seen her in the last two years. He was grateful Lilly had practically demanded Daisy take the job at the hospital, and it was evident getting out of the house and back into the workforce had done a world of good for her. She was holding Lacey in her lap, making a finger puppet out of her napkin, and talking in different voices to her. Lacey was bouncing up and down and giggling.

Daisy looked up and saw Jack watching her. Daisy smiled at her dad and with a look said, "I am finally getting happy again."

Jack's look back said, "You deserve it."

Ting. Ting. Ting. Lilly tapped her spoon against her glass and waited for everyone to be quiet. "My dad told me I had to lead the prayer today, so everyone will just have to bear with me since I usually don't do this." Lilly paused. "As I look around the table tonight, my heart is so full. I see and welcome our new friends, Andrew and Ren, along with old friends, Perry and Matt."

"Hey, what's with the *old* word?" Matt said, laughing. "Just because we hang out with Jack and he's old doesn't mean we are."

"You're right! I stand corrected. We are here with the perpetually young Perry and Matt! Is that better?"

Matt grinned. "I always said you were the smartest of the sisters!"

"Now that the serious age topic is settled, on with the prayer— or it's more of a toast, to be honest. I'm pretty sure everyone here at this table has things they're grateful for. I know I do. I'm grateful for my wonderful husband and children, for my fantastic father, for my beautiful sisters—" Lilly's voice cracked, and she looked down for a moment.

She cleared her throat and continued. "As you all know, like a lot of families, we've had our share of tragedies." Lilly gave a silent nod to Daisy. "But I think brighter days are ahead. My very talented and hard-working sister, Daisy, is going to revamp the way things are done at the hospital. She's already started by making friends with just about everyone there. I'm starting to feel a bit jealous of her! I have had so many people come up to me and ask me why it took so long for me to have Daisy come work there! So cheers to you, sis!"

Daisy laughed. "Stop! You're embarrassing me, Lil! Besides, I'm just riding on your coattails there. You are very popular, little sister!"

"And to my also very talented sister Rosie, who I have no doubt is well on her way to writing her first of many best-selling books! And, if there's one thing this family needs, it's our own personal vet. One who also comes with not one, but two huge dogs that will surely be able to hold their own with Big Shirley! Cheers, Rosie! Cheers, Ren!

"Not to leave out my other very talented sister Amy, who I have no doubt is well on her way to being number one in her law school class and who, I predict, will one day sit on a court of law . . . just not sure which one yet! We are all so proud of you, Amy! Cheers!"

"I know everyone's hungry, so I will finally finish this never-ending speech with one last toast. And this is to my wonderful husband." Lilly paused, smiled at Keith, and continued. "I cannot imagine my life without you. You are my best friend who I can tell anything to, my rock I lean on so many times a day, my clown because you make me laugh even when I'm not in a laughing mood, my love who somehow manages to make me love you more each day. Am I leaving anything out? Hmm. Well, yes, there is one more thing. You are my partner in this crazy business of child rearing. You are such a great father to Luke and Lacey, and I know you will be just as great to this next one. Congratulations, love! Are you ready for number three?"

Keith looked stunned for a moment, then leapt to his feet and yelled, "Hell yes!" He took Lilly in his arms and hugged her tightly.

Practically everyone was laughing and crying at the same time, with the sisters all getting up to congratulate Lilly and Keith. Rosie was saying she should not have been fooled by thinking Lilly was drinking gin, when in fact it was Perrier water, and Daisy and Amy were saying they knew Lilly wanted another one and asking if she knew if it was a boy or girl. Perry and Matt were telling Jack he would never be able to retire because he had to continue to put money in college funds for the grandkids, and Jack said he didn't want to retire because then all he would do was beat them at golf every day. Lacey finally broke Lilly and Keith apart by pulling on Lilly's dress and saying, "Up. Up. Up. Up, Mommy."

Keith lifted her up. "My little girl, you are going to be in for such a shock. You are going to have to make way for a new little brother or sister. Good thing it takes nine months for the new one to cook!"

They had discovered a perfect place to park the car where it could not be seen by the people in Jack's dining room. Watching the people inside—drinking, laughing, crying, hugging—made the hands on the steering wheel clench with rage, eyes glittering with hate. "Well, isn't that just a happy little Christmas family? Although, to tell you the truth, they make me sick. Sick. And I can't wait to fuck them up. All of them. Soon, very soon."

CHAPTER TWENTY-TWO

LATER, AFTER THE DUST HAD SETTLED from all the crap that would happen that year, the sisters agreed that the eight months leading up to the final shit storm were some of the best times of their lives.

Lilly got a promotion at work she ended up being thrilled about. The head nurse on the Progressive Care Unit had retired and recommended Lilly to take over the position. When the job was first offered to her, Lilly wasn't too sure she wanted to be involved in the day-to-day running of the floor. But after talking it over with Keith, she decided to take a chance. And was she ever glad she did!

Lilly discovered she rather liked being the one in charge, and her sisters were totally unsurprised at that. She had many ideas on how to make the floor run more efficiently and, better yet, she found out coming in from being on the front line gave her the street cred that made people listen to her. She felt like she was really making a difference.

Plus, she felt physically great with this baby. Working twelve-hour shifts like she had when she was pregnant with Luke and Lacey had taken a lot out of her. She'd never felt completely rested. She had either been resting up to go to work or resting up because she had been at work. Consequently, she'd always felt tired. Though now with her new job, she only had to be at the hospital five days a week, and she could be home by six, feed the kids, have an adult conversation with Keith, and still be in bed by 8:30.

Rosie and Ren were having a ball getting to know each other better. One of the first things they did was get Big Shirley, Walter, and Marilyn together for a doggie playdate. They decided to have the dogs meet on neutral ground, so early one Saturday morning, they all met at the dog park. Thankfully, there were no other dogs around to interfere with the meet and greet.

Ren brought Rosie a coffee, and they sat together and laughed at the dogs' antics. Marilyn, of course, initially decided she wanted nothing to do with Big Shirley, and she kept looking at Walter like she could not believe he was making such a fool of himself. And he was being a total goober. He would plant himself in front of Shirley, and when she tried to go around him, he would literally launch himself up in the air and practically do a 360-degree spin. How he was able to propel all his 180 pounds into the air was surely a feat of nature. And every time he did it, he looked at Big Shirley as if to say, "See? Pretty cool, huh? You want to play this game with me?"

Walter obviously did not know how Newfoundlands operated, or he would have known they're not exactly high energy dogs. Just getting out of the car and walking to the park was enough exercise for BS. Marilyn finally decided to get in on the action, if only to spare Walter any further humiliation. You could tell Walter really didn't want to play with Marilyn, but since Shirley was basically ignoring both of them, he made do with his sister.

After thirty minutes of dog craziness, all three of them decided it was time to take a nap. The early morning sun had just enough heat to feel good and all three of them stretched out on the ground and went to sleep.

Unless Ren had office hours, taking the dogs to the park became a weekly Saturday morning ritual. And every Saturday morning, Walter would go through his antics of trying to get Big Shirley to play with him. Sometimes he changed it up. Instead of jumping up in the air and turning in circles, there were times when he would take off running and do some serious laps around the doggie play area. Of course, two laps were enough to wear him out, and the result was always the same. Big Shirley would ignore him, and Marilyn would take pity on him and wrestle with him.

This particular Saturday had been a lap day, and now, the three dogs were snoozing at their feet. Ren and Rosie talked about the movie they had seen the night before.

"Last year's *A Star Is Born* movie was the best ever made," insisted Rosie. "Bradley Cooper and Lady Gaga made the most believable couple."

"They were pretty good but, ahem, well, being such an aficionado of older films, I have to say the Judy Garland and James Mason film was the best. Cooper and Gaga are a close second." While Ren was saying this, he was giving her such a goofy look and acting like he was some famous film critic that Rosie burst out laughing.

"You must have looked up all of the previous movies on Google because last night you knew nothing about *this* movie, much less any of the older ones!"

"Well, I do what I can to try and impress you. I am just a lowly vet, not a soon-to-be famous author."

Rosie snorted. "Yeah, right. In my wildest dreams. How about a not-so-famous girl who literally just stares at her computer every day hoping for some divine inspiration to hit?"

"You are being way too hard on yourself. You've only been

working on it for about nine months or so. Besides, I just read an article about an author who took *ten years* to write her best-seller. I have complete faith in you. I think you can do it in *nine* years! Ouch!" Rosie had grabbed and twisted his arm. "And if you decide writing a book is not in your future, then I know you will find something else that will satisfy your creative instinct."

"How long have we known each other?" Rosie asked. "Ten months? Give or take? How did you get to be so smart about me in such a short time?"

Ren leaned over and kissed her very gently on the mouth. He said softly, "Because when you're falling in love with someone, you want to know everything there is to know about that person, and the things that matter to them matter to you too."

"Oh, Ren. That is such a beautiful thing to say." Rosie's eyes filled with tears, and she reached out and laid her hand on the side of his neck. "I have been so hoping you were feeling about me the way I'm feeling about you, but I wasn't sure. Are you sure? Do you really mean it? You're not just saying that because you like my dog?"

Ren laughed. "Well, Big Shirley has certainly factored into my feelings about you, I've got to admit. Would I fall in love with you if you were a cat person? Or." And here Ren gasped. "If you liked one of those yip-yip dogs?"

"'Yip-yip dogs'? Seriously? Is that a tried-and-true veterinarian term? But trust me, I will never have a yip-yip dog. I mean seriously, could you imagine one of those dogs with this crowd?" Rosie pointed to Big Shirley, Walter, and Marilyn. The Danes were both sleeping on their sides with their paws tangled up, and Big Shirley had turned her entire body around so her rear end was facing the

Danes, almost like she just couldn't be bothered to even look at them.

Ren put his arm around Rosie, kissed her temple, and said, "Life could not be any better. I got my girl, my dogs, the sun is shining, and we have all day ahead of us to do, well, just about anything we want to do."

Rosie gave him a sideways look. "Anything?"

"Anything."

Amy's life as a law student was going much better than she had anticipated. She had been so stressed about taking the finals before Christmas, she'd almost made herself physically ill. Their study group met continuously in the two weeks before finals, and someone was always storming out of the group, complaining to high heaven that the stress was just too great. However, they must have done something right because everyone in her group came through finals with decent grades. Amy ended up twelfth out of 182 students, so she was ecstatic.

Even better, she'd done so well on her finals, she decided to write for *Law Review*, the scholarly journal put out by the law school focusing on legal issues. Being accepted onto the *Law Review* staff could have a significant impact on her future career, and though Amy still wasn't sure what kind of law she wanted to practice, she didn't want to close any doors. She was therefore thrilled when she was accepted. Joe and Brooke also got accepted, so they were all feeling pretty darn good about themselves.

However, Amy's love life was still nonexistent. She had gone out with Andrew a few times over Christmas break, but nothing seemed to click. He was a nice enough guy, but Amy couldn't seem to make herself want to go the extra mile. Maybe it was her. She'd dated a few boys during college but never seriously. She always thought she would get serious with a guy when she had her life figured out. She now justified not being serious with a guy by telling herself even though her life was figured out as far as a career, she was still very busy with school, and she had to devote all her time and attention to making good grades and doing all the extra crap that needed to be done to get ahead in the law profession.

Besides, she reassured herself, there was plenty of time to worry about romance. Whenever she would get to feeling blue about her lack of a boyfriend, she would think of Daisy and know that true love could be right around the corner.

And truth be told, Daisy and Jon were the talk of the Hurley sisters. Well, not specifically Jon. The sisters didn't know exactly *who* Daisy was seeing; they just knew she was seeing *someone.* Daisy had been seeing Jon for about six months when she brought up the idea of having her sisters and her dad meet him. Jon pointed out that Lilly already knew him, so technically he had already met one of her sisters, and so why should he meet any of the others? Daisy just scoffed at that remark. She said that Lilly didn't know the real Jon and just because he knew Lilly, it did not exempt him from meeting her other two sisters.

"What? A big, bad doctor such as yourself is afraid of meeting my sisters?"

"Sisters, not so much. I figure I can charm them. It's your dad I'm worried about. Just the thought is giving me flashbacks to my high school days. I'll probably wake up tomorrow with pimples, sparse facial hair, and a voice that goes up and down."

Daisy just laughed at him. It was a gorgeous spring day, and they were upstairs in Daisy's bedroom. The windows were open, and the breeze that came into the room smelled like freshly cut grass.

"Why do I doubt you ever had pimples or a fluctuating voice? I think you were born being Mr. Cool."

"Oh God. If only you knew. I was the ultimate nerd. Back in high school, girls didn't care how smart you were. The jocks were who they were looking at. And to be honest, I didn't help myself. For one thing, I didn't grow into this strapping six-foot-one hunk of muscle until I got into college, so I was not only a nerd, but a short one at that. And I really wasn't interested in team sports, mainly because I knew I would get my ass handed to me. Basically, I'm traumatized by my high school years, so only constant sex and kisses will make me a whole person."

Jon tried to put on a poor-pitiful-me face but he couldn't help but smile when he looked over at Daisy, who was just laughing and shaking her head at him. "Not working, huh?"

"Not one little bit," Daisy said. "And besides, I let you weasel out of not coming to Christmas, so you don't get another Get Out of Jail Free card. This Friday. My house. All the Hurley people are going to be here taking stock of you, and you better measure up!"

"Nooo! Anything but that! Can't Leo go in my place? Leo! Where are you? Come here, boy. I promise to buy you a whole box of doggie treats if you go in my place. Where is that dang dog?"

Daisy cracked up because Leo was lying in the sun at the foot of the bed and didn't even bother to open an eye.

"You need to offer more than treats, my good man. Maybe promises of more evening walks would work! And I'm not even sure that would sway him! Since he already knows everyone, your negotiating tool is nonexistent!"

CHAPTER TWENTY-THREE

DAISY WASN'T SURE WHY she was keeping Jon a secret. Yes, her sisters knew she was seeing someone, and yes, they knew she was truly happy for the first time since Tommy died, but none of them knew *who* she was seeing, especially Lilly.

She had discussed it with Miranda over coffee, and all Miranda had come up with was that Daisy was feeling guilty about being happy again and afraid to do anything that could potentially rock the boat. Right now, Daisy and Jon were existing in this wonderful bubble, and inviting her father and sisters in would pop it.

Daisy agreed she maybe felt a little guilty about being happy but scoffed at the bubble theory. Her father and sisters were the most important people to her, and she was excited about introducing them to Jon. Well, maybe not Lilly, but Daisy knew once Lilly met the real Jon, her attitude would change. That was why she decided to take the bull by the horns and have them all over at once, including Jack.

That Friday, Daisy took the day off work and did what one usually does when one invites people over to one's house. She vacuumed, dusted, made sure the toilets were presentable (including plenty of toilet paper and candles), called the BBQ place to make sure they would deliver dinner, and ordered liquor from the liquor store. Then she looked at the clock and saw it was only eleven in the morning, so she proceeded to sit down and have a mini breakdown.

"What in God's name was I thinking? Can't I, for once, leave well enough alone? Jesus!"

Since all the dogs in the Hurley households seemed to understand English, Leo knew Daisy was distressed about tonight, and he did what he could to distract her. He brought her his bone, dropped it in her lap, and then looked at her, as if to say, "Go ahead. Take a couple of satisfying chews on that and tell me it doesn't make you feel better!"

Daisy looked at the bone and started to laugh. "If only it was that easy! But thank you, sweet boy! You put it in perspective. Come on, let's go take a walk and let the chips fall where they may!"

During their walk, Daisy discussed with Leo all the reasons she had not yet introduced Jon to her family. Finally, she had to be brutally honest with herself and admit she was afraid Lilly would somehow, very inadvertently, let her feelings for Jon be known, and then the rest of her sisters and her father wouldn't be able to see Jon for who he was. Daisy knew Lilly would never do it intentionally, but if the relationship was sprung on her without warning, then she might say something. Daisy mentally kicked herself for not talking to Lilly sooner, and even Leo looked back at her with an expression on his face that said, "You had better fix this, like now. Walk faster!"

When they got back from their walk, Daisy phoned Lilly at her office. When Lilly's voicemail popped up, Daisy called her cell phone.

"Hey, Daisy. What's up? What do you need me to bring tonight? I know you said you had it under control, but I know you. There is always some last-minute item you need."

"Lilly. I need to talk to you about something, something very important to me."

"Sweetie, what is it? Are you okay?"

"I'm fine. I just—I don't know how to say this. But you need to know something before you come over tonight."

"What? What is it?"

Daisy sighed. "There is a reason I am having everyone over tonight, and it's not solely because I want to see everyone." Daisy hesitated. "Well, there's someone I want you all to meet."

"Daisy Wolf!" Lilly laughed. "Did you go and get yourself a man? Good for you! We were all wondering when you were going to let us in on the secret. You have been looking like the cat that swallowed the canary, you know. I'm so excited! Who is it?"

"Well, that's what I want to talk to you about. And I really don't want to do it over the phone. Have you had lunch yet? Could you meet me at that little diner by the hospital in about twenty minutes?"

"Sure, Daisy. I can meet you, but you're worrying me. Is everything okay?"

"Everything will be fine. I'll explain everything when I see you. I gotta go."

Daisy hung up in such a hurry that Lilly looked at her phone in surprise. *Something really must be going on. Daisy never acts like that!*

Thirty minutes later, Lilly walked into the diner and saw Daisy sitting at a booth in the back. Lilly walked over and sat down. "Did you order?" she asked.

"I'm not really hungry. I ordered some tea. You get lunch. You need to feed the little goofball you have growing in there."

"I will! My gosh, I feel like all I do is feed the goofball. It just feels so good not to be totally nauseated all day long, every day." Lilly ordered a Caesar salad and water, then sat back in her chair and looked at Daisy. "Okay, spill it. What's got you so nervous?"

Daisy sighed, and when her eyes met Lilly's, there were tears in them. Lilly reached across the table and covered both of Daisy's hands. "Honey, please tell me what's wrong. You have to tell me what this is, and then we can deal with it. I can't help you if I don't know what's going on."

Daisy grabbed a napkin, blotted her eyes, blew her nose, took a drink of her tea, and then finally sat back and said, "I have been seeing someone for about the last six months, and he really makes me happy. I haven't been happy for such a long time . . ."

"I know you haven't. But you say he makes you happy? That's a good thing. A great thing! Anyone that makes you happy is okay in my book. Are we going to meet him tonight? Is that why you're having the family over? Are you worried about introducing him to all of us?"

Daisy hesitated. "No, I'm not really nervous about introducing him to the family." Daisy looked at Lilly. "I am nervous to introduce him to you."

"Me?" Lilly looked so surprised that Daisy had to smile. "Why me? Wait, then it has to be someone I know, right? And I would think it would have to be someone at the hospital. Am I right? But what I don't get is why you are nervous, I mean, about me."

Daisy took a deep breath and said in a rush "I'm seeing Jon Booker, and oh, Lilly, you have him pegged so wrong. He's wonderful and nice and funny and . . . I really think I'm falling for him. But I know you don't like him, and I'm just afraid, oh, I don't know, that you might make Rosie and Amy not like him either. And I can't have my sisters not like him and I—"

"Wait." Lilly held up her hand. "Just wait. Did I hear you right? Did you say Dr. Booker? Dr. Dickhead? Are you kidding me?" She stared at Daisy as if she had grown two heads.

Daisy shook her head and said rather heatedly, "This is exactly what I'm talking about. You don't know the real Jon. He says he loves needling you and getting under your skin because it's so obvious you don't like him. He thinks it's funny. But I'm worried if you look at him tonight the way you're looking at me right now—with such a look of, well, disgust—then Rosie and Amy and even Dad are going to pick up on it and, of course, they'll take your side in this. And first impressions are very hard to overcome, you know that Lilly." Daisy was getting angry. "And I can't have you do that. I won't have you do that. If you can't promise me you'll meet Jon with an open mind and get to really know him, then I don't want you coming by the house tonight." And with that Daisy burst into tears.

Lilly was so astounded at first all she could do was look at Daisy with amazement. Daisy *never* got angry, ever. She was the peacemaker in the family, always ready to hear everyone's side to a story. This was just so unlike her, it took a minute for Lilly to realize her sister was crying across the table from her, and the reason she was crying was *because* of her.

Lilly got up and sat down in the booth with Daisy, putting her arm around her. "Shhh. It will be okay, I promise." Lilly was crying too. "Oh Daisy, if you only knew how all of us have hoped and prayed you would meet someone. We know how unhappy you've been since Tommy, and we also knew you and Tommy had a very special relationship, and well, we were afraid you wouldn't meet someone that made you feel like that again. I guess what I'm saying is, I trust you and I trust your judgment." Lilly paused. "If you say that Dr. Di—"

Daisy gave her a look.

"Dr. Booker is a great guy, then I believe you, and I promise to keep an open mind. I am just so surprised is all. I guess I really don't know him. I called him that in my mind the first time I met him, and it just stuck. And you're probably right. If I had walked in and seen him, I'm ashamed to say it but I probably would have made a comment or two to Rosie and Amy. And you know what else? I'm sad you were worried I wouldn't listen to you and keep an open mind. I love you and want nothing but the best for you. And if that's Booker, then okay. I just want you to be happy again." Lilly gave a self-deprecating smile. "And maybe, just maybe, I need to work on my own interpersonal skills. Seems like they might need some improvement."

Daisy gave her a hug. "You don't know how relieved I am to hear you say that. This has been eating me up inside. The first people I want to share good news with are my sisters, and it's been killing me that I couldn't. And just wait. You'll see how wrong you were about him."

"Well, he is cute, I'll give him that. So how long have you been seeing him? And has he ever confessed why he gives me so much shit?"

The next morning, the sisters gathered back at Lilly's house for an early morning coffee and to discuss the previous evening. Rosie and Amy particularly wanted to rehash the moment when Lilly walked in and saw Jon. Everyone was in the kitchen when Lilly, Keith, Luke, and Lacey came in.

Lacey immediately ran over to Daisy and lifted her arms so Daisy could pick her up. But once she was in Daisy's arms, she looked over to Jon and, to the surprise of everyone, leaned over with her arms outstretched to him. Lacey tended to stay back and study people for a while before she would even consider interacting with them.

Jon didn't hesitate at all but just picked her up, settled her on his hip, and said to her, "Did you know you look just like your momma? And did you know your momma is one of the best nurses I know? And did you also know I would play a game with myself to see how mad I could make your momma?" Lacey was nodding along to what he was saying and tapping her hand against his face, as if she really could understand him. "Don't ask me why I would do that, except your momma has a *very* expressive face and I was just waiting for her to tell me exactly what she thought of me."

And then he looked right at Lilly. "But you know what? I want to offer an apology for doing that. Not my finest behavior, I must admit. And so can we start over, please? Because" —and here he paused and looked at Daisy— "I really, really want to continue seeing your beautiful big sister, and that won't be happening unless I get the okay from you."

A collective "Aww" came from all the sisters, Lilly included.

Jack looked at Jon and gave him a slight nod, as if to say, "Man, you are good."

Ren couldn't help himself and said, "Now that's what I'm talking about."

Keith had heard the entire story from Lilly when she got home from having lunch with Daisy, so he was torn. On one hand, he was not at all happy Jon had upset Lilly, but on the other hand, he'd watched Daisy suffer so much after Tommy died that he was ecstatic when Daisy seemed to be content with her life again. He figured he would take his cue from Lilly, and he got his answer when he looked over at her. She had rescued Jon from Lacey and was talking and smiling at Jon, although Keith was pretty sure at some point in the conversation she would circle back and give him shit. *That's my girl. Dear Dr. Booker might not know just what he has gotten himself into!* Keith smiled to himself and went over to introduce himself to Jon.

CHAPTER TWENTY-FOUR

AMY WAS THE FIRST ONE to have an odd, unexplained occurrence. She had just finished her last estates and properties class and was heading to the *Law Review* office when she heard her name being called.

Amy turned and was surprised to see Susanna Durmeyer walking toward her. Susanna was the law school administrator and second in line to the dean.

"Amy. I'm glad I caught you. I was afraid you had already left campus."

"No, I was on my way to the *Law Review* office. Is there something I can do for you?"

"Yes, there is. I need you to come to the dean's office."

"The dean's office? Really? What for?"

Susanna was starting to look uncomfortable. All she said was that the dean needed to talk to Amy.

"Wow. Okay. Am I in trouble?"

Susanna just repeated the dean needed to see her, so the walk to her office was done in silence. Amy was frantically searching through her mind wondering what the dean could possibly want to see her for, because judging from Susanna's demeanor, it wasn't anything good.

Amy had never even talked one on one with Dean Alexander.

She knew who she was, of course. The dean had welcomed Amy's 1L class at the beginning of the school year, and she'd also given a speech to the group of students that ran *Law Review*. Other than that, Amy had never seen her. *Holy crap. Well, I am going to see her now.*

Susanna had Amy wait in the outer office while she went in. Amy could hear them talking to each other, but the words were too low for Amy to understand them. After about five minutes (which seemed like five hours), Susanna came out and told Amy to go right on in.

"Hello, Amy. Go ahead and take a seat." Dean Alexander was tall and slender, around forty-five years old with shoulder-length dark brown hair. She had a pair of readers perched on her nose, and she was reading something on her desk. She pushed the paper away and sighed. "I really hate doing some parts of my job. And this is one of them." She hesitated. "Amy, you do know we have a code, so to speak, requiring students to adhere to the highest degree of professional integrity and is based on the fundamental principles of mutual trust and respect. It is the honor code. You know about it, correct?"

"The honor code? Yes, I know about it. They talked about it in orientation. Is this why you needed to see me? Is it something about the honor code?"

Dean Alexander looked at Amy as if she was deciding how much to tell her. Finally, she said, "We received an anonymous letter stating you violated the honor code last semester."

Amy's stomach lurched. "WHAT? *Really?* I don't understand. When was I supposed to have violated the code?"

"I am starting a fact-finding mission but wanted to give you an opportunity to tell me anything you think might be pertinent."

"I haven't violated anything! Honestly, I'm freaking out here because I can't think of anything I've done that would violate it. Seriously. I'm—I don't know what to say! Can you give me any clue as to when or where I was supposed to have done this? I mean, how can I even begin to defend myself if I don't even know when this took place!"

"To be honest, this is not how we normally do an honor code violation. This is somewhat unusual. We received a report that you cheated on one of your exams last semester."

"Seriously? Which test? I swear I didn't cheat on anything! I really don't even know what you're talking about. I know I keep saying that, but it's true. Who said this about me?"

Amy was desperately trying not to cry, but she could feel her face getting red and hear her voice quivering. *This is all so fucked!* An honor code violation could get her a failing grade, kicked off the *Law Review* staff, or even kicked out of school altogether.

Dean Alexander held up her hand. "Amy, when I said this is not how a violation typically gets reported, I was telling the truth. Usually, a professor will notice a student cheating and report it, or another student can report someone, but we require all students who are reporting a violation to give their names and reveal exactly what they are accusing another student of. It is spelled out very clearly in the handbook. Otherwise, we would have to deal with a situation exactly like this one. You are being accused of a serious violation, but it was done anonymously and only stated that you cheated on your property law final last semester. I spoke to Professor Hernandez, and she said she did not notice anything untoward during the exam, and she usually keeps a pretty good eye out during finals. I guess I am just giving you a heads up. Obviously, if there is something you might want to tell me, then this is the time to do it."

Amy took a deep breath. "Dean, I really don't know what to say. No, I take that back. I know exactly what to say. I *DID NOT* cheat on any of my finals last semester. Whoever sent that is totally wrong."

"I don't want to bring this up because I don't want to even think one of our students could be doing this maliciously, but have you had any issues with another student? Anything you can think of?"

Amy thought for a moment. "No, I really can't. I get along with pretty much everybody. I mean, I obviously don't know every student yet, but I can't think of anyone who would want to do something like this. So, what happens now?"

"Well, I will table this complaint until there is more evidence. I have a sneaking suspicion nothing more will come of it, but I could be wrong. And I don't want to be wrong. I hear very good things about you, Amy. Your test scores last semester and being selected to be on *Law Review* are all positive things. I know you are very upset about this, and quite truthfully, I don't blame you. It might be difficult, but try not to worry too much. If further allegations come to light, then you will have a chance to defend yourself. I know it's not much consolation right now, but it's the best I can do."

When Amy left the dean's office, she was surprised to find she had only been in there about twenty minutes. She felt like she had been in there for hours. Amy knew she had to get her books and get off campus before she burst into tears. She was glad that her classes were over for the day, and she didn't have to face anyone. By the time she got to her car, the tears were beginning. She cried on the way home, she cried during her dinner, she cried during her shower, and then she cried herself to sleep.

Amy woke up at her usual time of six a.m. and was quite surprised she had slept through the night. She was sure she would have been awake most of the night worrying and crying about everything.

While in bed, she took stock of herself. Except for her eyes being swollen and gritty from all the tears, she felt pretty good. *No wait*, she thought. *I feel good physically, but mentally I'm very fucking pissed off! Who the fuck did this to me? And why? I can't think of anybody who would stoop so low as to file an honor code violation against me. I need to talk to Joe and Brooke. Like right now.*

With that, Amy jumped out of bed and sent a quick text to Joe and Brooke. They didn't have class until nine, so they agreed to meet at the Starbucks about five miles from campus.

Amy got there first and sat at their usual table in the back of the coffee shop. Starbucks was lenient about letting students' study there, as long as they kept buying food and drinks and didn't take tables away from other customers. There were days when Amy drank so much coffee, she was sure she was never going to be able to sleep again.

When Brooke and Joe came in, they hurried back to where Amy was before they even gave their coffee order. Thankfully, Amy knew what they drank, so she had their drinks already on the table.

"Okay, what is so important we had to be here at the bright and early hour of seven?" Joe asked.

"You guys are never, never, *ever* going to believe what happened to me yesterday. I am so mad right now; I think my hair is going to catch on fire.”

“Holy shit, what’s happening? Why are you so mad?” Brooke asked.

“What’s one of the worst things that could happen to us right now? I mean, that could happen to us regarding school right now.”

Brooke answered. “Uh, you could have to sit by creepy Donald in all your classes. That would be just about the worst.”

“Well, yes, that would totally blow, but this is even worse. Guess what happened to me yesterday afternoon? I got called into the dean’s office after class.”

“*What*? What for?” Brook’s look of surprise would have been comical if the situation had not been so serious.

“Well, supposedly someone anonymously sent a letter telling her I violated the fucking honor code by cheating on my property law final last semester.”

Brooke’s eyebrows went up. “No way! Oh my God. Who would do that?”

“That’s what I’d like to know. I mean, this is so incredibly bizarre. Why would someone do that? Is there someone in our class that hates me so much they want me kicked out?”

“What did the dean say exactly?” Joe asked.

Amy told them how the dean had been very nice about the whole situation and told Amy she shouldn’t worry too much about it, that the way to go about reporting an honor code violation was to not do it anonymously. Amy relayed that the dean had said that if more information came to light, then Amy would have every chance to defend herself.

“But I have just been racking my brain trying to figure out

who in the hell would do this. Have you guys heard anything? I mean, have you heard anything about someone hating me and you guys just don't want to tell me?"

"Get out," Brooke said flatly. "Everybody likes you. I don't get it either. It's such a sleazy thing to do to someone. You know, it probably was creepy Donald! Didn't he ask you out last semester? And you turned him down, which like, duh. I totally think he would do something like this." She shuddered. "He's just gross."

"Well, I agree he is super gross, but somehow, I don't see him being smart enough to think about doing something like this. It just seems so . . . malevolent and calculating. Someone had to put some thought into this." Amy seemed lost in thought for a minute. "Joe, remember that night I was running through the parking lot because I thought someone had been watching me and I got freaked out? I have felt like that quite a few times, but since nothing happened, I told myself I was being stupid. And I really haven't seen that red truck lately lurking in the parking lot like it was that night. But maybe I blew it off too soon. Maybe someone has been watching me and was just waiting for a chance to ruin my life. And they are using this honor code debacle to do it."

Joe shook his head. "Wow. This is so bizarre. Okay, we need a plan here. Brooke and I will keep our ears to the ground to see if we can find anything out about who would have done this. I doubt the person is going around bragging about it, but you never know. Amy, I think you need to listen to your inner voice, because it is probably trying to tell you something. Just be careful."

"Yeah, Joe and I don't want to have to break in another study partner," Brooke added.

Amy laughed. "You guys are all heart, you know that? Okay, I like this plan. And I promise, no more studying until late at night in the library. And I'll start using the eyes in the back of my head and listening to my gut. And I'll stay far, far away from gross Donald. And maybe I'll start carrying after all."

CHAPTER TWENTY-FIVE

AMY WAS FEELING PRETTY GOOD about the whole honor code fuckup, as she liked to call it in her mind. Joe and Brooke reported that they hadn't heard a word, even after they'd tried to randomly bring up the subject of the honor code with other students. Dean Alexander had not called Amy back into her office, and that was a *very* good thing.

Amy was paying more attention to her surroundings than she normally did and was no longer getting that uneasy feeling as if someone was watching her. All in all, she was prepared to write it off as some stupid prank, though how anyone could think that'd been funny was beyond her. Unfortunately, the stupid prank theory got blown out of the water when she went out to her car late one afternoon, about two weeks after she had been called into the dean's office.

As she was leaving school, she heard Joe calling her name. She turned and saw Joe jogging up to her. "Amy, please tell me you're leaving for the day and you're dying to take me to my car I left at Starbucks this morning."

"First of all, why would I be dying to take you anywhere, and second, why did you leave your car at Starbucks?"

"I really needed to get some exercise in this morning, so I ran from Starbucks. But now, I'm running late—get it, running late?—for my dentist appointment so I need you to take me back to my car. Plus, I know how much you love driving me places."

"Yeah, right. Most of the time, all you do is complain about how small my car is. Okay, but I gotta warn you, I parked in the back parking lot today, so I don't want to hear any bitching about how far away it is."

Since she hadn't had class until ten that morning, most of the spaces in the underground parking lot where she usually parked had been taken by the time she got to campus. When she couldn't find a spot on the street, she'd parked in one of the back lots, which were about a half a mile from school. Normally, Amy liked parking back there. It was an easy walk, and it gave her an opportunity to go over the day in her mind, plus it allowed her to be out in the fresh air and stretch her legs.

When they got to the parking lot, Joe suddenly stopped. "What the hell is wrong with your car?"

Amy's car looked like it was tilted over to one side. "Well, that's certainly weird. Do you think I have a flat?"

As they walked up to the car, they noticed the entire driver's side was about a foot lower than the other side. "What the hell?"

Both tires on the driver's side had numerous holes, as if someone had taken a knife and repeatedly stabbed them. It was easy to imagine that was what had happened because there was a knife with an eight-inch blade still lying by the front tire. There was an ugly scrape extending from the front of the car back to the fender. It was such a vicious scene; Amy swore later she could still feel the evil in the air.

"Joe. Oh my God, Joe. Look what someone did to my car!"

Joe looked around to make sure there was no one else in the

parking lot. "Call 911. Right now. Don't touch anything. Then call your dad and have him come out here if he can. There's no one else here in the parking lot, so hopefully whoever did this is gone. Wait, what's that on the windshield?"

There was a piece of paper that looked like it had been torn out of a notebook stuck under one of the windshield wipers. The other wiper had been ripped back and was hanging over the side. Amy reached out to take the piece of paper.

"Wait, Amy. Let me take a picture of it before you touch it. That way we can show the police how it was shoved under the wiper. Call 911 now."

"I'm getting seriously freaked out here. What the fuck is going on? I feel like I've been saying that for the last two weeks! Who hates me so much?"

"Don't know but you have really pissed someone off. Okay, I took some pictures. What does it say?"

Amy looked at the paper for a minute then handed it to Joe. She literally felt sick to her stomach, and she was trembling all over. She couldn't believe what was written on the paper:

YOU ARE A BITCH AND A CHEATER. YOU NEED
TO QUIT SCHOOL AND GO KILL YOURSELF.
YOU DO NOT DESERVE TO LIVE.

I AM WATCHING YOU.

AND I AM WATCHING YOUR SISTERS.

I AM GOING TO FUCK UP YOUR WHOLE FAMILY.

"Oh shit. This is really bad." Joe put his arm around Amy. "Hang on. The police are coming. We'll figure this out. It's going to be okay. Trust me. I'm right here." Joe continued to murmur reassurances to Amy, but all the while, he was scanning the parking lot to make sure they were alone. All he could think about was what might have happened had he not been with Amy. If she had been alone . . . he didn't even want to finish the thought.

The police and Amy's dad both arrived about the same time. Amy was glad to see the police officer was Danny Wright, Rosie's old boyfriend. Danny's partner began taking pictures of her car while Danny questioned Amy and Joe.

The first thing Danny asked Amy was if she was okay. Once he was sure she wasn't hurt, he asked if they had any idea who would do this. Amy showed him the note and filled him in on the whole honor code debacle, because she was pretty sure one thing had to do with the other, especially since the note had called her a cheater. Danny said they would file a report and told Amy and Joe to be sure and call him if anything else happened—and to be very careful.

CHAPTER TWENTY-SIX

LILLY WAS THE NEXT RECIPIENT of something dark and twisted. She got to her office earlier than normal because she needed to file reports in the hospital's quality database regarding a few incident reports. An incident report was filled out any time something out of the ordinary occurred. Usually, they were about patients' falls or perhaps a medication error or a physician's order that was not done properly.

Lilly was surprised how much she enjoyed the routine, the day-to-day attention to details needed to keep the floor running in a smooth manner. After six months on the job, she finally admitted to herself she was a nerd who really liked reading flow charts and tracking data. Who knew?

After an hour of data entry, Lilly left her office. She liked to go out on the floor numerous times a day to be a visible presence and to get a sense of how the day was going for the nurses. Lilly had once worked under a head nurse no one ever saw, and Lilly remembered what a dysfunctional floor it was. And not a great place to work, quite honestly. Lilly was determined to be a hands-on head nurse, and so far, it seemed to be working. She found out it was a hell of a lot easier to deal with an issue *before* it became a huge problem.

She spent about an hour on the floor, talking with the nurses and the few doctors who were making rounds, and visited all the patients' rooms. Some were still asleep, but the ones who were awake seemed to be doing fine, considering that they were in the hospital, after all.

Lilly especially enjoyed visiting Tina Moran, a patient who was recovering from open-heart surgery. Tina was an old Army nurse, and she kept all the nurses in stitches telling stories about how hard nursing was "in the old days" and how easy it was to be a nurse today in the age of computers. "Imagine," she would say. "You actually had to figure out the dosage of the medication in your head instead of just plugging numbers into a machine that does it for you."

When Lilly would ask how many medication errors were made back in the "old days," Tina would laugh out loud and tell Lilly she had a great point. Tina was being discharged tomorrow and Lilly was really going to miss her.

Lilly had about thirty minutes before she needed to be in the monthly meeting with the other head nurses and administrators, so she decided to check her computer. After scrolling through endless emails (it seemed like every time she would unsubscribe from one email list, twenty more would take its place), she paused. An email had just popped up, and while she did not recognize the sender, it was the subject line that got her attention. It read, in all caps, "LILLY, I WANT TO TALK TO YOU."

What the hell? Do people think we're stupid? Lilly thought to herself. She knew better than to click open the email, so she deleted it and even cleared out her trash folder, just to be on the safe side. She didn't give it another thought until three days later.

Lilly's mail usually landed on her desk around one in the afternoon. She typically didn't give it top priority because if there was something important she needed to know about, then it came via email or text, not through snail mail. But she would occasionally get a flyer for an interesting convention or notifications that it was time to get her continuing educational units, so she went through her mail right before she left the office. Along with the advertisements for purchasing state-of-the-art nursing equipment (Lilly would always laugh as she tossed those and think, *If only I had the power to spend money for all the updated equipment we need, then life here on the floor would be good*) was junk mail offering her great deals on everything from vitamins to remedies for constipation to the always amusing ads boasting about penis enlargement techniques.

Under the ads, there was a plain white stamped envelope with just her name, the hospital address, but no return address. *Strange.* She slid the letter opener under the flap. Inside was a single piece of paper with five typed sentences, all caps, and in bold print:

SO YOU THOUGHT JUST IGNORING MY EMAIL WOULD MAKE ME GO AWAY? NEVER GOING TO HAPPEN UNTIL YOU AND YOUR BITCH SISTERS ARE WIPED OFF THE FACE OF THIS EARTH. I AM WATCHING YOU. I AM GOING TO FUCK UP YOUR WHOLE FAMILY.

"Holy crap." Lilly threw the paper down on her desk as if it had burned her fingers and just looked at it for a minute, feeling like it was going to come off her desk and strike her in the face. She was sick to her stomach. Lilly knew about Amy's car and the letter she had received, so she wasn't completely surprised by this. But it still gave her the creepiest feeling knowing someone was out there with the desire to hurt her and her sisters. She hated that this person knew where she worked and where Amy went to school.

The sentences in both Amy's and her note were alike: "I am watching you. I am going to fuck up your entire family." These were such ominous words that Lilly felt cold all over.

After she locked her office door, she called Keith, mainly just to hear his voice and to have him reassure her the kids were fine. He told her to pick up the letter and envelope with tweezers and put them in an oversized envelope, but to stay in her office. He would come to her office and follow her home. He also said he was calling Danny Wright and the family, and everyone would meet at their house tonight. "We need to get to the bottom of this now."

CHAPTER TWENTY-SEVEN

"THIS MUST HAVE ALL STARTED WHEN Daisy received the call from Skylar Smith last spring."

The entire family had met at Keith and Lilly's house that evening, and this was how Danny started the informal meeting.

"Skylar's phone call insinuated Daisy had done something wrong and was nefariously involved in the accident that killed her husband. The investigation into the wreck showed that the front tire blew while you all were going around a curve, causing the car to hit the tree. Obviously, there was no criminal act involved. Approximately three weeks later, Dr. Buchanan, Lilly, and Rosie find Skylar's body in the woods behind his office, and to this day, that crime is unsolved. We assume she was killed in her apartment and then placed in the woods, but it is supposition because we have no direct evidence. We don't know how she was transferred to the woods, whether it was by car, van—hell, or even by a helicopter. Her apartment certainly didn't show any signs of a struggle.

"Skylar's family had no clue if she was seeing someone, but a couple of her sisters did report she'd seemed unusually nervous and scared the last three weeks of her life. Unfortunately, Skylar never divulged the reason to any of them. Nothing out of the ordinary happened for almost a year until a couple of weeks ago when Amy was first accused, anonymously, of an honor code violation. Then two weeks later, her car was vandalized in the school parking lot and she received a very threatening letter on her windshield.

"Now, add to all this the threatening letter Lilly received today. It was mailed to her office in the hospital. Lilly told me she also had an email four days ago where the subject line was, 'Lilly, I want to talk to you.' Lilly thought it was spam and deleted it. Our forensics people are dusting both letters for fingerprints to see if we get any matches and if anything matches the fingerprints found in Skylar's apartment. Plus, I've been thinking about the attempted break-in at your house about a month ago, Jack, and I think it's connected to what happened to Amy and Lilly. At the time, we thought it was just someone casing your neighborhood and trying doors to see if anything was unlocked, but now, I'm not so sure. I think it's the same person."

Jack's Ring alarm had alerted him to a possible intruder at three in the morning, but the lights and alarm had scared the person away. Neither Jack nor Danny had been able to tell very much from the Ring photos. The person looked to be about six feet tall, with a hoodie pulled up around the face and sunglasses on, even though it was the middle of the night. The person had done a good job of not facing the camera, so it was impossible to get any type of identification from the footage. There had been no unfamiliar cars along the street, so Danny had deduced that the person had parked around the corner from Jack's so the car could not be identified.

"That's all I can tell you at the present time, but I thought it would be a good idea to get everyone together to make sure we're all on the same page and to ask if there has been anything else out of the ordinary occurring. Any other weird or disturbing events that might now take on some significance? Something that seemed inconsequential at the time?"

Lilly and Daisy both looked at each other and nodded.

"Okay, this has happened about three times in the last couple of weeks," Lilly began. "Daisy and I usually walk out to our cars together at the end of the day. The parking lot is about half full at that time, and after a while you start to recognize most of the cars in the lot. Daisy and I both noticed this red truck always parked at the end of the lot, somewhat close to where we park. No lights are ever on, but the truck is running. You can kind of hear it, a low rumbling sound. Anyway, we can never see who is in the driver's seat. The visor is always pulled down, but we both think it is a large male. Normally, we wouldn't think twice about it, but with everything else going on . . ."

"Oh my God! Is the truck a rather dirty red color? Not bright red?" Amy asked.

"Yes. Why? Have you seen it?"

"Well, this happened a couple of times last fall. There was one night when I stayed too late at the law library, and when I went out to the parking lot, there was a red truck. It was running but no lights were on. And I could hear it too. That low rumbling. It was like it was waiting . . . and watching me. I realized I had seen it a couple of other times, but like you, I really didn't think too much about it. Until now. Danny, do you think this might be connected to whatever the hell is going on?"

"It very well could be, but we can't say for sure."

Everyone started talking at once. Rosie looked over at Ren and saw he was texting something on his phone. He looked up at Danny and said, "When you said something seemingly inconsequential might really be important, it made me recall an incident that happened the morning we found Skylar's body. I really haven't thought of it since, but maybe it will mean something. That morning, my assistant was coming to work, and she witnessed a car driving fast away from the woods. She noticed it because it hit a small dog that was on the side of the road. Claire, my assistant, said the car never even slowed down. I didn't even think maybe that was the car used to bring Skylar's body to the woods. She said it was a black car. Had no idea of the type, but she told me she memorized the license plate number. I just sent her a text to see if there's any way she happened to write it down. I'll let you know what she says."

"That would be great," Danny said. "It'd be the first break we've had in the case. This is what I'm talking about. Many times, it's the simplest thing that solves a case for us. Once you get the beginning of a thread, you can pull it until the whole sweater unravels. You just need that first piece of thread. And before I go, I have another piece of advice. Be very careful out there. We don't know why someone is doing this, or who might be doing it. Please do not take any chances. And call me immediately if you remember something."

After Danny left, the family sat around the dinner table and tried to make sense of what was happening. Amy and Jack both described in more detail what had happened to Amy's car, and Jack especially talked about how violent it had felt.

"I will be very honest with you. It made me sick to my stomach, and it made me angry," he said. "But it also made me realize we are dealing with someone who is very angry at our family for some reason. I don't know why, but I do know we all need to be on high alert here. No going somewhere at night by yourself—and yes, I am mainly looking at you, my youngest daughter who likes to study in the law library until late at night—but really, I am looking at everyone. And don't just be vigilant at night. Be always vigilant until the police catch this sicko. And remember, we also don't know if this is a male or female, one person or two, etcetera."

There was further discussion about who or what could have caused this, but no one could come up with any rationale.

Ren did make one further observation. "Daisy, you got the note from Skylar almost a year ago, in the spring. Amy noticed the red truck early last fall but has not seen it again. We have Amy's car getting trashed and the threatening letters to both Amy and Lilly just this last month. And now the mysterious red truck is back, although there may be many other times this truck has been around, but no one was paying attention. So why now? Why are things escalating? What's caused him—and you're right, Jack, it could be her—to resurface and start doing this crap? And believe me, it's not lost on me that Rosie's the only one who hasn't been a target yet. Damn, Jack. I agree wholeheartedly with you. I am pissed!"

Later that evening, Ren and Rosie were discussing the night's events in their living room over a glass of wine for Ren and a beer for Rosie. Big Shirley, Walter, and Marilyn were sleeping in their favorite spots on the floor, although Marilyn would occasionally lift her head and give them a look as if to say, "What the hell are you two still doing out here? My Tempur-Pedic mattress is in the bedroom, and that's where I'd like to be! Chop chop."

Ren had moved into Rosie's house about two months ago. He had been renting his house, and since they were spending most, if not all their time together, it just made sense for Ren to move in. It was a good thing Rosie had a large yard. Walter and

Marilyn were a complete package with Ren, and Rosie wouldn't have had it any other way. And once Big Shirley got a good look at their Tempur-Pedic dog beds, she had to have one. Navigating around the bedroom floor now took some figuring out, but somehow it had all worked.

"Wow." Ren said. "I knew Amy's car was pretty messed up, but I had no idea it was that bad. I'm so glad Joe was with her. She must have been freaked out of her mind!"

"Dad's livid with what's going on. And I know he's especially worried about Amy. I guess because she doesn't have a big strong man around to protect her."

"You got that right, woman. Not only do you have a big strong he-man protecting your ass, you also have about three hundred pounds of dogs ready to be fierce defenders at a moment's notice. I mean, these are some guard dogs."

Since all three of the dogs were presently sacked out on the floor, Rosie just looked at them and laughed. "I think the only one I can depend on is Marilyn. BS and Walter wouldn't have the first idea what to do."

"You would be surprised, but let's hope it never comes to that. And your dad is right. We really need to be on our toes. This person sounds sick and twisted. Maybe you should start coming to the office with me during the day. You can work on your book in one of the back offices; I know it would ease my mind."

"Honey, I'll be fine here. You just said we have three hundred pounds of ferocious flesh-eating dogs. And remember, I have my license to carry. I'll keep my gun with me and all the doors locked. I wouldn't get anything done at your office. I'd be playing with all the dogs and cats and hanging out with Julie and Claire."

"I don't know about the flesh-eating dogs, but I do like the idea of you keeping your gun with you. Especially since I know you're a regular Annie Oakley."

They had gone to the gun range a couple of weeks ago, and Ren had been very impressed with how accurate a shooter Rosie was. He'd also been surprised by how turned on he got watching her shoot her gun. Her toned arms, slim hips, and total concentration on the target were quite a sight. Of course, his thought about whispering in her ear how hot she was making him disappeared when she turned to him and told him it was his turn to shoot. Rosie was determined to turn him into a Wyatt Earp to go with her Annie Oakley, but Ren was pretty sure she was wasting her time.

He didn't mind learning about guns and being somewhat proficient with them, but that was as far as he wanted to go. He had no problem letting Rosie be the gunslinger in their little family.

CHAPTER TWENTY-EIGHT

WHEN REN WENT TO THE OFFICE the next morning, he was surprised to see Claire already there, since she usually didn't get to work until nine. "Hey, Claire. Did you set your alarm clock for the wrong time?" Ren teased. "It's only eight, you know."

"I know! But Ren, I found the license number!" Claire was practically jumping up and down with excitement. "I remembered putting it in my desk drawer, but I was afraid I'd thrown it out. I couldn't wait to come to work today to see if it was still there, and it was! It was in the very back, but I found it, thankfully. Maybe this will crack the case wide open, and whoever is terrorizing Lilly and Amy will be caught and put in jail." She handed Ren a small piece of paper with some numbers scribbled on it.

"I certainly hope so. Whoever it is deserves to be put away. They have serious issues, if you ask me. I'll give Officer Wright a call and give him the license. And I promise never to make fun of your rather—um, how do I put this? Your rather unorganized desk? Especially since you may have saved the day!"

Ren took the paper into his office and placed a call to Officer Wright. Danny took down the number and told Ren he'd get back with them when the plate was run. Ren next called Rosie to tell her that Claire had found the license plate number and hopefully they would soon have some answers as to who in the hell was terrorizing the Hurley girls. He also wanted to make sure she was okay. Rosie laughed and said yes, nothing had happened in the thirty minutes he'd been gone, but he was very sweet to be worried about her. And that the dogs were doing their very best to try and stay awake to protect her, but they were fighting a losing battle.

Ren had a hectic office day scheduled, with Dwayne Cooper and his bulldog, Leonard, as his first patient. Ren always had to fight a battle with himself when he saw Dwayne. On one hand, he wanted to chew him out and ask why he even bothered having a dog, but on the other hand, he wanted to keep his office open, and cussing out his patients was not the way to do that. Keeping his office open won every time. Vet school 101. So, Ren pasted a fake smile on his face and went in to see what complaint Dwayne had this time.

Finally, around two o'clock, Danny called. He said they'd gotten a hit on the plate, but there were a few things about the driver's license linked to the car that didn't add up. He wondered if Ren could gather everyone over to their house that evening, where Danny would tell everyone all together what he had found.

"We're hosting the family for dinner at our house anyway tonight, so just come over around six and join us for some salad and pasta."

Danny said he would see him there.

That evening, after everyone had filled up on Rosie's famous lasagna (which was frozen Stouffer's, but she preferred to think no one could tell), Danny told them what he had found out.

"When we ran the license number Claire copied down, it turned out to be a rental car, but the driver's license used to rent the car was a fake. The name on the license was Lance Smith from

Asheville, North Carolina. Sad to say, it's extremely easy to obtain a fake driver's license. They won't pass muster when the police run it, but they're certainly good enough to rent a car. We contacted the car rental agency this guy rented from, and they went back into their records, but unfortunately there was nothing that stood out to them about the actual license.

"However." Danny paused. "Remember how I said the littlest thing can unravel a case? So Ren remembered Claire saw the car, Claire remembered where she put the license number she copied down, and now we got lucky again. I talked to the actual agent who rented the car to this guy, and let me tell you something, I want to hire this lady. She actually remembered him—said there was something about him that gave her the major creeps, so much so that when her shift ended, she made sure the manager walked her out to her car. I asked about any specifics that caused her to be so unnerved about this guy, and she said there wasn't just one thing, but his whole persona. She said when she asked him if he was in town for business or pleasure, which was what she asked everyone just to make small talk, he jumped down her throat and demanded to know why she wanted to know what he was doing.

"She also said he would step away from the counter and carry on a conversation. She originally thought he had earbuds in, but the more she thought about it, the more she realized he was carrying on a conversation with just himself. And a few times he seemed agitated about something. But the good news is that the rental agency instituted a program a few months ago where they keep a copy of each driver's license on file for a year in case a customer sells or abandons the car. Anyway, I have a couple of printouts of the guy, so hopefully someone will recognize him."

Danny put the pictures on the table and stood back. Everyone crowded around to get a look. Lilly and Daisy were the first to see the photos, and both shook their heads and said they had never seen the guy before. Same with Keith, Jon, and Jack. When Amy and Rosie bent over the table to look at the picture, Amy heard Rosie take a quick intake of breath.

"Do you know him?" Amy asked.

"What?"

"Who is he?"

"What's his name?"

"How do you know him?"

Everyone was speaking at once, but Rosie just kept staring at the picture, slowly shaking her head back and forth. "I'm not entirely sure," Rosie said slowly. "But he looks like someone. Someone I knew in New York. But it doesn't make any sense. No, I think I'm just seeing things. I don't know this person."

"Rosie, are you sure? Maybe it *is* someone you knew in New York."

"No, I'm sure. I thought at first it might have been someone I knew. But no, it can't be. I'm sure of it." Rosie turned to Danny. "Sorry this didn't work out. I wish I could have been more help."

As everyone was getting ready to leave, Danny reiterated his warning to be very careful and not to take any chances. He said they would continue to work the case and hopefully another clue would drop that would allow them to find the jerk who was doing this.

CHAPTER TWENTY-NINE

AFTER THE DISHES WERE CLEANED UP, Rosie and Ren took the dogs for a quick walk around the neighborhood.

Big Shirley hadn't decided how she felt about this new and completely unnecessary addition to her nighttime routine. Before Ren and *those other annoying dogs* (which was how BS thought about Walter and Marilyn), her nighttime ritual consisted of her going out into the backyard around nine and then enjoying a bedtime biscuit before making her way to her bed. Not any more though! Ren had said Walter and Marilyn were a wee bit more high-strung and needed the extra exercise. *What a joke,* thought Shirley. Great Danes were not high energy dogs, but compared to a Newfoundland . . .

"Are you okay, Rosie? You seem lost in thought. Anything to do with the picture Danny showed us tonight?"

Rosie looked at Ren for a long moment, then seemed to come to a decision. "I'm not totally sure about the picture, but it does factor into what I need to tell you. I should have told you a while ago, but it's not something I like to think about. Let's get the dogs home, and I'll fill you in on my wonderful time in New York." Rosie snorted. "Such a swell time."

"You know, babe, if you don't feel like talking about it, I certainly understand. I don't want to pressure you into anything, but I'm here if you need a sounding board."

Rosie grabbed Ren's hand and gave it a squeeze. "I still feel ter-rible about that Skylar Smith girl we found, but I thank my lucky stars every night Lilly and I decided to go on a run that day. I think you're special; you know that don't you?"

"Of course I do!" Ren joked. "We're meant to be. Even our names go together. Ren and Rosie. Hmmm. Makes me think of ice cream every time. Ben and Jerry's. Let's get these very large and tired animals' home, and I will bring up wine and ice cream. Every story is better when told with them."

Rosie was curled up in bed with ice cream when Ren brought wine from the kitchen. The lights were turned down, and the dogs were already snoring. He poured Rosie a glass of wine and said, "You do know there isn't anything you can tell me that will make me feel different about you? I just want you to know that."

Rosie took a deep breath. "So, you know I went to New York to intern at the *Times Express News* after college. And I had every intention of staying in New York and working as a journalist at ei-ther a paper or magazine, or any job having to do with words, real-ly. I was just so excited. I really felt like I was this sophisticated ca-reer woman making my way in the Big Apple." Rosie looked down at her empty ice cream bowl and sadly shook her head. "Guess it didn't turn out that way, huh?"

Ren took her bowl out her hands and placed his hands on either side of her face. It killed him to see the shine of tears in her eyes. "You are a success whether you're in New York, Texas, or on the moon. The physical place is not important. What matters is in here." He placed his hand on her heart. "And here." He smoothed her hair back and tenderly placed a kiss on her forehead. "I've said it before, and I'll say it again. You have so much potential, and I have no doubt you will succeed at whatever you do. I love you and I'll support you for all the days of your life."

"I love you too. Very much." She chuckled. "Don't think I haven't thought there's some divine intervention going on with us. If I had stayed in New York, I would probably never have met you, or if you kept your practice up in Kansas we never would have met, or if you had decided against taking a walk behind your office that day. There are so many what-ifs, I'm convinced we were meant to be. So, top me off and sit back and be prepared to listen to the story of my life—or at least the story of my life in New York."

CHAPTER THIRTY

GWYNETH STILES WAS STANDING at the front of the
conference room expounding on the rollout of the new format
for the newspaper to the interns. And expounding . . . and expounding . . . and expounding. *My God, she can turn a ten-minute
idea into an hour discussion,* Rosie thought to herself.

Even though she had been at the newspaper in New York City
for only a month, Rosie thought she already had Gwyneth's number. The woman loved to hear herself talk, especially if the subject
revolved around herself or the newspaper. Rosie just hated to go to
her office with a question because she knew she would be in there
for the better part of an hour. It was unfortunate Gwyneth was
such a pain in the ass because she really did know the newspaper
business.

Gwyneth had the coloring of a true redhead, with pale skin
and scattered freckles. She wore small frameless glasses, and when
she got excited (either about herself or the newspaper), her voice
would go up a couple of octaves. Rosie was waiting for the day
when she would start to sing about the newspaper. She had a nose
that started out normal from between her eyes, but then took a
sharp left and did an upturned number, as if she had been trying
to wiggle her nose with her finger but it got frozen to the left
instead. When Gwyneth was speaking in front of people, Rosie
would watch Gwyneth's hand start to creep up, like she wanted

to cover the middle part of her face. She always managed to halt her hand at about breast level and Rosie would find herself leaning forward in anticipation, willing the hand to go all the way to the nose. So far, it hadn't happened.

Rosie glanced over to Steve Gaynor, one of the other interns she had met on her first day on the job. He was looking straight at her, and when she made eye contact with him, he crossed his eyes and made a face. Rosie stifled a laugh and turned back to Gwyneth.

Unfortunately, Gwyneth was looking right at her. "Rose, is there a problem? Did you not understand the roll out? I can always go back over it for you."

"Oh gosh, no, that's okay, Gwyneth. I totally got it the first time."

"Well then, if there are no further questions, I think we're done here. Rose, could you and Steve come to my office in about ten minutes? I have something I would like to discuss with you."

The other four interns looked over at Rosie and Steve curiously, then filed out.

"What do you think she wants with us?" Rosie asked Steve.

"I have no idea."

"She probably wants to yell at you for making faces and at me for laughing at you. You know she expects everyone to worship this paper like she does."

"Yeah, I've picked that up about her. But come on, how excited are we supposed to be? We're just changing the format, not discovering a cure for the common cold. Come on, I'll buy you a coffee before we go in there. We're going to need something to keep us awake!"

Ten minutes later, Rosie and Steve were sitting in Gwyneth's office watching her finish an email. That was another habit of Gwyneth's that drove Rosie crazy. She would make you come to her office, but then you sat there like a bump on a log waiting for her to finish whatever it was she was doing. Like she was so busy, every minute was not to be wasted. It had to be a power thing.

"Okay, that's done," Gwyneth said as she hit the send button. She turned in her chair and faced Rosie and Steve, looking at both with an appraising stare. "Well, have you two enjoyed your time at the paper so far? You've been here for about a month, correct? Isn't it everything you could have hoped for?"

Rosie dared not look at Steve, because she knew she would start smiling, and she was sure smiling was not exactly the response Gwyneth was looking for. "It's been great, Gwyneth," Rosie managed to say. "I've learned so much already!"

"I agree," said Steve. "I think there's going to be a lot of opportunity to experience different aspects of the newspaper business, and—"

"Exactly." Gwyneth interrupted Steve before he could finish his thought. "This is what I love about this place. It's so challenging, and it has so much to offer everyone!" Gwyneth stopped for a moment and clasped her hands to her chest. The rapturous expression on her face told Rosie and Steve that she thought she was solely responsible for the entire success of the newspaper, even though it had been in existence for almost eighty years.

"You know, you two are extremely fortunate to have been picked as interns. There are just so many applicants, and every year I must be cruel and disappoint all those wannabe interns because they just don't make the grade." Gwyneth didn't look too disappointed. In fact, she looked delighted she was able to hold so much power over people, and Rosie could just bet Gwyneth was in seventh heaven during the two weeks every year she held interviews for the intern positions. Rosie was sure the thought of monopolizing someone's time carrying on about the paper was enough to make Gwyneth give a little happy wiggle.

During Rosie's interview with Gwyneth, Rosie had thought Gwyneth was just an enthusiastic and happy employee. Little did she know Gwyneth believed herself to be the heart and soul of the paper.

"Um, Gwyneth? Is there a reason you wanted to see us?" Steve asked. "Are we doing anything wrong?"

"Oh no! You two are the best of the bunch. I want to offer you both an experience I think you'll be crazy about. What would you say to spending the next couple of months on the crime unit desk? Of course, you would work with the seasoned reporters at the beginning but eventually you would have your own stories to follow. I'm envisioning you two starting out together as a team, but when you get comfortable with the work, it can be split up. Well, is this not the best thing?" Gwyneth looked at both like she expected them to jump up and do a jig around her office, and she seemed a bit disappointed when they stayed in their chairs.

"Is there a problem?" Gwyneth asked. "This is a plum assignment, and I can always give it to someone else."

"No, no, there's no problem," Rosie said. "I don't know about Steve, but I am so surprised at the offer I'm just trying to digest it."

"Yeah, me too. I'm blown away. I was hoping to eventually be put on the crime unit desk, but I didn't think it would be so soon."

"Normally, we would only allow one intern to do crimes, and

that would be only after the intern had been at the paper for over six months. But one of our reporters is out on maternity leave." Gwyneth's face showed a mild disbelief that anyone would pick a baby over the paper. "And another reporter, well, he's gone to work with a different paper." Her face revealed exactly what she thought about that reporter. "Excellent. It will take me about a week to get everything set up, so let's plan on you both starting this assignment a week from Monday. Does that work?"

Rosie opened her mouth and started to ask specifics about the assignment but then thought better of it. She knew she could get all the information she needed from the reporters who worked crimes, and she assumed they would give it to her straight and not through rose-colored *Times Express News* glasses.

"Are you thinking what I'm thinking?" Steve asked Rosie as they left the office later that day.

"What, that Gwyneth Stiles has a screw loose, and if we don't act like this new assignment is all we've been pining for since the day we were born, she'll take it away and make us work the obituary desk? Is that what you're thinking?"

"Damn girl, you are a mind reader. That's *exactly* what I've been thinking. Well, that and wondering if you'd want to go to dinner with me."

Rosie looked at him with surprise. "Dinner? Uh, well, I don't know. I mean, what about Angela?"

"Angela? What does she have to do with anything?"

"Well, she was telling everyone in the break room you and her were going out tonight."

Angela Steffens was another intern at the newspaper, and she'd made it clear from the beginning she had her sights set on Steve.

Angela was from Alabama, and her southern twang became more pronounced whenever there was a man around—especially if that man was Steve. She would practically be swimming in the "y'all"s and "over yonder"s.

A frustrated expression crossed Steve's face. "I did not ask her out tonight. She said something to me about getting together later for a drink, but I told her I was busy."

Rosie was surprised at the warm feeling inside her when she heard Steve's words. "Well then, I would love to go out to dinner with you! We should probably do it before Gwyneth decides we can't fraternize outside of work because we are working on the same desk! Why don't I meet you at Gino's in a couple of hours?"

When Rosie walked into Gino's around seven that night, she was not surprised to see Steve sitting in a booth, but she was surprised to see he was not alone. Rosie stood for a moment in the crowded entryway, trying to gauge Steve's body language. For some reason it gave her pause. The way he was talking to Angela seemed just a bit off.

Steve looked over at the door and when he saw Rosie standing there, he gave her a big, relieved smile. *Why are you always trying to psychoanalyze things?* Angela had probably gotten wind of where they were going to dinner (and since Gino's was about the only place everyone from the paper met, it didn't take a genius to figure it out) and decided to crash the party. Typical.

Rosie walked over to the table. "Hi, Steve. And Angela, how are you?"

"Well, I'm meeting my girls here for a drink and saw poor ole Steve sitting over here all by his lonesome. I thought I would come cheer him up. I was trying to get out of him what y'all talked about with Gwyneth today, but he's not budging on any secrets, are you, Steve?"

"Nope. There are some super hush-hush covert pieces of information about the newspaper Gwyneth only tells a few select individuals, and surprisingly, Rosie and I are those select individuals. If we told you, we would, of course, have to kill you."

"Well, I guess I'll mosey on along." Rosie could have sworn Angela looked at Steve as if she expected him to ask her to stay, and when he didn't, she gave a little shrug and slithered out of the booth. How she was able to stick her boobs and butt out at the same time she was sliding across the booths seat was impressive, Rosie thought.

After Steve was sure Angela was across the room, he turned to Rosie. "Thank you. Thank you. Thank you for coming in when you did! I swear she was about to do some Southern ritual to put me under her spell! She scares me!"

Rosie just laughed. "Why do I not believe that? A big strong man like yourself surely can resist her wiles and shenanigans! Okay, enough about Angela. This is supposed to be a working dinner. We need to figure out how we're going to get the most out of this new assignment and not kill Gwyneth in the process!"

The next couple of years at the *Times Express News* were everything Rosie had hoped the job would be. Instead of their being on the crime desk for only a couple of months, the assignment became permanent. They worked with Bob and Pam; two veteran reporters who had been partners for so long they could practically finish each other's sentences. In the beginning, Bob and Pam had no problem with letting Steve and Rosie venture out on their own with a few of the easier projects, as long as they were kept in the loop.

"We're okay with just about anything," Bob said when they all got together the first time.

Pam finished his thought with, "Just no surprises. We don't like surprises."

So "no surprises" became the code Steve and Rosie lived by. Every morning, the four of them would have a huddle at Bob's desk and go over the assignments. In the first couple of weeks, Gwyneth would hover around on the edges, but since Bob and Pam pretty much ignored her, Steve and Rosie followed suit. Typically, Steve and Rosie went out on an assignment together, did the interviewing needing to be done (or, truth be told, spent most of the time in the library or on the computer doing research), and then came back to the news station to begin the tedious chore of writing up the story. Rosie was always amazed at the rewrites required before a story would appear in the paper.

She'd been relieved to find Steve to be such an easy-going partner—at least, at first. They split the work according to their strengths. Steve was a whiz at finding just about anything on the computer, and Rosie could take the information and write it out in such a way that it was easy to read but managed to hit all the important ideas. And when they did manage to score an actual interview, Steve had such a charm about him that people (especially women) would tell him anything.

It was a work relationship made in heaven, and their away-from-work relationship was doing just fine too. At the end of the day, Steve and Rosie, along with any of the other interns who were free, would end up at Gino's or one of the other cheap restaurants situated near the newsroom for dinner and drinks.

Surprisingly, Rosie and Angela became very good friends. Rosie liked to think it was because Angela thought she was fun, but it was probably because Angela saw which way the wind was blowing between Steve and Rosie and, being a practical girl, turned her sights (and everything else) toward John, another unmarried journalist working in the department with them. Either way, the four of them had a lot of fun—before the bottom dropped out and everything went to shit.

CHAPTER THIRTY-ONE

THE DAY STARTED INNOCENTLY ENOUGH. If for some reason they had not spent the night together, Rosie would meet Steve at their usual spot on Greenwich Street. The corner was two blocks east of Rosie's apartment and three blocks west of Steve's, and Rosie never failed to giggle when he acted like he was so out of breath when they met. He teased her and told her she was the only girl he would go an extra mile for, even though Rosie consistently pointed out he would need about twenty blocks to make up a mile.

It was always a special way to start the day. Every morning, he kissed her neck and told her she smelled better than the bakery across the street selling cinnamon rolls, or better than the pizzeria with the spicy tomato sauce, or better than the flower store with the fragrant roses—every day, a new place she smelled better than. She was waiting for him to start repeating himself, but so far, he had a perfect record.

They spent the day doing research on one of their projects that had been on the back burner for a while, so after eight hours of staring at computer screens, they were looking forward to meeting John and Angela at Gino's.

At first, the evening was just like all the other ones they had spent together. After they got their drinks and were seated at their booth, Angela started telling a story about how she finally ended up getting some much-needed background information on the person she was going to interview by managing to connect with his high school teacher. Since Angela had a habit of going into way too much detail (something Steve and Rosie had laughed about numerous times), when Rosie shot Steve a look, she'd expected to see him smiling at this typical Angela monologue. Instead, he was glaring at Angela like she had just told his darkest secret.

Angela noticed his stare. "Sugar, you okay? You haven't said five words this whole night."

"Well, maybe I haven't said five words because you keep telling the same stupid story in your fake stupid accent and no one else can get a word in edgewise."

"Steve!" Rosie gasped. "What in the world are you talking about? Why are you saying that to Angela?"

Angela and John both looked at Steve like he was crazy. Angela said slowly, "Steve, I really don't know how to respond to that. I am not saying the *same* stupid story. In fact, it is a *different* stupid story." And she gave him a small smile that said if he apologized everything would be okay.

Angela was trying to let Steve off the hook, and Rosie appreciated her friend trying to be nice about the awkward situation. She looked at Steve, fully expecting him to at least look a tad bit ashamed about what he'd said to Angela, but instead, he just looked angrier than before. Except this time, he was also including Rosie and John in his angry glare.

"You know, I can think of about a thousand things I'd rather be doing than sitting here, listening to this bullshit. I'm out of here." Since he was sitting on the outside of the booth, he stood up and walked out the door.

Rosie, Angela, and John just looked at each other, wondering if Steve was playing a gigantic practical joke on them.

Finally, Rosie said, "What the fuck just happened? Did he just walk out? Do you guys know what's going on?"

The look John gave Angela made Rosie immediately say, "Wait a minute. Do you all know something I don't? Is Steve okay?"

"Rosie, um." John paused. "Have you noticed anything different about Steve lately?"

"What do you mean, different? Has he said or done anything to you? What are you talking about?"

"Sweetie, has Steve been under a lot of stress lately? I mean, more than normal? He seems . . . tense."

"Angela, you're being nice about this. Rosie, in the last couple of months, Steve has had a couple of incidents in the newsroom that concern us, to say the least. It's never when you're around, but he's been lashing out at us and at a couple of the other reporters over really stupid stuff. Almost accusing us of trying to undermine his work or going behind his back to talk shit about him with Bob and Pam. I finally confronted him a couple of days ago, asked him what the hell was going on with him, and he laughed it off, said he had some work issues really bugging him. He apologized and said if he was coming on too strong, then he was sorry. He seemed so sincere about everything, I just chalked it up to—I don't know— something else going on in his life we don't know about."

Rosie was flabbergasted. "Guys, I don't know what to say. He has never talked to me about anything bothering him. I mean, you know this story we're working on is bugging the shit out of him, but I don't think there's anything else going on. He certainly hasn't lashed out at me."

Their back-burner story involved searching for background information on a city council member who was being accused of fraud and having an inappropriate relationship with one of his clients. The member had been involved in New York politics for many years and was friends with many of the city's powerful elites. It had been difficult to get anyone to talk to them about the councilman, and they had found themselves blocked on all sides. Yes, it'd been frustrating, but Steve seemed to take it personally. Even though Bob and Pam, and even Gwyneth of all people, told them this was just how the political system worked and not to worry too much about it, Steve couldn't seem to let it go. He would brood about it, for lack of a better word, and then he would seem to give himself a mental shake and be back to normal, funny, loving Steve.

"I mean, no, I really can't think of anything else. You know, I've got to go after him and find out what's the matter. I'll talk to you all tomorrow."

"Let me just pay the bill and we'll go with you."

"No, I'm good. I really think I need to just go talk to him by myself. Let me know what I owe you."

"Rosie, please. We want to go with you to make sure everything's okay."

"John, this is *Steve* we are talking about. Funny, doesn't-know-a-stranger Steve? What are you not telling me? You're scaring me, John."

John shook his head. "It's just that he can get so angry so quickly. And he won't listen to reason when he's like that, and it takes him a while to calm down. I know everything is probably fine, but I would feel a ton better if we walked with you. Besides, this is New York, and you're from a small Texan town. And I'm the man, and I want to protect my women." Rosie and Angela both snorted and rolled their eyes.

Rosie looked at them both for a long moment and then shrugged. "I appreciate your help, John. Let's go."

As it turned out, they were not able to track Steve down. It was a straight shot to Steve's apartment from Gino's, but he'd obviously taken another route. Rosie tried calling his cell phone, but it went straight to voicemail. John and Angela walked Rosie to her apartment, where she gave them both a hug and thanked them. She also made them promise to tell her if he had any more outbursts at work—not that she could do anything about it.

Rosie had never been so glad to have kept her own apartment as she was that night. They had talked about moving in together, if for no other reason than to save money, but Rosie always held back. For one thing, they each only had a one-bedroom unit, so if they moved in together, they would either have to get a bigger place or be really cramped. And while they frequently spent the night together at Steve's place, there was just something to knowing her own apartment was still there.

Rosie left two more messages on Steve's cell phone, then thought, *To hell with it*, and went to bed. She figured she would deal with it in the morning.

Unfortunately, going to bed and going to sleep were two very different things. She was really having a hard time reconciling the Steve she knew with the Steve that John had talked about. He was very popular at work, and everyone seemed to like him so much.

Although now when she thought about it, the mood in the newsroom had subtlety changed. Rosie had thought it was because everyone was working hard on various stories, but maybe it was because no one wanted to make Steve mad, and no one wanted to tell her that her boyfriend was becoming an asshole. On that pleasant thought, she fell asleep.

As it turned out, Rosie didn't have to confront Steve at their usual corner. She waited for about fifteen minutes, but he never showed up. She walked on to work and when she went into the newsroom, lo and behold, there was Steve, sitting at his desk and working on his computer. Rosie was torn about how to handle this. On one hand, she wanted to walk over to him and smack him upside his head, but on the other hand, she wanted to freeze him out and make him come to her. She walked to her desk, which, unfortunately, was right across from his, and noticed a single white rose laid across her keyboard. When she looked over at Steve, he was looking straight at her with such an embarrassed look on his face, she immediately forgave him.

"I have no excuse for my behavior. It was inexcusable, and all I can say is that I'm sorry and it won't happen again. I've already apologized to John and Angela, and I promised to buy everyone drinks tonight at Gino's. That is, if you still want to go out with me."

Rosie sighed. "Of course I still want to go out with you. But Steve, you really worried me. That outburst was so unlike you and so mean." She didn't know if she should bring up what John had said, but then thought, *What the hell?* "John said you've been getting angry here at the office about stuff. What's going on? Are you okay? Do you feel okay?"

Steve got up and came over to her side of the desk. She could tell he wanted to put his arm around her, but the look she gave him stopped that. She was willing to hear him out, but not yet ready to drop the whole thing.

He finally said, "I've had some issues with family stuff. And some other stuff too. There's really nothing I can do about it, but it's been bugging me. I know I should have told you, but I just want to ignore it and hope everything goes away."

Rosie knew Steve had a brother a year younger than him who still lived in the small town of Branson, Missouri, where they had grown up.

"Well, okay, I can respect that Steve, but if this is bothering you so much that you're lashing out at your friends, then maybe ignoring it is not the right answer. I mean, you were mean and hurtful to Angela last night. I've never seen you act like that."

"I know, I know. I promise it will never happen again. If I start feeling stressed about things, I'll come talk to you. Is that a deal?"

He looked so worried about what she was going to say, she took pity on him. "Okay, but you had better keep your promise. And thank you for the rose. Oh, and you owe me ten bucks. I had to buy your drink last night."

"Tell you what. I'll give you a twenty if you promise to meet me at our usual corner tomorrow and kick the shit out of me if I ever act like that again!"

"Done!"

CHAPTER THIRTY-TWO

FOR A WHILE, things went back to normal, although it took Rosie a couple of weeks to stop tensing up every time Steve started to say something. Rosie thought of it as the "new normal." There was underlying tension between them, but whenever she brought the subject up with Steve, he blew her off or changed the subject. She made John promise to tell her if Steve went off on people, but so far all had been calm.

Steve and Rosie's assignment about the councilman finished after about four months, and even though they never did get any substantive information about the man, there was enough information that they were able to write a decent article.

Their new assignment was a fun one. It wasn't the usual assignment that came through the crimes desk, but a couple of reporters were out of the office, so Steve and Rosie had volunteered. One of the smaller museums in New York had sent out a survey to the surrounding schools asking the kids what type of exhibit they would like to see. Steve and Rosie were working with the museum by helping them go through the answers to the survey and publishing the different responses in the newspaper each week.

"Who knew little kids could be so bloodthirsty?" Rosie asked Steve.

It was a beautiful fall day in New York, and Rosie and Steve had decided to walk to the museum instead of taking a cab. They were going to listen in on a tour given by one of the docents at the museum and then write a report. All the results from the surveys were in, and the overwhelming request from the kids had been to see an exhibit about the ancient Egyptians and mummification—how the mummies came to be mummies, to be exact!

Rosie had done some research the night before on the specifics of the mummification process, and she was skeptical that kids would want to know all the details. She'd described to Steve on their walk how it took seventy days for the embalmers to prepare a body and how the embalmers stuck a hooked instrument up the nose to pull the brain out. "Do you really think little kids want to know all that?"

"Of course they do. Little kids nowadays know more about gross stuff than we ever did at that age. And the gorier the better. Besides . . ."

"What? Besides what?" Rosie asked.

"Nothing." Steve paused. "Um, do you really need me to come on this tour with you? I have some other stuff I need to get done, and I'm afraid if I don't do it now, I won't get to it."

"What do you have to do? I thought we were going to report on this together. Steve, what's going on?"

"Rosie, nothing is *going on*." The words "going on" were said in such a way that Steve clearly thought she was being crazy. "I just have something else to do, and I would rather not spend a morning doing some fluff piece about a museum."

"Are you kidding me? What brought this on? You were excited about the whole mummy exhibit last week. And it's not a fluff piece. That's not a very nice thing to say."

Steve sighed. "Look Rosie, you told me to tell you if things were starting to get weird with my family again. Well, they are. I just need some time by myself to think things through, okay? Am I asking too much here? Could you give me some space?"

Rosie blew some air out in a huff. "Fine. Go do what you have to do. Could you just give me some warning before you upend our entire schedule for the day?" Rosie could tell Steve was getting irritated with her, but she really didn't care. Things had been fine between them for the months after the Angela incident, but Steve was getting tense again. She had tried a couple of times to talk to him, but he always made a joke or changed the subject.

"I just have to get some stuff off my plate regarding my family."

"You know, maybe if you told me about what's going on with your family, then I could possibly help you."

"Well, since the only thing we do talk about is *your* family, I'm thinking it won't work to try and talk about my family. Your sisters, your dad, your dead mother—"

Her stomach dropped. It was happening again. "Are you fucking kidding me? Why do you do this? Turn the entire argument around and make it about me? This isn't about me. This is about you and your weird problems with your family—at least, I think they're weird. How would I know? You never talk to me about it!"

At this point, they had stopped in the middle of the sidewalk and were glaring at each other. People were having to navigate around them and, of course, since it was New York, someone told them to either move out of the way or get pushed out of the way.

They moved off the sidewalk and into a small doorway, neither one willing to look at the other.

Finally, Rosie said, "I have to go. The tour starts in thirty minutes, and I want to get to the museum and get oriented." She looked at Steve, thinking he would say or do something that would take the tension down a notch between them, but he just stood there, looking out onto the street and clenching his jaw.

"You might as well go and figure out your problems." Rosie hated being such a bitch about the whole affair, but she was suddenly tired of always trying to read Steve and trying not to say something that would make him mad. Sometimes, when a relationship took more time and effort to keep it going than to end it, it was time to call it quits. Rosie was starting to think she was putting a little too much effort into keeping Steve happy.

Rosie pushed past Steve and continued down the sidewalk toward the museum. She really was expecting him to call out or to start walking next to her, and when he didn't, she was surprised by how relieved she was. *Well, that should tell me something*, she'd thought.

Rosie met Angela later that afternoon for an early happy hour, even though Rosie was not too happy. "I really think I need to pull the plug on this relationship. Steve was so much fun to be with when we first started hanging out. He always seemed to know what to say to make me laugh or just feel good about myself. But now . . . there is absolutely nothing fun about it anymore. I spend our entire time together trying to gauge him. Is he mad? Is he about to go off on me because I said the wrong thing? Shit, I don't even know what the right thing to say is anymore. I keep thinking all the problems have to do with his family and we are still good, but I'm not sure anymore."

Angela reached out and patted Rosie's arm. "I know, sugar.

It's obvious to us you guys are going through a rough patch." She hesitated for a moment. "He isn't hurting you or anything, is he?"

"No, nothing like that. And I hope I would tell you if it was like that, although you never know. He's just changed so much in the last year. I swear he's like a different person. When he does deign to talk to me about stuff, he always just says it's a problem with his family. And when I press him for details, he clams up and either changes the subject or gets up and leaves. I get the impression it's his brother that's the problem, but I could be wrong."

Angela looked relieved to hear things had not gotten physical between them but still seemed hesitant to say what was on her mind to Rosie. She sat there, pulling at her lower lip (which was a habit when Angela was really thinking about things) and looking at Rosie.

Finally, Rosie said, "Either I have a booger hanging out of my nose or you're trying to tell me something I don't want to hear. I'm guessing you have some news that will not make me happy." Rosie sighed. "Spill it. I already know it must be about Steve."

"Well, I guess I'm not betraying a confidence, but I don't care if I am. I was walking by Gwyneth's office yesterday and just happened to notice Steve in there, talking to her. I heard your name, so I stopped. And I wasn't eavesdropping, really. Steve was talking so loudly, there was no snooping needed. He was saying how you've been riding on his coattails this entire time you've worked together. That you aren't pulling your weight, and half the time he has to go back and redo your work because it's sloppy and incorrect. I was surprised Gwyneth hadn't shut the door, but I got the impression she was taken off guard with the whole diatribe."

Rosie was immediately drenched in a red heat. "Why, that son of a bitch! I can't believe he would go behind my back that way, and to Gwyneth, of all people! What the fuck is wrong with him? We do these projects together, but we both have separate jobs. He never even sees my work! I'm going to kill him! If he went to Bob and Pam behind my back, I'll scratch his eyes out!"

"I know, I know. I don't blame you for being furious. Gwyneth pushed back at him, saying she had never received any negative reports about you, but I thought I had still better tell you. You need to watch your back around that guy. I just don't get it. Why has he changed so much? You really don't know?"

"I have asked and asked him to confide in me, thinking I could somehow help him. Gee, little did I know while I was trying to be the good little girlfriend and help him out with his problems, the whole time he was going behind my back and making me look like I don't know what the hell I'm doing. I am going to kill him the next time I see him!" Rosie raised her glass of wine to Angela. "Drink up, girlfriend. This time tomorrow, I will be back on the market. And I hope I pick someone who is not an asshole. Now that's a lovely thought!"

Rosie was going to wait to confront Steve in person, but she was just so mad! She felt like her head was going to explode if she didn't get a hold of him to yell at him and tell him in no uncertain terms what she knew and how she felt about him. She called his cell phone, but when he didn't pick up, she left a message asking if he wanted to come over to her place around seven for dinner. She said she was making spaghetti and he was welcome to join her. She kept her tone light and casual, even if she gagged almost the whole time she was leaving the message. She didn't want him to have any clue she knew about his treachery. Rosie was already going over in her mind how she would act like everything was normal and then hit him right between the eyes with the news that she was breaking up with him and never, never ever wanted to see him again.

Of course, she hadn't figured out how she was going to navigate the whole work situation, but she decided it was more important to let him know how she felt about him first. She was going home for an extended weekend trip the next morning, and she wanted to cut any ties to Steve before then.

By nine, Rosie had eaten, cleaned up the kitchen, and started to pack for her trip. Steve had neither called nor texted her, and the more she thought about it, she had to admit to herself she was relieved he hadn't come over. Rosie had never been great with confrontation (that was more Lilly and Amy's style) so she figured she would talk the situation over with her sisters when she was home, and the two confrontationists could give her pointers on what to say.

She was smiling to herself just thinking about going home to see her sisters when the doorbell rang. *Shit, shit, SHIT!* She briefly debated not answering the door, but she figured that was the chickenshit way out. *Let's get this over with.*

Rosie didn't know what to expect when she answered the door. She thought he might bring her flowers and give them to her with that sheepish look on his face that told her he knew he'd screwed up. Or he could still be nursing a grudge and he would look at her with a defiant, angry glare telling her he thought she was the one with the problem. What she didn't expect was to open the door and find him flat-out drunk as a skunk. He was literally holding onto the door jamb to keep from falling over, and it looked like one eye was rolling to the right while the other eye rolled to the left.

"Steve! What's going on? Where have you been?" Rosie reached out, grabbed his arm, and began pulling him into her apartment.

He took a few steps, then started to lean over to the right. He did the two-step dance shuffle to get his balance back and tried to over-compensate by leaning to the left, which just succeeded in bringing both Rosie and Steve to the floor with Rosie underneath him.

"Oomph. Get off me. God, you're too heavy!" Rosie pushed at his shoulder and managed to turn him over on his back and wiggle her way out from under his dead weight. "What in the world have you been doing? How much have you had to drink?"

But Steve just lay there on the floor, his arm thrown over his eyes. Rosie poked him in the side, then poked him harder, but he didn't even move. She pulled his arm off his face, and it dropped to the floor with a thud. He was totally passed out. She leaned over him and got a whiff of bourbon. *Bourbon?* She had never seen him drink anything stronger than beer. Maybe a glass of red wine here and there, but that was it. *What in the world were you doing tonight, you asshole?* Rosie thought. *And with who?*

She thought about getting a blanket and a pillow, but then replayed what Angela had told her in her mind and decided he could just lay on the floor all night long. She turned out the light and started into her bedroom, but turned back into the kitchen, brought out a bucket, and put it next to him. No sense in taking any chances. She didn't care if he puked on himself, just not on her floor. With that thought, she went into her room, locked her door, and went to sleep.

CHAPTER THIRTY-THREE

ROSIE HAD HER ALARM SET for 5:30 a.m. because she was taking an early flight back to Texas. After she turned her alarm off, she laid there and listened to her apartment. It was quiet. She got out of bed and opened the door of her bedroom. She looked out into the living room, fully expecting to see Steve still sprawled out by the door. She was surprised to see the room was empty. The bucket was dry, and there was a note taped to the side of it:

> SORRY I WAS SUCH A FOOL LAST NIGHT. I DON'T KNOW WHAT GOT INTO ME, EXCEPT A TON OF BOURBON! THANKFULLY, I DID NOT HAVE TO USE THE BUCKET!
>
> :) STEVE

There you go, Rosie thought. *So much for having the talk about our relationship and what I think about him. I guess now I can get some hints from Lilly and Amy on how to do the dirty deed with minimal pain to myself and maximal pain to the asshole.*

———

Rosie got back to her apartment in New York late Sunday evening. She was exhausted but also so happy she had been able to spend quality time with her sisters and her father. As she suspected, Lilly, Amy, and even gentle Daisy, had been so pissed when they heard how Steve had gone behind her back and talked shit about her to Gwyneth. Rosie really hadn't wanted to get into the whole story about how Steve had changed so much, so she'd kept it simple and focused on his betrayal. The sisters had never met Steve, but, of course, they immediately hated him.

"Fuck him," Amy had said. "Go total blackout on him. Don't call, don't text, don't answer his texts or calls—just freeze him out."

When Rosie explained that she would still have to see him at work, Amy had told her to just think of him as one of those people at work nobody wants to have anything to do with. No eye contact, no talking, nothing. And if he said something to her, then she should look at him as if she couldn't believe he'd dare talk to her.

Lilly hadn't been quite as insistent as Amy that she should ignore him because she knew Rosie was dying to tell him exactly what she thought of him. After that, *then* she could go blackout on him.

Daisy—to her sisters' surprise—had been the most bloodthirsty of them all. She'd suggested sending an email immediately to Gwyneth, Bob, and Pam to set the story straight, then send the same email to the upper management and demand Steve get fired immediately. She'd also mumbled something about fire-bombing his apartment, but when all the sisters had looked at her, she'd said she was just kidding.

Rosie hadn't even bothered discussing Steve with her dad, because she knew his solution would be to go to New York himself and handle it "mano y mano." Rosie suspected that while their dad gave voice to how proud he was of his independent daughters, he secretly wished they were all still toddlers so he could take care of them and their problems. Of course, when they'd been toddlers, those problems had consisted of dealing with one sister wearing the other sister's shorts without asking or whether they were going to wear pigtails or a ponytail.

The next morning, Rosie had to admit she was surprised Steve hadn't tried to call her last night and failed to meet her at their usual place. *There is really something really going on with him. And I, for one, am tired of trying to figure it out!*

When Rosie walked into the newsroom, the first thing she noticed was John and Angela standing by her desk. They were obviously looking for her, and they both had the most stricken looks on their faces. She knew right away something terrible had happened and quickly looked over to Steve's desk to see if he was there. His computer was shut down, and his chair was pushed all the way in. If he was in the office, then he had not been by his desk yet.

"John? Angela? What's wrong? Is everything okay?"

John just looked at Rosie. He started to speak and then just shook his head. "I don't know how to tell you this, Rosie."

"What? What is it? Is it . . . Steve?"

John hesitated, then looked at Rosie with tears in his eyes. "There's no good way to say this. We just got word Steve was killed in a car accident late last night."

Rosie's felt like she might faint. "What? What are you saying? That can't be true . . . I mean . . . I saw him Thursday night . . . and . . . I mean, I didn't talk to him this weekend . . . but . . . what? Where? What time?"

Angela put her arm around Rosie, and they both started to cry. She led Rosie over to her chair and sat her down. Rosie kept repeating, "He can't be dead." She was looking at John as if he were truly the crazy one and saying stupid shit just to mess with her.

"All I know is that the newspaper got a call from the highway patrol this morning. I guess Steve had been spotted driving erratically down the turnpike around midnight last night, and an officer started to follow him. Steve supposedly sped up, and when he went around the curve, his car hit the guardrail . . . and . . ."

"And what? Did it stop the car? Did it flatten the tire? And since when does Steve even have a car? He doesn't have a car here! Are they sure it's Steve? Have you tried to call him? I'm going to call him right now, and I bet he'll be able to clear this up." Rosie started frantically going through her purse, looking for her phone. "Where is my phone? It's in here somewhere."

John crouched down in front of Rosie and gently put his hands over hers. "Rosie, it was Steve in the car. They found his wallet. I don't know where he got the car or why he was driving like that. We don't really know any answers at this point. The police are contacting his brother to let him know what's happened. Have you ever talked to his brother? Do you want me to call him for you?"

"The last time I saw Steve, he was drunk. He came to my apartment Thursday night. Angela, remember, we went for a drink, and I told you I was going to break up with him? That I was so mad at him because of what he had done? I never had a chance to even talk to him. And now he's dead? This can't be right. I haven't told him how mad I am at him. How can he be dead when I haven't been able to talk to him? This is all wrong!"

Angela sat on the other side of her and took her hand. "Of course, honey. I know you wanted to talk with him."

"But I never got the chance! He came over later that night, and he was so drunk. Like falling over drunk! He smelled like bourbon! Have you guys ever seen him drink bourbon? I mean, bourbon! What was he doing that for? What was going on with him? Why wasn't I able to talk to him?" Rosie was beginning to cry in earnest at this point. "The last time I talked to him, we were arguing about the fact he was being so weird about everything. That was the last time I talked to him. He didn't call me this weekend, and I was glad! I was glad, I said! I was with my sisters, and I was talking about breaking up with him and how I didn't want to talk to him. Why didn't I want to talk to him? I want to talk to him now!"

Angela took Rosie in her arms. Rosie put her head on her shoulder and just sobbed. John looked like he wanted to say something else, but Angela shook her head. She knew what he wanted to say to Rosie, and this was not the time.

Angela let Rosie cry for about fifteen minutes, then gently said to her, "Come on, sugar. Let me take you home. John is going to talk to the police again and then he'll come over and tell us everything you want to know."

Rosie didn't respond for a minute, but then nodded, took a very deep breath, and let Angela help her up. Angela wasn't sure Rosie was going to be able to walk past Steve's desk without breaking into fresh tears, but all she did was stop for a minute and look at his desk with the saddest expression Angela had ever seen. She reached out and, with a shaky finger, gently touched the picture Steve had on his desk. It was a picture of Rosie taken about a month ago. She had been waiting for Steve at their usual meeting place and looking down at her phone when Steve had called her name. She'd looked up and smiled, and he'd taken her picture. Rosie remembered the weather that morning had been perfect, sunny with a slight chill in the air. Everything looked like it had been freshly washed. The kind of morning that made you want to take a deep breath and say, "Hello, world. What a great day!"

"I remember that day. We had finally gone a whole week without fighting, and I really thought everything was going to work out." She paused for a moment. "I guess I was wrong, huh?"

Before they were able to get out the door, Rosie heard her name being called. She turned and was surprised to see Gwyneth hurrying toward them. Unless Gwyneth had something specific to say, she usually ignored them. And Rosie was doubly surprised when Gwyneth reached out to her and pulled her into a hug. Yes, it was an awkward hug, as if Gwyneth didn't have a whole lot of experience hugging people, but when she murmured to Rosie how sorry she was to hear about Steve, Rosie relaxed and hugged her back. "Thank you, Gwyneth."

"You take all the time you need to get through this, you hear? Please let the paper know if there is anything we can do for you."

After she hurried away, Angela and Rosie just looked at each other. They had spent enough evenings dissecting Gwyneth and all her weird social peculiarities that they knew exactly what the other was thinking. *That was so weird but also kind of nice.*

———

Later that afternoon, John softly knocked on Rosie's door. Angela opened it. "Shh. She's finally sleeping."

"How is she?"

"About how you would expect. She was like a zombie on the cab ride here. Said absolutely nothing. No tears. Just stared at the back of the seat. When we got here, I asked her if she had anything like a Valium around, and she just looked at me like I had two heads. I was expecting her to break down and cry some more, but she just went into her bedroom and shut the door. I looked in every thirty minutes, and she would be just staring at the ceiling. She'd shake her head when I asked if she needed anything. She finally fell asleep about an hour ago. So, what did the police tell you? Anything more on what they found in his apartment?"

"I'm not asleep. What did they find in his apartment?"

John and Angela both jumped when they heard Rosie's voice. She was standing in the doorway to her bedroom and holding onto the door jamb like she would collapse if she let go. Her face was parchment-paper white except for the redness around her eyes. It was obvious she had been crying, but her eyes were dry now.

Rosie made her way slowly over to the couch, walking like she was a ninety-year-old lady. Angela told John later she'd sworn she could hear Rosie's joints creaking when she walked, as if Rosie had cried all the fluid out of her body and there was nothing left to lubricate her joints.

"Sugar, do you want any water? How about a cup of hot tea?"

"I don't want water or tea. I just want to find out what the police found in his apartment."

John hesitated and looked over at Angela. She slowly shook her head. John shrugged his shoulders as if to say, "There is nothing I can do about it now," and went over to sit next to Rosie. He looked at her for a moment, then took her hand. "Rosie, I'm not sure if this is the time or place to talk about that. I don't want to cause you any more pain."

Rosie closed her eyes and gave a small sigh. "I'm not sure I can be in any more pain than I am right now. But if you know something that can shed some light on this absolute nightmare, then I really want to hear it. No, I take that back. I *need* to hear it, even though I am getting the impression this is not going to make me feel better. Probably worse, huh?"

John took a deep breath, held it, then let it out. "I really don't know where to start."

He looked so miserable that Rosie took pity on him. "John, you and Angela are two of the best friends a girl can have. I love you both, and I know you would never do or say anything to hurt me. But I need to know what's going on. I've gone over every stupid thing Steve did or said in the last year since he got so weird, and I can't make heads or tails out of it. Where did he get a car? Why was he speeding and running away from the cops? Why was he drinking bourbon and getting shit-faced? I mean, did I even know him at all? Were the last couple of years just one big, fat, stupid lie?"

She was crying now, so John put his arm around her on one side and Angela sat next to her on the other side. They held her and let her cry, and there were tears on their end too. Finally, Rosie let out a big, "Ugh . . . I *hate* this! I *hate* crying! I have a horrible headache, and I'm sure I won't be able to open my eyes tomorrow! I'm just so mad at him and sad for him and . . . and . . . sad for me. I don't know how to feel!" She threw herself back against the cushions on the couch and just stared at them.

Angela stood up. "Fuck water and hot tea. I'm opening a bottle of wine, and you, my very good friend, are going to have a healthy glassful." Angela poured each of them a glass, and they solemnly, silently, toasted to Steve.

Then Rosie simply said, "Tell me."

CHAPTER THIRTY-FOUR

JOHN TOOK ROSIE'S HAND and proceeded to shatter her world all over again. "According to the police, they were actually on their way over to Steve's apartment to talk to him regarding some pretty serious allegations."

"Allegations? What allegations? What had he done?"

"There's no easy way to say this. He is . . . was . . . whatever. Okay, I'm just going to say it. They wanted to question him about child pornography."

Rosie's mouth dropped. "What! Child pornography? Are you fucking kidding me?" Rosie was staring at John like he had suddenly sprouted two heads and five legs and was doing a dance on the coffee table naked.

"I know. I *know*! I can't wrap my head around it either! Steve and child porn? It's crazy! But let me get through what the police told me this morning, and then we can try to figure this cluster out."

Rosie couldn't even speak. She just nodded and took Angela's hand.

"When the police came by this morning, we could tell they had bad news. It started out casual, I guess. They asked me how long I had known Steve and if I knew where he'd been last night. I told them I had no idea, and then they told me about the car wreck. My first response was like yours, Rosie. I told them he didn't even own a car that I knew of. And I knew you were out of town, so I told them I assumed Steve was just hanging out at his apartment over the weekend since he hadn't tried to get in touch with me to grab a beer. You know, normal stuff. Then the whole conversation veered off the rails and went totally crazy!

"They said he'd been under an investigation—a sting operation of some sort. They were working with the FBI to try and catch people downloading child pornography. I swear, I wanted to laugh! I almost asked them if it was some kind of joke, but from the looks on their faces, I knew they were dead serious. I couldn't believe it! I still can't! When they went to his apartment, he wasn't home, so they put an APB on Steve, and about twenty minutes later, they got a report that a car was speeding on I-287. I guess the patrol car spotted Steve, turned on its lights, and gave chase. According to the police, the patrol car wasn't too aggressive, because why should they be? They just wanted to talk to Steve at this point, and when a police car comes up behind you and turns on their lights, people usually pull over. Steve upped his speed, and ten minutes later, he went around a curve and hit a concrete pillar. The police said they don't think he even touched his brakes. Just drove right into—"

"We get the picture." Angela gave John a look that said, "TMI."

Rosie was just looking at John and slowly shaking her head. Suddenly, Rosie stood up and said in a high, strained voice, "I'll be right back." She practically ran into her bedroom and before she could get the bathroom door shut, John and Angela heard her coughing and retching. There was nothing in her stomach to even bring up, but that didn't stop her body from trying.

After about twenty minutes, Rosie came back out to the living room. It was obvious she had washed her face and brushed her teeth, and even though she was still pale, there was a bit of color in her cheeks.

"Okay, let's think this through. Is there any way the cops could be mistaken? I mean, don't you think I'd know if he had a thing for little kids? There was never even a hint that he was like . . . that . . . or . . . I mean . . . everything was okay on that end. Quite truthfully, it was the only thing that stayed okay in our relationship these last couple of months. I mean, could they have targeted the wrong Steve Gaynor? That stuff must happen, don't you think? Who do you think we should call to ask them if they had the right guy? Maybe I'll go do some research on—"

John reached out and took her hands in his. "Rosie, I would like nothing more than for the cops to be wrong about Steve. Obviously, it wouldn't bring him back, but I know it would make us all feel so much better." John paused. "The way the cops were talking…I think they had the right guy."

Rosie just sat there with a stunned look on her face. "It just doesn't make any sense. No sense. None."

"There's more."

"Oh my God. How can there be more? John, what are you talking about? How can it get any worse?"

"It does. It gets so much worse."

"Angela, what's he talking about? Do you know?"

"Sugar, the only way to tell you this is straight out. And I know it's going to hurt. But here goes." Angela took a deep breath. "He had pictures of you on his computer—compromising pictures of you and him."

Rosie felt like she was going to throw up again. "What? *What?*

Are you kidding me? I don't believe this. This seriously cannot be happening! I'm living in the goddamn Twilight Zone! I can't believe this! Angela, John, you guys knew him. What did I miss? What did we miss? Surely there were clues. Did I miss something? How could I have been with such a twisted person and not know about it? I just . . . I don't even know what to say! I'm so pissed! So. Very. Fucking. Pissed. I . . ."

Rosie grabbed a pillow from behind her back, put it up to her face and screamed into it—then took another breath and screamed some more. She took a third breath and screamed even louder, if that was possible. Then mid-scream, she just stopped and held her face into the pillow, like she was trying to suffocate herself with it.

"Sugar?" said Angela. "Honey, are you okay?" Angela looked at John, who just shrugged.

"A truly horrible thought occurred to me in the middle of my screaming." Rosie said into her pillow. "And I don't know what I will do if it's true. I really don't."

"If what's true?"

Rosie took a deep breath and still talking into her pillow asked, "How do I find out if he sent out the pictures of me? Out into the world for everyone to see? For my sisters and my father to see? So any creep who wants to get his jollies by looking at naked women could see me? Why did he hate me so much? Why did he do this to me? I swear to God, if he wasn't dead, I would rip his throat out with my bare hands. I swear to God, I would."

Somehow, Rosie got through the next couple of weeks. When she would later think back to that time, which she avoided at all costs, it all seemed like one big recurring nightmare. A perpetual Groundhog Day. Talking to the police, emailing with Steve's brother to coordinate some type of service they could possibly have in New York (Lance, Steve's brother, had made the arrangements to have Steve's body shipped back to Missouri), struggling to get some work done at the newspaper, but most of all, trying to reconcile the Steve she thought she knew with the true Steve.

Rosie had thought, before things got weird between them, he might have been the one. She had indulged in a fantasy where they would get married, move back to Texas, and have a couple of kids. That daydream had gone by the wayside when everything fell apart, but she still could not believe she had missed so many signals he was into kiddie porn, to say nothing about being so deviant he would take naked pictures of her. That thought still made her want to throw up all over Steve after she cut his balls off with a very dull knife. Although she supposed that was the way with many deviant behaviors. *Look at all the people who've said they had no idea their neighbor was killing and cutting people up!* Rosie thought. *The usual refrain was, "He seemed like such a nice guy!"*

They never did have any type of formal memorial service for Steve. Rosie just didn't have it in her to push the issue, mainly because she would start to shake with anger every time she thought about him. Lance had made it clear through emails that he had no intention of coming back to New York, and he'd also made it very clear they were not welcome in Missouri. Rosie never even knew if his family had any proper funeral for Steve, which seemed so unbelievably sad to Rosie, even though she hated his guts now. After Daisy's husband died, the outpouring of condolences and friends sharing their stories about Tommy was about the only thing that had made it possible to keep Daisy going during that dark time. Rosie couldn't imagine a family being so cold and hurtful. Of course, maybe that was why Steve had turned out to be such a deviant!

CHAPTER THIRTY-FIVE

"ALL I CAN SAY IS that if he were still alive, I would kill him. Slowly. And I would make it hurt."

Ren and Rosie were lying in bed, and Ren had his arms around her. Rosie had cried more than a few times telling him about her time in New York and its horrible ending, but she admitted she finally felt like she had exorcised the ghost of Steve. She almost hadn't told Ren about the photos Steve had taken of her, but she was tired of feeling like it was all her fault that Steve had turned out to have been a degenerate fuckhead. Besides, she'd had numerous conversations with Officer Rice, the forensic police officer who'd overseen the case. She'd assured Rosie that they had done a complete sweep of his computer, and the pictures of her hadn't appeared to have been posted to the web, dark or otherwise.

"Trust me," Rosie said. "There have been many nights when I couldn't sleep until I played the scenario through my head where I come upon Steve hunched over his computer, wait for him to turn around to make sure he sees me, and then blow his fucking head off. What he did to me was terrible, but I just see red when I think about those poor kids trapped in the child pornography hell. Those men, and I guess probably some are women too, deserve every horrible thing that happens to them. In my mind, Steve got off way too easy."

Ren kissed her forehead again. "Come on, my little vengeful Annie Oakley, let's get some sleep and tackle the rest of this tomorrow. It's been a long night for you." Ren turned her around so she was facing him. "Thank you for confiding in me. I know it wasn't easy to have to relive that time in your life. He was the pervert; he was the asshole. People like him are so very good at manipulating people and making them feel like it's *their* fault. He fooled everyone into thinking he was an okay guy, but he wasn't. And it's probably not very Christian of me, but I'm glad he's dead."

"So am I."

————

The next morning, Ren called his office and told the staff he wouldn't be in until after lunch. He had wanted to let Rosie sleep in, and he also wanted to talk to her about the picture Danny had shown them. No way was he buying her story that she'd been mistaken about who she thought it was.

But Ren also knew last night had been particularly trying for her, so he had not wanted to press. Today would be soon enough.

Ren fed the dogs and took them out on a leisurely stroll to the park. When he got back, Rosie was sitting at the breakfast table, enjoying her first cup of coffee. She looked up when they came through the door and laughed at the sight of all the dogs trying to get into the house first. They had briefly discussed putting in a doggie door but decided against it because they knew there would not be a doggie door big enough to handle them. Instead, they'd hung up a mesh screen with magnets down the middle so the dogs could come and go, but bugs couldn't get in the house.

Predictably, it'd taken Walter longer than the other two dogs to figure out how to navigate it. He would poke at it with his nose but always hesitated to push his whole body through. Marilyn, of course, would look at him as if to say, "Once again, you are making a huge fool of yourself. Pull yourself together, man!" Big Shirley, as usual, ignored both.

"You're going to be late for work if you don't hustle. I would have walked them."

"I know. But you looked so peaceful sleeping, I figured if I took the dogs out and let you sleep in, you might do me a favor. And I already called Julie at the office and told her I won't be in until after lunch."

"And what would that particular favor be, hmm? Didn't I just let you rub my back and have your way with me, like two or three nights ago?"

Ren laughed. "Well, if you can't even remember when it was, then I must not have been rocking your world! I might have to change some of my moves!"

Rosie got up from the table and put her arms around Ren, resting her head on his shoulder. She smiled into his neck. "I like your moves just the way they are. Although you could make the back rub last a little longer than five minutes!"

"I can't help it if this old vet gets excited just by looking at you! I'm around animals all day, and you turn me into one at night!"

"Jeez, how many times are you going to use that line? And how many times am I going to smile at it? Okay, if the favor is not having sexual relations with you at eight in the morning, then what exactly is the favor? Should I even ask?"

Ren took his time filling his coffee mug and refilling Rosie's. He sat down at the kitchen table with her and took her hands in his. He looked at her for a moment, then bent over and gave her a kiss. "I know your time in New York was not what you hoped it would be. I still feel a murderous rage come over me when I think of what Steve put you through, and I admire you more than you know when I see how strong you are when dealing with it. And the last thing I want to do is cause you any more distress. But I do think there is a connection between New York and the picture Danny showed us last night. I could be wrong, but I don't think so."

"No, you're not wrong." Rosie sat for a minute, staring into her coffee mug and looking like she was a million miles away. "I only saw a picture of Steve's brother once, just in passing. Steve had bought a new wallet, and he was taking stuff out of his old one and putting it into the new one. He had old ticket stubs, receipts, stuff he was throwing away, and it was in a pile on the bed. Steve had left the room to get something, I don't remember what, and I noticed a picture on the pile. This is so weird. I haven't thought of this in forever, but I can remember it distinctly. The picture was of Steve and another man, a younger man, and he looked a lot like Steve. I wasn't able to look at it very long because Steve came back in the room and kind of yanked it out of my hand. I remember saying, 'Hey, is that your brother?' I joked and said something about how his brother must have gotten the looks in the family, and Steve didn't answer, just pushed all the trash together, including the picture, and said something like neither of them were very photogenic or they didn't like getting their picture taken, I really can't remember exactly what he said. But I do remember him angrily wadding up the photo with the rest of the trash, like he couldn't wait to get rid of it.

"I knew even then Steve didn't have a close connection with his brother. Which is so strange to me, given how close I am to all my sisters. But I know not everyone has that kind of relationship, so I didn't press him too much over it. I got the impression that his brother had some problems, but I never knew what they were. Steve *never* talked about his family. Like I said, I knew he had a brother, and when we first started dating, he told me his parents had been killed in a highway accident of some sort. I think Steve said he was in college when it happened. Nothing about any other siblings that I can remember. Steve just had a way of deflecting anything he didn't want to talk about. He would change the subject or make a joke or ask me something to take my mind off whatever I was asking. I think I was trying to be the good girlfriend, you know, to support him, but after a while, I just stopped trying to get any information about his family out of him." Rosie looked at Ren with angry eyes. "He really did a number on my head, now that I think about it."

"Hey, you are being way too hard on yourself. It's like we talked about last night. People like Steve are not normal people, like you or me. They have an uncanny knack for knowing how to use unfair or insidious means to make people do what they want them to do. He didn't want to talk about his family, so he was able to always turn the tables on you to make you feel like you were being an intrusive bitch if you pressed him on the subject. This is not in any way your fault."

"But Ren, the picture. The one the car rental agency sent to Danny." Rosie looked at Ren. "I'm pretty sure it was Lance, Steve's brother."

"Shit."

"Yeah. No shit."

Ren and Rosie just looked at each other. Finally, Ren said one of them should probably call Danny. Rosie agreed, but said she wanted to write down everything she could remember about Steve's brother before they went to the police. She also wanted to do a bit of research on her own.

"Go ahead and go to the clinic. Even though I'm sure Julie and Claire can handle just about anything that walks through the doors, I know you get antsy when you're supposed to be there and you're not. It's crazy. I've spent the last year and a half doing everything I can to not think about Steve and everything that happened in New York, and now, it's like a floodgate has opened in my brain and I'm remembering all sorts of shit. I swear that twisted bastard must have been drugging me every day so I would let him get away with all his crap! It's making me angry all over again!"

"He knew exactly what he was doing, so you should not beat yourself up about it. Besides, do you really want to give him any more satisfaction by letting him get you all upset? Even though he is dead and doesn't know you're upset, so there is that. But still, I am going to put on my wise and loving boyfriend hat and suggest you go for a nice long run. Listen to that one podcast you like where they talk politics about the jerk who is alive and trying to ruin our world. That'll take your mind off Steve. Plus, that podcast always gets your ire pointed in the right direction. Then, I think it is a great idea to write down what you can remember. Maybe even call Angela to pick her and John's brains about that time."

John and Angela had gotten married a few months ago, and Rosie and Ren had traveled to New York for the wedding. They had all carefully avoided the subject of Steve, preferring to focus on the joy of the wedding and of seeing old friends. The four of them spent one hilarious night getting tipsy at Gino's. There was so much gossip to catch up on, but nothing could compare to the news that Gwyneth not only had quit her position at the newspaper but was also pregnant!

According to Angela, one of the sports editors from a rival newspaper had come by the newsroom to see one of the *Times Express News* sports editors, and it had been love at first sight for Gwyneth. And also for the rival sports editor. After dating for about six months, Gwyneth had announced her resignation and moved in with her sports guy. Angela said Gwyneth had been by the newsroom a couple of times since, and she was a totally different person.

"You know how she used to channel all her energy and focus into the newspaper?" Angela had asked. "Now all that focus is going toward the baby. But you know what? It's great to see. And we really get a kick out of her. John and I have been out with them a few times, and we really enjoy them. Besides, it ended up being a great career move for us." Angela and John had been named co-editors of the paper, and they were having a blast instituting all sorts of new and innovative practices. All in all, there'd been a win for everyone.

"Those are great ideas, oh wise and wonderful boyfriend. Especially going for a run. I'm so keyed up right now, my thoughts are going every which way but straight."

Rosie got up from the breakfast table and headed toward the bedroom to change into her running outfit while Ren poured himself another cup of coffee and started scrolling through his phone to catch up on any messages. Something made him look up, and there was Rosie in the doorway, in all her naked glory. "Did I hear there was an animal out here, just waiting to show off some jungle moves?"

"Grrrr."

Rosie smiled to herself and snuggled deeper into the sheets. His jungle moves had been exactly what she'd needed. He could be Tarzan and she could be Jane any day of the week.

Since her thoughts were still centered around her time with Steve, she couldn't help but compare the two men.

Before their relationship hit the skids, she'd really thought she was happy with Steve. But in retrospect, Rosie realized there had always been this feeling, though very subtle, that Steve was holding something back. Perhaps it was because Steve had never really opened up to her. Oh sure, at the beginning, like all new relationships, they'd shared stories about their backgrounds. But now that Rosie thought about it, Steve's stories had been generic and lacked any type of depth. Rosie just wished she had caught on to him sooner, before he . . . *Stop it. Do not go there,* she thought. *He is in hell, and you are in a fantastic place with your own jungle boy. So be happy.*

Ren was in the shower, the dogs were sleeping in their beds, and Rosie couldn't decide whether to join Ren in the shower or join the dogs in slumberland. Maybe a little nap, then a shower, would be the way to go.

CHAPTER THIRTY-SIX

ANGELA USUALLY GOT BACK into the office around one after lunch, so after Rosie fixed herself a sandwich, she called Angela's cell phone. After about ten minutes of catching up, Rosie said, "Ang, I'm calling for another reason. Do you have some time to help me with something?"

"Well sure, sugar. One of the great things about co-editing with John is I can make him do his job and mine if needed! So, what's going on?"

Rosie realized she hadn't shared all the crap happening to her family with Angela, so she spent the next twenty minutes filling her in.

"Oh my God, that is terrifying! I am so glad your sisters weren't hurt, but this could easily swerve out of control. Do you have any idea who's behind this madness?"

"Um, you are not going to believe this, but yes, I do think I know who is behind this. And you will never guess in a million years who it is."

That evening, Rosie shared with Ren the notes she had written down, detailing everything she could remember about Lance, Steve's brother. Not that there was much to detail. The main thing had been that whenever Steve would mention his brother—and it didn't happen very often—he always prefaced it by saying something like his brother had trouble with life, or his brother had some problems, or his brother always just got into trouble. And whenever Rosie had questioned Steve about it, he would just shrug off her questions by saying everyone had shit going on in their life and then change the subject. Since Rosie was now reliving those days in her mind, she could not get over how often she had let him get away with it. Absolutely crazy.

Rosie contacted Officer Rice; the forensic police officer who had made sure the photos Steve took of her had not gone out for the entire world to see. Rosie would still feel an overwhelming sense of shame whenever she thought about those photos, even though she hadn't known he was taking them. She told herself repeatedly that Steve was the bad guy, and after sharing her story with Ren, she was almost starting to believe it. Officer Rice told Rosie she would do some research on Lance to see what she could find.

Rosie also called Danny and set up a time for her to go to the police station tomorrow. Rosie figured the more people who had eyes on this situation, the better. It had been a couple of weeks since Lilly had received the letter at the hospital, and everyone was on eggshells, afraid of when or where the crazy person would strike next.

And finally, Rosie texted her sisters, asking if they could meet up tomorrow evening. Their bimonthly get-togethers had been somewhat curtailed by what had happened to Amy and Lilly. Rosie knew she needed to tell her sisters about how Lance was the guy in the picture and give them the full story about what'd happened to her in New York. She'd never worked up the nerve to tell them before. Again, the whole "blame the victim" mentality had been in play.

That is no longer applicable, Rosie thought. *Steve was the bad guy, not me, and I refuse to lay any more of the blame at my feet. There is only one thing I can be blamed for, and it is taking too long to see Steve for what he was. I could start with A for asshole and go through the entire alphabet and still have some derogatory names left to call him.*

CHAPTER THIRTY-SEVEN

THE LATE AFTERNOON SETTING was eerily similar to when the sisters first found out that Daisy had received the call from Skylar. They were in Daisy's backyard, and everyone had their drink of choice in front of them, just like before. The birds were still singing their same song about how hard life was and how some man bird had done them wrong, and Rosie, of course, was late again. The sisters were speculating as to why Rosie had been so insistent on meeting today.

"I think she'll tell us she's going to propose to the handsome town vet, and I have no doubt he'll say yes. I love the way he looks at her when he thinks no one's watching. Or maybe they already are engaged, and she just hasn't spilled the beans yet. Yay, a wedding!" Amy said.

Daisy said "How cool would that be! But I think you might be getting a tad ahead of yourself, Amy, don't you think? Maybe she just wants to get a little bit of normalcy back in our lives. And knowing Rosie, she's probably run out of Hendrick's gin and wants to drink some of mine, now that she knows Jon also drinks Hendrick's." Rosie had introduced Jon to Hendrick's at one of the family dinners, and he'd declared himself a fan.

"Or maybe I just miss my sisters and want to share this absolutely gorgeous day with them!" Rosie said as she came out onto the porch. "And speaking of how someone looks at someone when they think no one's watching. Can you say, 'Jon'? Hmmm, Daisy? And no, I have not proposed to the handsome town vet, but that's not a bad idea. I might have to work on it!"

Rosie pulled her chair over to the table and raised her glass in a toast. "To the absolute best sisters anyone could ask for. We can handle anything life throws at us, as long as we handle it together!"

"Hear, hear!"

"Actually, there is a reason why I asked to meet today, besides just the desire to see my sisters. And I want to apologize in advance. The reason I haven't shared this with you guys is, well, I just wasn't ready. I needed to come to terms with this in my own mind, you know. But wait, I'm getting ahead of myself." Rosie took a deep breath. "I need to tell you what happened to me in New York, because oddly it has to do with what's going on with our family."

"What? How is even that possible?" Lilly asked.

"I know it sounds bizarre or like something you would read in a badly written murder mystery. But there is a connection, crazy as it sounds. So let me get this story out first, and then we can try to make sense of it. It all starts with Gwyneth Stiles, our managing editor at the *Times Express News*, and her decision to put Steve and me together on the crime desk."

Rosie told the sisters exactly what had happened to her in New York. She managed to get through the story only tearing up twice, which was an improvement on when she'd told the story to Ren. And she left nothing out—not the child porn, not the pictures he took, not how she felt so much shame and blamed herself.

"Oh, sweetie, I am so sorry you had to go through something like that," Lilly said after Rosie had finished her story. The sisters had gathered around Rosie, giving her physical support by hugging her and verbal support by calling Steve every name in the book.

"We knew something bad went on in New York. Remember when you came home that weekend and told us you were going to break up with him? We all just thought he was a total idiot who didn't deserve you. And break-ups are hard, especially since you guys were together for a couple of years. But we had no idea something like this was going on."

Daisy shook her head. "Seriously, what is it with some men? The guilt trip he laid on you was just the worst. Making you carry that around with you. I agree with Ren. It's a good thing he's dead, or he would have some Hurley sister badasses to contend with. All I can say is that we're pretty darn lucky to be with the guys we have now."

Amy nodded. "Totally agree with that sentiment. So, how is this connected to what's going on around here?"

"Well, one asshole is gone—that would be Steve—but unfortunately, he had a brother. His name is Lance. And I am almost one-hundred percent sure the picture Danny showed us the other night was Lance. I never saw him in person, but I did see a picture once. Now granted, I only saw the picture in passing, but I was struck with how much Lance looked like Steve. And the person in the picture Danny showed us could have been Steve's twin. He used the name Lance on the fake ID—which is stupid, if you ask me—but he was probably trying to keep it simple. And the way the lady at the car rental place described him? Being agitated? Talking to himself? The very few times Steve mentioned his brother, he always said he had some problems with life. Although I'm not sure why I would think anything Steve told me was true, I think this was."

Rosie told them she had talked to Officer Rice and Danny, and they were going to do some checking up on Lance and get back with them. She also gave each one of the sisters a copy of the driver's license photo. "Keep your eyes peeled, girls. Danny said to call him ASAP if anyone sees him. Quite truthfully, I am sick to think my New York problems have followed us here, but at least now we have a name and a face. It was so maddening not knowing who, what, why, or where. And let me tell you, I, for one, cannot wait to confront this guy and get some answers. Like, how did he even know about Tommy's accident? Or the shit with Amy and Lilly? And Dad! I mean, I know you can get just about anything off the Internet these days, but it's not like we post our entire lives online! I'm not even on Facebook, for God's sake!

"So drink up, girls. Hopefully, this is going to be resolved shortly, and we will be able to sleep easier knowing this horrible person, Lance, is behind bars. Now, I have one last thing to do tonight, and I'm sick to my stomach thinking about it."

"What else do you have to do?"

"Go tell Dad."

The conversation with Jack about New York was as hard as Rosie had predicted. It had been one thing to tell Ren and her sisters about the sexually explicit pictures Steve had taken of her, but then to have to tell her dad, who probably could have gone his entire life without thinking about his daughters having sex—well, it was about as awkward as you'd expect. Knowing Rosie blamed herself was enough to make Jack want to punch something, preferably the dead Steve.

He was very intrigued by the new development with the Lance angle, and he and Rosie sat up until midnight trying to figure out what exactly Lance's endgame was. They were assuming that Lance was solely responsible for Amy's car, the honor code letter, Lilly's letter, the phone call from Skylar to Daisy, the mysterious red truck, and the attempted break-in of Jack's house. They put themselves in Lance's shoes and concluded fairly quickly that Rosie was the ultimate target. The others had just been window dressing.

CHAPTER THIRTY-EIGHT

TWO DAYS LATER, Rosie was in her office when she got a call on her cell phone from Danny. "Good morning, Danny. I really hope you have some good news for me, because I'm kind of starting to freak out a bit here thinking about Lance."

"I have quite a bit of information for you—stuff you won't believe. I didn't want to make you come to the station, so I'm out in your driveway. I even brought you a coffee, hoping I could bribe you to let me come in and talk to you."

"Are you kidding me? I'll make you eggs and bacon, plus biscuits and gravy, and even oatmeal if you'll come tell me what the hell is going on!"

"Be right there."

When Danny came into the house, the first thing he said to Rosie was that Lance was no longer a threat to them because he was in jail in Missouri. He'd figured she would want to know that as soon as possible. Then he proceeded to tell her the rest of the strange Lance saga.

One of the first things Danny and his partner had looked for was a connection between Skylar and Lance, since solving Skylar's murder still ranked high on their priority list. Danny thought it would be a good idea to work backward and concentrate on Skylar's public profile, since they had come up with absolutely nothing on Lance. No job history, no social media posts, no nothing. It was as if the guy had never existed. Danny called Skylar's sister Jessie, who had been the point person for the Smith family during the investigation and asked where Skylar had gone to college. It had turned out Skylar had attended Northwest Missouri State University for a few years but had dropped out before she got her degree.

Jessie told Danny she'd always suspected something terrible had happened to Skylar at school because she'd abruptly quit in the second semester of her second year. Skylar had never told her exactly what had happened, but Jessie remembered Skylar being very happy and excited about school, even tossing around the idea of possibly going to nursing school. After she'd left school, however-er, she had never talked about nursing school again and would get very angry at anyone who brought up the topic.

Skylar's siblings had decided to respect her desire for privacy, and they'd quit asking about what had happened to her at school. But after Skylar had come home from school, she never seemed to be the happy, outgoing sister Jessie remembered. And Jessie said she regretted, to this day, not pushing Skylar to tell her what had happened.

Danny had asked Jessie if she remembered ever hearing Skylar talk about a guy named Lance Gaynor. Jessie said she didn't recognize the name but couldn't be sure if Skylar had ever talked about him. She had apparently talked about a lot of boys. When Danny had asked if Skylar had been on Facebook, Jessie had laughed. "Of course! Who isn't?"

Jessie had given Danny Skylar's Facebook information, and Danny had spent the afternoon scrolling through her account. Her Facebook profile had been searched in the investigation, but the new information about Lance Gaynor gave them something different to focus on. And lo and behold, Danny did find some pictures of Skylar and Lance together. Not many, and they had all been taken in the last month or so that Skylar was at school, but it did conclusively prove that Skylar and Lance had at least known each other. It did not prove Lance had killed her, but they were a hell of a lot closer to figuring out the truth now that they had a name and face. And they had their ace in the hole, which was the DNA found under three of Skylar's fingernails. They were in the process of using the DNA sample Lance had to give when he'd been booked into jail to see if it was a match with the material under Skylar's fingernail. Danny expected they would have the results in a day or two.

Danny had done a little more digging to see if there was anything else connecting Lance to Skylar. The only thing he'd discovered was a small story in the college newspaper about a student's body being found in the woods behind one of the dorms. That had been a month before Skylar dropped out of school. The autopsy showed that the twenty-one-year-old woman, Melissa Greller, had died of alcohol poisoning. Danny had called the police officer in charge of the case and gotten a few more details, the most important being that Skylar had been Melissa's roommate.

According to the officer in charge, officials had ruled it an accidental death. In the interviews with Melissa's friends, they'd all told them the same story. Melissa had been at a party on campus and drinking heavily. No one had seen her leave. When she hadn't shown up at a scheduled event the next morning, a couple of her friends had tried calling her, but her phone kept going to voicemail. By that afternoon, her friends had been concerned enough that they contacted the campus police, who sent out a campus-wide text message asking for any information regarding Melissa. The next morning, a student out walking his dog in the woods behind the school had spied her body. According to the report, she'd been slumped against a tree. It'd been difficult to determine if she had just sat down there or if she'd been purposely placed. Nothing had been done to try to conceal her. Her clothes had been intact, and there hadn't been any visible injuries. The autopsy showed she'd recently had sex, but nothing to indicate it wasn't consensual—no bruising or lacerations.

Two hours later, Rosie was sitting at her breakfast table just shaking her head at Danny. "Wow. This is the craziest turn of events. Guess it's true. Truth is stranger than fiction. I'm just glad that now we know. Wait until I tell the rest of the family. They'll be so relieved! So, you think Lance was responsible?"

"It's just a hunch. Maybe I'm trying too hard to find a connection between Skylar, Lance, and Melissa. I mean, it makes sense that Skylar would drop out of school after her roommate died. But if Skylar and Lance were involved . . ." Danny trailed off. "I'm flying out to Missouri tomorrow to interview Lance. I'm going to ask him specific questions about Melissa, Skylar, and everything that has happened to your sisters and dad and see what response I get."

"What's he in jail for?"

"You mean this time? This guy is not a good guy, let me tell you. You remember we were wondering why there was a long period between Daisy's phone call from Skylar and the incidents involving your sisters and dad? About a year, right? Except for the period in the fall where the red truck seemed to be following Amy, which was just conjecture that it was him, but let's assume it was him because the timeline fits. We found Skylar's body mid-April, over a year ago. Lance was not in jail at that time. He went to jail from May to October for selling drugs to minors, so that could very well be the reason nothing escalated after Skylar's body was found. After he was released, he was free until January. This would match up with the red truck following Amy, although if Lance was indeed driving the red truck and tracking Amy, it seems odd that nothing further happened.

"He went back to prison in January for a minor infraction and was again released in March. Amy's car gets trashed in May, and the red truck is back, this time stalking Lilly and Daisy. Lilly gets the threatening letter, and Jack catches a possible intruder on his Ring. And then nothing. We all were wondering when the next incident would occur. Well, the reason nothing happened was because our friend went *back* to prison in June, this time for assault. It appears he beat the crap out of a woman named MaryAnn Lewis, who he met at a bar one night in Branson, Missouri. It was a very vicious assault. He broke her jaw and cracked a couple of ribs, just because she wouldn't go home with him. Nice guy, huh? I'm hoping I can get some answers out of him when I do the interview, but, Rosie, this has to be the asshole who's been harassing your family and we know exactly where he is. If the DNA report comes back with a match, then Lance will hopefully be in jail for the rest of his life."

"Sounds like the best place for him. Oh my God, just think if Joe hadn't been with Amy the day he trashed her car. It makes me sick to my stomach thinking about what could have happened!"

"Trust me," Danny said. "That was the first thing I thought of when I was reading the report on his assault. He deserves to be behind bars."

"I cannot wait to tell my sisters and dad! You know how on edge we've been. Looking over our shoulders all the time, being afraid to even go out to the grocery store. And to think that I'm responsible for bringing this psycho into our lives—"

"You are *not* responsible for this, Rosie. Lance is responsible, no one else. He's a sick man who revels in preying on people. He's exactly where he needs to be and that's behind bars so he can't hurt anyone else. Remember that."

———

When Rosie got a call from Danny two days later, she was sure he was going to fill her in on what information he had gathered from the interview with Lance. Instead, what Danny told her angered her, saddened her, sickened her, but most of all, frustrated her.

When Danny got to the jail for his interview with Lance, the head of security met him and took him back to his office. According to the cameras and the reports from the guards on duty, Lance had gotten into an altercation with another inmate that morning in the cafeteria. Apparently, the fellow inmate was someone Lance had history with, and there had been bad blood between them. Lance had been in line when that particular inmate walked by with a tray full of food. Lance had waited until he passed, then body slammed him hard from behind. The other inmate ended up breaking his arm when he fell to the floor, and a brawl broke out quickly. Lance had ended up getting stabbed in the neck. Supposedly, the injury hadn't been too deep, but Lance's carotid artery was cut, and he had ended up bleeding to death.

Rosie's mouth dropped. "Holy shit. Wow. I don't know what to say. I was really expecting you to tell me you had solved the question of how in the heck Lance was able to do all the stuff he did. And why he was doing it. I never even met him, so I could not figure out why he was so angry at me and my family. And according to Steve, they really didn't even have a relationship to begin with. With both of his parents dead, this is the craziest and saddest thing I have ever heard!"

"I know it's frustrating not getting the answers to all your questions. But at least you have some closure. You won't ever know exactly why he did it, but you know he will never bother you or your family again. That must give you guys some comfort. Like you told me, having to constantly be looking over your shoulder was really wearing everybody down. There is something to be said for being able to put this horrible chapter behind you."

"There is that. And I am grateful we can take a deep breath and get on with our lives. It was like we were frozen; just waiting for the next horrible thing to happen. By the way, did you get the results from the DNA yet?"

"No, but I am expecting the report to be on my desk this afternoon. As soon as I get it, I will let you know."

"Danny, I'm not sure we are ever going to be able to thank you enough for all you've done. Keeping us in the loop with all this information has gone a long way in making this terrible situation at least slightly more tolerable. We owe you big time!"

"Hey, as long as you keep inviting me over for some of that" —he coughed dramatically— "homemade lasagna, then I figure we're square."

Rosie laughed. "So, Ren spilled the beans about my secret

ingredient! That rat! Well, I guess I'd better get on the phone and spread the word about Lance. What a fucked-up, sorry ass family."

CHAPTER THIRTY-NINE

IT HAD BEEN ABOUT TWO MONTHS since Rosie had sat down with the family and informed them that they could finally put this terrible chapter behind them. They were free!

Daisy and Jon decided to celebrate by going on a quick weekend getaway to Port Aransas. They booked a rental right on the ocean and spent most of Saturday morning walking on the beach. They took turns throwing a tennis ball into the ocean for Leo to fetch, taking bets on how soon the yellow lab would tire out. Jon bet that Leo would tire out after an hour, but Daisy said she knew her dog and was certain that Jon's arm would wear out before Leo. Sure enough, Jon had to admit defeat and concede to Daisy. Of course, the bet was that the loser had to buy the ice cream, so it turned out they were all winners. Even Leo got a scoop of vanilla.

Later that afternoon, with Leo snoring softly in the corner of the bedroom, Daisy woke up from a nap of her own, only to find Jon sitting on the bed staring at her. "Oh my God, you scared me to death. What's wrong? Why are you just sitting there looking at me?"

"Because you are beautiful. Because you look angelic. Because I like watching you sleep. You get the cutest frown on your face, like you're trying to figure out the answers to all the questions in the universe. So maybe you have the answers to some questions I have. For instance, who do you think was the first person to open an oyster shell, look inside, see stuff that looks like it came out of your nose, and say, 'You know, this might taste great'? And then actually put it in their mouth and *eat it*? Same could be asked of the first person who ate a snail. Who would even think of putting that stuff in your mouth?"

By this time, Daisy was lying back on the pillow and laughing. "Your brain goes to some bizarre places, my man. Must be all that schooling you had to do to become a big bad doctor. And I can answer your questions. It had to be a guy. A woman would never do something so gross. Women are way too refined to even think about doing that!"

"Okay, then here's one for you. Who was the first person who saw what a laser could do and think, 'I should have someone burn my face with a laser to make me look younger?' Hmm? I'm thinking that would definitely be a woman because most men aren't as into looking younger. Maybe looking more buff or getting a certain body part to look bigger . . . but even then, no man I know would let a laser come within fifty feet of that part of the anatomy." Jon shuddered. "I know I wouldn't, no matter what I was promised."

Daisy was shaking her head and smiling. "A CT scan of your brain would be interesting. No telling what parts would light up like a pinball machine. Why are you thinking about all these crazy questions? Who even thinks about stuff like this?"

Jon moved off the bed until he was kneeling. He said softly, "I have one last question. Who was the first man to get on his knees, open his heart up to the woman he loves, and ask her to marry him? To me, that takes more guts than eating a whole plateful of snails." He lifted one of Leo's favorite dog toys, a red fish that squeaked when Leo bit it in just the right place. Tied around the fish was a beautiful diamond ring. "I was originally going to have Leo bring this to you while you were having coffee one morning, but I was afraid he'd get distracted and either start playing with it and swallow the ring or drop it and go hunting for squirrels. So, I decided to do it this way. Daisy . . . will you marry me?"

Daisy had both of her hands up to her mouth, looking at Jon with tears in her eyes.

"Um, can you say something? I've never done this before, so I'm not sure of the protocol, but I can only guess you're supposed to say something or do something or run out of the room screaming."

Instead, Daisy leaned over, took Jon's face in her hands, and kissed him very gently on the mouth. "I thought you only got one opportunity to have a once-in-a-lifetime love affair. I thought my time with Tommy was it, and I would never again feel for someone what I felt for Tommy. But I was wrong. Thank you, God, I was so wrong. You make me laugh, you make me smile, you love my family, you love my dog, and you love me. You're hitting all the goalposts. I'm not sure what I did to deserve this, but whatever it was, I'll take it. I am not going to run out of the room screaming; I am going tell you yes so many times you'll get tired of hearing it." Daisy threw her arms up in the air, practically shouting. "And I'm going to put on this gorgeous ring and only wear it and nothing else, and we can discuss certain body parts that want nothing to do with lasers."

Daisy stopped abruptly. She looked at Jon. "But before we get crazy, I want you to know how much I love you. You have made me the happiest person in the world." She smiled and looked down at her hands. "I was hoping this weekend was going in this direction. And since you know I discuss everything with my sisters, they were all encouraging me to ask you to marry me! They've been on Rosie to do the same with Ren for quite a while, but recently they've set their sights on us. So just know, this will elevate your status big time because you did it first!"

"I figured I could arm wrestle Ren for the top dog position, if it came to that. Although, wait a minute, he does hoist those big animals around for a living while I stand at the bedside of patients and type on a computer. Never mind! Why am I wasting our time talking about this? Right now, I'm only interested in what you were saying about *only* wearing this ring and nothing else. Cover your eyes, Leo!"

The next morning found Daisy and Jon again walking on the beach and throwing the tennis ball for Leo. The sun was shining, the seagulls were singing their songs and diving into the water for their breakfast, the sand crabs were burrowing back into the sand every time a wave washed over them, and Daisy and Jon were oblivious to all of it but each other . . . and Leo, of course.

"You really do look like the cat that ate the canary. I'm surprised there aren't some small yellow feathers poking out of your mouth."

Daisy just smiled and looked at Jon. "Could this day be any more perfect? Although I must admit, even if it was storming with cold wind gusts and sleet, I would still think it's a perfect day. And don't even get me started on last night, which was pretty perfect too."

"Go ahead and tell me about the perfect night. Was it when

you . . ." Jon leaned over and whispered into Daisy's ear. "Or was it when I did . . ." More whispering.

Daisy laughed. "I think both of those times cover the perfect night scenario. And why are you whispering? There's no one on the beach yet but us."

"Well, Leo had to be in the same room with us last night, so I didn't want to scar him even further by talking about it. He is sensitive, you know."

"Yeah, he really looks traumatized. So much so I'm surprised he can manage to run into the ocean to retrieve his tennis ball. And do it over and over and over. We'll have to ask Ren if he can recommend a doggy shrink!"

They were enjoying one last meal by the beach before they had to head back to the city when Daisy clinked her wineglass against Jon's. "Okay, tell me the truth. You just want to marry me so you can retire and live a life of luxury on my unit clerk salary. Very devious!"

"Dang it! I was hoping to get the wedding over with before you figured it out!"

"Too late. I am curious about one thing, though, and I can't believe I haven't asked you yet. Why have you never married? I mean, you check a lot of boxes, and you are a doctor, which is still, even in this day and age of enlightened females, pretty high on the wish list of many a mother. You're pretty darn handsome—at least, I think so. You don't embarrass yourself in public by farting, belching, or scratching yourself in private areas. You watch other things on TV besides sports. You listen to NPR. You vote the way I want you to vote! Come on, putting all of that together should make you extremely marketable. So how did you escape until now?"

"You mean I didn't tell you about Melinda, Cathie, Barb, Jane, Rita, Dana, and Mary? And I can't believe I forgot to tell you about all the kids! How could they have slipped my mind?"

"Not funny. So how have you managed to live almost forty years on this earth as a single male?"

"I will admit I came close a couple times. I don't know why I was never able to pull the trigger. Just when the time came to ask someone to marry me . . . I couldn't do it. It never felt right, you know? I was focused on getting through med school and starting my practice, but it wasn't like that was the only thing I was focused on. The romantic soul living inside of me is saying I was waiting for you." Jon toasted Daisy with his wineglass. "Because I have been wanting to ask you to marry me since our first date. But I was pretty sure you would have run for the hills if Dr. Dickhead declared his love for you after knowing you for all of six hours!"

CHAPTER FORTY

LILLY AND ROSIE WERE SITTING OUTSIDE in Lilly's backyard, soaking their feet in the baby pool, and watching Luke and Lacey splash each other (and the two women) with their pool toys. Lilly had finally convinced Luke to point his water gun at the flowers and trees in the backyard instead of at them, so they were at least able to say more than two words to each other before getting blasted in the face.

"Luke has a pretty short attention span, so get all the interesting stuff out now." Lilly was leaning back in her lawn chair in the shade, breast-feeding her newest arrival, baby Claudia Grace, named after the sisters' mother. Claudia had made her appearance in the world two weeks early, when she woke Lilly up at five in the morning by breaking her water. The contractions had started soon after, and Keith had to tell Rosie on the phone that no, she could not finish breakfast before she came over to watch Luke and Lacey, she needed to get there now!

Thankfully, the staff at the hospital knew Lilly, so when she came into the ER and said she needed to go to the OB floor *right this second*, no one challenged her. As it turned out, one of the labor and delivery room nurses working had been Kandy, the same OB nurse who had helped deliver Luke and Lacey. So when Lilly stood up from the wheelchair and yelled that the baby was coming now, she'd calmly had Keith help Lilly onto the bed, and among the three of them, baby Claudia was delivered without too much of a fuss.

Lilly would later joke that in all her years of working in the hospital and hearing over the loudspeaker, "ANY OB DOCTOR IN THE HOUSE TO THE DELIVERY ROOM STAT," she'd never thought it would be about her. And Keith liked to tell people how he told Lilly's doctor she should reimburse them because they did all the work. Of course, that was never going to happen, but Keith still liked to say it.

"I still can't believe Lance did all those shitty things." The topic of Lance and Steve still dominated the sisters' conversations, even two months later. They were still trying to process the fact that such an evil person had come so close to doing a lot of harm to them, and how easy it had been for him to find out intimate details of their lives. Since the skin under Skylar's fingers had matched Lance's DNA, the sisters were doubly grateful nothing worse had happened to them, especially Amy. They all agreed Amy's guardian angel had been working overtime the day her car was vandalized. If she had been alone in the parking lot with him—well, none of the sisters could even finish the thought.

Danny had also told them that Skylar's family was finally able to find some peace now that they knew who killed her. There were still unanswered questions regarding what exactly had happened to Melissa, Skylar's college roommate, and if Lance had been responsible for her death too, but months later, it seemed like those questions would never be answered.

Lilly finished feeding Claudia and asked Rosie if she would watch the kids while she put Claudia down for her nap. "And keep your fingers crossed she stays asleep, at least for an hour. Lately, she's been waking up every twenty minutes or so. It makes for a very long day, trust me."

"Go put the little one down. I'll watch the goofballs. Lacey and I just might take Luke on in a water pistol fight!"

When Lilly came back into the backyard twenty minutes later with the baby monitor in one hand and a beer for Rosie in the other, she laughed to see the fully clothed Rosie sitting in the baby pool with both Luke and Lacey. The kids were having a ball pouring water over Rosie's head.

"It's a good thing I don't have a hot date with Ren tonight, because I'm not sure my hair can be resurrected from this impromptu water boarding! I think we decided on frozen pizza, beer, and watching the Kansas City Chiefs play football, so a robe and a towel around my head will work just fine."

"Here's a beer to get you started for your night and to thank you for being on lifeguard duty with these monsters. Although I should have brought out dry clothes instead!"

CHAPTER FORTY-ONE

ROSIE WAS SURPRISED TO GET A CALL from Danny one morning a few weeks later. "Rosie, once again I am sitting in your driveway with a cup of hot coffee and with hopefully the last bit of information about the very dysfunctional Gaynor family. You up for a disturbing conversation?"

"When you put it like that, I would really like to say no, but I guess I need to hear the ending. Hard to believe this has been going on for over a year now! Come on in."

Danny and Rosie sat at the dining room table again. "We thought Steve was the sicko, and believe me, he was. But little brother Lance truly had some issues."

According to Danny, the Missouri police had gained access to Lance's apartment after Lance was killed in prison. One of the first things they'd noticed was the dark red pickup truck parked in front. "Now that we know for sure Lance had a red truck, we can be even more grateful he never did anything worse to Amy, Lilly, and Daisy besides following them and watching them in the parking lot. Given what we've discovered about this guy, your sisters dodged a huge bullet."

Besides the apartment being absolutely filthy, there'd been quite a bit of evidence that Lance had had a serious issue with the Hurley family, especially with Rosie. He blamed her for Steve's death and decided that he was going to hurt or kill one or all her sisters, so Rosie would know what it felt like to lose a sibling. The police found evidence of this in a paper trail Lance had left on his computer. Lance wasn't much into email, but when the officers accessed his Notes app, they found a treasure trove of letters Lance had written to a person named Martha, letters that described, in sickening detail, what Lance had planned for the Hurley sisters. Danny didn't go into a whole lot of detail, mainly because Lance was dead and unable to perpetrate the acts, but he told Rosie enough to make her sick to her stomach.

"My God, this is just crazy! Steve barely even talked about Lance. And when he did, he was so dismissive of him, like Lance didn't even matter. I just assumed they were estranged. I think Steve went home exactly once in the three years we were in New York together. I used to feel sorry for him, especially during the holidays, because he didn't have anywhere to go. I would always ask him to come home with me, but he said the holidays just weren't important to him. He told me that his parents were killed right around Christmas, and he dealt with everything by keeping his head down and not acknowledging the holidays at all. And since he never talked at all about his brother, I just assumed Lance was not a big part of Steve's life." Rosie closed her eyes and shook her head. "Man, did I miss the memo on the very weird and dangerous Gaynor brothers. Maybe I should hire a private detective to investigate Ren, just to make sure he's not hiding some psychopathic sibling in the wings who'll want to kill me if we ever break up."

Danny smiled. "For some reason, I think you hit the jackpot with Ren. And haven't you met his parents and sisters already? Weren't his parents just down here visiting?"

"How do you know that? Did I tell you that? Wait a minute." Rosie's eyebrows went up. "Who have you been talking to? It has to be one of my . . . Oh my God. Are you seeing Amy? You are, aren't you?'

Danny groaned and put his head down on the table. "She's going to kill me. Amy really wanted to tell you herself."

"The cat is out of the bag now, so you need to fess up, mister! I can't wait to get ahold of Amy. I want details now! And just so you know, I think it's great! We've all been wanting Amy to start seeing someone, if for no other reason to let her think and talk about something other than law school. Don't get me wrong, I love that she loves law school, but at this point, I feel like I know as much about estates and trust law as a regular attorney. That should give you some idea of what she discusses with us. Until we change the subject, that is!"

Danny laughed. "I know what you mean! I finally told her I'd only listen to cases from her criminal law class. At least that's interesting to me, and I can contribute some real-life information about the justice system. You know how it is when you only get one side of the story from a textbook. Sometimes it's not very practical."

"You're side-stepping the major story here. How long? When did it start? When was she going to tell us?"

"Jeez, you should come to work in the interrogation room! When did we start seeing each other? I don't know if you remember about six months ago when I came to one of your family dinners to give some information about the case. Well, when I was leaving, Amy was standing next to me and mentioned she had to leave because she had to study. This was when everything was going on, and I didn't want her walking out by herself, so I waited for her. She said her goodbyes to everyone and—"

"You guys have been seeing each other for six months? And she hasn't told us?"

"If you would quit interrupting, I can finish this story before I turn old and gray. No, we didn't start seeing each other that night. But I do think it was the first time I started seeing Amy as someone other than your little sister. You know how that happens. I've known Amy for forever.

"Anyway, we just talked about the crazy situation regarding whoever was messing with you girls, and I made sure she got in her car safely. I admit, I did think about maybe asking her out then but figured the timing wasn't exactly the best. Then a couple of months ago, I got off my shift and went into Starbucks to get a coffee, and Amy was there, in the corner, with about a million books around her, staring intently into her computer. I almost didn't want to bother her because she was concentrating so hard, but I thought, *Hey, what the hell?* You Hurley girls have no problem letting someone know if you don't want to talk to them. And I know that from firsthand experience!"

"Hey, when did I ever blow you off? Absolutely never is my answer!"

"Let's just say I've always been in awe of you and all your sisters. You all are smart, and none of you take any shit. That's a good thing in my book."

"You're still dodging the question! When did you get together?"

"Well, that day at Starbucks, I went over to her table and asked her if she wanted a coffee. I've since discovered when your sister is concentrating on something, boy, she really concentrates! At first, she just looked at me, almost like she didn't recognize me, but then smiled and said she would love a fresh coffee. Anyway, we sat there and talked for over an hour. When I finally got up the nerve to ask her if she'd like to go out some time, she looked at me, shook her head, and said it took me long enough to ask her! The rest is history."

"History, my ass. That was a bland recital of what I'm sure were some exciting dates. I guess I'll have to get all my info from my main source, my little sister!"

CHAPTER FORTY-TWO

ROSIE PULLED INTO HER GARAGE, turned the car off, and reached into the back seat to get her yoga mat and towel. She had just come from her 8:00 a.m. class with Audrey, after which she had told Rachel the latest update on the Gaynors.

"I mean, we are talking one sick, twisted individual. Oh my God, when I think of what could have happened . . ." Rachel had just shuddered and gave Rosie a hug. "It's too horrible to even contemplate. What makes some people become so evil? I am trying to be a good person, but I must admit, I'm glad they're both dead. Thank God everybody is safe."

"And I haven't told you the good news. Guess who Amy is going out with!"

When Rosie walked through the door into the kitchen, she just started laughing. There were three floor-to-ceiling windows looking out to the backyard, and when the sun hit just right, the windows put out three perfect four-by-six blocks of sunlight. The dogs all vied to be the only one laying the sun, but always ended side by side and laying nose to rear end.

Marilyn was in the first block of sunlight with her back to Big Shirley and Walter. Big Shirley was in the next block, facing Marilyn with her face snuggled right up into Marilyn's backside. Rosie couldn't believe Marilyn was allowing this, because usually she would give BS a dog look translating to, "I can't even believe you have the nerve to get close to me. Hanging out with Newfoundlands is not something I do!" Walter, as usual, looked like an idiot. He was laying on his side with his two front paws pulled up tight to his chest, but his head was stretched out as far as it would go—and yes, it was in BS's butt.

What happened to a dog's fantastic sense of smell? Or maybe that certain aroma is to them what a nice lavender-vanilla scent is to us, Rosie thought. *I will never know, I guess, and I'm okay with not knowing!*

After Rosie showered and rinsed off her yoga mat, she stopped by the kitchen to get some water and came out into the living room. The living room had a rather odd configuration, but it worked perfectly for Rosie's new office. Her original office had been the guest bedroom, and Rosie had always felt a little claustrophobic when she worked in there. She'd wanted something different to focus on when she needed some inspiration (which was often) to kick-start some new ideas in her brain. She had a few posters on the wall from Walt Whitman and Audrey Hepburn that declared: "Keep your face always toward the sunshine, and shadows will fall behind you," or "Nothing is impossible. The word itself says, 'I'm possible.'" These quotes had lost their luster a long time ago.

She'd decided she needed a whole new room, and the little alcove off the living room had turned out to be the perfect place. The big bay window was situated sideways, so it looked out into the street and at the house next door to them. While there usually wasn't a whole lot of activity outside, there was enough to keep Rosie entertained when she needed a break from staring at her computer screen.

And entertained she was by the goings-on in the house next door. Aaron and Vlad had moved into the house about six months ago. They had an adorable eleven-month-old baby boy named Whitley, and their two Pomeranians were always up to something in the backyard. Surprisingly for two yip-yip dogs, Rosie rarely heard them bark.

Aaron was a lawyer, and since he owned his own law firm, he could also be a stay-at-home dad who was able to work around Whitley's schedule. Vlad was a human resource manager at one of the top tech firms in the city, so he had the typical nine-to-five job. Rosie and Ren really got a kick out of the new family, and already they had established a routine of meeting for a happy hour drink on Friday nights.

Rosie still chuckled when she remembered the first time the Pomeranians saw BS, Walter, and Marilyn. Aaron and Vlad had lived there about a week. Rosie had been sitting at her desk, encouraged because she had written about two thousand words already and it was only nine a.m. There were times when it would take her days to write that many words—although, to be honest, writing the words was not the issue. Not deleting the words after she reread them was the issue. She kept telling herself to just get the words on paper and she could revamp later, but telling herself was one thing and doing it was another.

That September morning had been beautiful. It had rained the night before, so everything had looked fresh and clean. The back door had been open, and Rosie heard the dogs go out to the backyard. She always knew when the dogs went out because even though Walter had figured out *how* to go through the mesh, he had not figured out how to do it *quietly*. He thought that unless he charged the door like it was a flapping red cape and he was a bull, then he would not make it out alive. Needless to say, he made quite a bit of noise going out into the yard.

Rosie had seen the Poms (named David and Goliath, which was a hoot since they maybe weighed fifteen pounds between the two of them) slip out their doggie door and go into the back yard to do their business. Suddenly, both Poms had stopped what they were doing and turned in unison toward Rosie's back yard. Because she could see her dogs at the wrought iron fence, Rosie had figured David and Goliath were about to go crazy with the barking, but instead it had been as if they were frozen. They'd just stood and stared at her dogs. Rosie had told Ren later that evening, "I swear to God, their eyes sort of bulged out, almost like they could not even begin to process dogs could be that big!"

Marilyn, as was her wont, had just looked at them and turned away. BS and Walter had been intrigued, though, and they'd pushed their noses as far as they could go through the opening between the bars. Rosie had expected the Poms to at least come a bit closer to smell Big Shirley and Walter, but they were having none of it. It was as if they'd both been thinking the same thing, "This is just like the T-Rex in *Jurassic Park*. Don't move a muscle!"

What Rosie found even more hilarious was that the Poms still did this whenever all the dogs were out in their respective back yards, even after all the dogs had been introduced to each other in a controlled environment and were now seeing each other several times a day. Getting the dogs together was one of the first things Rosie and Ren had suggested after Aaron and Vlad moved in.

For one thing, Rosie did not want to get off on the wrong foot with them. The last people to own the house had not been dog people, and they'd made it quite clear they had no intention of becoming fun neighbors together. Which was okay by Rosie since she hadn't been fond of them either. But with new people living next door, Rosie wanted to start the relationship out right. And she really wanted them to know that the dogs, for all their size, were gentle and very unaggressive.

Rosie and Ren had invited Aaron, Vlad, and Whitley over for an introductory get-together about two weeks after they had moved in. Rosie had also invited Lily and Keith, plus Luke, Lacey, Claudia. Dogs, babies—everyone was invited. Rosie had known they'd scored a home run with the new neighbors when the first thing Vlad had done when he got to the living room was to get down on the ground with BS and Walter and play with them. The Poms and Marilyn had stood on the sidelines with identical expressions on their doggie faces. "WTF?"

CHAPTER FORTY-THREE

ROSIE WAS OUT IN FRONT watering the lantanas she had planted a couple of weeks ago. She was ambivalent about the lantanas. There were other flowers she thought were prettier, but having lived in Texas most of her life and in neighborhoods with plenty of green space where deer lived, she knew the lantanas were about the only thing deer didn't eat. She'd also planted some Pride of Barbados plants, and so far, they were holding on.

"Those are very pretty flowers. What kind are they?"

Rosie turned. An older woman stood on the sidewalk in front of Rosie's house. She had on one of those roll-up straw sun visors with a very wide brim. She had short spiky gray hair that stuck up through the opening of the hat, and a pair of oversized aviator sunglasses completed the look. A small, elderly golden retriever flopped down at the woman's feet as soon as she stopped walking.

Rosie shut off the hose. "Thank you! They're lantanas. I take it you're not from Texas. Down here, we know these are the only kind of flower the deer won't eat."

"So that's why you see these in almost every yard in the neighborhood. I wondered about that. And you're right. I just moved here from Arkansas a few months ago. My apartment complex was too close to a busy highway, so I never saw any deer."

"You'll learn fast that if you don't want to throw your money away, you only plant these out front. All the other gorgeous flowers need to be in backyards, behind fences!"

"I will remember that. Come on, Evie. Let's finish our walk. Have a great day! And thanks for the advice!"

"Anytime."

Rosie would see the woman a couple of times a week walking her dog in the neighborhood. She always had on her visor and sunglasses, and Rosie would go back and forth trying to guess her age. Originally, Rosie had her pegged as middle-aged, mainly because of the gray hair and the rather frumpy way she had of dressing. The capri pants with white bobby socks and white tennis shoes felt like a dead giveaway to someone's advanced age, but Rosie had to admit she just wasn't a fan of the style, and it really had nothing to do with how old someone was.

You can have bad fashion sense at any age, she thought. All Rosie had to do was call Gwyneth to mind. Every day was a fashion *don't* when Gwyneth walked into the newsroom.

A couple of weeks later, Rosie was out again watering her flowers when the visor lady (that was how Rosie thought of her) came by with Evie. Once again, she stopped, and once again, Evie flopped down like her legs just would not carry her any farther.

"I took your advice and planted some of those flowers. No deer have eaten them yet, so that's good! My name is Cheryl, by the way, and this lazy dog is Evie."

"Nice to meet you. Hello, Evie. Can I pet her?" Rosie walked over and put her hand down for Evie to smell, and when her tail started wagging, Rosie ran her hand over her head. "Who's a pretty girl, hm? Yes, you are! Such a good girl."

"She's been such a joy. I adopted her when I moved down here.

I figured we could be the two old ladies in the neighborhood!"

"I think as long as you are out and about, then age is just a number. I'm Rosie, and I'm the proud owner of the two Great Danes and the Newfoundland you might have seen."

"Oh my gosh! I have seen you and your husband walking them. They're beautiful animals, but I must admit they would be too big for me. But they seem very well trained."

Rosie chose to ignore the husband part. "Yeah, having those big guys requires a fair amount of training. Although both those breeds are known for being gentle and laid-back. They can scare people because of their size."

"I certainly can see that. Well, Rosie, I will let you get back to watering. I think this one wants to get home and take a nap. It was nice talking to you."

"Have a good one."

Cheryl and Rosie usually chatted about once a week. Cheryl was open about her life, to the extent that there had been a few times Rosie wished she weren't quite so open. One of the first things Cheryl had told Rosie was that her son had recently died, and his death had been one of the reasons she'd left Arkansas and come to Texas. She said everything in Arkansas reminded her of her son, and she'd needed a fresh start. She never mentioned a husband, and the only time Rosie had broached the subject, Cheryl just threw her hands up and said he'd been dead for years.

After a while, Rosie would deliberately wait until Cheryl and Evie had passed by the house before she went out to do yard work or go on a walk of her own. It wasn't that she didn't like Cheryl, and she did feel sorry for her, but the conversations were the same every time. The weather first, then the dogs, then somehow Cheryl would manage to bring the conversation back around to her dead son. Rosie never knew what to say, though Cheryl never seemed to be looking for a response.

Rosie had talked about it with Ren, and he'd said that was probably her way of working through her grief. Besides, it sounded like she didn't have a whole lot of people to talk to. "Fine then. I'll send her your way, and she can talk to you about her problems!"

"How did her son die? Does she give you any specifics?"

"That's part of why this is getting so weird. I could swear the first time she talked about him, she told me he died of cancer, but just last week, she mumbled something about a car wreck. I really don't want to get too far into the weeds with her about her son. I feel awful for her—or for anybody, for that matter, who loses a child. But you can only say 'How terrible' or 'I am so sorry' so many times before it gets a little redundant and, well, creepy. It doesn't sound like she has any family or friends. The one time I asked if she had siblings, her response was almost the same as when I asked her about a husband. Like they are all in the past. So, I guess I'll continue to scout out the street to make sure she isn't around before I go out in front, and make you water the plants on the weekends!"

CHAPTER FORTY-FOUR

ROSIE HAD SUCCESSFULLY EVADED Cheryl for about three weeks and was hoping she was taking a different route for her walks, or perhaps had finally found someone else to talk to, when she looked out her window and saw Cheryl walking down the sidewalk in front of Aaron and Vlad's house. It took Rosie a minute to notice that something was different.

First, Cheryl didn't have Evie with her. Rosie had never seen her without her dog. Second, Cheryl was walking . . . oddly. Rosie's first thought was that she was drunk. She was walking like she was having trouble putting one foot in front of the other, and there was a weird sway to her gait. It was also the first time Rosie had seen her without her visor, but there was no mistaking the spiky gray hair and her capris and tennis shoes.

Suddenly, she put one hand on her chest and stretched her other hand out to grab the tree near her. Her knees started to buckle but she caught herself before she fell to the sidewalk.

Oh shit, she's going down. Rosie ran out of the house and over to where Cheryl was still gripping the tree trunk and weakly massaging her chest. "Cheryl, Cheryl, are you okay? Do you feel faint? Are you having chest pain? Do you feel like you're going to pass out?"

Rosie put her arm around her to steady her. Cheryl shook her head no.

"Hey, I really need you to tell me what's wrong, if you hurt somewhere. Let's just sit down here on the grass and talk about it." Rosie was afraid that if Cheryl fainted, she wouldn't be able to prevent her from taking a bad tumble. Cheryl probably outweighed Rosie by about forty pounds and was a couple of inches taller. She figured if she could at least get her to sit on the grass, then if she did faint, she wouldn't fall face first onto the concrete sidewalk. And she wouldn't take Rosie with her.

Rosie grabbed Cheryl around her waist and slowly lowered her to the ground. Rosie had left her phone back in her office, so she looked around the street to see if anyone else was out. Of course, no such luck. "Cheryl, do you have a cell phone on you? I don't have mine, and I really think we need to call for help."

Cheryl continued to just shake her head back and forth. Rosie bent farther over to peer up into Cheryl's face. Her eyes were scrunched shut, and she seemed be mumbling something over and over, but Rosie couldn't make out the words.

Her color was surprisingly good. Rosie thought for sure she would be the color of day-old oatmeal. Rosie still had her hand on Cheryl's arm, and she noticed the skin was warm and dry. Rosie had never forgotten the film she saw when taking a first aid class that described what happened when someone was having a heart attack. The pictures of the heart attack victims showed them to be pale, sweaty, and clammy. Cheryl, however, was looking nothing like that. *So maybe it's not her heart.*

"Cheryl, you must talk to me. I can't help you if I don't know what's going on. What are you saying? I can't understand what you're saying. Okay, I am going to go get my phone. Just sit here against this tree and wait for me to get back. I promise to hurry."

Just as Rosie started to get up from the grass, Cheryl grabbed her arm. "No. Please. Just please sit here with me. I—I think I'm starting to feel better." She continued to rub her chest, though, and she still wouldn't open her eyes and look at Rosie.

"But Cheryl, I think you need some medical help. You almost fell, and you keep rubbing your chest like it hurts. I think someone needs to look at you."

Cheryl gripped Rosie's arm tighter and slowly raised her head. She opened her eyes, turned toward Rosie, and just stared at her. There was no mistaking the hate and malice in her eyes.

Rosie gasped. "Cheryl, why are you looking at me that way? What the hell is wrong with you?"

Cheryl didn't answer. She just kept staring at Rosie. Her left hand was still tightly gripping Rosie's arm, and her right hand went into the front pocket of her sweatshirt. She slowly pulled out a small handgun and pointed it at Rosie's stomach.

Rosie went cold all over. "What the fuck, Cheryl! What is going on? What are you doing?" Rosie tried to stand up, but Cheryl kept yanking at her arm, keeping her off balance.

In a cold, hard voice, Cheryl hissed, "Shut up, bitch. Just shut up or I swear I will shoot you. And let me tell you, nothing would make me happier than to put a couple of bullets in you. Maybe one in your knee and one in your stomach. I'm a very good shot, but even if I weren't, there's no way I could miss at this close range."

All Rosie could do was gape at her. None of this made any sense. It was as if a small gentle kitten had suddenly turned into a snarling tiger that was looking, for all intents and purposes, like it was going to pounce and eat her at any minute. "What? I—"

"I just told you to shut the hell up. I am done with talking. I don't want to hear your voice." Cheryl continued to hold tight to Rosie's arm, her voice low, controlled, and full of hate. "You need to do exactly what I tell you to do. And quit looking at Aaron's house. Do you think I'm stupid? Huh? I made sure they were going to be out of town. Jesus. Look at you. What did he ever see in you? You're just a stupid, small-town whore. You'll probably thank me for putting you out of your misery."

"He? Who's he?"

"If you're lucky, maybe I'll tell you all about it before I put a bullet in you. This is what we are going to do. You are going to stand up. Don't even think about running or screaming. If you do, I will shoot you. Won't shoot to kill, but it'll put you down. Maybe I'll shoot you in the back and paralyze you. Then I'll walk into your house and put a bullet in the heads of those three ugly dogs you're so proud of. And then guess what? The next person I shoot will be your oh-so-precious vet. And I'll go down the line. Your sisters. Your father. Your nieces and nephews. I know where everybody lives. Hell, I'll shoot their dogs too. And you won't be able to stop it. You'll just lay there knowing I am completely destroying your world. Just like you did mine."

Rosie felt like she was frozen. She heard the horrible words coming from Cheryl's mouth but was still not comprehending them. The visor lady? Owner of the gentle, lazy golden? With a gun threatening to shoot everyone she loved? Saying Rosie had destroyed her world? While none of this was making any sense, Rosie had no doubt Cheryl would do exactly what she'd promised if Rosie didn't do what she wanted.

"Now act like you're helping an old lady get up. Once we're standing, you're going to help me walk to that black car there."

Cheryl pointed to a car parked three houses up from Rosie's house. "You're going to get into the driver's seat and stay there while I get into the passenger side. And make no mistake about this. I will do exactly what I promised to do to you and your family if you don't do what I say. I can see you thinking that you can outrun me. Which is true, but you can't outrun a bullet. So let's go."

Rosie didn't know how she managed to stand up, but she did. Her legs were shaking, her teeth were chattering, and now she felt like *she* was going to throw up or faint. It was finally dawning on Rosie that Cheryl was dead serious about taking her someplace at gunpoint, but the idea was still so ludicrous that she could not form a single coherent thought in her head. Run. Stay. Walk. Scream. Faint. Puke. Get the gun. Wish she had never looked out her window this morning.

"Where are you taking me? And can you please tell me why?"

Rosie and Cheryl walked side by side to the car. Anyone looking at them would think that Rosie was helping Cheryl, but in reality, Cheryl had a strong grip on Rosie's arm and the gun was jammed painfully into Rosie's side.

Rosie knew the gun was a SIG Sauer P238 because it was exactly like her gun, which was, unfortunately, locked up in her gun case in the bedroom. Rosie had kept her gun on her person when everything was happening with the family, but since they'd gotten word that Lance was dead, she'd gone back to keeping it in the locker. She had a brief fantasy that she had her gun in her pocket and could blow Cheryl away. If only.

"Remember my promise, bitch. I am very sure you wouldn't want to live in this world knowing you were responsible for the deaths of your whole family. Oh no, here come the tears. I'm sure next you'll start begging, but it won't help, so save your breath."

Rosie was trying to hold back the tears but to no avail. "Cheryl, please—"

"Stop calling me Cheryl. I hate that name!" Cheryl barked out the words. She took a deep breath and expelled it forcefully. "Hate, hate, hate that name. It was *her* name, and the only reason I said it was mine was because I figured *she* would wear these stupid clothes. And would walk around like an old lady with a good-for-nothing dog. Now quit fucking around and get in the driver's seat before I really lose my temper. And you don't want to be around me when I do."

Rosie was standing by the open door on the driver's side. Everything in her was telling her not to get into the car, that she would be doomed if she got into the car, but she kept hearing Cheryl's—or whoever the hell she was—words in her head describing in detail what she would do to her family, and she had absolutely no doubt this horrible, wicked woman would do precisely what she'd said. And that was something Rosie could never let happen. She took a jagged breath, looked one last time at her house, and got into the driver's seat.

"Where am I supposed to drive to?" Rosie had her hands at the ten and two positions on the steering wheel, using the wheel to ground herself. She was gripping it tightly with both hands because she knew if she let go, she would launch herself at Cheryl. There was a rage building inside her. A rage directed at this woman who she didn't even know, but who seemed to know everything about her.

Cheryl settled herself into the passenger seat and turned toward Rosie, dangling the car keys. She smiled her cold, dark smile at Rosie. "Well, I'm not sure exactly where I want to go to first. I was thinking maybe we could take a drive down memory lane and talk about old times."

Rosie gripped the steering wheel even tighter. "I really think you have me confused with someone else. I don't know you. The first time I laid eyes on you was about two months ago when you walked down my street and asked me about flowers. I mean, can you let me in on your secret? How do you even know me? And if your name isn't Cheryl, then what is it?"

"You can call me Martha."

CHAPTER FORTY-FIVE

"MARTHA? MARTHA? I-I don't know anyone named Mar—" Rosie stopped in mid-sentence. A cold chill shot up her spine. She could hear Danny's voice in her head describing letters they had found on Lance's computer: *The police found evidence that Lance had had a serious issue with the Hurley family, but especially with you. He blamed you for Steve's death and decided he was going to hurt or kill one or all your sisters, just so you would know what it felt like to lose a sibling. The police found evidence of this in a paper trail Lance left on his computer. Lance wasn't much into email, but when the officers accessed his Notes, they found a treasure trove of letters Lance wrote to a person named Martha, letters that described, in sickening detail, what Lance had planned for your sisters.*

"Who in the hell are you? If you're Martha, how are you involved in this? What are you to Lance? How do you know everything about my family?"

Martha threw the car keys at Rosie. "Pick those up and start driving. I'll tell you where to go. I might fill you in. Or maybe I'll just kill you, and you can go to hell still wondering. When are you going to get it through your thick skull that it makes no difference to me what you do or don't know? You ruined my life, and now, you are going to pay." Martha pointed the gun at Rosie's midsection. "Just go. DRIVE!"

With trembling hands, Rosie put her seat belt on and picked

up the car keys that were on the console between them. She put the keys in the ignition and started the car. She could feel the hot prick of tears behind her eyes, but she sensed the only way she was going to get through this alive was to keep Martha talking and then maybe—*God, please just maybe*—something would happen that would allow her to get the gun away from Martha.

Rosie was thinking furiously, still trying to come up with something, anything, that could change this nightmarish scene when she pulled away from the curb. She thought about just accelerating and running the car into something big enough to stop them, but unfortunately, they lived in a newer part of the neighborhood, and most of the trees were still only saplings. Besides, Martha had put her seat belt on when Rosie did.

Martha sneered at her. "I'm not stupid. You need to remember that. I saw the movie where the good guy put on his seat belt and floored it, and the bad guy went through the windshield. Not going to happen here, honey. In case you haven't figured it out yet, I really don't care if I live or die. My life is already over. It's your fault my life is over. You took away everything I loved. And now I'll do the same to you."

Rosie started driving slowly down the street, and for the next thirty minutes, the only sound in the car was Martha's terse commands.

"Turn left here."

"Go straight through the stoplight."

"Go right at the next stop sign."

"Pull in here. On the right."

At first, Rosie couldn't see where there was even a road to turn into. They were on a two-lane road that Rosie had never been on. She hadn't seen one other car in the last fifteen minutes. She slowed down and then saw a very small trail, hardly even a road. "You want me to turn here? There's no space."

"Yes. Just do it. Turn here."

Rosie eased the car onto the small path and slowly moved forward. Branches slapped at the windshield and scraped the sides of the car, but Martha appeared unconcerned. She never once took her eyes off Rosie, as if she knew Rosie would try to escape if she turned away. And Rosie would have, if she thought she could get away with it. It was all Rosie could do to resist grabbing the door handle and hurling herself out the door. She might have tried it if she didn't have her seat belt on. The creepy way Martha was staring at her told Rosie she would never be able to get the seat belt off before Martha shot her. And Rosie had no doubt that was exactly what she would do.

"Stop."

They pulled into a small yard overgrown with weeds and scattered with trash, old tires, discarded yard equipment, and a rusted-out shell of a car. It was the setting of every scary Halloween movie, down to the small cabin complete with broken glass in the windows and a sagging porch with holes scattered throughout the wood. The only thing missing was a man in a mask holding a bloody chainsaw. *The Texas Chainsaw Massacre Part 2.*

"Turn off the car and get out." Martha hissed the words and gave a small, triumphant laugh. "Not so high and mighty now, are you, missy? The Hurley name can't help you out here. I bet you're just ready to piss yourself, you're so scared. Get moving."

Rosie unbuckled her seat belt. She slowly turned her head and looked at Martha. "I see the resemblance now. I should have seen it earlier. Steve always had that exact look when he thought he was the smartest person in the room. Because he always thought he was better than everyone else. Even though he never was."

"You shut the hell up. You know *nothing* about my boy. NOTHING. My boy who *you* killed. He would still be here today if he hadn't taken up with a bitch like you. Now, I am serious. Either get out now or eat a bullet. Your choice."

Rosie opened her door and stepped out. It had only been about an hour, but she felt like she had been living in this nightmare forever. She knew she was going to have to think of something to save herself; otherwise, she was going to die here. The trouble was, what could she do? Martha handled the gun with ease, which told Rosie she knew how to shoot. The very thought of running and waiting for a bullet to tear into her was terrifying.

Somehow, she needed to get the gun away from Martha. That meant she needed to distract her. Rosie doubted she could take her on one-on-one. Even though Martha was older, she outweighed Rosie and, unfortunately, looked like she was still in pretty good shape.

She needed to come up with another plan that didn't involve practically arm-wrestling Martha. She took a deep breath and almost gagged. Even the air surrounding this hellish house and its grounds stunk. It was like the entire property was composed of dead or dying things.

"Pick up that sack in the back seat. And quit taking all day. The calvary is not going to come to save you."

Rosie opened the door and reached in to grab the paper sack sitting on the back seat. She noticed there were two bottles of wine, two glasses, and what looked like five or six framed photos face down in the bag. *Jesus. Can this get any more fucked up?* Rosie thought to herself. *Does she think we're going to have a party? Exchange gossip and recipes? Think, Rosie. Try to come up with some sort of a plan!*

"Bring the sack into the house and set it on the table."

Rosie gingerly stepped up the stairs, doing what she could to avoid the holes in the porch. She could hear Martha breathing behind her and knew the barrel of the gun was pointed at her back. The door creaked eerily when she pulled it open, and Rosie braced herself for what she could only imagine would be a nightmarish scene. Couches with the stuffing coming out, mouse droppings everywhere, the table where the termites had eaten away part of the legs so it would be tilted to one side, a dirty and rusted out sink—and Rosie's mind couldn't even go to the bathroom.

But instead, surprisingly, the inside of the cabin was, if not clean, at least livable. There was a new table that had four chairs placed around it. The floor had been swept recently. Instead of a couch, there were two chairs placed side by side facing a small, clean coffee table. Even the sink looked like it had been rinsed out recently.

"Home away from home. Does it meet your approval? Not that I give a shit, but I'm trying to be a good hostess. Now put that sack on the table."

Rosie walked to the middle of the room and placed the sack down. Just as she was about to turn, Martha grabbed her arm, spun her around, and roughly shoved her into one of the chairs at the table. Before she could even react, Rosie felt a circle of cold steel around her right wrist and heard the *click* of the handcuff as Martha fastened it to the leg of the table. Rosie's initial reaction was to jump up and try to pull her arm away, but the chain of the handcuff yanked her back down. To her dismay, the table did not even move when she pulled on the cuff. She looked down and saw the table had been bolted to the floor. Rosie pulled again at the handcuff, but the table didn't move.

"Yes, I've been planning this for quite a while. Let's both sit down and get comfortable. We have a lot to talk about, starting with how you ruined my life." Martha dropped the gun into her purse that sat on the floor by her chair. "Don't think I'll be needing that right now—you're not going anywhere for the time being. So, do you want a glass of wine?"

Rosie's gut reaction was to accept and then throw the wine in Martha's face, but instead she said "*What?* No, I don't want any wine. Martha, like I told you before, I really don't know what you want me to say." Rosie could no longer hold back tears. "If you think I did something wrong, then I am so sorry, but I didn't—"

"Stop. Just stop right there. I don't want to hear any excuses. Because of you, my Stevie is dead, my Lance is dead. Now, in my mind, you need to pay for that. Because you just went on with your charmed life while I— Oh, you make me so mad!" Martha literally gripped both sides of her head and squeezed. "Okay, Martha, get a grip. Let's lay out all my evidence. Where did I put those pictures? Oh, here they are." At this point, Martha was just talking to herself. She pulled the framed photos out of the grocery sack, along with the wine. "Are you sure you don't want any wine? I'm going to have some. I know it must be five o'clock somewhere, as they say."

Rosie watched with dread and fascination as Martha segued from glaring at Rosie and threatening to kill her to offering her a glass of wine like they were at a girls' happy hour. And Rosie wasn't sure which Martha she should appeal to. Mad, angry Martha was bad enough, but simpering, smiley Martha was just downright twisted. *Where, oh where, is my knight in shining armor? Where is Ren? What am I going to do? I don't want to die in this cabin. Why did I ever go out to help the bitch?*

CHAPTER FORTY-SIX

ROSIE DECIDED her best course of action was to not say anything to antagonize Martha, so she kept quiet and watched as Martha poured herself a glass of wine, swirled it in the glass a few times, and inhaled the scent as if she were at a wine tasting in Napa Valley, for God's sake. Rosie watched incredulously as Martha downed one glass, then two, then three, then the entire bottle of wine, all the while making occasional comments to Rosie, mostly having to do with how Rosie had ruined her family.

"Stevie would still be alive today if you hadn't pushed your way into his life."

"I just know Stevie wanted to get rid of you, but he probably felt sorry for you."

"You think you are so great, but Stevie thought you were stupid."

Martha had pulled a stack of framed photos out of the sack and was lining them up on the table facing Rosie. The first one was of two boys, about nine and ten, wearing identical sweatshirts declaring, "We won our football league!" Rosie recognized the older boy as Steve, so she assumed the younger one was Lance.

The next photograph was of the same two boys, around the same ages, posing with people Rosie could only guess were their mother and father. The woman in the photo was not Martha.

Martha appeared in the next two photos though, holding Steve in one photo and Lance in the other. It was hard to tell their exact ages, but they looked to be around five and six. Rosie assumed the photos had been taken the same day—both taken in front of the same Christmas tree, Martha wearing the same outfit.

The final picture was of the couple Rosie assumed to be the parents, obviously taken on their wedding day. The woman was in a wedding gown, and the man had a black tuxedo on. They were posing cheek to cheek, and together they were holding a knife, getting ready to cut into the wedding cake. Rosie thought the man looked quite a bit like Steve, but again, the woman was definitely not Martha.

"My boys were the best-looking kids in their class." Martha was gazing at the pictures where she was holding each boy in front of the Christmas tree. Rosie thought she saw tears form in her eyes, and Rosie felt an unexpected jolt of sympathy for her. Of course, that sympathetic feeling disappeared when Martha, once again dry-eyed, looked at Rosie with true hatred. "You destroyed my boys, and you have destroyed me. It's only fair that I destroy you." She reached down into her purse and pulled out the gun. She raised it and pointed it at Rosie.

"Wait. Wait, Martha, please. *Please!* I . . . um . . . I have something to tell you." Rosie was desperately trying to think of something, anything, to say to Martha so she wouldn't shoot. "Something about Steve that I know you'll want to know. Something he told me about. Things he talked a lot about. He talked about you, you know, and what you meant to him. And Lance. He talked a lot about Lance too."

Rosie held her breath and looked at Martha to see if her words had made any difference. Because she knew, deep down, if they didn't, then Martha was going to pull the trigger and her life would be over.

Rosie had never been so frightened in her life. She started to cry, and under her breath, she started saying the Hail Mary. She wanted to break eye contact with Martha—looking into her cold, flat eyes made her even more scared—but she found that she couldn't. It was like she was hypnotized.

For an agonizing moment, Rosie thought her words hadn't penetrated. That Martha was going to pull the trigger, no matter what she said. When she saw Martha's hand that held the gun slowly lower, Rosie thought she was going to pass out or throw up. She took a couple of very shaky breaths and slowly let them out.

"Okay, missy, you bought yourself a little bit of time. Spill it. What did my Stevie say about me?" Martha poured herself yet another glass of wine from the new bottle. Even as frightened as Rosie was, because she was sure Martha was going to blow her face off any minute, she still couldn't help but marvel at the amount of alcohol Martha was putting away, seemingly without any effects either. No slurring her words, no unsteadiness in her hands or feet, no disjointed conversations. Just cold, flat shark eyes and a steadfast grip on her gun.

"Okay. I will. But can you clear something up for me? Steve told me his parents were killed in a car crash right around Christmas when he was in his late teens. I'm confused. I mean, well, if you're here, then what happened?"

At first, Rosie didn't think Martha was going to respond. Finally, Martha said, "Well, I guess I can tell you about it, especially since you won't live long enough to tell anyone else." Again, she stopped, as if she was waging an internal debate with herself. "I'm not really their mother. But I should have been, and I would have been if not for my sister." Martha spit those words out. "My sister, Cheryl. Perfect, perfect, perfect Cheryl. God, how I hated her." Martha picked up the picture of the bride and groom and stared at it intently. "Perfect Cheryl. Thought she could have whoever she wanted, no matter that *he* was supposed to love someone else. No matter that *he* was supposed to belong to someone else. She always thought only of herself. *Always* herself. *Always* herself. *Never* me. *Never* me. NOT ONCE. NOT ONCE. NOT ONCE!" Martha banged the framed photo against the table, shattering the frame. She yanked the picture out and began tearing it into little pieces, the entire time muttering, "Not once," over and over and over.

Rosie went perfectly still. She sensed if Martha turned her anger to her now, it could be deadly.

After about five minutes, Martha seemed to calm down. She was still looking down at her lap, where all the torn pieces of the picture had ended up, but at least she was no longer saying those words with such fury, with such anger—and yes, with such hurt. It was so painful to watch her, and Rosie again felt a stab of sympathy.

"You were in love with Steve and Lance's dad?" Rosie asked softly. "And he loved you?"

Martha didn't answer. She continued to stare into her lap and roll the small pieces of the torn-up picture into balls, dropping them on the floor. "It's the tale as old as time, really." Martha snorted and shook her head. "Older sister, not as pretty, not as popular, finally gets the attention of the guy of her dreams. We met in college, you see."

Martha looked up from her lap, but Rosie could tell she really wasn't seeing Rosie or the inside of the broken-down cabin in the woods. She was back in the heady days of first love. Back when anything was possible. Back when you felt like if you didn't spend every single minute with him, then your life would be over.

"I never really had any boyfriends in high school. Even though Cheryl was three years younger than me, boys always seemed to want to be with her, not me. I tried so hard. I really did. I just didn't know what to do. But they either laughed at me or just ignored me. I actually preferred being laughed at, as weird as that sounds. At least they were seeing me. And I would try to talk to Cheryl. I would ask her to tell me what I should be doing different—I never knew what exactly was wrong with me—but she never had time for me. Did I tell you she was very popular? Always had a bunch of friends around. She just didn't have any time for me." Martha focused on Rosie, and her face was such a naked picture of hurt, puzzlement, longing, and grief that Rosie's breath caught in her throat.

"Oh, Martha. That must have been very painful. I am so sorry."

"His name was Gabriel, but he went by Gabe. And he was tall, and so handsome, and everybody knew him. He was on the baseball team—he was the pitcher, of course—and he told me, the first time he saw me, he thought I was the prettiest girl he had ever seen." Martha was smiling, lost in her yesteryear when life had been perfect. "Can you imagine that? He said I was pretty. No one had ever told me that before. I would go sit in the stands while they practiced and pretend to do my homework. But I wasn't doing any homework. I was watching Gabe because the first time

I saw him, I knew he was the one for me. And then when he told me I was pretty, I knew right away our life together was going to be perfect. We would get married, have two darling little boys, never fight or fuss with each other, and grow old together. And it would have been exactly like that. If it wasn't for *her*."

CHAPTER FORTY-SEVEN

REN PARKED HIS CAR in the driveway and reached over to grab the two Whataburger hamburger sacks. Rosie had been craving a jalapeño cheese Whataburger with mustard and pickles, and since she rarely ate meat, Ren was keeping his fingers crossed this meant what he thought it meant. He didn't want to read too much into it, though. They had only discussed babies once before—and besides, it seemed to Ren that everyone in Texas craved a Whataburger at some point or another.

Ren was a Winstead's man himself—the iconic hamburger joint had opened on the Country Club Plaza in Kansas City, Missouri, in 1940—but slowly, Whataburger was winning him over. Mainly because Whataburger was here, and Winstead's was not. Ren was a "bird in one hand was worth two in the bush" kind of guy.

When Ren came around to the front of the house, he was holding the Whataburger sacks behind him so Rosie couldn't see them. Her office desk looked out onto the street through their big picture window, and Ren knew she would be sitting there working on her novel.

Lately, she had been re-energized about the direction her book was going in. She'd told Ren it was like a key had finally turned in her head and she could envision the storyline, and better yet, the ending. Of course, she was a long way from that, she would hasten to tell Ren, but just having a basic outline and being able to flesh out most of the characters was enough to get her to plant her butt in the chair for most hours of the day. She still had times when staring at the blank screen was enough to make her crazy, but at least those times were the exception now and not the rule like in the early days of her writing career.

Ren was surprised to see Rosie wasn't at her desk. *Well, maybe she's peeing or something,* he thought. *Or, most likely, she's playing with the dogs.* The dogs were the one thing that could entice Rosie from her computer. Laying with all three of the dogs in the sun and laughing at their different personalities was a highlight of her day. Walter was the most eager to please. Wherever Rosie would lay, he would scooch over to lay beside her. Big Shirley would then have to try to crowd him out, determined to be the closest to Rosie, and, of course, Marilyn stared at them like they were on drugs.

Ren was walking up to the front door and pulling his house keys out of his pocket when he noticed the front door was slightly ajar. *That's odd.* Since they'd heard the news about Lance dying in prison, both Rosie and Ren had relaxed their heightened vigilance, but not enough that Rosie would leave the front door open. While it was true she no longer walked around the house with her gun in her pocket, she'd admitted to Ren that she still felt uneasy. She said she was amazed at how simple it was for Lance to gather all the information about her family and how easy it was to use that information to terrorize them.

"Rosie? Hey, babe, where are you?" Ren pushed open the front door and walked into the living room. Everything looked just like it had when he'd left that morning. All three dogs were lying in their respective places, and Walter was the only one who even opened his eyes.

"Rosie?" Ren walked into the kitchen. No Rosie. Into the bathroom. No Rosie. Into their bedroom. No Rosie. "What the hell is going on? Where are you, babe?"

Ren opened the door going out to the garage, expecting to see her car gone. Maybe she had run to the store. Instead, her Cadillac SUV was in its usual place. He walked over and put his hand on the hood, mainly because that was what all the cops did in the shows they watched. *Cold as ice, so she hasn't driven her car this morning. This is starting to freak me out.*

Ren went back into the living room and went over to Rosie's desk. What he saw made his heart sink. Rosie's phone was right next to her computer. No way would she have gone somewhere without it. Even if she'd decided to take a walk, she would have taken her phone and gone out through the garage.

Okay, think this through. She is not in the house. Not in the back-yard. Car is in the garage. Front door was unlocked and ajar. Phone at her desk. What the fuck?

Ren stood there for a minute, looking out on the street. All was quiet. Wait a minute. He grabbed Rosie's phone, punched in the passcode, and brought up the Ring app. They had just installed it last week, and Ren still wasn't too sure how to use it.

What the hell? At 9:18 a.m., a notification had come through about motion at the door. Ren clicked on the video, and sure enough, the camera had picked up Rosie hurrying out the front door. Ren watched her run down their walkway and veer to the left, toward Aaron and Vlad's house. Then she disappeared out of frame. Ren tried expanding the picture, but the angle of the video only showed their front walkway. *Damn it. What were you doing? Who was out there? Where did you go?*

Ren called all the sisters, but no one had heard from Rosie all morning. Not one phone call or text. Jack said the same thing. But they all agreed that Ren should call Danny. It was now 11:45 a.m., and Rosie was nowhere to be found. All the sisters, Jack, and Ren were becoming plenty worried.

CHAPTER FORTY-EIGHT

"I'LL NEVER FORGET the first time I brought Gabe home. It was during spring break, and we had been dating for about five months. Neither one of us had much money, so we couldn't afford to go to some of the fancier places, like Cancun or the Bahamas. Although it was interesting, my parents were able to pay for *her* to go away to some place in Mexico for her senior-year spring break. When I asked my parents why they would pay for her and not me, they said, 'Martha, you're in college now. You don't need to go on spring break. It's Cheryl's last year in high school, and we want to make it special for her.' When I tried to point out they had never paid for a spring break trip for me in high school, had never tried to make anything special for me, they fell back on the same old excuse that Cheryl was the youngest and more sensitive than me. That was their reasoning every single time I tried to point out the inconsistencies in how we were being raised."

Martha was once again in her relaxed, storytelling mood. Gone was the red-faced, angry, bitter person who'd torn up her sister's wedding photo into little pieces. She seemed . . . reflective, like she was enjoying this trip down memory lane.

But Rosie was not at all reassured Martha would remain like that. In just their short time together, Rosie had seen Martha go from zero to sixty in about one second. Rosie figured her only chance of getting out of this situation alive would be to keep Martha calm and relaxed, and for some reason, talking about Gabe seemed to calm her down.

"That must have been very hard on you, Martha. Nobody likes to be treated unfairly. I don't blame you for being upset."

"Hey, would you like some coffee? I'm going to make some."

Rosie again could not help but marvel over Martha's swift mood changes. Just fifteen minutes ago, she'd been pointing a gun in Rosie's face, and now she was offering to make her some coffee? Batshit crazy.

"Actually, that would be nice. And is there any way I could . . . maybe . . . use the bathroom? I really have to go."

"Well, of course. Why didn't you say something earlier?" Martha dug into her front pocket and took out a key. "You'll have to unlock it yourself. And I really would not recommend trying anything stupid. My very reliable friend here is known for never missing a target." She held up the gun and waved it. "Especially not one as close as you are."

It took a bit of maneuvering on Rosie's part, but she finally managed to unlock the handcuff around her right wrist. She sat for a minute at the table, massaging her wrist and shifting her weight from foot to foot. Even though she had only been sitting in the chair for a couple of hours, her legs felt stiff and weak. Rosie slowly got up from the chair.

Martha was standing about six feet away, pointing the gun right at Rosie's chest. "Better hurry up and go, missy, while I'm still in a good mood. And there's no window in the bathroom, so don't think you can jump out and save yourself. Not going to happen, I'm afraid."

Rosie walked across the room and went into the bathroom. Martha was right. There was no window, just a toilet and sink—a surprisingly clean toilet and sink, Rosie was glad to see. She had to go so bad it wouldn't have made any difference, but it was nice just the same.

After she finished, she sat for a moment on the toilet trying to think of any way she could turn this around. But with every idea, from trying to run out the door to trying to physically overcome Martha, the image of the muzzle of the gun with a bullet exploding out toward her let her know she had to think of something else.

She couldn't outrun or overpower a gun. She somehow had to get the gun away from Martha, but she'd already figured out that Martha, unfortunately, knew exactly what she was doing. Martha had mentioned she'd worked as a guard in a federal prison, and Rosie could see she knew guns.

"Come on, come on." Martha rapped on the door. "I've given you plenty of time to do your business. Besides, the coffee's ready."

Okay, Rosie thought. *I just need to keep her talking. Maybe she will pass out from all the wine she's been drinking. And maybe pigs will fly or hell will freeze over. I am going to die in this hellhole.*

"Seriously, girl. Get out here now. I hate drinking a cold cup of coffee."

Rosie slowly opened the bathroom door and stepped out. Martha was again standing about six feet away, far enough away that even if Rosie had been stupid enough to think she could wrestle Martha for the gun, the distance between them was just too great.

"Go to the table. Sit down. You're going to have to handcuff yourself. It's easy—just snap one around your wrist. I'll even be nice and let you decide which wrist you want to use."

"Martha, can we not do the handcuff? I promise—"

"Now. Do what I say. Don't argue. It won't get you anywhere. You'll just make me angry, and you really don't want to do that. Just ask my poor dead sister. She made me angry. And look at where she is now." The look of satisfaction and gloating on Martha's face frightened Rosie more than anything else that had occurred on this totally bizarre day. She was looking at a face that was pure evil.

CHAPTER FORTY-NINE

EVERYONE MET AT REN'S within the hour. Keith and Lilly got there first, mainly because Lilly and Keith were both working from home that day and Keith's mom was already at their house watching the kids. Danny and Amy arrived together (something Lilly filed away in the back of her mind for later), followed shortly after by Jack and Daisy. Daisy said Jon would be there as soon as he could get away from the hospital.

Once everyone was there, Ren played the Ring video showing Rosie hurrying out the door and veering off to the left. All looked outside the picture window, as if there would somehow be a clue they had missed in the yard that would point them to where Rosie had gone. But no. Outside the window was a quiet residential street, an occasional car driving by. No clues. No fingers pointing to where Rosie had gone. No GPS tracking Rosie's whereabouts.

"Ren, who are your neighbors to the left of you? Do you know if they have a camera on their doors?" Danny asked.

"You know, I'm not sure. They just moved in a couple of months ago, but I'll call them right now."

While Ren was on the phone trying to get in touch with Aaron or Vlad, Danny gathered the family in the living room and asked if anyone had noticed anything out of the ordinary or had received any more threatening letters in the last couple of weeks.

Jack, who was pacing around the living room, stopped and said, "I think I can speak for the family. After what we went through, with months of living on edge because we weren't sure where the next attack would come from, or against whom, for that matter, I have no doubt we would have gone straight to you, Danny, if there had been even an inkling of a threat. But no, nothing. Right, guys?"

"Everything has gone back to normal for us," Keith said.

"Life's been quiet, thank God," Amy agreed.

Just then, Ren walked back into the room, still speaking on his phone. "Excellent. Thanks so much, guys. Send anything you think is worthwhile. We'll keep you in the loop. And keep your fingers crossed, please." Ren hung up and turned to the family. "Aaron and Vlad are out of town, but they do have a Ring. I gave them the times to look at, and they're going to send any videos they have over to us."

His phone vibrated to let them know a text was coming through. "Please let this work," Ren muttered as he punched in his passcode. "What the hell?"

Everyone gathered around Ren to see what the Ring videos showed. Aaron and Vlad's camera had picked up Rosie hurrying on the sidewalk in front of their house toward a woman who was bent over and holding her chest.

Ren held the phone out so everyone could watch the video. They saw Rosie running up to Cheryl and helping her down to the ground. Rosie's back was to the camera, but they watched Cheryl shaking her head at whatever Rosie was saying. The angle of the camera didn't show Cheryl's hand emerging from her front pocket with the gun, but it did show Rosie and Cheryl slowly standing and walking away together. They could tell Cheryl was grasping Rosie's arm, but it seemed on the camera that Rosie was helping Cheryl walk.

"Ren, do you know who that is? Does Rosie know her?"

"Yeah, Rosie knows her. Her name is Cheryl; she moved here a couple of months ago. She walks an old golden around the neighborhood. That's how Rosie met her. She started talking to Rosie one day about the flowers Rosie was planting, and so they would talk whenever they saw each other outside. It was all very casual and neighborly. Although lately, Rosie had been trying to avoid her. I guess she had a son who passed away, and Rosie said that was all she wanted to talk about. And it sounded like the story of his death had changed. Rosie swore when Cheryl first told her about her son, she said he'd died from cancer. But just a couple of weeks ago, she told Rosie he died in a car wreck. Rosie did feel sorry for her, but it sounded like the conversations were getting a bit awkward. But it looks like Cheryl was having some medical problem and Rosie went out to help her. But why wouldn't she have come back here for her phone? She could have called 911."

"Do you know where she lives in the neighborhood?" asked Danny.

"No. I mean it would have to be close, I would think. Her dog never looked like it could manage to walk more than a few blocks. I don't even think Rosie knows where she lives. Danny, what do we do?"

"The first thing we need to do is to call around to some of the local hospitals or urgent care centers to see if Rosie took her to get some treatment, though you'd think Rosie would have called you, Ren, to let you know where she went. Do you know Cheryl's last name, by any chance?"

"I don't. I'm not sure Rosie knows her last name."

Just then, Ren's phone rang. He looked down and shook his head. Not Rosie, but Aaron calling back. "Hello?" Ren listened, then said, "That's great. Thanks, Aaron. I'll tell Danny. At this point, anything might help." Ren nodded. "I know. As soon as she's back safe and sound, I will let you know. We appreciate your concern. Thank you."

"What did Aaron say? What did he find out?"

"They widened the video. He said he would send it." Just then, Ren's phone vibrated again. "Aaron said the video showed a portion of the left back bumper and the first two numbers of the license plate. A five and a three. He couldn't tell what kind of car or where the license plate was from but thought maybe you could do something with it." Ren nodded to Danny.

"Perfect. I'll hand it over to the lab guys. And don't worry about Cheryl's last name. It doesn't really matter. I'll have my partner start making the calls to the medical facilities. There aren't many around here, so it shouldn't take long. Also, text me those Ring videos. I want to see if Cheryl's face comes up in any of our databases. Might be a long shot, but it's worth a try. And unfortunately, you all will have the hardest job. Waiting to hear anything from Rosie. Keep your phones on and charged, just in case she calls one of you. I'm hoping she's still helping your neighbor lady and time has gotten away from her."

CHAPTER FIFTY

ROSIE STOOD THERE FOR A MINUTE, unable to make her legs work. She was convinced that if she went back to the table and closed the handcuff around her wrist, she would die at that table, and the handcuff would be the only thing to keep her from falling off the chair. The visual in Rosie's mind of Martha calmly pointing the gun at her and pulling the trigger filled her with terror.

She felt paralyzed—not only physically but mentally. For the life of her, she could not come up with any scenario that would save her life. If she ran at Martha, she would be shot. If she meekly went to the table, she would be shot. If she ran for the door, she would be shot.

"Come on, come on. I told you I don't like cold coffee." Martha motioned for Rosie to sit at the table. "Now."

"Martha, please. Isn't there—"

The sound of the gun going off in the enclosed cabin was deafening. Rosie felt a severe burning in her left upper arm, and the impact of the bullet forced her backward, practically into the restroom.

"Oh my God. Oh my God. OH MY GOD. You *shot* me!" Rosie went down on her knee and grabbed her left arm where the bullet had hit. She could feel the hot gush of blood running down her arm and her vision blurred around the edges. The pain in her left arm was excruciating. *Don't faint. Don't faint. DON'T FAINT!* Rosie kept repeating this to herself because the thought of fainting in front of Martha and lying motionless on the floor in front of her was unbearable.

"Oh, don't be so dramatic. It's only a graze. I told you I'm an excellent shot. If I had wanted to, I could have blown your whole arm off, but I decided to be nice. Besides, I didn't want to clean up the mess. Now GET UP AND GO SIT AT THE TABLE!"

Rosie stayed on her knee for another moment, then slowly grabbed the door jamb and pulled herself up. Her right hand left a bloody handprint. She made herself stand up straight and hold pressure on the wound in her left arm.

Martha was right. It was only a flesh wound, and Rosie could already feel the flow of blood slowing. Nonetheless, the sheer horrifying realization that she'd been shot was something Rosie couldn't wrap her head around. She had been shot! Rosie knew she would hear the sound of the gunshot in her nightmares. That is, if she lived long enough to have nightmares.

Rosie walked over to the table, sat down, rested her left arm on the table, and used her other hand to pick up her coffee mug and take a sip—the whole time glaring at Martha.

"Well, well, well. You have more gumption in you than I gave you credit for. I thought for sure you were going to be curled up in the fetal position for the rest of the day. Maybe my Stevie was wrong to quit on you."

Rosie snorted. "Do you really think he quit on me? I was fully prepared to kick him to the curb, but instead . . . um . . ."

"But instead, what? Go ahead and say it. But instead, my Stevie decided to drive his car into a bridge going eighty miles an hour? I still can't believe he did that. He was not raised to take the easy way out. I just wonder what was going on in his head."

"I'll tell you what was going on in his head! He was going to be arrested on child pornography charges! He was going to go to jail!" Rosie practically screamed the last sentence at Martha. She could not believe she was saying all this to Martha. It was almost as if the gunshot to her arm had jolted her out of the cocoon of fear enveloping her since she had first seen Martha stumble outside her window.

The entire morning, Rosie kept thinking, *What if she shoots me? I better not make her mad. I need to placate her. Just tell her what she wants to hear. Let her talk it out. I don't want her to shoot me.* Well, Rosie had done all that, and Martha still shot her. And yes, her arm hurt like a son of a bitch, and yes, Rosie was still terrified of Martha and the power of the pistol, but she was getting a glimmer of an idea. Martha responded favorably to strength and resolve—she had practically beamed at her with pride when she'd stood up and walked over to the table after she'd been shot.

Rosie took a breath. "I'm sorry. I didn't mean to yell. But you honestly have me curious about Steve and the way he grew up. It sounds like you practically raised him." Rosie figured if she could get Martha talking about the past, then it would give Rosie more time to try and turn this trainwreck of a day around.

"I know what you're trying to do," said Martha. "But it's okay. I like talking about my boys. It might be nice if someone was around to tell the world that my Stevie and Lance were not the monsters people thought they were." Martha chuckled. "Although they could be hellions, I will give them that." Martha's look on her face was one of benevolent bemusement, like she was talking about simple childhood pranks Steve and Lance had pulled.

Rosie had to steel herself to just sit in her chair and nod her head in agreement when what she really wanted to do was point out to Martha all the way her "two boys" were not cute little hellions. Cute little hellions usually didn't end up in prison or being chased by the police. But Rosie was sure Martha would dismiss those allegations.

"So, did I raise them? Good question. I tried to be there as much as I could for them. But once again, *Cheryl* fucked up my plans. These pictures?" Martha was pointing to the two Christmas pictures where she was holding Steve and Lance in her lap. "The boys were around five and six. Cheryl had finally relented and let me come over to the house to see them, although she'd made sure Gabe wasn't around when I was there. You see—" Martha leaned in and lowered her voice, like she was letting Rosie in on a secret no one else could hear. "Gabe had finally figured out he'd married the wrong sister and, well, he kept telling me he was going to divorce her and take the boys, and we were going to go away together and live happily ever after. I think Miss Cheryl figured out Gabe wanted to be with me instead, so she never let me come over when he was there. Shortly after these pictures were taken, she banned me from seeing the boys. She always knew exactly how to cut me the deepest. Everyone always thought she was so sweet and nice, but let me tell you, she had a mean streak in her a mile wide." Martha's voice was rising, and Rosie could tell by the way she was staring at the photos she was once again back in her very hurtful past.

Rosie was hesitant to ask this question, but despite everything that had happened that day, she needed to know more about Steve, his upbringing, and if Martha had played any further role in raising him. It would explain a lot, in her opinion. "Did Gabe ever ask for a divorce from Cheryl?"

Martha tossed her head back. "Of course he did! Numerous times. And each time she would cry and beg, threaten to take away the boys, promise to be a better wife—I don't know what she would say. But every time she managed to pull him back in. Always. I know he wanted to be with me, but he loved the boys. He was a good man, you understand, but he just couldn't stand to not see his boys. I told him we could get married and take her to court, but he never wanted to do that. Said he didn't want to use the boys as a bargaining chip. Said he was afraid she would take it out on the boys if he left. Said he just couldn't do that to his boys."

Rosie was startled to see tears on Martha's face. She was still staring intently at the pictures and shaking her head back and forth. "Said he couldn't do that to his boys, but he had no problem doing it to me."

Martha looked at Rosie. "Who cares if Martha gets left behind and never gets to have a life? Who cares if Martha's left to grow old without a husband or family? Did she care? Not on your life. As long as she had Gabe and I didn't, then she was satisfied. I don't think she ever loved him, not really. Not like I did. But she couldn't stand for me to be happy. Everything was always about her, never me. And, well, after a while, Gabe just stopped coming over. You know, he never even told me goodbye. Just stopped seeing me, wouldn't take my calls. He left me, just like everyone else."

Martha reached up her trembling hand to wipe the tears off her face. Slowly, the look of sadness on her face passed. Once again, she looked over at Rosie with anger in her eyes and a determined look on her face.

Rosie's heart sank. Even in the short period of time she'd been at the cabin, she'd come to know that look. Martha had left the past and was back in the present, looking for revenge against the one person she blamed for both her boys' deaths. And that person was Rosie.

CHAPTER FIFTY-ONE

AFTER DANNY LEFT, everyone just seemed to deflate. Keith and Lilly were holding hands on the couch, Daisy was on the floor cuddling with Big Shirley, Amy had her arms around Marilyn's neck, Ren stood next to Walter and absently stroked his head, while Jack was still pacing around the living room, each time stopping at the picture window and glaring out at the empty street, as if he could make Rosie appear if he just wished hard enough for it.

Jack cleared his throat. "This waiting around is driving me crazy. Does anyone have any other ideas? Even if Rosie took that lady to the hospital, she would find a way to let us know what's going on. Especially since she left her phone here. Ren, do you want to take the dogs out walking in the neighborhood? Maybe something, anything, might happen that will give us a clue as to what in the hell is going on."

Keith and Lilly needed to get back to their house, mainly because Lilly had to breastfeed the baby. They hugged Jack and Ren and told them to call immediately if there was any news. Amy had brought her books, so she said she would sit at Rosie's desk, study for her estates and trust test, and monitor any activity on the street. Daisy volunteered to stay on the floor with a napping Big Shirley.

Jack and Ren leashed the dogs and left through the front door. They automatically turned left, walking in the direction they last saw Rosie go. They slowly walked along the sidewalk, staring intently at the ground just in case Rosie had left a clue.

"So, this Cheryl lady," Jack started. "Any clue as to where she lives? I know you said she can't be very far because her old dog wouldn't be able to walk long distances. Which way did she usually come from?"

"Most of the time, I would look out the window and see Rosie talking with her. Gosh, I wish I had gone and found out where she lives. The one time I saw her walking down the street, she came from this direction. It's funny the things that stand out. She always had this stupid hat on—you know, the ones you see elderly women wearing when they're out gardening. Her gray hair was always spiky and sticking up through the slit in the hat. And now that I think of it, I'm just assuming she was old, probably because of the gray hair. But I guess she could be anywhere from forty to sixty."

Walter and Marilyn were taking their time sniffing every blade of grass for any potential smell given off by another dog. Marilyn certainly did not feel the need to mark her scent, but Walter felt like it was his doggie duty to do just that, so Jack and Ren's walk was more like a slow stroll. They made it to the corner and turned right.

The houses in that part of the neighborhood were, for the most part, modest ranch homes built in the fifties. Most of the owners were working couples, some with young children, some trying to get their careers to take off. There were a few retirees still living in the neighborhood, and Ren and Rosie always said they could tell those houses apart because the yards were pristine, not a dandelion to be found anywhere.

They had been walking for about fifteen minutes when Ren abruptly stopped. "I don't believe it."

"What? What is it?"

"That house there. The blue one." Ren was pointing to one of the smaller houses on the street. It was painted dark blue and had yellow shutters.

Jack excitedly said, "Is that Cheryl's house? I thought you said you didn't know where she lived?"

"I didn't. But look in the backyard. This cannot be a coincidence."

Sure enough, sunning herself on the patio in the backyard was an elderly golden retriever.

"Are you sure, Ren?"

Ren smiled. "I might not have a clue how old some lady is, but I know my animals. That's Evie, Cheryl's old golden. Notice her tail. See the strip of dark red fur going down her tail? I noticed it the first time I saw her."

Ren walked up to the chain-link fence with Marilyn and whistled softly. "Here, Evie. Come here, girl."

When Evie didn't move, Ren whistled louder. "She probably has some hearing loss. EVIE! Come here, girl!"

This time, Evie raised her head and looked over at Ren. Marilyn gave one loud bark and wagged her tail once or twice, which for Marilyn was like jumping up and down. Evie slowly got to her feet, shook herself, and ambled over to where Ren was standing. He bent down to pet her through the fence while Marilyn and Evie did the sniff test on each other. "You're an old girl, aren't you? But you're a good girl. Yes, you are. Where's your mommy, huh? Is she in the house? And where's my Rosie? God, I wish you could talk."

"Hey, Ren. It's unlocked."

Ren looked up from petting Evie to see Jack at the front door. He had the screen door open and his hand on the doorknob. "It's not breaking and entering if the door's unlocked. Besides, we need to go in to make sure Rosie's not here. We can call Danny after."

Ren walked over to Jack. "Trust me, I'm not going to try and talk you out of it. Let's go."

Both men kept a firm grip on the Danes as they opened the front door. Jack had already knocked once and rang the doorbell with no answer, so they were certain no one was home. Jack went in first, with Ren close behind.

They both stopped dead in their tracks in the foyer. "Holy shit. We have to call Danny."

CHAPTER FIFTY-TWO

MARTHA CONTINUED TO STARE at Rosie, and Rosie stared right back. She didn't know what else to do. Rosie was drawing a complete blank on trying to find another Steve topic to get Martha talking again. It was like her brain was frozen. Rosie was pretty sure that once they had exhausted the topics of Steve and Lance, her time would be up, and Martha would raise that goddamn pistol again.

"Uh . . . Martha . . . um. What's your favorite memory of Steve?"

Martha still didn't say anything; she just looked at Rosie, and slowly the angry look on her face was replaced by one Rosie could not figure out. It was like the lights were on, but no one was home. She was looking at Rosie as if she were trying to figure out exactly who Rosie was and how she ended up in the cabin with her. "You know what? I am going to take a nap."

With that, Martha got up, walked over to the bed in the corner, laid down with her back to Rosie, and appeared to fall asleep all within a couple of minutes. Rosie was so surprised by this that all she could do was gape at Martha's back. *Could this fucked-up day get any weirder?*

She looked at her watch and was amazed to see it was 3:20 in the afternoon. "Crap. I've been in this hell for over six hours. Ren is probably going crazy by now." She glared at her left wrist, hand-cuffed to the table leg. Every couple of minutes she would pull her arm toward her, hoping against hope that something would give. Already bruises were beginning to form. She had the almost un-controllable urge to just start yanking as hard as she could against the cuff, in hopes somehow the metal cuff would break, but she knew that wouldn't help the matter.

She tried to lift the table, hoping the leg would come off the floor so the cuff could slide down and she could run, but the table didn't budge. She'd never felt so helpless. Being forced to sit, hand-cuffed to a table in a cabin in the middle of God knows where, and know with a sick certainty she'd probably not survive the day—Rosie did the only thing she could think of to do. She lowered her head down on the tabletop and began to pray.

CHAPTER FIFTY-THREE

THE SCENE INSIDE THE BLUE HOUSE was something Ren thought he would only see in the movies. Various pictures of Rosie were thumbtacked to the walls, along with photos of their house, their dogs, one photo of Amy, and two of Daisy and Jon walking out the front door of Rosie and Ren's house. A chill went through him just thinking about someone surreptitiously taking pictures of them.

"ROSIE! Rosie, are you here?" Ren yelled Rosie's name a couple of more times, but the house was eerily quiet. "That bitch has been taking pictures of us! Jesus. What a creepy, twisted thing to do!"

"And she's certainly fixated on Rosie," Jack agreed. "I'm calling Danny right now. Walk through the house just to make sure no one's here, but don't touch anything. We have got to find my daughter."

The pinned pictures of Rosie and family were scattered across the living room walls. There was one chair in the room, but that was it. No table, no TV, no couch, no lamp. Just a rather uncomfortable-looking chair placed in the middle of the room. Almost as if Cheryl didn't need anything else to look at except the pictures of Rosie. It was beyond creepy.

Ren took Marilyn with him as he walked around the corner

into the kitchen. It was a perfectly normal kitchen, except, like the living room, there was hardly any furniture in it. No table, no dishtowels, no chopping block—just one straight-backed chair in the middle of the room.

There was a small doggie door leading out to the backyard, and a bowl of dog food and a water bowl were placed nearby. Ren looked into the water bowl and saw the water was clear. *So obviously she gave Evie fresh water this morning . . . before she took off with Rosie. How very nice of her.*

Ren took the stairs leading up to the second floor by himself, since neither one of the Danes would go near stairs. The one and only time Ren took Walter up to a second floor was at his friend's house in Missouri. Walter went up the stairs just fine, but totally froze trying to get back down. Ren practically had to carry him down, which was no small feat.

The upstairs had two bedrooms and one small bathroom. The first bedroom was completely bare of any furniture. The closet was empty except for some wire hangers. The second bedroom had one twin bed, neatly made, and a small end table with a lamp. Nothing in the drawer. No books or magazines on the bedside table. No TV. The small closet had three pairs of capris and a couple of T-shirts. The funny-looking sun hat was on the upper shelf in the closet. Ren shuddered. *I don't even want to think about where she keeps her underwear. Gross.*

Ren went back downstairs. Jack was still in the living room, shaking his head while looking at the pictures of his family plastered around the room. The Danes were sitting next to Jack, and Evie had come inside and lay down in the middle of the floor, watching the Danes out of the corner of her eye. Marilyn, of course, was ignoring her. Walter had done the requisite sniffing of her backend and decided she was not a threat.

"Danny's on his way," Jack said to Ren. "This is beyond messed up. Who the hell is this lady? And what does she want with Rosie?"

"It's got to all be connected to Steve and Lance. Steve didn't have any other brothers or sisters, did he? I certainly don't remember Danny saying anything about any other siblings."

Ren frowned. "Who was the lady Lance was communicating with? Remember, Danny said Lance told her all the horrible stuff he wanted to do to the family, Rosie in particular. Marsha? Margaret? Something with an M. Martha! That was her name. It cannot be a coincidence. I mean, what are the chances of some strange lady moving into the neighborhood, talking to Rosie all the time—remember, Rosie thought there was something off about her—and then the Ring showing Rosie helping her. And now they're both gone!"

"Do we know what kind of relationship she had to Steve and Lance?"

Ren shook his head. "But she must be connected to all of this. Don't you think a sane person would go to the police if they'd gotten those letters where basically Lance said he was going to kill an entire family? God, I hope Danny has found something out. He's pulling up now."

Jack went to the door and stepped out onto the front step. Danny motioned to his partner to go around the back, while he walked up to Jack. Jack couldn't help but notice both Danny and his partner had their hands on their guns, holsters unbuckled.

"We went through the house, and it's empty," said Jack.

"Danny, have you found out anything? This is one seriously disturbed individual. She has pictures of Rosie everywhere."

"We're working on it." Danny slipped past Jack and went into the living room. His reaction to the photos thumbtacked on the walls was the same as Jack and Ren's. His partner came in through the door leading out to the backyard. "Backyard and kitchen are clean. Nothing in the kitchen closet."

"Check upstairs, please."

"Have you found anything out? Anything at all?" Ren was becoming increasingly agitated. "We've got to find her."

"I know, Ren. We're working on it. The forensics team is on their way."

Ren's face went pale. "Do . . . do you think . . ." Ren could not finish what he was going to say.

Danny put his arm on Ren's shoulder and squeezed. "No, this place is too neat. But I want to make one-hundred-percent sure. Plus, we need to run this lady's DNA."

Danny's partner came back into the room. "Upstairs is empty. I'll canvass the neighbors to see if anyone has information about her."

"Okay. I'll follow Jack and Ren back to Ren's house. Keep an eye out for forensics. Let me know when they're done here."

Ren went into the small laundry room and came back with Evie's leash. "No way am I leaving this dog with a crazy person. Come on, girl. You're coming home with us."

CHAPTER FIFTY-FOUR

"HEY, MISSY. WAKE UP."

For just a moment, Rosie kept her eyes closed and tried to hold onto the blessed sleep she had slipped into. For just a moment, she tried to convince herself the horror of the day was just a bad dream, and she would wake up in her bed, smile at a sleeping Ren, and listen to the soothing breathing sounds of three large dogs. For just a moment, she tried to forget a deranged woman had kidnapped her, had handcuffed her to a table, had shot her in the arm, and was now, at this very moment, probably getting ready to finish the job. For just a moment—

"HEY. Wake up."

Rosie slowly opened her eyes. Martha was back in her spot across the table from Rosie, gun next to her right arm and the ever-present glass of red wine next to her left arm. Rosie liked red wine, but she was pretty sure if she ever got away from this nightmare, she'd never drink it again.

"I had a great nap, thanks for asking," Martha said. "And I think I owe it to you to tell you the rest of the story of my life. Where did we leave off? Oh yeah, when Gabe quit coming around. Turned out he wasn't such a nice guy after all." Martha took a hefty swallow of her wine. "I had no husband, no kids, no life. I had graduated from college with a get-you-nowhere liberal arts degree, but I was so sure I wouldn't need to work. That Gabe and I would get married, and I would stay home with our kids. If there's one lesson you should take from all of this, it's to *never* depend on someone else. *Never* pin all your hopes and dreams on a man who will tell you what you want to hear, just so you'll go to bed with him."

Martha snorted. "You girls today, though. Everyone wants a career. Everyone thinks they can have it all. Because you were told from the very first day of your life that you could, and should, do it all and have it all. Being told you were something special." She grimaced. "I wonder what that would have been like."

Martha paused, then just looked at Rosie and shook her head. "Well, when I figured out my life was not going to turn out the way I wanted it to, I needed to make some changes. I needed a job. I told you about my job, didn't I? The only time in my life I ever caught a break was when I got hired at the women's prison. That place taught me all sorts of things—how to be in control, how to handle myself in any situation—hell, where do you think I learned to handcuff someone so quickly, hmm? Taught me all sorts of things I never knew I needed."

Martha poured herself another generous glass of wine. Rosie couldn't believe how much alcohol Martha had to have in her system, and yet she walked straight, was not slurring her words, was still making sense. It was like she had been drinking water all day, instead of almost two bottles of red wine.

Rosie also could not figure out where Martha was going with all her talk about finishing up with her life story. Rosie had seen Martha be angry, sad, hateful, and sarcastic. But she had not seen her in this contemplative and thoughtful mood. It seemed like the

Martha show was coming to an end, and Rosie was almost positive she knew what would happen then. And the thought of that ending scared the shit out of her.

CHAPTER FIFTY-FIVE

REN, JACK, WALTER, MARILYN, AND EVIE slowly made their way back to the house. At one point Ren thought he was going to have to pick Evie up and carry her, but after she rested for a moment, she stood up and walked the rest of the way.

"You guys were gone for a while. And who is this cute little girl? Where have you all been?" Amy asked while bending over to pet Evie.

Jack and Ren shared a look.

"What? What did you find? What are you not telling us?" Amy got up from the office chair, and Daisy stood up from the floor. They both looked somewhat panicked at Ren and Jack's expressions.

"We haven't found Rosie yet, but we finally had some luck. Ren recognized this girl—whose name is Evie, by the way—in the backyard of a house a couple of blocks over. And . . ."

"And what? Was anyone home? Dad, you have to tell us."

"Okay, but we need to keep calm. There were pictures of Rosie thumbtacked on the walls in the living room. There were pictures of all of us. Someone's been watching this house." Amy and Daisy both gasped. Daisy put her arm around Amy and held her close. "We called Danny. They want forensics to sweep that house—I guess to get fingerprints. The rest of the house was empty. It barely had any furniture in it. But at least we have something to go on."

Daisy looked at Amy. "We are going to find her. Everything is going to be okay. I know it."

Amy had tears in her eyes. "But what if everything is not going to be okay? What will we do? I'm really scared. This is just so bizarre."

Jack walked over and hugged both Amy and Daisy. "We must keep strong and trust that Danny will come up with something we can use. At least now we have a house and an address. Hopefully we will be able to figure out Cheryl's last name and how in the hell she is involved in this."

They all heard a car door slam outside. Danny came through the front door. "Bingo. We have a name, Martha Fonda. Not only is she renting the house with all the pictures, she's also—and this is so weird—Steve and Lance Gaynor's aunt."

"Fuck!" Ren cried. "I knew this had to be connected to those two psychos." He was the one pacing now, running his hand through his hair before stopping to glare out into the street.

Danny went on. "Her sister, Steve and Lance's mother, was named Cheryl. Martha's picture popped up in our facial recognition system because she's worked in a federal women's penitentiary for the last twenty-five years. People who work in a federal prison go through a yearly employment background check. I have no doubt her fingerprints will also come up in our system. Her record at the prison was clean until about nine months ago. Seems she just stopped coming into work. The HR person I talked to said they'd tried numerous times to get in touch with her, but she never responded to phone calls or letters. The HR person said they'd been surprised because Martha had worked there for a long time and never had any personnel issues. If fact, it sounds like she was well liked at the prison."

Jack said "Martha. Wasn't she the person who Lance wrote to all the time, telling her all the horrible things he wanted to do to the family? That Martha?"

"We are making that assumption due to the fact she is their aunt and is obviously obsessed with Rosie and you guys. Plus, it appears she was the last person Rosie interacted with."

"What do we do now?" Amy went over to Danny and put her hand on his arm. "Do we have any other information about this woman? Can we find out her car's license plate, and you can put an APB on it? We need to be able to do something else. This sitting here waiting is terrible!"

Danny agreed. "Waiting is the hardest thing you can do. I know you feel helpless right now. As for her license plate, it was listed on her employment record. It matches the five and the three shown in the Ring video. The entire force has been briefed, and everyone is keeping their eyes and ears open. That's all we can do at this point. We have a patrolman watching the house now, so if or when she comes back, we'll question her and try to get some answers."

"And there's nothing else we can do?" Jack asked. "Is there anyone else at the prison we can talk to? Maybe she had a good friend she confided in. It's worth a shot, right? Hell, at this point, anything is worth a shot. I know Rosie was brought up to be strong and resourceful, but I doubt she has any idea this Martha woman is an evil person that wants to harm all of us."

CHAPTER FIFTY-SIX

JACK WAS WRONG about that. Rosie knew firsthand how evil Martha was. She knew exactly how Martha wanted to hurt her and her sisters because she'd told her, more than once. And having to sit there and listen to Martha relate the story of her life was maddening, especially when the whole time Rosie was on edge worrying about when the dreaded gun would make its appearance again.

Since her nap, Martha appeared to be a bit calmer. Almost as though she had made a decision and was now comfortable with it. Although Rosie wasn't sure she wanted to know what exactly the decision was.

"So, blah, blah, blah. I went to work at the prison. If I may say so myself, I was a great employee. And why wouldn't I be? I had no family. No husband. No kids. I was always available to work any holidays, do overtime, cover everyone's shift because I had no life. Cheryl and Gabe made it clear they didn't want me in their life. The boys barely remembered me. I didn't really have any friends. I honestly thought I would work at the prison until I died. A sad, lonely life with a sad, lonely death. I sound like a real loser, don't I? Huh? A real big fucking loser."

Rosie's heart sank watching Martha transform back into the angry, bitter woman she had been most of the day. *So much for thinking that Martha had calmed down,* she thought. *Why won't that wine knock her out?*

Martha was still talking. "Not like you and your charmed life with your sisters and your vet boyfriend. I hate people like you. Always lording your good fortune over everyone else. Did you ever once stop to think maybe there are people in the world who don't have such a great life? Did you ever think maybe you should take off your rose-colored glasses and see how other people live? No, you never did. And why not? I'd really like to hear your sorry excuses for being such a bitch. Go on. Talk to me."

Rosie saw Martha's right hand reach out and pick up the pistol. She knew she was going to have to say something quick to divert Martha. But what? Rosie was truly out of thoughts and ideas.

So she decided to go for broke. "You know what, Martha? I don't think I am a bitch. I'm actually a very nice person. And so is my family. And I'm very sorry to hear about your life. It must have been awful and lonely and very, very sad. But wasn't there something you could have done to change it? I know Gabe didn't work out, but there are plenty of men in this world. And you don't even need to be with a man. There are plenty of relationships you could have with other people that don't include sex. So why didn't you? What were you so afraid of?"

Sweat was trickling down Rosie's back, and she felt like she was either going to throw up, pass out, or shit herself. Probably all three at once. But the same weird dynamic that had played itself out after Martha shot Rosie was happening again. Almost as if Martha was proud of her for speaking up and challenging her, like this was what she'd wanted all along. Rosie thought, *I don't know how many times I have thought it today, but this is one seriously fucked up person.*

"Hmm. Well, looky who decided to get a backbone. It's rich to have you lecture me on what I should have done differently with my life. As a matter of fact, I did try to have other relationships. But for some reason they never worked out, and after a while I stopped trying. Why put yourself out there just to continually get your heart stomped on, time after time after time? I admit it. It was easier to just go to work, do my job, come home, and—well, where do you think I developed my taste for the vino? A couple of bottles a night and you sleep like a baby. You don't care your life turned out to be this ungodly, horrible mess."

Martha paused, then carried on. "Or when you get a phone call from your doctor telling you your liver enzymes and values are a mess and the pain in your stomach and the itching and the weight loss are all signs of something wrong. And you realize there's absolutely no one to call—no one you can tell who might come over and put their arms around you; no one to take you to chemo and sit with you when you're puking your guts up and bring you a cup of tea. And you finally, *finally* realize you are truly alone in the world. Let me tell you something missy. I have had dark days in my life. Gabe leaving me, Cheryl being an absolute bitch to me most of my life, knowing my parents preferred Cheryl over me, knowing I'd never have kids of my own. But this . . . I always told myself I was strong. That I wasn't like everyone else and therefore I didn't need anyone else."

Martha looked down at her hands. She almost seemed surprised to see the pistol in her right hand. She put it down on the table and sort of pushed it to one side. Rosie was very glad to see Martha put the gun down. Because when Martha started in on all the wrongs that had been done to her for her entire life, Rosie was quite sure those thoughts would again lead to Martha blaming Rosie for absolutely everything. Irrational? Yes. But there was nothing rational about this day or the broken-down, defeated woman in front of her.

"But this crushed me. Why this? I don't know. But it did. And it made me think about Steve and Lance, that maybe there was a chance I could see them again. I didn't know Cheryl and Gabe had died in a car crash. I hadn't heard from them for years. But when I got the diagnosis, I thought, 'I'll try to find them, and maybe, just maybe, before I die, I can have a relationship with someone.'"

Rosie started to say she was sorry to hear about the cancer, but that seemed too normal of a response. Almost like something you would say to a friend, or even a passing acquaintance. So she kept her mouth shut. And for the first time, she really looked at Martha. Her skin was a faint yellow color, but Rosie had just assumed it was because Martha didn't get out in the sun very much. She was thin, but now that Rosie was looking at her with a more discerning eye, she could tell Martha's abdomen was fairly enlarged. Like all the weight she'd lost went directly to her gut. Rosie remembered an older employee at the newspaper in New York who had liver cancer, and that was exactly how he'd looked too.

"I decided to see if I could find my boys. And my word, what a mess they had made of their lives." Martha gave a disgusted laugh. "Trust Cheryl to totally fuck things up. I'm sure that once the boys started having problems, little Miss Cheryl threw her hands up in the air and told Gabe she just couldn't handle it. It sounds like she gave up on them from the get-go and persuaded Gabe to give up on them too.

"Oh, I heard plenty from Lance," Martha said. "Once I tracked him down and told him I wanted to be in his life, that his parents had denied me at every turn, he turned back into that little boy that loved to sit on my lap. We had the best conversations, staying up late at night, drinking wine together, plotting the destruction of your family. Don't look so surprised, missy! Lance told me all about what you had done to Steve and how the only way Steve could see a way out was to drive his car into a bridge at about seventy miles an hour. You see, Lance had been in prison before and knew how the other inmates treated someone in for child pornography. He knew Steve wouldn't be able to handle it. And even though he'd sworn all that stuff on his computer wasn't his, they both knew he was going to get nailed for it."

Martha got up, once again made her way over to the counter where the wine was, and once again poured herself a hefty glass. "You'd think as bad as my liver is, that I wouldn't be able to drink this stuff without falling down drunk after a couple of sips. Nope, doesn't happen! If you're thinking and praying I'll pass out and you can walk right out of here, well, think again."

Rosie just looked at Martha, her face giving away all she was feeling.

Martha smirked. "You should see yourself. That is exactly what you were hoping would happen. Or else hoping I would somehow grow a conscience and heart and let you go. Again, not going to happen.

"So, we are at long last coming to the end of our story. And there are some remarkable coincidences coming up. For instance, the phone call your sister, Daisy, got from that whore, Skylar? Lance had come to Texas to see what kind of trouble he could make for you guys. He told me all about it. He went into a greasy little diner over off Tremont Street and lo and behold, little Skylar was his waitress. They'd known each other in college, and I guess they used to be an item. Lance didn't share with me all the details, but something happened at the college. Something to do with drinking, sex, and a girl dying. That's how Lance was able to get Skylar to make that phone call. Because he had something on her, something that if he went to the police with, she would be in trouble too. That phone call would just be the first of many 'misfortunes' that were going to impact all of your lives."

Martha sighed. "But you know what they say about the best laid plans. My Lance was not able to stay out of prison. I told him and told him to keep it together, to think about how great it would be to do everything we had planned to your family, but he just couldn't help himself. Stevie had always been the leader of them. I don't think Lance knew how to execute all our plans without Stevie telling him what to do. He told me how he would drive his truck down to Texas to follow you girls, and when I said, 'Why in the hell didn't you run over a couple of them?,' he said he just never thought of it. I'm not trying to be mean, but my Lance was not the brightest person. But he loved me, and that's all that mattered. And if he hadn't gotten his sorry ass thrown in jail, then I probably wouldn't have been able to find him and reconnect with him in the first place. Really, it was a win-win for everyone."

CHAPTER FIFTY-SEVEN

AT NINE THAT EVENING, the whole family was still at Ren and Rosie's. At this point, Rosie had been gone for about twelve hours. Keith's mom was still watching the kids, so Lilly and Keith brought over a big pot of chili, and while everyone had a bowl in front of them, not a lot of actual eating was happening.

Danny was working a double shift, keeping the family informed of any progress via cell phone and personal visits. So far, there hadn't been any hits on the APB regarding the license. Danny had gotten back in touch with the head of HR at the federal prison where Martha had worked, but all she could tell Danny was that Martha stopped coming into work about nine months ago and she really hadn't had any close friends at the prison. It seemed Martha would come to work, do her job, and then go home.

Danny spoke with Martha's immediate supervisor, and he'd confirmed Martha had been a loner; while she'd been very pleasant, she'd kept to herself. As a matter of fact, he'd said he couldn't remember her ever even having lunch with another employee. Everyone had known to just leave her alone and let her do her job.

"Wow. What a lonely life. If I didn't hate her so much, I might actually feel sorry for her." Daisy was sitting on the couch with Jon, Big Shirley sleeping on their feet. "I just feel so helpless. And I know we all do. If only there was something we could—"

At that moment, Ren's cell phone rang. He looked down but didn't recognize the number. "Hello?"

"Ren? Ren, you need to come get me. Please. I need you. Come get me." Rosie's voice was high-pitched and breathless, like she had been running for the last hour. She started sobbing, and the sound of her voice, broken and forlorn, tore at Ren's heart.

"Rosie! Rosie, where are you? Are you all right? Where are you, baby?" Once Ren said Rosie's name, everyone jumped up and crowded around him. Ren held up his hand to keep everyone quiet. "Honey, where are you? Do you know where you are?"

"I . . . I don't know. I'm so scared. Please come find me, Ren."

"Rosie, um . . . look around you. Is there a street sign? A store? Anything?"

"It's—" Ren could tell Rosie was trying to stop crying. "It's just so dark. And I can't go back into that house. I just can't. Please don't make me."

"Rosie, whose phone is this? Is there someone there with you? Someone that can help you until I can get to you?"

Suddenly, a male voice came over the phone. "Hey, mate? I think I may be able to help out here. Is this Ren?" The fellow on the other end of the phone had an Australian accent.

"Yes, I'm Ren. Where are you? Is she hurt? Hold on." Ren lowered his phone. "It sounds like she's all right, but she's scared. I'm trying to get directions to her. Someone needs to call Danny and tell him what's going on." Ren turned back to his phone. "Okay, can you tell me exactly where you are?"

"Well, I'm not sure of the exact location; I haven't been here very long, but I can give general directions. I was driving down the road and your lady was just sitting there, right in the middle of the road. Scared the shi—uh—scared the heck out of me, I can tell you that. Let me tell you, mate, it's a good thing no one really drives along here. There really aren't any streetlights around—"

"Don't mean to interrupt, but you said you could give general directions? I have a police officer on the other line, and hopefully, he can send an officer out right away."

While Ren got the directions from Phil Laughlin (the Australian mate), Amy was on her phone with Danny filling him in. Together, they pinpointed an approximate location, and Ren told Phil an officer could be there within fifteen minutes. Danny also told Ren to keep Rosie on the phone, talking to either Ren or one of her sisters. He said an officer would be there soon, and he had also called for an ambulance.

Ren asked Phil if he could speak to Rosie again. "Honey, the police are going to be there in just a few minutes. I want you to sit in Phil's truck and lock the doors. We're coming to get you and bring you home."

Rosie spoke so softly Ren could barely hear her. "I just can't believe she did that. She wanted to kill me."

Ren handed the phone to Daisy. "Just keep talking to her and telling her we will be there shortly."

Daisy nodded. "Sweetie, it's Daisy. How are you, hon?"

Jack had a pretty good idea where Rosie was, so he would take the lead car with Lilly and Keith. Ren would follow with Daisy and Jon. Amy knew someone had to stay behind, so she just said, "You all keep me informed *every minute* of what is going on!"

Jack said that it would probably take at least thirty minutes to get to the location, but thankfully, there shouldn't be too much traffic trying to get there. They loaded up and took off down the highway.

They could see the flashing red and white lights from miles away. There hadn't been any sign of life for the last fifteen miles, just an open road and faint lights out in the distance. Jack said a buddy of his used to have a hunting cabin not too far away and that was the only reason he somewhat knew where they were going. They were all heartened to see that the police were there already. No one had any idea what to expect, but judging from Rosie's heartbreaking phone call, it didn't sound like it would be a fun story.

Daisy had kept Rosie on the phone until the police got there. She'd said she sounded very un-Rosie-like. Rosie had cried, at one point she'd had to throw up, then she'd cried some more. But even with Daisy gently asking her to tell her what had happened, Rosie had just kept repeating that she couldn't believe she wasn't dead, she couldn't believe what Martha had done. Her voice had been very thin and strained, and it seemed like she was having trouble taking a deep breath. Jon had said she was likely in shock, and it was a good thing the ambulance was on its way.

They crested the hill and saw three police cars and an ambulance parked on the side of the road. There was an older white Ford F-150 on the other side of the street, and a tall young man was leaning against the front of the truck. Jack pulled over and practically had the door open before the car had turned off. Ren was right behind him.

They could see Rosie sitting in the back of the ambulance with an EMT, staring ahead with a blank look on her face. She had her arms wrapped around herself as if she was freezing, even though there was a heavy blanket draped across her shoulders. Her face was dead white, and her eyes looked huge in her head. Jon had said she would be in shock and, boy, was he right.

A police officer came up to them. Ren explained who they were, and the officer said he had been expecting them. Danny had called the Harris County Sheriff's office when he got the information about Rosie's whereabouts. The officer introduced himself as Officer Williams and said that Rosie, so far, appeared to be relatively unhurt. She did have a bullet wound on her left upper arm, where it appeared the bullet had grazed her arm, right above her left bicep.

"A fucking bullet wound? Have you found the crazy lady who did this?" Ren demanded. "I need to go to Rosie."

"Sir, if you would just let the EMT complete his exam of her, I would appreciate it."

Just then, another police car, lights flashing, pulled up behind Jack's and Ren's cars. Danny got out and walked over to the group. He held up his hand when they all started talking at once. "Here's what I know so far about the situation. The officers have questioned the young man over there, the one who found Rosie in the middle of the street and stopped. He told basically the same story he told you guys. Rosie was sitting in the street when he crested the hill, and it was a good thing he had his bright lights on because he could see her from a distance and was able to slow down. The ambulance arrived about fifteen minutes ago, and, as you can see, they are taking care of her. There are three other officers searching the area for this Martha woman. So far, there's been no sign of her or her car."

They could see flashlights moving through the trees to the

right of them. Danny looked over at the EMT, who gave a nod. "Okay, Ren, you and Jack can go over to Rosie now. If the rest of you don't mind, let them see her first."

"Rosie? Honey? We're here," Ren said.

Jack and Ren climbed into the ambulance and sat on either side of her. The EMT had started an IV in her right hand, and she was receiving some oxygen, The heavy blanket was still draped around her. She was rocking slightly, and there was a faint keening noise coming from the back of her throat. She stared straight ahead, not appearing to notice them until Jack took one hand and Ren the other.

Her hands are ice cold, Ren thought.

She stopped rocking and slowly, so slowly, turned her head to look at Ren. Her pupils were dilated, but there seemed to be a bit more color in her face than when they first saw her. The EMT returned with a cup of hot tea, which he gave to Jack, and told him to have Rosie try and drink some of it.

"Ren. You came for me." Rosie's eyes filled with tears. She reached out a trembling hand to touch his face, as if she needed to feel him to reassure herself he was really sitting next to her. To reassure herself that she was finally safe.

"Of course I came for you. I would do anything for you. I love you. We were all so worried about you, honey. But you're okay now. You're safe, and we are here with you."

Jack held out the cup of tea to Rosie. "Come on, little rosebud. Drink this. It'll make you feel better."

Rosie took the hot tea and held it between her hands, drawing comfort from the heat from the mug. Slowly, she lifted it to her mouth and took a swallow. "Dad, I was so scared. I thought I was never going to see any of my family ever again. She kept telling me she was going to hunt all of you down and *kill* every one of you! She told me that over and over and over." The dazed look was gone from Rosie's face. It was replaced by a look of abject terror, almost as if what Martha had promised *had* come through and Rosie was alone in the world, just the way Martha had been.

"Shh. You're safe now." Jack had put his arm around Rosie and was holding her close. "We're all okay. She will never hurt any of us. The police will find her and give her the help she needs. It's going to be okay."

Ren and Jack both noticed the increased activity by the police outside the ambulance. Two more police cars had arrived, and the officers all seemed to be heading off to the right toward the flashlights.

Rosie finished her tea, closed her eyes, and rested her head on Jack's shoulder. Without opening her eyes, she said softly, "Martha is dead."

CHAPTER FIFTY-EIGHT

THE CABIN OF HORRORS was situated about a half a mile from the main road. One of the officers had stumbled upon the very faint path, and Danny and four other officers were approaching the cabin with their guns drawn and flashlights pointed at the front door and windows. The car in front matched the description and license plate number from the one in the Ring video, the car Rosie and Martha had driven away in. The car was unlocked, but there were no keys in the ignition. Danny motioned to one of the officers to go around to the back to make sure no one would be able to get out that way.

"This is the police. Come out with your hands above your head. We are armed, and we will shoot if you do not comply." The officer repeated the order twice more with no response at all from the cabin. Danny and Officer Williams slowly walked up the stairs to the porch, paying heed to the broken areas. Falling through and breaking an ankle would not be a great idea. The other two officers stationed themselves at the front of the house.

Danny stood to the side of the door and slowly pushed it open with his gun. Officer Williams stood on the other side and shined his flashlight into the room. The room looked empty, but both officers could still smell the acrid whiff of gunpowder and the oily scent of blood just beginning to dry. There was a table with three chairs in the middle of the room, a coffee table off to the side. Danny and Officer Williams advanced into the room, both shining their flashlights into the corners.

Once Danny was far enough into the room, he saw why there were only three chairs around the table and where the smell of blood was coming from. The fourth chair had tipped over, and when Danny shone his flashlight, he saw a woman he assumed to be Martha still sitting in the chair, arms at her side, legs draped over the seat, wearing the same clothes she had on in the Ring video. The only difference now was that half of her face had been blown away by a pistol shot. The presumed pistol lay about two inches from her outstretched hand. She was obviously dead, but Danny still reached out and felt her neck. No pulse detected.

Officer Williams came up behind Danny and informed him the house was secure. The only other room was the bathroom, and it was empty. There were no doors or windows along the backside of the house.

"May God have mercy on your soul," Danny said softly to Martha's prone form. Then he turned back to his colleagues. "Okay, even though it looks like a cut-and-dried suicide, I'm going to treat this as a crime scene until we're sure. Let's get some generators in here, and I'll call the forensics team. I guess I'll also go see if Rosie is in any shape to answer questions." Danny looked at Officer Williams and said, "And I would like you to come with me when I question her. We've been friends since grade school, so I want to avoid any conflict of interest."

Rosie was still sitting in the ambulance with Ren and Jack. Keith, Lilly, Daisy, and Jon were standing outside the open doors of the ambulance, speaking quietly to Rosie. Danny couldn't hear what they were saying, but when the officers came up to the group, they all turned as one, seemingly putting a protective barrier between Rosie and the rest of the world.

Everyone looked questioningly at Danny, but he just shook his head. "We need to talk to Rosie now. I will come talk to you all in a minute."

Jack looked like he was going to object, but when he saw the look on Danny's face, he got up, squeezed Rosie's hand, and simply said they would be back.

Danny sat down next to Rosie, and Officer Williams stood outside the ambulance. "Rosie, I need to ask you some questions now. Are you going to be able to answer them? Are you feeling okay now?"

Rosie just looked at Danny for a moment, her eyes big and unblinking. Finally, she nodded. "Did you find her?"

Danny hesitated. "We need to know what happened in there. Can you walk me through what happened to you today?"

Rosie gave a shaky laugh. "Wow. You don't want much, do you? I'm trying so hard to forget what happened and now you want me to tell you about it?"

"I'm sorry, Rosie. But we need to know. I really don't want to take you down to the station, so if you can tell me what happened, we can use it to determine the course of our investigation."

"Okay. Okay. Right. Of course, you do. Do you want the long or short version of my day from hell?" Rosie was grateful for Danny bringing it up and making her angry. She was finally starting to shake off the overwhelming lassitude and fatigue that made her feel like she was encased in cotton, and everything being said to her sounded like it was coming from underwater.

She was smart enough to realize this was her body's way of handling the trauma she had experienced, but it also was making her mad. She had spent the entire day catering to the whims of a deranged woman and not being able to change any of it. Martha had done a great job of not only shackling her physically but shackling her mind by constantly repeating the worst thing imaginable to Rosie—killing all her family. She had been at Martha's mercy, and they'd both known it.

Rosie took a deep breath. "She kidnapped me by sticking a gun in my side, she made me drive her car to the cabin, which has to have been in every scary movie ever made, she handcuffed me to the table, she poured two bottles of wine down her gullet, and she spent the whole time talking. *ALWAYS* talking. About her poor life, about the deviants, Steve and Lance, about her sister, about her job. But you know what? I could listen to that all day long. I actually would start to feel sorry for her! But then she would swivel, stick that gun in my face, tell me she was going to shoot me either in my face, my back, my legs . . . or sometimes all three . . . and then she would go on and on about what she was going to do to my family. Danny, she knew *everyone's* name! Ren, Jon, my sisters, my dad. For fuck's sake, she even knew the names of my *dogs!* And she told me, over and over and over, how she was going to kill all of them. Just shoot them in the head. Then I would be alone in this world, just like she was. I would become a poor, sad, lonely, pathetic person, just like her."

At this point, Rosie was practically shouting the words at Danny. She was crying and pushing the words out, almost like they were going to choke her if she kept them inside her. "And then . . . and then . . ." Rosie put her hands over her mouth and just looked at Danny with terror in her eyes. He could tell she was reliving whatever hell had happened to her in that cabin.   Rosie whispered, "She picked up the gun . . . and pointed it at me . . . like she had been doing all day. I knew I was going to die." Rosie stopped talking. It seemed as if everyone was holding their breath, waiting for the next heartbreaking words out of Rosie's mouth. "I shut my eyes and started to pray. But all I could come up with was, 'Oh my God, oh my God, oh my God.' I hoped God was going to understand that I was terrified. Then . . . then . . ."

Rosie stopped and began looking frantically around the floor of the ambulance. Danny knew what that look meant. He reached over, snagged the wastebasket, gave it to Rosie, and stood up to block the view of her from the others outside. Even though she hadn't eaten since that morning, there was still enough in her stomach to make her gag. She held her face over the wastebasket for a few minutes, then shakily gave it back to Danny. She looked at him, and then at the crowd out by the ambulance, her family, the young man who had essentially rescued her, the other police officers. She could tell Ren wanted to jump up next to her and hold her.

She held her hand up and said in a clear voice, "Martha was a very sick woman, and there were times today that I pitied her. There were also times I hated her for what she was doing. But I never thought she would turn that gun on herself. I thought she was reserving that bullet for me."

CHAPTER FIFTY-NINE

THE FORENSIC TEAM ARRIVED at the cabin within thirty minutes. They swabbed the skin on Martha's hands and swabbed Rosie, even though gunshot residue can be easily wiped off. The coroner got to the scene and deemed it a suicide. There would still need to be an autopsy, but the cabin was no longer considered a crime scene.

The EMT wanted Rosie to come to the hospital for observation, but she adamantly refused. Her only physical injury was the gunshot wound to her arm, and that had been cleaned and bandaged, no stitches needed. She kept repeating that all she wanted to do was go home.

Danny told her she would have to come to the station in the next week or two to make a formal statement, but as far as he was concerned, Martha had died by suicide.

"Thank you, Danny. Really, thank you so much for being there for us. It helped so much knowing you were there." Rosie was standing by Ren's car, getting ready to get in the front seat. Jack, Keith, Lilly, Daisy, and Jon had just pulled away, and Ren was waiting patiently for Rosie in the driver's seat. He sensed that she had something more to say to Danny, and he wanted to give her space.

"What's going to happen to her now? I mean . . . her body?

What, um, do you do when there's no one to claim it? Does she get cremated? I can't believe I'm even saying this but, well, if there's any way, I would like to pay for her burial. For some reason, it feels like something I need to do. Am I crazy?"

Danny took her hands. "No, you are not crazy. You are someone who's been through a very traumatizing situation, a situation where you had no control. And I know you, Rosie. You like to be in charge." They both chuckled. "You are also a very caring and sympathetic person, one who is cognizant of the fact you have a great life with a great family that loves you. And you can't help but think how different her life was from yours. So quite truthfully, I think it's admirable you would want to do that for her." Danny smiled. "You're something else, Ms. Hurley. You know that, don't you? If you ever forget, I'll remind you—or Amy will."

Rosie squeezed his hands. "I'm going home now. You know where to find me." She reached up, kissed his cheek, and turned away. "But do me a favor. Don't come to find me for about a week, okay? That's how long I'm going to sleep!"

"Understood."

CHAPTER SIXTY

ROSIE DID SLEEP for practically a week. Even though she was sleeping around eight hours a night and her nights were surprising-ly nightmare-free, she still was so tired during the day, she usually ended up taking an hour-long nap around two in the afternoon. She would bring the dogs into the bedroom (the dogs followed her everywhere, as if they sensed she needed their physical presence to feel safe), get under the covers, and slide into a deep sleep.

The family was doing their best to give Rosie enough time and space to clear her head. Lilly brought a roast crockpot dinner over one night, and Daisy brought by a handle of Hendrick's. Amy sent her humorous texts every day. Jack purchased pizza from the pizza parlor he used to take the girls to on Saturdays, and when he stopped by the house with it, conveniently around six in the evening, he ate with Ren and Rosie but didn't linger too long after the meal. He'd pulled Rosie close, kissed her forehead, and told her that when she was ready to talk about what had happened, then he was ready to listen, but if she was never able to talk about it, then he would accept that. "Just know we're here for you, rosebud."

Rosie knew the family all thought she was talking to Ren about the trauma, but surprisingly, she wasn't even sharing things with him yet. It was as if she needed to analyze and deconstruct internally what had happened to her. And she was certainly doing that. There was a running movie in her mind, right on the edge of her consciousness, where the entire day played out, over and over. Rosie would wonder if she could have said anything different, or if she could have somehow managed to get the gun from Martha—or her favorite, wondering what might have happened if she'd never gotten in the car with Martha at all. But ultimately, the end was always the same. And each time, when the movie in her mind approached the ending, she would do everything possible to try and change it, or at least stop it from happening again and again. But she never could.

On a Friday morning, two weeks after she had been kidnapped, Danny called and asked if she would come down to the station to make a formal statement. Ren wanted to come with her, but Rosie told him she was fine and he could go to work. He had two surgical cases scheduled for the day, and she didn't want to be the one responsible for any delay in treatment for an animal.

It was a beautiful November day, the kind where there wasn't a cloud in the sky. Rosie put her Caddy in reverse and made her way to the police station, which took about twenty minutes. She knew she needed to tell Danny everything about that fateful day, and truthfully, she was hoping that if she could get it all out on paper, even the horrifying way the day had ended, then maybe she could shut off the movie projector in her mind.

At the station, Danny led her into a small office off to the side of the main floor. "Let me explain how this works. I will ask some basic questions about what transpired that day, and I want you to just tell me what happened. If you are ready, I will call Officer Clifford to come sit in with us. You met him the day you and Lily found Skylar. Is this okay with you?"

Rosie nodded, although she wasn't exactly sure she was ready or okay. She knew she had to expel, somehow, the memories of that horrible day to get her life back. "Let's do this." She sat up straight and squared her shoulders. "Today is the first day of the rest of my life."

Danny watched as she put on her game face, and he had to admire her grit. Amy had told him that Rosie was still processing everything, that she hadn't even spoken at length to the sisters about what had happened. Danny was familiar with victims having a very difficult time coming up with the words to describe what had happened to them. Violent situations could be such out-of-body experiences that it was hard for the normal person to even begin to formulate thoughts about the event, much less find the proper words. Danny was counting on Rosie's background as a budding author and former newspaper reporter to help her find the words needed to flesh out the story.

But it was not an easy task. Danny knew this first-hand. He had been involved in numerous witness statements, and inevitably, the victim would break down and sob. But Danny also knew that, at times, talking about the situation was the only way to exorcise the demons. In more cases than not, the victim would be noticeably calmer and at peace with themselves after giving their statement. Danny was hoping it would be the same for Rosie.

Officer Clifford entered through a door in the back of the room and nodded to Rosie. Danny went through the usual introduction. He had Rosie state her full name and the date, and then had her acknowledge the date she was kidnapped by Martha. Then Danny simply said, "Rosie, can you tell us in your own words what happened?"

Rosie took a deep breath, folded her hands together and placed them on the table in front of her, looked straight into the camera, and started speaking. She started with the weeks leading up to being taken by Martha. She described how Martha had initiated their original meeting by asking her about the flowers she was planting. She said they would talk once a week or so, usually about their respective dogs and the weather. Nothing very specific. It was only when Martha started talking more and more about her deceased son did Rosie start to feel uncomfortable. But she hadn't registered a creepy vibe from Martha, just a bit of a pitiful vibe.

I was right, Danny thought as he watched Rosie speak. She was a natural in front of the camera. It was like she was delivering a well-rehearsed play, which told Danny just how much she had been thinking about what had happened to her.

She told Danny how she saw Martha stumbling down the street, clutching her chest, and how she was sure Martha was going to have a heart attack right before her eyes. How she had the first inkling something was not right when she grabbed Martha's arms to keep her from falling and found her skin to be warm and dry, not cold and clammy like Rosie had been expecting. And how before she could even react to that, Martha had pointed the gun at her, and her nightmare had really begun.

Rosie told Danny about the bizarre situation with the wine and the pictures of Cheryl, Gabe, Steve, and Lance. She described how Martha would go from speaking calmly about her life to shoving a gun in her face and threatening her life in a matter of minutes. How shocked she had been when Martha shot her. How loud the gunshot had been in the cabin. How Martha had kept her handcuffed to the table. How Martha had shown a heartbreaking side to her when she talked about her life and how Cheryl had stolen Gabe and kept the boys from her.

Rosie had been speaking for about forty-five minutes when she abruptly stopped. She lowered her head and stared at her hands. Danny could see from her body language just how tense she was getting, and he figured it was because she was coming to the end of her statement and was going to have to tell him about the gut-wrenching conclusion of her saga.

"Rosie, do you want to take a break? Get some water or coffee?"

At first, Rosie didn't respond. She finally raised her head and looked at Danny, then gave an almost imperceptible shake of her shoulders, like a horse's skin twitching to get a wasp off its back. "Yes, actually. That would be wonderful. Thank you."

Rosie used the restroom, and as she was washing her hands, she looked at herself in the mirror and gave yet another pep talk to her image. "You can do this. You are a strong woman. She cannot hurt you anymore. You have the power to banish her from your memories. Let's get this done."

Settling back in the chair across from Danny, Rosie took a sip of water. "I know you saw what was in the cabin." She thought for a moment. "And I'm not sure I can fully relay to you what happened; it's all such a blur in my mind. I've been going over it all for the last two weeks, and I'm still confused about what happened. Well." She grimaced. "I'm not confused about what happened exactly, but I am confused about why—why she did that."

"Rosie, I don't know if it will help you to think of it this way, but maybe there is no why. In my experience as a cop, so many things happen that truly make no sense. And we all would go crazy trying to bring some semblance of order and rationality to the unthinkable. So just tell us what you remember. Act like you're reading from a book, written by an unknown author. The words have nothing to do with you."

Rosie gave a small laugh. "As if." But she smiled. "Okay, life coach, here goes nothing. It was getting late. There were no clocks in the cabin, but I could see it was getting dark outside. My God, it seemed like we had been there forever. Just Martha and me, stuck in that cabin for eternity. But I knew things were ending. Maybe it was a slight shift in Martha's posture, or something in her voice, or maybe it was some unknown presence telling me to be on alert. That this was it. That I might . . . die . . . very soon. That thought was like a hamster on a treadmill in the back of my mind. Going around and around and around. I could die. I could die. I could die. Do you have any idea of the absolute terror those three words brought?"

Rosie's hands were clasped tightly together. Her whole body was rigid, and her eyes took on the haunted look she'd worn right after she was found. Danny knew she was back there, in that cabin, reliving the nightmare that took place. He also knew there was nothing he could do to help her. That she had to follow through and put into words what had happened. Even though there were no adequate words to describe the horror.

"She'd been drinking steadily all day. I told you that, didn't I?"
Danny nodded.

"I kept praying that she would pass out, or stand up and fall and hit her head, or just go to sleep. Anything to get her to stop talking and looking at me like I was the most despicable thing in the world. Of course, I'm not sure what I would have done if she had passed out. I'd probably still be sitting there, handcuffed to that table. I told you she'd nailed down the legs of the table, so even if she had left me alone, I don't know how I would have been able to get that handcuff off. I was a sitting duck. All gussied up for her to do to me whatever she wanted. And I knew, *I knew,* she wanted to kill me. All because she blamed me for Steve and Lance's deaths. Crazy."

Rosie paused. "I keep asking myself over and over—why didn't she kill me? I mean, she had every opportunity in the world to shoot me. She knew she was dying of liver cancer, so she wasn't worried about spending years in jail. She professed the desire to be done with this world more than once. She said she wanted to be with Steve and Lance. So why not shoot me and be done with it? And the only reason I can come up with is that somewhere, buried deep in that twisted mind of hers, was the fear that she would not meet up with Steve and Lance in the afterlife if she murdered me."

"She said something odd, or odd for her, right before . . . before everything ended. She said, 'I only hope there is a benevolent being somewhere out there who knows everything I have been through and will have mercy on me.' I mean, this was not a particularly religious woman, or, at least, I don't think she was. I think she had one last moment to be a caring human being. One last time to atone for everything she had done. And then . . . then . . ." Rosie looked so haunted. And so very sad. She whispered, "And then she put the handcuff key on the table with her left hand and brought the gun up with her right hand. She shot herself in the head. My God, she shot herself."

Rosie shook her head as tears formed in her eyes. She continued speaking in a low voice, like if no one could hear her, then it wouldn't be true. "She shot herself right in front of me. Danny, I have never seen anything like that. It was . . . Blood went everywhere. She fell backward, and the chair tipped over."

Rosie was speaking with urgency now, trying to get it all out at once. "I don't exactly know how long I sat there. Everything was so quiet. The cabin had seemed so noisy all day, but it was because Martha talked literally the entire day. And now, it was so quiet. I kept expecting Martha to jump up and say something like, 'You are so stupid to have fallen for that old joke. Of course, I didn't kill myself. I'm going to kill you.' So I waited. Waited for her to get up. Waited for the bullet that I knew was coming my way. Waited for someone to come tell me it was over, and I was okay. Waited to feel relief . . . but I just felt so very sad. For her. For me. For those little boys who grew up to be such monsters. For all the lonely and desolate people in the world who have no one to turn to, no one to help them. I kept thinking how different Martha's life would have been if maybe she had connected with just one other person. Would it have made a difference? We will never know. We will never know."

Danny sat quietly next to Rosie and gave her time to collect herself. As he had hoped, she appeared to be at peace with herself—at least for the time being. He knew she was going to have many days and nights in the future where she would relive the horrors of that day, but by speaking about it, she'd taken the first steps toward healing herself.

Rosie finished her statement by telling Danny she had no idea how long she'd sat at the table. It had seemed like hours but was probably no more than twenty minutes.

She'd finally reached out, taken the handcuff key in her right hand, and then had to sit quietly some more to try and get her trembling under control. When Rosie finally unlocked the cuff, she'd been amazed at the cuts and bruises it had left around her left wrist. She had pulled and jerked on the cuff, trying to get it off, but she'd never felt any pain in her wrist until the handcuff came off. She'd sat there rubbing her wrist, her mind a blessed blank. She'd known she needed to get up and try to find help but was unable to make her legs obey her brain.

She'd eventually pushed back from the table and stood up on shaky legs. Rosie had considered for a moment going around the table to make sure Martha was . . . was . . . but Rosie had just stood there and whimpered. She'd known that if she saw what lay around the table, she would never be able to get it out of her mind. Instead, she'd said a brief prayer for Martha and turned toward the door.

She'd stopped before she went out to the yard and slowly turned. She'd taken in the wine bottles on the counter, the three chairs around the table, the handcuff dangling from where it was still fastened on the table, the door left ajar leading to the bathroom. She'd known then; she would never forget this place. Then she opened the door and walked out to freedom.

CHAPTER SIXTY-ONE

REN WAS AT THE HOUSE when Rosie got back from giving her statement to Danny. He was standing in the living room, looking down the street and waiting for her. In the last two weeks, Ren would pace in front of the big picture window when Rosie was gone. He couldn't help but relive the horrifying day when Rosie went missing.

When she came in the back door, Ren took one look at her face, crossed over to her, and pulled her into his arms. "Oh, babe, I wish I had been there with you. I hate that you had to do it alone."

Rosie just pulled him closer. "I think it was exactly what I needed to do. I . . . I keep going over that day in my mind. Over and over. What I should have done differently. *If* there was anything I could have done differently. I'm even going back to my time spent with Steve in New York and wondering if there was a sign or a clue or something that would have alerted me.

And . . ." Rosie shrugged. "And nothing. I don't think there was one thing I could have done that would have changed what happened. And I think coming to terms with that is slowly helping me get over what *did* happen. I talked to Danny after I gave my statement, and what he said gave me hope. He said that being able to talk about it and facing your fears about that day is the first step in healing. He said many times it takes months before a victim is ready to share all the details with the police. He thinks it's healthy I was able to do it today. And I am going to hold onto that thought and keep reminding myself *none* of this was my fault."

"I've never doubted how strong you are. Remember, one of the first times I saw you, you were kicking everyone's butt in yoga, and, well, doing certain contractions in an unnamed body part at the same time." Ren could feel Rosie smile against his chest. "Good times, right?"

"Absolutely. There is one more thing I am going to do. Danny gave me the name of a therapist who deals in aiding people who have been through a traumatic experience. At first, I was somewhat offended when Danny gave me her name. I mean, I have always thought of myself as not only a physically strong person, but also as a mentally strong person. I can handle just about anything. But you know what, Ren? I'm not sure I can handle this on my own. And I don't just want to handle it. I want to deal with it and put it in its proper place so I can go on and live my life the way I want to. And as much as I know I have the support of you, my sisters, my dad, my dogs, none of us are equipped to deal with this without professional help. I'm going to call her tomorrow and set up an appointment."

"I think that is a brilliant idea!"

Rosie leaned back in Ren's arms. "I just wish there was something the two of us could do right now, together, to take my mind off my troubles. I just can't think of anything, can you?"

Ren's eyebrows shot up and he got a gleam in his eye. "Um, are you sure, hon? It's not too . . . well . . . soon or something?"

Rosie laughed softly. "Martha fucked with my brain, not my body. Besides, I know there are things Martha took from me, and

I don't know if I will ever get them back. My sense of invincibility, for one thing. She did a number on my ability to trust someone, or even my ability to trust my instincts about someone. I mean, I never got any weird vibe from Martha, except maybe thinking she talked too much about her dead son." She snorted. "The reoccurring nightmare of her dead sons—or, should I say, her dead want-to-be sons. But what I won't let her take from me is my desire to be with you, to be held by you." Rosie said softly, "I don't think anyone could do that."

———

Rosie spent the next six months doing exactly what she told Ren she was going to do. She started seeing Andy Holderness, the therapist Danny had recommended. Rosie felt a connection to Andy from the very first meeting. Andy was about ten years older than Rosie, but there was something about her that made Rosie feel like she could trust her with her darkest secrets. Andy was very open to using different types of trauma therapy, so the first couple of months were spent working out which was the most therapeutic for Rosie.

Rosie had found that she responded best when Andy would give her certain "homework assignments" to complete before their next session. She found it soothing and enhancing to her well-being to be able to write about the various emotional pitfalls she'd encountered that fateful day.

Plus, it was encouraging to find she could write at all. The first time she'd tried to resume writing on her novel, she found her mind blocked, and her hands seemed to not remember where any of the letters were on the keyboard. It was as if she was afraid to let her mind wander because she was afraid it would wander down the wrong path. The path that would take her straight back to Martha and that dreaded house of horrors.

Her homework assignments, for now, were taking the place of her novel. If she concentrated on just one aspect of that day, say the absolute fear she felt every time Martha pointed the gun at her, then she could analyze it from various points of view and strip it of its power to take over her mind and make her lose control.

Rosie also requested her family to take part in group therapy. She realized she was not the only one traumatized by that day, and Andy encouraged Rosie to talk her family into therapy. And one of the most surprising outcomes of the group talk was how everyone felt they had let Rosie down in one way or the other. Ren had discussed his anger at himself for not stepping in and stopping Martha from continuing to talk to Rosie, even though there had been absolutely no indication Martha would turn out to be the psycho bitch from hell. The sisters all felt some guilt, irrational as it was, because they hadn't physically been there with Rosie on that day. They all felt like they could have prevented the kidnapping. Jack was plagued with both anxiety and anger—anxiety when he relived that day in his mind, knowing full well the outcome could have been very different, and anger toward unseen forces allowing someone like Martha to terrorize his family.

Andy was particularly effective during group therapy. She encouraged everyone to voice their most hidden fears about that day, and by doing so, allowed the family to see there was nothing they could have done to prevent what Martha did. She was very skillful in steering the family to come to that conclusion on their own. She had been a therapist long enough to know that telling someone something, even if it was the truth, wasn't nearly as effective as the person determining the outcome by themselves.

Rosie also incorporated physical exercise on her journey for the mentally stable Rosie. She had always been very active with yoga and running, but she upped the stakes by adding a weightlifting program. Rosie still struggled with feelings of helplessness and being powerless when she would think about that day. For every weight she lifted, for every newly defined muscle in her arms, for every push-up she did, she felt like she was taking back her life and telling the world, "Never going to happen to me again!"

Andy was very supportive of the increased exercise regimen. She knew feeling powerful in your body went a long way in feeling powerful in your mind. Andy also encouraged Rosie to continue going to the shooting range once a week. It was unspoken between them, but they both knew every time Rosie discharged her weapon at the silhouette target, she was shooting Martha.

CHAPTER SIXTY-TWO

"OH, DAISY! You look beautiful!" Lilly, Rosie, and Amy were all crowded into the dressing room. Daisy was trying on dresses to wear at her wedding to Jon in six weeks.

"I still think you need to wear a long white gown," said Amy.

"Yeah, right. How weird would I look, huh? A thirty-six-year-old woman getting married for the second time wearing a long, flowing, white wedding gown? I suppose you also want me to have it cut super low between my boobs, wear a tiara with a veil twelve feet long, and be proceeded by eighteen bridesmaids? Do we want a sophisticated wedding or one that would be at home on a reality TV show?"

"Hey, I vote for the reality TV show wedding. It would certainly give everyone something to talk about!" Amy laughed. "I can just see Dad's face if you walked out wearing something like that! He would shit!"

"Well, so would Jon, I guarantee you. He would shit first, then bolt for the door. He would be perfectly fine with a quick stop into the justice of the peace, followed by dinner at the local diner. The man has simple tastes. But I told him he's only getting married once in his life, hopefully, so it would be nice to have some type of ceremony. Also" —Daisy paused— "I think he's worried I'm going to be comparing this ceremony with my last one."

"Really?" Lilly said. "Daisy, that surprises me. Jon seems so—I don't know—so self-assured about everything."

"And he is. Don't get me wrong. He's never come right out and said anything, but I just get the sense he's worried or nervous about it. I'm only saying this because of something he said a couple of weeks ago. We were talking about the wedding, and he got kind of quiet. When I asked him if there was anything wrong, he looked at me for a moment, and then said that he hopes he can live up to the memory of Tommy." Daisy smiled a sad smile and wiped a tear away. "I told him he could be assured that Tommy was up in heaven, looking down at us, and high fiving everyone around him, including my mom. I've told him more than once I think he and Tommy would have been very good friends."

"So, you talk about Tommy with him?" asked Rosie.

Daisy nodded. "Not all the time, of course. That would be crazy. But Jon asks about him every now and then. He knows about the accident and that we had been together for a long time. I also told him *because* I had such a happy marriage, I am so very excited to do it again! All right. Enough of this talk! Which dress am I going to wear to the wedding and which one to the reception?"

Since it was going to be an afternoon June wedding in Jack's backyard, the girls decided on a simple halter maxi dress in a soft blue-green color with gray teardrop earrings. The dress was such a flattering fit on Daisy that she decided to heck with getting a different dress for the reception. She would not wear heels for the wedding but would consider some fancy flats. She was sure that if she were stupid enough to wear heels, then she would fall flat on her face walking down the aisle. Heels had a nasty way of sinking into the ground and refusing to move forward. Daisy also decided she would change into sparkly Sketchers flip-flops for the reception. A girl must be comfortable to dance the night away!

Daisy and Jon had decided to have a simple wedding, but they both wanted their family members to participate in the ceremony. Jon's mom and dad, Camille and Dave, would walk Jon down the aisle. Then Jon's two sisters, Jean and her husband Tim, and Nancy and her husband Kevin, would walk down the aisle and be seated. Amy and Danny, Lilly and Keith, and Rosie and Ren would follow. They'd debated whether to have Leo somehow participate in the festivities, but in the end decided that it would be too much for him.

Since neither Daisy nor Jon were particularly religious, they decided to ask Jack if he would perform the marriage. At first, Jack had been a bit hesitant, but after doing some research and finding out it was common and easy these days to become a legally licensed minister, he became very excited about it. After having a couple of conversations with Daisy and Jon to find out exactly what they wanted him to talk about, he threw himself into drafting the best wedding ceremony ever!

With the wedding plans in full swing, the sisters decided they needed a weekend away from the men to properly plan the ceremony. Of course, the planning involved sitting around the pool, getting massages and pedicures, and just enjoying each other's company. They all met at the Trailway Spa in Austin. Jean and Nancy joined them, and it was a great weekend to really get to know Jon's sisters.

And since the wedding had already been planned—everyone walks down the aisle, Jack marries them, a buffet and a couple of bars would be set up under a tent—the girls did not have any decisions left they had to make. The only question left unanswered was if they should have a DJ or a band.

In the end, they decided on both, only because the band they wanted to use was the Justice League, a band comprised of four lawyers, with Keith being the lead guitarist. The Justice League had garnered a bit of fame in Brunswick, and they frequently played at some of the local bars, usually on a Friday night. They played mostly oldies and country western, which fit perfectly with what Daisy and Jon wanted. They figured the DJ could play newer songs afterward. Keith's band was more than happy to play for about an hour, but then Keith wanted to be able to enjoy the rest of the reception.

On Saturday morning, Daisy woke everyone up by texting, "It's competition day! Get up, put on your workout clothes, and join me at the pool for some yoga. Then we're going to see who gets to be crowned Miss Fitness Queen!"

"What the hell is she talking about?" groaned Amy as she buried her head under her pillow. "I thought we were here for rest and relaxation before the big weekend. Besides, I haven't been able to sleep in on a Saturday for, like, forever!"

Rosie jumped out of her bed, stretched, pulled Amy's covers off her, and tickled her feet. "Wake up, sleepyhead! Remember, this is all about Daisy. If she wants us to go on a fitness hike or whatever, we will smile, maybe curse her under our breath, but do it for her."

"Easy for you to say. You have turned into the female equivalent of the Rock. I, on the other hand, have to spend my days toiling away in a dark and musty law library, hunched over my computer, usually trying to find some obscure case I can use to bolster my arguments for my Appellate Advocacy class. Why did I take that class again? It is driving me crazy! Plus, I no longer have any muscle tone. I feel like a little old lady. I may need a walker if we go on a hike."

"No, no, no. No law talk today, no crazy woman kidnapping people talk today, no being angry at our body talk today. Today, the only talk will be about Daisy, the wedding, and what activities she wants to do today to make her happy. Okay, and maybe we can talk about what drinks we are going to have this afternoon at the pool, but that is it! Come on, my lazy little sister. Let's go conquer the world!"

At seven-thirty, the temperature was a very comfortable seventy-two degrees with a brilliant blue sky. Since this was Texas, the temperature was supposed to climb to a toasty eighty-seven by mid-afternoon, but the girls figured the pool would keep them cool.

Daisy, Lilly, Jean, and Nancy were all sitting on yoga mats in the grass in the field next to the pool. The class had just begun, and the twenty or so women and men were all sitting crossed legged and doing their yoga breathing. In through the nose and out through the mouth. Rosie and Amy silently made their way to the two empty mats next to Daisy, sat down, and joined the class.

An hour later, after numerous sun salutations, down dogs, up dogs, tree poses, mountain poses, warriors one-two-three, cobras, and cat/cow poses, the girls all relaxed during savasana. "If it's all the same with you, Daisy, I'll volunteer to stay here for the rest of the day. I heard the pool gets full in the afternoon, so someone has to be here to get our six chairs." Amy sighed dramatically. "It's a hard job, but someone has to do it."

Amy turned her head to Daisy and opened one eye to see if Daisy was buying her bullshit. Daisy was still lying in the corpse pose but she was smiling and shaking her head. "I have always thought you were the most selfless of the sisters, Amy. To make an offer like that—you should be nominated for sainthood! But—and I know I speak for everyone here—the day just wouldn't be complete without all of us being together. Besides, I already spoke to the lifeguard yesterday, told her it was my bridal shower weekend, and she promised to put a reserve sign on six of the chairs. Plus, I just know you would be pissed if you missed out on some of the activities scheduled for the day. And speaking of, the next activity starts in thirty minutes, so go pee, grab some coffee, and meet me out in front of the main building."

CHAPTER SIXTY-THREE

"GIRLS, THIS IS NICK. He is going to be our sort-of tour guide today," Daisy said.

Nick was a six-foot-two, blond, blue-eyed young man. He gave the group a big grin, revealing (of course) perfect, straight white teeth. He was muscular but had the lean look of a runner.

"Okay, ladies, this first activity is to just get us into the swing of things here." Nick led them into a big, cavernous barn. There were six archery targets on one end of the cabin and six archery bows with arrows placed at the other end. "I know y'all did yoga this morning, so everyone's muscles should be limbered up and ready to go. But archery is also a thinking sport, and I would be remiss if I let anyone start shooting before I am positive your brain is ready to go. To make sure of that, there are a few questions that need to be answered." Nick seemed very intent and serious. "And I hate to say it, but if these questions are not answered correctly, then there will be no archery in this barn today."

The girls were standing in a line behind the bows and arrows, and Nick was pacing in front of them. "Okay, Daisy, you get the first question. Here goes. Question—what did the archer get when he hit a bullseye?"

Daisy started smiling. "Uh, I don't know, a high five from the crowd?"

Nick made a buzzing noise. "Wrong answer. But since this is our first question, I will take pity on you. The answer is . . . a very angry bull!"

All the girls just groaned and laughed. "Second question. This is for you, Lilly. Question—what did the lustful maiden say to the handsome archer?"

Lilly laughed. "I have no idea, but maybe something like, I don't know, something about Cupid shooting an arrow to her heart?"

Nick made the buzzing noise again. "Nope. The answer is . . . wait for it . . . you make me quiver! Get it?"

They were all laughing now.

Jean said, "I have a question for you, Nick. Since you are probably in your twenties, how did you get all these archery dad jokes?"

"Those were not archery dad jokes! *This* is an archery dad joke. Question—why couldn't the pepper do archery? Anyone? Anyone? Because he didn't habanero!" Before anyone could respond, he went on. "All right, even I am rolling my eyes with that one! What say we do some archery?"

———

The next activity Daisy pulled them to was wall climbing.

"You have got to be kidding me. Shooting an arrow is one thing, but this is just torture! My upper body strength is, like, non-existent. There is no way I am getting up that wall." Nancy was laughing but seemed pretty determined to bypass this exercise.

"You sure, Nance?" asked Jean. "They strap you in and hook you up with all these pulleys and straps, so there's no way you can fall. Look, Nick is up on the platform. I just bet he has some awesome wall-climbing dad jokes!"

"Even that is not enough to make me try this. I'll be the climbing wall monitor!" Nancy pointed. "I mean, maybe if I had some back muscles like Rosie!"

Jean turned to see Rosie and Amy start up the walls. There were two climbing walls, side by side, approximately thirty-five feet tall. Both girls wore helmets and harnesses. Rosie got off to a great start, and Nancy was right about her upper back muscles. She was very toned. Amy was having some difficulty navigating and coordinating her hands and feet. She would grab a hold with her hand but then would have trouble finding the hold for her foot, which she needed to propel herself upward. Rosie, on the other hand, scaled the wall like it was something she did every day and twice on Sundays.

When Rosie reached her platform, she stood and rooted Amy on. "Come on, girl. Almost there. You can do it." When Amy finally made it to the top, both sisters jumped up and down, pumping their fists in good imitations of Rocky.

Lilly and Jean were the next two to scale the wall. No one did it as quickly as Rosie, but each managed to make it to the top, with just a small amount of assistance from the belayers. Daisy said she was going to try and come up with some spa jokes for Nick and stayed on the ground with Nancy. After the girls made it up the wall, each had to do a small zip-line that took them back down.

"Please, please say our next activity involves sitting down at lunch and maybe, just maybe, cracking open a nice cold beer," Amy begged.

Daisy just laughed. "I have saved the best for last!"

———

THUNK.

"I hit it!" Jean yelled excitedly. "I hope you all saw that! It was a perfect throw, if I may say so myself."

THUNK. THUNK.

"Damn it! What a showoff! Have you been practicing?" Jean glared at Daisy. "And remind me to tell my baby brother to never piss you off!" The girls had signed up for an axe throwing class, and Daisy had turned out to be a natural. She would bring the axe straight back behind her head and then throw it straight forward, releasing the axe when her arm was extended and parallel to the ground.

There were seven wood targets with bullseyes marked on them about twelve feet away. Jean had hit the first target, and she had turned just in time to see Daisy throw two axes, one in each hand, and hit two more of the bullseyes.

"Holy crap. Jean is right! Have you been practicing? I can't even hit one target, and now you hit two like it's no big deal! Must be the luck of being the bride!" Lilly had thrown four axes already, and none of them had even come close to hitting the targets. "In order to save my pride, I'll just stand here. Since Nancy got to be the climbing wall monitor, I will be the axe throwing monitor."

Daisy just laughed and shrugged. "I have never done this in my life, but I just might make it my second career. Jon can quit doctoring and be my manager. This could be very lucrative!" Daisy was wearing a pair of black yoga pants and a fuchsia-colored tank top. Her hair was pulled up in a high ponytail, her cheeks were flushed, and her eyes were sparkling. All the sisters took note of how happy she looked and gave a big silent "thank you" to whatever higher power was responsible for giving Daisy her life back.

The Trailways Spa prided itself on their farm-to-table restaurant. Nick and the girls were seated at a table for eight on the patio with a fantastic view overlooking Lake Austin. As promised, the weather was in the low eighties, but with the gentle breeze blowing from the lake, it felt like a very comfortable seventy-five degrees. They were all laughing and peppering Nick with questions about his life.

"So, Nick. What are you going to do with your life? Or do you think you might be able to go on the stand-up comedy circuit? I mean, I'm sure those jokes would be a huge hit! Although I really thought nothing could be worse than the archery jokes. Turns out I was wrong! The axe jokes are not even worth repeating!"

Nick laughed. "What? How can you not like the all-time favorite, 'How can you tell that an axe thrower loves his assistant?'"

All the girls answered as one. "Because he misses her!"

"Okay, I knew I needed a more realistic life plan than taking my comedy act on the road, so I applied to get my doctorate in physical therapy."

"Where are you going, Nick?" asked Lilly. "There are quite a few excellent programs in physical therapy right here in Texas."

"Well, I realize this might be sacrilegious to say, but I really wanted to study someplace other than Texas."

"*What?*"

They all laughed.

"Don't say that too loud! They might spit in your food or something!" Lilly joked. "So where have you applied?"

Nick got a big grin on his face, showing off those beautiful straight white teeth. "Not only did I apply, but I found out three weeks ago that I was accepted. Pretty darn excited about it too!"

"Where?"

"Rockhurst University in Kansas City, Missouri. Right in the middle of the heartland!"

"Wow," Rosie said. "Congratulations! My boyfriend is from Kansas City. Small world!"

"True confession time. I doubt I would have even considered Kansas City because it's almost too far north for me. I want to study somewhere outside of Texas, but I don't want to freeze while I'm doing it." He laughed. "But it's amazing what you'll do for true love. My girlfriend of three years is starting med school there in September, and she convinced me to give it a try. And I guess I can always go buy a parka!"

CHAPTER SIXTY-FOUR

FINALLY! The wedding day was here. The ceremony was scheduled for four in the afternoon. The girls gathered at Jack's at noon, and the guys all went over to Rosie and Ren's to get ready. Daisy had arranged for a light lunch at the house and for the makeup and hair girls to arrive at one. Daisy had to be talked into getting her hair and makeup done by the sisters.

"Come on. When do we ever get to get all fancy? And since Amy is the only one who really knows how to apply false eyelashes, I need an expert to do mine so I don't look like I have tarantulas on my eyes." Rosie had batted her eyes at Daisy, who just rolled hers.

"Your eyelashes look perfectly fine to me. I'm afraid I will look like a clown or something since I rarely wear much makeup at all. I don't want Jon taking one look at me and deciding he made a big mistake."

"Nope. You are going to get overruled on this one." Amy had displayed her imaginary judge's gavel and brought it down on the table. "I happen to have a friend who does make-up for a living. Remember the wedding I was in a couple of months ago? Brooke and Joe, my law school buddies? Anyway, Brooke's best friend does this for a living, and let me tell you, she did a fantastic job. Brooke is like you, Daisy. She doesn't wear much make-up, but, my God, she looked like a model or something after Harper was done with her. And it looked very natural, so don't worry."

Harper got to the house at 1:00 p.m. and brought Madelyn, who was going to do their hair, with her. Thankfully, Jack had a big master bathroom, so all the girls gathered in there to watch, and, of course, to comment on Daisy getting the royal bridal treatment. It was decided that Harper would start with Daisy's make-up. She positioned Daisy with her back to the mirror and was done in about thirty minutes. After spritzing Daisy's face with a make-up setting spray, she said, "Okay, Daisy, I am going to turn you around, and you must promise me you will tell me if you don't like something. We have plenty of time, and I can fix anything. Here goes."

"I'm afraid to look," Daisy said, keeping her eyes shut. "What do you guys think?"

"Oh my God, Daisy. Jon is going to take one look at you and his jaw is going to drop. You look so beautiful! Come on, open your eyes."

Daisy slowly opened her eyes and then just stared at her face in the mirror.

"Say something, anything, Daisy. I can change whatever you don't like," Harper said, standing behind Daisy and looking at her in the mirror.

A small smile spread across Daisy's face. She raised her hand and softly felt her cheek. Daisy's skin really looked flawless, and combined with the eyeliner and false eyelashes, it really did make her look like a different person. "Wow. Can you come over to my house every morning and do this to me?"

Harper smiled at Daisy in the mirror. "You don't know how relieved I am you like it. You are a beautiful bride!"

All the sisters agreed, and over the next couple of hours, everyone else got ready. Hair was pulled up in messy buns, false eyelashes were applied, and when Daisy came out of the bedroom in her halter wedding dress, all the sisters gathered around her and started talking at once.

"You are beautiful!"

"I love that dress!"

"Jon is going to fall over!"

"I want to get married again!" That was from Lilly.

"I just want to get married now!" That was from Amy, and the sisters all turned to her.

"Really? You want to get married?"

Amy laughed. "Actually, no. I just got caught up in the moment. I mean, I do want to get married someday, but not yet. Have to get my career settled first. I think I just want to look like Daisy when I do eventually get married."

"Get out. And enough about me! I think we all look like a million bucks! Look at us together." They all turned and looked in the long bathroom mirror. Daisy was the only one in the soft blue-green color. Everyone else wore various shades of deep blue or purple, which really made Daisy stand out. "We look like a watercolor by Monet! Harper and Madelyn, you all did a fantastic job! And thank you to my wonderful sisters for talking me into doing this. I'll feel like a fairy princess today."

There was a knock on the bathroom door. "Is everyone decent in here? The photographer is here. Time to get this show on the road," Jack said.

CHAPTER SIXTY-FIVE

"PLEASE BE SEATED."

Jack looked at Daisy and smiled at his oldest daughter. As was his way, he talked to Claudia in his mind. *She is so beautiful and happy again. We are truly blessed.*

"First, I'd like to begin by welcoming everyone and thanking each and every one of you for being here on this most happy of days." Jack paused and cleared his throat. "We are gathered here together for an occasion that I know is not only monumental for the wedded-couple-to-be, but for all of us who are lucky to know and love them as individuals and even more so as a perfect pairing."

"The most remarkable moment in life is when you meet the person who makes you feel complete. The person who makes your world a beautiful and magical place. The person with whom you share a bond so special that it transcends normal relationships. I was very lucky and met that person in high school when I looked across the cafeteria and saw the most beautiful girl in the world. Her name was Claudia, and she became my wife and the mother of Daisy and her sisters. For Daisy and Jon, it happened at a later period in their lives, but the bond nonetheless is so pure and so wonderful, and they are loving the fact that they get to spend the rest of their lives together. I know how deeply these two care for and love one another, and I feel privileged to be here today among all of you as a witness of their commitment to a lifetime of love for one another. So, without further ado, let's get Daisy and Jon officially married!"

Jack looked at Daisy and gave a slight nod. "We are gathered here to join Daisy and Jon in the union of marriage. This contract is not to be entered into lightly, but thoughtfully and seriously, and with a deep realization of its obligations and responsibilities. We have now come to the point of your ceremony where you are going to say your vows to one another. But before you do, I ask you to remember that love—which is rooted in faith, trust, and acceptance—will be the foundation of an abiding and deepening relationship. No other ties are more tender, no other vows more sacred than those you now assume. If you can keep the vows you take here today, not because of any religious or civic law, but out of a desire to love and be loved by another person fully, without limitation, then your lives will have an abundance of joy and exaltation."

"Daisy, if you would, please turn to Jon and recite the vows you have written."

Daisy turned to Jon, took his hands in hers, took a deep breath, and began. "I, Daisy, take you, Jon, to be my husband. When you need a friend, I will be your best friend. When you need help, I will be there for you. When you need care, I will support you. In you, I have found a partner in life, a lover, a friend, a safe place, and most of all, a place to rest my weary head at the end of the day. You have taught me that two people joined together with respect, trust, and open communication can be far stronger and happier than each could ever be alone. You are the strength I didn't know I needed and the joy I didn't know I lacked. And most importantly, thank you for allowing me to experience true love for the second time in my life. And I can't believe I made it through without crying!"

Jon smiled down at Daisy. "I hope I can do the same. So here goes. Daisy, I was drawn to you from the first day we met. I remember making reasons to talk to you, just so I could be in your presence. You have the purest heart and a warm, loving soul. In every person you meet, Daisy, you not only find, but brighten, their inner light. With you, I feel like half of an unstoppable whole, and I can't wait to take on this life with you as my best friend and partner. You have also shown me what unconditional love feels like, so I promise to treat you with kindness throughout the rest of our lives together and always love you unconditionally. I promise when we are old and gray, we will look back on our lives together and have no regrets. From this day forward, you will never walk alone."

After the rings were exchanged, Jack instructed Daisy and Jon to face the crowd. "By the power of your love and commitment and the power vested in me, I now pronounce you husband and wife."

A loud cheer erupted from the audience. Daisy and Jon were beaming from ear to ear, and the cheers got even louder when Jon reached over to Daisy, bent her into a classic dip, and gave her a big kiss. It was such a totally non-Jon thing to do that all the sisters, including Daisy, gave a resounding cheer.

Daisy turned to Rosie, hugged her, gave her the bridal bouquet, then hooked her arm with Jon and started down the aisle. Rosie looked startled by this. In the rehearsal, Daisy had carried her bouquet while she and Jon were walking out. Rosie and Ren were to follow, then Lilly and Keith and Amy and Danny. So Rosie wasn't sure what exactly was going on. But then the craziest thing happened.

Daisy and Jon stopped, turned around, and went back toward the wedding party. Rosie, Lilly, and Amy were standing in line, and Daisy went and stood by Amy. Jon stood by Danny, as he was the last one in line on the groomsmen side.

"What the hell?" asked Rosie. She turned to look at her sisters to see if they were as confused as she was, but all three of them were standing together, holding hands and smiling at Rosie. "What's going on?"

Just then, she heard Ren say, "Rosie?"

She turned and there was Ren, on his knee and holding up a beautiful diamond ring.

"Ren," Rosie whispered, appalled. "What are you doing? Why are you doing that here?"

The audience had gone from cheering for Daisy and Jon to absolute silence. Everyone was sitting at the edge of their chairs, watching intently to see what was going to happen next. The only ones who did not seem confused by the sudden shift of events were Daisy, Jon, Keith, Lilly, Amy, Danny, Jack, and Ren.

"Dad? What is going on?"

"I think Ren is going to clear everything up."

"Rosie. I am kneeling before you and your family and all our friends to formally ask you to marry me. I—"

Rosie was still holding Daisy's bouquet in her left hand, so she put her right hand up in a "stop now" position. "Have you lost your mind?" Rosie hissed. "This is Daisy and Jon's wedding. Why are you doing this now?"

Rosie felt Daisy's arm go around her shoulders. "Rosie, look at me. You do know that you can't say no to the bride on her wedding day, right? And that you have to do exactly what the bride tells you to do? Well, Jon and I talked to Ren, and we told him this is what we wanted. We wanted to share our very special day with you and Ren. As a matter of fact, sharing it with you makes it even more special. We knew Ren wanted to propose to you, and we thought this would be the perfect time and place. We're all here. It's a beautiful day, a day where love is all around us. A day where when you look back, years from now, you will still be able to feel all the love that everyone here has for you."

Rosie was looking at Daisy, tears forming in her eyes. "Daisy, are you sure? This is supposed to be your day, not mine."

Daisy put her hands on Rosie's shoulders, leaned in, and whispered "This is our day. We have come out of the dark and into the light. My dark days after Tommy and yours after Martha. We are strong Texan women and absolutely nothing keeps us down. I am so excited for my future with Jon and to be able to witness yours with Ren. I love you, and this is the best wedding present you can give us." The sisters hugged each other for a long moment. Daisy gave Rosie one last squeeze and then turned back to Ren. "I, for one, cannot wait to hear this proposal. Ren said he had something special planned."

"Something more special than this? Is that even possible?"

Ren stood up and slid the ring onto Rosie's left hand. It was a perfect fit. "Rosie, if you want to kill me when we are alone, I won't stop you. I know the timing is a shock to you, but the proposal shouldn't be. I knew you were the one for me from the moment I saw you. You are brave, you are beautiful, you are my best friend, and I want to spend the rest of my life with you. Daisy and Jon . . . well, the way they explained it to me, they want everyone to feel the joy and happiness that they have in their life and thought this might be a great way for us to carve out some of those feelings for our own. Or" —Ren paused— "I never thought about it but maybe they just want me to publicly humiliate myself when you turn me down in front of all these people."

Everyone laughed. Rosie just kept looking at Ren, shaking her head but with a smile starting on her lips. Ren was starting to look a bit nervous. "Uh, you do know I was *kidding* about turning me down, right?"

"I just want to see you sweat a little bit, big boy. Now, what is the 'something special'? I'm waiting for that before I give you my answer."

Ren turned toward the house and gave a shrill whistle. At first, nothing happened. But then everyone could hear some faint laughter that got louder and louder. Finally, from around the corner of the house came Julie Jones, Ren's office manager. She had Walter and Marilyn. Next came Claire Graham, the office assistant, being led by Big Shirley and Leo. Lastly, Maggie Redcamp, who'd happened to be at the vet's office when Julie and Claire were discussing bringing the dogs to the wedding and thought it was such a great idea that she begged to help, brought up the rear of the procession, walking with her dog Lois, and the newest addition to the household, Evie the elderly golden retriever.

The mixed procession of animals and humans walked right up the aisle to Ren, and then, miraculously, they all sat at the same time. It was as if the dogs knew they had to be on their best behavior. Rosie and the sisters were cracking up, especially after they saw the message Marilyn had around her neck. It was a sign saying, "PLEASE SAY YES TO MY DAD SO I CAN GET THIS STUPID SIGN OFF AND GO BACK TO IGNORING ALL THESE ANNOYING ANIMALS!" And the look on Marilyn's face was priceless.

"You didn't think I was going to make one of the most important decisions in my life without my squad behind me, did you? Plus, I knew they would help make my case! And Daisy and Jon gave me permission, as long as Leo got to join in the fun."

Rosie walked up to Ren, put her arms around his neck, and whispered something in his ear.

Ren got a big grin on his face, gave her a quick kiss on the lips, and turned to everyone. "It could have gone either way, but the dog parade sealed the deal. She said YES! Now let's go celebrate Daisy and Jon!"

TWO YEARS LATER

It had been two years to the day since Daisy and Jon's wedding and Ren's proposal to Rosie. Once again, they were gathered in Jack's backyard with chairs lined up on either side of the aisle leading to the wedding arbor that was decorated with garden roses, larkspur, and fuchsia bougainvillea. Keith's bandmates, the Justice League, were tuning their instruments under the tent by the house. On the other side of the yard, the long tables were ready to be covered with the BBQ buffet, and both bartenders were busy polishing glasses and putting out the different beers and wines they were going to serve.

Jack looked at his daughters, smiled, and as was his way, said in his mind to Claudia, *I will always love you.*

Rosie and Ren were the first ones to walk up the aisle. They held each other's hand, and when they got to the wedding arbor, Ren leaned over, gently placed his hand on Rosie's very pregnant belly, and gave her a kiss. Daisy and Jon were the next to walk up the aisle, along with Rowen and Frankie, their fourteen-month-old twin girls, all holding hands. Lilly walked up with Luke, Lacey, and baby Claudia. Amy and Danny were the last ones to walk the aisle. They took their places, and everyone turned as one when the band began to play the song "You Are the Reason" by Callum Scott and Leona Lewis.

Jack reached over, took Sarah's hand, and looked into her eyes. "I will be forever grateful Matt stood me up for golf that day. Now let's go get married."

A year ago, on a beautiful day in June, Jack had been at the driving range of the local golf course. He was supposed to have met his friend Matt for a game and had decided to get to the course early to practice. The last couple of times Jack had played, he'd struggled to hit his three wood straight, so he figured he might try to work out the kinks on the driving range instead of during a round. Jack had thought perhaps his stance or grip might have been the problem, instead of LOFT, as Matt liked to say—LOFT, of course, standing for Lack Of Fucking Talent. *Why do I even play golf with him?* Jack asked himself.

Jack had noticed the woman who was about six slots to the right of him. She'd been practicing with her driver, and Jack stopped what he was doing to watch. She'd addressed the ball, took her club back slowly, and then swung down to hit the ball about two hundred yards straight down the middle. *Great swing. Wish I could hit it that straight,* he had thought as he went back to practicing his own game.

Thirty minutes later, Jack's cell phone had rung. It had been Matt saying something had come up at work and he wasn't going to be able to play after all. *Rats. I guess I can play as a single. I might meet up with a group and join in.*

Jack had his pushcart next to him, and as he put his three wood and driver back in the bag, he'd again noticed the woman with the great swing. She was still practicing. As he would tell people later, he didn't know what got into him. Normally, he would never have approached her, but there had just been something about her that caught his eye. She was slim, about five-seven, had glossy dark brown hair in a ponytail that was pulled through the back of her ball cap, and wore a golf dress that showed off her shapely, muscular legs.

Sarah later would joke that it was the dress and her legs that had caught his eye, but Jack would always deny that and instead would say he was just impressed by her swing. One golfer to another, he would insist.

"Is there any way you might want to play a couple of holes?"

The woman also had a pushcart and had been gathering up her clubs when Jack walked up. She'd turned to face Jack and looked around, as if to make sure he was talking to her. "Me?"

"Well, it is a beautiful day, I have a tee time in five minutes, my friend stood me up, and I really hate playing golf by myself. I'm always afraid the people, when they drive by in their carts, are thinking I either don't have any friends or I must be a crappy golfer. I thought you might take pity on me and save my reputation.

Also, I noticed you have a hell of a swing, so I'm hoping you might give me some pointers!"

The woman had laughed. "This must be the day for having things get cancelled on you. I just got word my meeting got postponed until tomorrow, so actually I'm free to play. But . . . was that a joke about being a crappy golfer or are you trying to warn me?"

Jack had raised one eyebrow and smiled. "Are you willing to take a chance?"

The rest, as they say, was history. That day on the golf course had been the beginning of the relationship between Jack and Sarah that started out as friends and ended with their wedding. Both had lost spouses early on, and neither one had thought they would ever get married again. Sarah didn't have any children by her first husband, and she'd managed to fill that void by always having a couple of cats around and throwing herself into her work. She was a pediatrician, and she always said that she had hundreds of kids instead of just one or two.

Jack introduced Sarah to the sisters about two months after their first "date" on the golf course. He had joked with Sarah that he wasn't worried about his girls accepting Sarah, but he was worried about all the dogs accepting the cats. As it turned out, he'd had nothing to worry about. Jack had been right about his girls welcoming Sarah with open arms. She had a warm and engaging personality, and it was obvious from the start that she adored Jack. The sisters had long wished for Jack to find someone, but he'd seemed so content with his life that they never pushed the idea.

Introducing the cats to the dogs in the family had taken some strategizing, but they finally decided to introduce Leo and Evie first, since they were a little less imposing than the other ones. As it stood, the family could have brought all the dogs together at once because Sid and Caesar (the cats) had been totally unimpressed and uninterested in anything the dogs had to offer. Once it became obvious the cats did not want to play, they'd all found some sunshine on the carpet and taken a nap. However, the meet-and-greet with the Danes and the Newfie had been a bit different. Marilyn and Big Shirley had sniffed at the cats and then given a canine shrug and walked away, as if to say, "Not too sure what those two little balls of fur are, but it is nothing we have to concern ourselves with."

Walter, as usual, had been the one to put on a show. Just like when he'd met BS for the first time, he'd tried every trick in his book to get the cats to notice him. The jumping up and spinning in circles, doing the downward dog pose to get closer to their faces, the sudden stop and then the explosive run around the yard . . . all for naught. He'd finally admitted defeat, but not before staring at Sid and Caesar with such a hurt look on his face that Sarah had gone over to him and given him a big hug. "It's not you, big guy," she'd whispered in his ear. "They're like that with everyone!"

Jack and Sarah took a deep breath, nodded to each other, stepped out into the sunshine, and took the first steps toward their new lives.

"Please be seated."

Keith had been nominated to perform the wedding ceremony, and just like Jack, he took his responsibilities very seriously. The ceremony was short, but what it lacked in length, it more than made up for in the beautiful and heartfelt messages of love and gratitude in second chances for happiness.

After the rings were exchanged, Keith instructed Sarah and

Jack to face the crowd. "By the power of your love and commitment and the power vested in me, I now pronounce you husband and wife."

And when a familiar loud cheer came from the guests, Jack said, "I am quite a bit older than Jon, and if I tried to dip my new bride here, we both would probably tumble to the floor. In interest of not breaking her back, I will give her a traditional kiss." And he did.

Sarah turned to Amy, hugged her, gave her the bridal bouquet, hooked her arm with Jack, and started down the aisle. But halfway there, they turned around and went back to the wedding party, with Sarah standing by Rosie and Jack by Ren.

And like before, Amy turned to her sisters and new stepmother and saw them holding hands and grinning at her. Just then, she heard Danny say, "Amy?"

Acknowledgments

First and foremost, I would like to thank the people at Wildling Press. I knew absolutely *NOTHING* about publishing a book, and they took me under their wings and made the publishing process, if not enjoyable (after all, you are talking about putting yourself out into the world for all to judge!), then certainly as stress-free as possible. Christina Kann, Mary-Peyton Crook, Allison Tovey, and Michael Hardison, thank you all very much. You all did a great job!

Christina Deptula, at Authors Large and Small, had the unenviable job of assisting me with the marketing of the book. Since I wasn't even on social media before all of this, you can only image how difficult her job was! And special thanks to Alyssa Hernandez and my daughters Jessie Williams and Maggie Peeples, who composed and monitored my Instagram and Facebook page and made wonderful posts. Another shout-out to my computer genius son, Nick Peeples, who did such a great job in designing my website.

I also want to thank all my children and their partners. Nick, Andy, Jessie, Frank, Alex, Maggie, and Lee: I always knew you were pulling for me, and that is one of the things that kept my nose to the grindstone.

Included in this acknowledgment is my squad of friends, both in San Antonio and Kansas City. The Kansas City squad includes the Hens and the Car-dog . . . you all know who you are. Your support and kind words about this writing journey has kept me centered and focused.

To my beautiful, *older* (I always have to include this) sister, Amy: although there are sixteen months between us, many people think we are twins. Heck, I think we are twins! We think alike, talk alike, think the same things are funny when no one else does . . . I am you and you are me. I am so grateful you are my sister. Much love to you.

And finally, my husband Keith. When I first laid eyes on him, during freshman English class, I thought he was . . . the biggest idiot I had ever seen! But he does have a way of growing on a person, so we became friends, then best friends, and when he asked me out on a date in September 1974, I was hesitant to go, if for no other reason than I didn't want to ruin our friendship. But I did go, and later that night I told my sister, "I am going to marry him." And I did. Been happily married for forty-three years. He has been my mainstay, my constant, my rock in our years together. As a matter of fact, he is one of the reasons I finally finished this book. About two years ago, we were walking Hudson (aka Walter), and I was bitching about the book. Keith stopped, looked at me, and said, "Babe, I love you. I will support you in anything you want to do in this life. But either finish the book or shut the hell up about it!!" And the rest is history.

There is no limit to what we, as women, can accomplish.

—*Michelle Obama*

<u>ABOUT THE AUTHOR</u>

SHANNON PEEPLES started her career as a coronary care nurse in Kansas City, Missouri. Knowing that she always wanted to be a lawyer, she went to law school at the young age of forty-five and worked at the law firm of Shook, Hardy, and Bacon. Shannon has four children and five perfect grandchildren. She lives in San Antonio with her husband Keith and Hudson, her two-hundred-pound Great Dane. This is her debut novel.

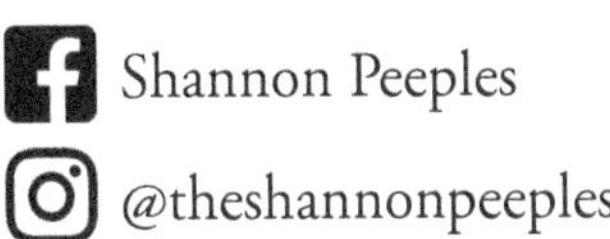 Shannon Peeples

@theshannonpeeples

1) The dogs almost talked in this book. How do you think that added to the story? Which dog would you like to own?

2) Which sister did you relate the most to, and why?

3) Jack was widowed fairly young. How do you think he managed to raise four well-adjusted daughters? What do you think of his choice not to date or marry while the girls were young? If you think that was the right thing, why?

4) What were your impressions of the various romances the sisters developed in the book and do they all seem to be on the track to matrimony? What was your reaction to Jack's announcement?

5) How will the sister dynamic change when they are all married and their father has a new wife?

6) Jack and Daisy had both lost a spouse. What did they display regarding the grief process?

7) Did you wonder if the threat made to Daisy that Tommy was having an affair had any truth to it? The other threats and accusations were resolved but that one wasn't.

8) In the suspense of the book, did you think another character was going to be the stalker? If so, who?

9) Did you think Martha's dog Evie was a "prop" to get to Rosie or do you think Martha actually cared about the dog?

10) Have you ever had a relationship like Rosie did with Steve where you missed or overlooked a serious character flaw? What red flags did Rosie miss?

11) It seems the author really tapped into the feelings of Rosie during her ordeal. For those that have experienced shock or trauma, how did you relate to the description?

12) The author described Rosie as being "un-Rosie like" immediately after her escape due to the trauma. Have others experienced this effect?

13) Talk about Martha and her anger. How did she get so emotionally attached to Steve and Lance? Could she have done anything to steer them in a better direction?

14) If you have sisters, could you relate to the love and their friendship? Did you pick up any reasons for their closeness?

15) What was your overall impression of the story from this first-time writer?

16) Would it have been helpful to have a list of characters and pets in an index at the back of the book to refer to? It did require concentration while reading to keep track of the names and associations. Do you think the author wanted to give the readers more choices of a possible villain?

FUN FACTS ABOUT
GREAT DANES AND NEWFOUNDLANDS

<u>GREAT DANES:</u>

The Great Dane is a German breed which descends from the hunting dogs of the Middle Ages. These dogs were used to hunt bears, wild boars, and deer. They were also used as guardian dogs for German nobility, with the favorites staying in the bedchambers of their lords at night. The Great Dane is one of the two largest dog breeds in the world, along with the Irish Wolfhound.

Due to the Great Danes size, it is often dubbed the "Apollo of dogs". Over the years, the tallest living dog has typically been a Great Dane. The current record holder is a black Great Dane named Zeus that stood 44 inches at the shoulder before his death in September 2014. The current Great Dane holding the record for the world's biggest dog is Atlas, who is a German Harlequin Great Dane living in Florida. At six years old, he weighs 225 pounds.

The Great Dane's large and imposing appearance belies its out-going and friendly nature that can make it a loving and devoted addition to any home. The breed is often referred to as a "gentle giant".

The Great Dane was named the state dog of Pennsylvania in 1965 and the University of Iowa had Great Danes, Rex I and Rex II, as mascots before the Hawkeye was chosen. "Great Danes" is the nickname of the University of Albany. Their mascot is a Great Dane. The animation designer Iwao Takamoto based the character of Scooby-Do on a Great Dane.

<u>NEWFOUNDLANDS:</u>

The Newfoundland is a large breed of working dogs. They can be black, grey, brown, or black and white. They were originally bred and used as working dogs for fisherman in Newfoundland.

Newfoundlands are known for their giant size, intelligence, tremendous strength, calm disposition, love of children and loyalty. They excel at water rescue/lifesaving because of their muscular build, thick double coat, webbed paws, and swimming abilities. The double coat makes the dog hard to groom, and also causes a lot of shedding to occur. The droopy lips and jowls make the dog drool, especially in high heat. Sounds like Big Shirley!

As noted, the breed is wonderful with small children, and are often referred to as "nanny dogs." The breed was memorialized in "Nana", the beloved guardian dog in J. M. Barrie's *Peter Pan.*

One famous Newfoundland was named Seaman, and was one of the most traveled dog in human history. He accompanied American explorers Lewis and Clark on their expedition from the Mississippi to the Pacific and back, a journey that took three years.

Males normally weigh 143-176 pounds and females weigh between 120-143 pounds. The largest Newfoundland on record weighed 260 pounds and measured over 6 feet from nose to tail!

All information acquired from Wikipedia

Printed in the USA
CPSIA information can be obtained
at www.ICGtesting.com
CBHW032222070324
5073CB00004BA/13